Murder at
MONT ST. MICHEL

ROBERT HARDAWAY

WESTERN REFLECTIONS PUBLISHING COMPANY®

ISBN: 978-1-937851-49-1

First Edition
Printed in the United States

Text design by Steve Smith
FluiDesigns

Western Reflections Publishing Company
P.O. Box 1149
951 N. Highway 149
Lake City, CO 81235
www.westernreflectionspublishing.com
(970) 944-0110

BOOKS BY ROBERT HARDAWAY

Novels (Western Reflections Publishing)
Alienation of Affection
Lily Queen
The Papyrus
Six Queens Naked
Dreamlet

Academic Books on Law and Public Policy
Colorado Evidence (Lexis-Nexis, co-authored, 14 editions)
The Great American Housing Bubble (Praeger)
Marijuana Law and Politics (Praeger)
Saving the Electoral College (ABC-CLIO)
Airport Law and Regulation (Greenwood Press)
Crisis at the Polls (Greenwood Press)
America Goes to School (Praeger)
Population, Law, and the Environment (Praeger)
The Electoral College and the Constitution (Praeger)
No Price Too High: Victimless Crimes (Praeger)
Preventive Law Casebook (Anderson)
Aviation Law and Regulation Treatise (co-authored) (Butterworths)
Preventive Law in corporate Practice Treatise (Mathew Bender)
Colorado civil Rules Annotated (West Publishing, co-authored)
Aviation Law and Regulation—student Edition
        (Butterworths, co-authored)

DEDICATED TO
JUDY TREJOS

CHAPTER ONE

DECEMBER 11

Dean "Zach" Higgins swung his recent model Lexus sharply around the corner leading into the very small law school parking lot in uptown Manhattan. Normally a sedate and patient driver, Dean Zack was in a foul mood, and this uncharacteristic maneuver belied his agitation about a most disconcerting article which had appeared on page nine of this morning's New York Times. Thank God it had not appeared on page one.

Plunging the car into his much coveted reserved parking space before slamming on the brakes and coming to a squealing stop, he resisted the urge to immediately exit the car and storm into his office. That would certainly have alarmed the usually sedate staff in the dean's suite consisting of the registrar, academic dean, and his private staff assistant. Instead, he took a deep breath, paused for several moments to gather his thoughts, and do what he himself so often counseled both students and Professors to do when they blustered into his office to complain about some new perceived outrage: calm down.

As Zack had soon found out after assuming the dean's chair, it was not easy being a law school dean. Like professional football coaches, most law school deans around the country didn't last more the three or four years. If prima donna law Professors and students perpetually outraged over some perceived slight or other did not do them in, then dissatisfied alumni generally finished the job. But the perks offered him had been seductive, which they would have to have been to lure him away from what had been a most lucrative law practice with the thriving mid-town law firm of Steiner, McDonnel, and Rowe. While the salary offered him was significantly lower than his average annual partner's share had been at SMR, it was steady and firmly in the middle six figure range. This enabled him to keep his three million dollar condo on Park Avenue.

On the verge of being burned out at the firm, he had imagined that the stress level of running a law school would be far less than at the law firm where he often worked sixty-hour weeks. But what had clinched his decision to leave the firm and accept the offer to be a law school dean was the perk of a ground floor personal parking space only a few feet from the back door of the law school building. Even the law firm had not provided him with such a perk, relegating him to a general parking pass to a ten story parking garage several blocks away where he often had to roam for a space. It did not need to be said that in traffic-challenged Manhattan where even parking space "condos" sold for six figures if any were even on the market, a dedicated ground floor parking space only steps from one's working office was a luxurious lagniappe to be treasured far more than mere money.

In an area of town where square footage was measured in the thousands of dollars per square foot, it was not surprising that the entire law school parking lot consisted of but three dedicated spaces, one of which was for the exclusive use of the dean. The other two were set aside for visiting dignitaries or celebrity lecturers. Students and Professors generally made their way to classes by subway, or Uber.

The Oliver Wendell Holmes School of Law in Manhattan had been established some twenty-eight years before with a generous bequest by a great grandniece of the distinguished Supreme Court jurist, and had received its accreditation from the American Bar Association (ABA) six years later. It competed for students with nine other law schools in New York City, and because it was the most recently established had struggled in its early years to attract the most qualified students, especially those applicants who's Law School Aptitude Tests qualified them to be accepted in such highly ranked law schools as Columbia or New York University.

In more recent years, however, the Oliver Wendell Holmes Law School had risen in the *U.S. News* standings, and it could now boast that among its graduates were a number of successful and respected practicing lawyers and judges. The school had also begun to be nationally ranked, primarily for its innovative programs, especially its Exoneration Clinic.

Students accepted into that program by the supervising Professor earned credit for investigating real cases that came to their attention in the form of desperate letters sent to the clinic by prison inmates claiming to have been unfairly convicted. Several years before, the law students and supervising Professor, in that clinic had enjoyed national media acclaim for having investigated a case and found old D.N.A evidence thought to have been discarded many years before to successfully convince the Texas Supreme Court to reverse the murder conviction of a man who had spent eight brutal years on death row.

Since then, however, no similar success had been achieved despite the expenditure of countless hours screening letters from inmates and undertaking no less than four major time consuming investigations that led nowhere. Despite the lack of recent success in righting unfair convictions, however, the clinic was highly popular with the students, many of whom aspired to careers in criminal law. The supervising Professor Robin Hammond, strictly limited student participation in his clinic to no more than six or at most seven students. This allowed him to select only the most dedicated and competent students, as well as to keep the number of students to be adequately supervised to a manageable size. As a result the clinic was considered to be the most elite in the law school and the most touted in the recruitment brochures sent out to career counselors at colleges and universities around the country.

But now the newspaper clipping that Dean Zach Higgins held in his hand threatened to derail the law school's reputation that had been so patiently and diligently built up by a succession of law school deans over the past decade. Worst of all, the damage would occur under his watch—damage which might even result in the demise of the law school itself. So much for his hope that his term as dean might exceed the average three- to four-year terms of law school deans.

"Good morning Dean Higgins," came the cheerful greeting from Rebecca, the dean's chirpy, platinum blonde, and always meticulously groomed staff assistant. "Your regular decaf this morning?"

Zach managed a smile, but only barely. "No thanks, Rebecca, not now. Has Dean Mason arrived yet this morning?" Rebecca walked over to the office of Academic Dean Roger Mason and peered in. "Yes sir, about twenty minutes ago but he must have stepped out. Shall I go find him?"

"No that's all right. When he returns ask him to come in and see me." Zack lost his smile, entered his office, and firmly closed the door.

Zack read the article again and again, hoping against hope to find some redeeming part of it that might cheer him up. But there was little of that. He was already aware that the bar passage rate of his law school was in the bottom quartile of accredited law schools. That rate had been gradually improving over the last several years. But now the New York Times was reporting that the ABA Section on Legal Education and Admissions was proposing to require that 75% of law graduates pass the bar within two years of graduation. Law schools whose graduates fail to meet this requirement would risk loss of accreditation. The Oliver Wendell Holmes Law School's previous year's pass rate was only 58%. If the proposal were enacted, it would spell the end of the Oliver Wendell Holmes Law School—of that Zack was sure.

"Come in!" Zack called out in response to the brisk knock on his office door.

Dean Mason entered and saw the Times article laid out on the desk. He smiled and shook his head. "Morning Zack. I see you saw the article this morning. I wouldn't worry about it. Really. It's only a section proposal. The House of Delegates will never approve it."

"You're sure of that, Roger?"

4

"Yeah, pretty sure. I know a lot of the delegates, and they all plan to vote against it. The California bar is already raising hell over it. The California bar passage rate is less than 40%. If enacted, this proposal would shut down half the law schools in that state alone."

"The thing of it is, Roger, I actually agree with the proposal. There are too many damn law schools in this country, too many lawyers, and more to the point, too many unqualified lawyers. Universities are using their law schools as cash cows, cramming 100 or more students into large classrooms, charging 60k or more a year for tuition, and then unleashing their hordes of law graduates on to the market where there are not half as many jobs as applicants."

"Zack, you knew coming in that we'd have to admit applicants with lower Law School Aptitude Tests scores in order to fill our class. And you know that there's a high correlation between LSAT scores and bar passage."

"I know, but what can we do? The applicants with high LSAT scores apply to Columbia or NYU."

"Sure, and applications are down across the board. But we've got top notch Professors from the real world of law practice here. They don't spin their wheels writing mindless law review articles no one reads. And not all our students have lower LSATs. We have a good group of students with high LSATs—good enough to get in to Columbia—but they came here anyway because of our nationally ranked programs."

"Granted. Our immigration clinic is ranked in the top ten in the nation. And I think our civil litigation clinic will probably be ranked next year."

"You should be proud of that. And don't forget our Exoneration Clinic. They gave the school some great publicity when it made national news after convincing the Texas Supreme Court to reverse that murder conviction. The best lawyers in the country have a hard time getting that court to do that."

Zack shook his head. "But that was several years ago, and I don't know that it's done much since."

Roger sat silent, for he had a pretty good idea where this was going. He waited.

Zack leaned over his desk. "Roger, I'll be honest. The fact is that I'm fifty-two, too young and not financially secure enough to pay off the rest of my mortgage on that damn condo in the sky, and Lorene wouldn't let me retire even if I wanted to. But I can tell you I'd prefer a new edition of the Spanish Inquisition to going back to SMR. So here I am, and I'll do whatever it takes to make sure this school survives. As I see it, there's only one way to do it. We've got to get our bar passage rate up. That's the bottom line. If we have to shut down some of these expensive programs to release resources for bar prep classes, cut out all our boutique courses—you know international law, jurisprudence, feminism and the law, you know which ones I'm talking about, and who in God's name approved that course in art law—and concentrate on courses which cover actual bar exam subjects, then that's what we'll have to do."

"Teach to the test, then."

"If that's what it takes to save this law school, then yes! Once we're out of the woods on bar passage, we can bring back some of the programs and esoteric course offerings."

Roger waited for the dean to calm down, and then said "I'm not sure the faculty will go for that. It's our programs that attract many of the good students we do have, especially those with higher LSATs who could have gone to higher ranked schools. And many of our faculty are also here because of these programs."

Zack thought for some moments before adding, "I take the point. But maybe we can have our cake and eat it too. Let's take a look at some of these programs and figure out if they can be done at lower cost. Maybe you could give me a spreadsheet showing the costs of the programs we now offer."

"I can do that."

As soon as Roger left, Zack picked up the phone. "Rebecca, tell Professor Hammond I want to see him."

CHAPTER TWO

DECEMBER 11

Professor Robin Hammond placed his books and copy of the Federal Rules of Civil Procedure on the podium and called the class to order. He pulled out the deck of cards containing the names of the ninety two students in his Civil Procedure class, shuffled them, and plucked a card at random from the middle of the deck. He used this random method of calling on students to recite the assigned case in the belief that it was the fairest way to keep all students on their toes and prepared for every class. It didn't always work.

When he saw that the name of the student whose card he had plucked, he was tempted to put it back in the deck and choose another. Cindy Leibowitz was known as a "front bencher," sitting on the front row with her hand perpetually up and frantically waving either to ask a question or answer a question posed to the class as a whole. This had led to her reputation as a "flamer" among her exasperated classmates, a group of whom had inserted her digital photo from the class picture on to the center square of the "flaming bingo" game they played on their laptops. Every time she raised her hand another "x" was checked with her name until she formed a bingo. She'd won the bingo game four times already, and there was still a week left in the semester.

There were low groans among the class. By calling on her name to recite, the good Professor had unwittingly enhanced her chances of winning a fifth bingo before the end of the semester.

"Doctor Leibowitz, can you tell us how Harris v. Balk laid the conceptual foundation for quasi-in-rem type two, and how Shaffer v. Heitner altered the legal basis for that foundation?"

Professor Hammond always addressed his law students in class as doctors, believing that if medical students studying for a medical doctorate degree could be so addressed in medical school, then law students studying for a juris doctorate degree deserved the same title. It also saved him having to choose between the undue informality of addressing students by their first name, and the formality of calling them by their last name as Mr. or "Ms." It had the added advantage of only requiring him to memorize one name for each of his students rather than two.

"Yes Professor," Cindy eagerly and excitedly responded. "Balk, a North Carolina merchant owed $344.00 to Epstein, a Maryland merchant. Harris, a North Carolina acquaintance of Balk owed $180.00 to Balk. Harris' debt to Balk was not formalized in any written instrument..."

"Actually, Doctor Leibowitz," the Professor interrupted, "we can dispense with the facts of that case here, if you could just tell us the legal principle of quasi-in-rem jurisdiction type two as set forth..."

At just that moment, the classroom door opened, and the young woman who had since the beginning of the class in the fall sent the male students' hearts aflutter, gracefully entered. Uncharacteristically, she was several minutes late for class. Usually she was at least ten minutes early and unobtrusively took her seat at the very back of the class. Not once had she ever raised her hand to ask a question, nor had her card ever come up to be called upon.

Typically she wore only a t-shirt or sweatshirt, jeans, and tennis shoes. But her beauty could not be so easily camouflaged, and her late entrance now provided her with the closest the large classroom could provide to a catwalk as she elegantly climbed the stairs to the back row and took her seat.

Visibly annoyed by this distraction, Cindy paused to change the gears of her recital, but her rare opportunity to take the limelight and shine had been eclipsed by this beauty from California. What was the matter with all the guys in the class? For the rest of the class Cindy did not raise her hand.

As the class ended and the students shuffled quickly out of class for the lunch hour, only one student came up to the podium. Usually there were several who approached the Professor to ask questions, but since Cindy was now the only one at the podium she felt she could make a personal observation out of earshot of her classmates.

"Professor," she whispered "that Judy Alexander. Sure, she's beautiful and all, but I think I know why she's never said a single word the entire semester. She's probably got a terrible voice, and just doesn't want anyone to hear it."

Professor Hammond shrugged and pretended not to have heard this inappropriate comment from his doubtless brilliant, but pushy and exasperating student.

"Cindy, I'm sorry," he replied, "but I'm late for my meeting with the Exoneration Clinic. Please feel free to email me with any questions, or come by during office hours."

"Oh yes, Professor, sorry, of course. I'll come to your office next Tuesday."

"I'm sure you will, Cindy, but I really have to go now."

As Professor Hammond exited the classroom he was met by the dean's staff assistant in the hallway.

"Professor Hammond?"

"Yes, Rebecca, what is it."

"Dean Higgins wants to see you in his office ASAP. He says it's important."

Robin Hammond scowled. "I know. It's always important. Can it wait until after lunch? I have a meeting during the lunch hour."

Rebecca considered. "I suppose so. I think he's going out to lunch with a possible donor, so that's probably OK."

"Great. Tell him I'll come by after my meeting, about one. OK?"

"I guess so."

******

The Exoneration Clinic met every Friday during lunch hour in the mock courtroom on the third floor of the law building. They also met there in the evening after classes when necessary to discuss an ongoing case.

9

All seven of his students were waiting for him, seated around the counsel tables. Hammond took out a file from his briefcase. "This Gordon Gage case. Julie, any progress there?"

"I'm afraid not, Professor. As you know, we finally got the D.N.A results, but the Denver D.A. says they don't prove anything, so he's not going to budge. He admits that some of the D.N.A on the victim's dress was not Gage's, but says that at least seven witnesses have signed statements that they danced with the victim the night before at the bar—apparently quite vigorously—which can account for the some of their D.N.A on her dress. And the dress she was wearing at the crime scene is the same dress. The D.N.A of three of those who danced with the victim was on the dress—they all gave D.N.A samples—but none of them have motives, and they all have alibis for the hours after she left the bar and went home. Gage, on the other hand had plenty of motive, and his blood was found at the scene which the D.A. claims was the result of wounds on his hand incurred while stabbing the victim."

"So dead end, then."

"We can still work on finding the person Gage says could be his alibi. Jerry, you were working on that weren't you?"

Jerry Hill was the most experienced student in the clinic, having worked on three other cases during his three years in the clinic. He said, "Gage didn't give me much to work on. Just says he gave a ride to a hitchhiker on his way home, and they both then went out to a field to smoke pot all night. But he doesn't know the guy's name, so that angle looks pretty hopeless. I suppose I could try talking to the alibi witnesses for the people whose D.N.A was on the dress, but right now they're pretty firm, and they're not talking anyway—all of them lawyered up."

Hammond shook his head. "Sounds like we're wasting resources. Sophia, do you still think he's innocent?"

Sophie, a second year student who had brought the Gage case to the clinic, nodded. "Yes, I do Professor. Absolutely. The police held him all night before he finally confessed, and then turned on the video recorder for him to repeat the confession.

He says he asked for a lawyer before he confessed, but of course the police deny it. And his mother claims..."

Hammond held up his hand. "Sophie, the matter of the confession was litigated all the way up to the Colorado Court, and has been upheld, and the U.S. Supreme Court has denied cert. That ship has sailed. There's very little we can do with purely legal questions. As always we need actual evidence. We've spent thousands of dollars on the D.N.A tests, which we thought would at least cast some doubt in the Gage case, and I know he claims he's innocent, but of course they all say that, so we can't just go by that. We have limited resources, and we've got to spend them where we have a real chance of proving that there has been an unjust conviction."

There were several moments of silence before Hammond sighed and said: "Guys, here's the deal. Javier and Jennifer, I know you're still waiting on the D.N.A results on the Cravens case. We've already paid for these tests, so we can continue to wait for the results. Maybe something will come of that, but I'm not holding my breath. What I'd like to ask the rest of you to do now is to scour the crime reports, media, newspapers, not just the big ones, but local, rural newspapers. Maybe interview local public defenders. There are just too many ways out there in what passes as a fair system of justice in which innocent people can be convicted—coerced confessions, lack of resources, incompetent lawyers. If we can find and exonerate just one innocent person facing death or a lifetime of imprisonment, it will be worth all our efforts. I know you've been screening a lot of letters from inmates. Have any of them been promising? Amy, Reid?"

Amy Yeager and Reid Underwood shook their heads. Amy said, "We've looked at over a hundred letters, and gotten backgrounds on about twenty of those. But nothing yet that we're ready to report as showing evidentiary grounds for exoneration."

"OK, keep looking everyone. See you all next Friday."

Hammond waited until all his students had left, packed his briefcase, and headed for the dean's office.

CHAPTER THREE

DECEMBER 12

Professor Hammond filled his coffee cup and paced with cup in hand as he waited outside Dean Zack's office. There were times he regretted leaving his criminal law practice to teach at a law school—especially since he had not even been allowed to teach in the specialty for which he considered himself most qualified, but had rather been consigned to teaching Civil Procedure—a subject in which he had little interest and considered quite boring. Nevertheless the opportunity Dean Zack had offered him offered to establish an Exoneration Clinic had induced him to enter what he considered to be the stultified and pompous world of academia.

"The Dean will see you now, Professor," chirped the ever smiling Rebecca. "Can I offer a refill?"

"I'm good, thanks," nodded Hammond as he kept his cup in hand and entered the dean's inner sanctum.

"Afternoon Robin, thanks for coming in on such short notice," said Zack with a smile too broad to suggest that the meeting was going to be anything but a pleasant one.

Robin fell back into the dean's plush leather chair, which required its occupant to look up at an angle of several degrees to interface with the boss.

"Love this chair, Zack. Really comfortable," said Robin.

"Yes, I get a lot of compliments on it. How's the Civil Procedure Class going?"

"Just fine—considering that's it's not my area of expertise."

"Yes, sorry about that, but when Winokur decided to retire I had no choice but to assign you that class, and Tishman has been teaching the criminal law class since day one."

"I understand, Zack," said Robin with some impatience, "so what's up?"

Zack's smile disappeared as he picked up the New York Times article and handed it over to Robin. "Have you seen this?"

Robin hadn't seen it and paused to read it. After a short glance he shrugged. "I've heard about it. From what I've heard it won't be approved by the House of Delegates. The 75% cut-off would shut down half the law schools in California. The bar passage rate in that state is only about 40%. And look at Brooklyn. I think their pass rate was 73% last year. I wouldn't give this a second thought. It's not going to happen."

"Hopefully not, but we can't rely on that. The bottom line is that we have to get our bar passage rate up. We've got to compete for students with nine other law schools in the New York area. And as you know, LSAT scores are the best predictors of bar passage."

"Yes, but we've got a number of students now with LSATs that could have gotten them into Columbia. But they came here instead because of our innovative programs. The Exoneration Clinic..."

"I know," Zack interrupted. "Actually that's what I wanted to talk to you about. Roger just gave me those figures. Your Clinic billed $167,000.00 for D.N.A tests, transportation and lodging costs just last year alone. And nothing to show for it. For that we could set up an internal bar refresher course right here in the law school, give the at-risk students' academic credit for taking it, and get our bar passage rate above the danger zone. We wouldn't call it a bar refresher class, of course—I know that ABA doesn't approve of such courses within the law school curriculum—but we can offer it under some kind of legal practice or legal analysis course name, and require our marginal students to take it. How many students do you even have in the clinic? Five or six?"

"Seven," Robin corrected, "and I don't judge the success of the clinic by how many exonerations we achieve. The students gain experience in investigation, witness interviewing, legal analysis..."

Zack raised his hand. "I get it. I do. But my primary responsibility is to make sure this school survives as a going

13

concern. The only way I can keep that clinic on the course list is if you can conduct it without billing the law school for any expenses."

Robin stood up, trying to hide his anger. "But that's impossible! No expenses at all? Almost all exonerations are based on D.N.A tests, and they cost plenty when the state won't pay for them, which is most of the time, and students have to travel out of state to interview witnesses, to gather evidence, to..."

Zack resisted the urge to shout back at his recalcitrant Professor but interrupted in as calm a voice as he could muster, "I've made up my mind on this! If you want to teach the clinic as an overload to your regular teaching load..."

"I already teach it as an overload."

"Well, you'll have to continue to teach it as an overload because I also need you to teach Contracts, which is a multi-state bar subject. And as for the faculty, I can tell you right now that most members of this faculty are more concerned about keeping their job and their tenure right now than about your damned Exoneration Clinic."

Defeated, Robin saw no point in further resistance. "Without funding, it would just be an ordinary practicum," he said resignedly as he fell back into the giant leather bean bag that passed for a chair. "I wouldn't be interested in teaching it."

"That's entirely up to you. If you do decide to keep teaching it, you can call it anything you want. Maybe you could apply for some grants."

"Maybe, but that can take years. I'll let you know. So you're saying the course can stay in the curriculum if we don't bill for expenses, and if I continue to teach it as an overload?"

"I said it could, Robin. Look, you're a good teacher and I knew you would be, which is why I recruited you. Did you know I attended some of your CLE lectures before you came on board?"

"I didn't know that."

"You were excellent, just like your old law school mentor Irving Younger. His lecture "Ten Commandments of Cross-

Examination" is still the gold standard for the trial bar. And it surely wouldn't be the end of the world if you feel you have to let this clinic go."

Robin got up and headed for the door. "I'll let you know."

"One more thing. If you do decide to keep teaching the clinic as a practicum, would it be possible to add a few more students? It would still be a very small class, and we have very few small classes as it is."

Robin had always limited the size of the Exoneration Clinic to seven in order to insure that he could adequately supervise all the students. Without such supervision, he knew inexperienced students out in the field or in a courthouse by themselves could get themselves—and him—in to all kinds of trouble. If the clinic was to be downgraded to a practicum that was taught only by simulations—all within the walls of the law school—perhaps he could take in a few more. But he was still not resigned to such a downgrade. He would have to think about it. In fact he would have to think about whether he wanted to continue teaching at all. At the age of forty-eight, divorced for five years, there was still time to go back to his law practice if his two former partners at Hammond, Riley, and Jessup would agree to take him back.

"I'll let you know, Dean." Robin took his leave, throwing his coffee cup in the trash as he left the Dean's suite.

******

Robin had always considered himself fortunate that he had never acquired a taste for alcohol. Even later in life he much preferred a diet coke, or God forbid, a chocolate milkshake. In his fraternity social circle at University and at NYU Law School he had kept this idiosyncrasy—as it certainly was among trial lawyers—hidden by slowly sipping on his beer at keg parties and in bars, or camouflaging his drink with virgin coke which all assumed must be rum and coke. He had even become adept at feigning tipsiness. And so after a particularly stressful day trying a case, he much preferred to go home to his modest apartment on the north side of Washington Square, relax on his couch with the New York Times crossword, listen to some Chopin or Gershwin, and sip on either a flask of Voss water or a diet coke.

But today he had endured stress of a different kind. Uncharacteristically, he now found himself at the uptown Hilton bar sipping a...real rum and coke. He thought about how he would break it to his eager and idealistic students in the clinic that they wouldn't be going into the real world to be champions of justice anymore; rather, they would just be conducting trial simulations in the artificial and unrealistic world of the law school moot courtroom. How many of them would want to sign up for the clinic in the spring semester? And without real witnesses and defendants could it even be called a clinic? Would it be worth suffering through teaching Civil Procedure—and now Contracts?

But as he began sipping on his second rum and coke, he determined to divert his mind completely and not think about any of that until the next day, or maybe even not until the next week. Instead he moved over to a booth where the light was better, opened his briefcase and took out the Times crossword puzzle he had cut out that morning. As he did so, out tumbled the deck in which each individual card contained the name of a student in his Civil Procedure class. But now with the light inadequate to read the fine print of the crossword clues, he allowed his mind to wander.

Several months later he would ask himself why at this moment he thought of what Cindy Leibowitz had said in a hushed tone after the last Civil Procedure class:

"That Judy Alexander. Sure, she's beautiful and all, but I think I know why she's never said a single word the entire semester. She's probably got a terrible voice, and just doesn't want anyone to hear it."

Why Cindy's asinine comment had stuck in his mind he had no idea, but despite himself Robin's curiosity had been piqued. After the second rum and coke he decided to do what he had never done before: he would rig the deck.

At the last Civil Procedure Class of the semester, the beautiful Judy Alexander would be called upon to recite the case of Mullane v. Hanover Trust.

CHAPTER FOUR

DECEMBER 14

"So, what are you saying, Professor, that we can't sign up for the Exoneration Clinic next semester? It was supposed to be a two semester course, with the option to take it for two additional semesters without credit."

The face of Sophie Shapiro, the senior member of the seven student clinical team, revealed an expression of both concern and alarm.

"Not at all," Hammond assured her. "The second semester of the clinic will be offered in the spring as usual. However, as I explained, our budget for the course will be—well, there will be no budget as such. I will continue to supervise the clinic as an overload. We can continue to use the D.N.A tests we have already paid for, but the administration has said it will be re-allocating the funds which have previously been made available to us. Those funds will instead be used to hire adjuncts to teach legal analysis classes."

Amy Yeager, never one to shrink from speaking her politically incorrect mind, showed her skepticism by shaking her head vigorously. "You mean remedial bar refresher courses for the dummies in the class. But we can already sign up for such private courses outside the law school, though I admit they cost a bundle. And how can we ever exonerate anyone without D.N.A?"

"Now Sophie, you know very well that there are other ways, though I confess those cases are harder to convince an appellate court to grant a new trial."

"In the Draper case last year we submitted the depositions of two witnesses who retracted their testimony at trial, but without D.N.A we weren't even able to get a hearing. And he had a public defender who had never tried a capital case before. "

"Well, Sophie, there was no D.N.A in that case to be had, but I understand and sympathize. The alternative is to eliminate the clinic entirely. I'm hoping you will all want to continue in the clinic next semester. I guess you all know there's a waiting list of twenty-seven students who want to be in the clinic. Can I have a show of hands of those who intend to register for the second semester?"

All but Reid Underwood raised their hands. "I don't know, said he. "I'll have to think about it. But I guess I will."

"Glad to hear it, Reid. Now, the rest of you—you'll recall that last week I asked you to screen the rest of our mail from prisoners and also look at the newspapers and internet to find some cases, interesting cases, we could look in to."

Jennifer Morrison raised her hand. "I found an interesting case in Alabama. A man was arrested and convicted for handing out leaflets to prospective jurors as they were entering the courthouse telling them that they had a constitutional right to vote not guilty if they thought the law was unfair even if they thought the defendant was guilty of that law."

"Jury nullification," said Hammond. "Yes, it's true that juries have the ultimate constitutional power to render a not guilty verdict if they don't approve of the law under which the defendant is being charged. But judges aren't required to advise the jury of this power, and in fact always instruct the jury that they must follow the law."

"But doesn't the guy who passed out the leaflets have a First Amendment right to tell jurors the truth—that they have the power to nullify?"

"Good question, I don't know. But this is a case which would depend entirely on the law—in this case first Amendment law—and we really aren't equipped to argue the law. We need cases in which the facts are in dispute. And there's also the practical problem of expenses now. Anybody here financially able to pay for a trip to Alabama, hotels, meals, transportation, to meet with witnesses?"

This question was met by a stone silence.

"Well, keep looking, and focus on cases here in New York where costs won't be a factor—and cases where we can make a difference. All right, keep looking and we'll meet again next week."

The last Civil Procedure Class of the semester was a review class in which Hammond asked a student what principle of law was set forth in a particular case, statute, or rule. He plucked out the card which he had preselected.

"Judy Alexander?" he called out, looking around the class as if he didn't know where the conscripted student chosen to recite was sitting.

There was silence again as the entire class turned around to hear the response of the silent beauty who had sat in the back row corner all semester without so much as a single word. Cindy Leibowitz's expression and wide open eyes belied her excited anticipation as she turned around to listen.

"Can you tell us the holding of the case of Mullane v. Central Hanover Bank and Trust?"

Everyone in the class seemed to hold their breath to see if the goddess talks.

After a short pause came the response in the most crystal clear and melodious voice Hammond had ever heard:

"The 1950 U.S. Supreme Court case of Mullane v. Central Hanover Bank raised the question of the constitutional sufficiency of notice by publication only to beneficiaries of a common trust fund established under the New York Banking Law. It held that service by publication does not violate the procedural due process clause of the Constitution if the appellant uses due diligence to discover the whereabouts of the absent beneficiaries, and after failing to find said whereabouts gives notice that is reasonably calculated to reach said beneficiaries under the circumstances."

There was a hush as this exquisite and virtually perfect recital hung in the air.

On the front row Cindy Leibowitz sat back and rolled her eyes.

After class as Cindy filed past the podium she gave her Professor a look and just shook her head.

CHAPTER FIVE

DECEMBER 16

A week after the last class of the semester, the halls of the Oliver Wendell Holmes School of Law were almost deserted. Hoping to catch up on some paperwork in the early morning without distractions, Robin Hammond walked briskly down the fourth floor corridor toward his office. As he turned a corner he nearly bumped into Judy Alexander, causing her to drop several books. Both apologized profusely to the other.

"Not at all," said Robin as he leaned down to retrieve the books he had caused Judy to drop. "I didn't expect to see many students around today."

"Thank you, Professor," replied Judy as she accepted the books. "Actually, I was looking for your office as I wanted to talk to you about something. I was hoping you might be in."

"I don't have office hours during the exam study period. I assume you're studying for the exam and have some questions about the material? As I told the class, you can ask questions by email."

"No, it's something else, if you have a minute."

"Oh. Well, OK, but I need to take care of some things first. Could you possibly come by a little later?"

"Sure, I'm just studying in the library downstairs. I'll come up later. When do you leave for lunch?"

"I won't be going out to lunch, but will be leaving my office for the day by two or so."

"Thank you Professor. I'll come by later."

Having finished his paperwork more quickly than he expected, Robin would have left the office to go home had he not remembered that he had told Judy that he'd be in the office until two. To kill the time until she appeared, he took out the previous day's New York Times crossword and began trying to fill in a word that had stumped his efforts to complete the crossword the night before. He was having little success.

He was shaking his head in frustration when Judy appeared at his open door. "Professor, do you have time now?"

Laying down his pencil, Robin looked up from his crossword. "Sure, come on in. You can leave the door open. Please have a seat."

Robin Hammond always made sure the door was open when meeting with female students. He had heard too many horror stories from colleagues who had been caught up in gossip or worse based on rumors which started with what occurred behind a Professor's closed doors with a female student.

This was the first time Robin had been in such close proximity to the woman whose beauty had created such a stir around the school over the past semester. As usual, she was dressed casually in blue jeans and sweatshirt, rubber boots to deal with the recent snowstorm, her hair pulled back in a ponytail, and wearing no make-up that he could discern.

"I'm Judy Alexander. I'm in your Civil Procedure class." "Yes, of course I know. You gave an excellent recitation of the Mullane case, by the way. Now what can I help you with?"

Judy knew her request would require a departure from one of Professor Hammond's known policies, so she was hoping a little chit chat might soften what appeared to be his brusque demeanor and possibly some discomfort at having her appear at an inconvenient time for him.

"I see you're working on a crossword."

"Yes, just a hobby of mine," said Robin with some embarrassment—as if he didn't have anything better to do with his time—and just enough shortness to suggest he really wasn't in the mood for chit chat and would just as soon she got on with whatever she wanted to talk about. He also knew that the mere presence of Judy Alexander in his office during the exam reading period could very well set tongues wagging if anyone happened by and saw them. And he knew from experience that once wagging, their effect on reputation could last for years.

"Any particular clue giving you a problem?" she asked, surmising that she might just have found his soft spot.

"Well, yes," Robin replied, warming slightly. 'Refrain from piracy.' I can't imagine a word that describes how one would refrain from piracy."

"That's it? 'Refrain from piracy?' That is a stumper. Can't imagine. How many letters?"

"Um, six."

"Do you have any letters to help?"

"The third letter may be an 'H,' but not sure. That's all I have."

"I'm sure you'll figure it out."

There was a long silence as Robin continued staring at his crossword, waiting for Judy to get to the point of her visit.

"Professor, a friend of mine I met here at the beginning of the semester, Jennifer Morrison, is in your Exoneration Clinic. We were at Starbucks a couple of weeks ago, and we were talking. She told me what a great experience it was working in the clinic—examining cases in which there were indications of a miscarriage of justice."

"Yes, it is most satisfying work. You may have heard that we were successful in having a murder conviction reversed."

"Yes, I did hear that, and that's what I wanted to talk to you about. I'd really like to join the clinic."

"This coming spring semester?"

"Yes, I'd really like to."

Robin shook his head. He considered asking her what were her reasons, or what experiences in life had led to her interest in correcting miscarriages of justice, or her interest in criminal law in general. But that could take a long time to listen to, and there were reasons why he didn't admit 1Ls (First Year Law Student) into his clinic.

"But you haven't taken criminal law yet."

"Yes, but I will be taking it next semester at the same time as I would be in the clinic, if you can admit me."

"As you have probably heard, I don't admit 1L's. And there's usually a fairly long waiting list of applicants for the clinic. Why don't you go ahead and take your criminal law class, and then apply after next semester."

"But you could admit me if you wanted to? I mean you do have the discretion to admit me even if I am still a 1L?"

Robin had no doubt that the young woman before him —surely she could make a fortune modeling, so why on earth would she be interested in entering the stressful and problematic life of a lawyer—was probably used to using her looks to get what she wanted. As he gazed into a face that reminded him of the face of Egyptian Queen Nefertiti, he sensed himself melting and was determined to resist it.

"I'm sorry Ms. Alexander," he managed to say curtly. "I think you'd better wait until you've finished your first year. I suggest you concentrate on getting a good grade in criminal law next semester, as that's one of the factors I look at in deciding who to admit to the clinic. So if that's all..."

"Jennifer told me that you asked students in the clinic to look for interesting cases. I think I have one. I'd like to tell you and the other students in the clinic about it."

"Again, I'm sorry. Apply next fall, and I will give your application due consideration at that time. Thanks for coming in."

As Robin turned back to look at his crossword stumper, Judy managed a polite smile. "I understand. Thank you, Professor."

"Sure. No problem." Judy rose, but then paused at the door and turned around.

"Yes?" asked Robin, looking up from his crossword.

"Yo-ho-ho."

"Pardon?"

"Yo-ho-ho. A refrain from piracy. Six letters, with an "H" for the third letter."

With that, Judy turned and walked out.

"Of course. Why didn't I see that?" Robin mumbled to himself. He went to the door and called out to Judy. "Ms. Alexander! I have an idea if you can come back for a moment."

Judy returned. "Yes, Professor."

"As I said, I can't admit you to the clinic for next semester, for the reasons I gave you. But if you want to audit the clinic— that is come to our meetings without getting credit—I think we could do that. Next Tuesday we're having our last meeting of the semester before the exam period begins if you'd like to attend. I'm sure we'd be interested in any case you've found."

"I'll be there. Thanks, Professor. Next Tuesday, then?"

"In my office, at 9:00 A.M. sharp."

"I'll be there."

Watching her walk down the hall, Robin let out a big breath, wondering if he'd been manipulated.

Surely not.

CHAPTER SIX

DECEMBER 17

"Let's see. Looks like everyone's here except..."

The meetings of the Exoneration Clinic were always elbow to elbow since Professor Hammond insisted on conducting the class in his office. Extra chairs had to be brought in.

"Julie had to head back to visit her family in Utah," piped Sophie, who was crammed into a chair between Reid and Javier. Judy, the newcomer to the group had found a chair in the back corner of the office.

"All right, so the rest of you are here. This will be our last meeting before the start of the spring semester. Also, as you can see we have a visitor today, Judy Alexander, who would like to share a case she found. She won't be eligible to take the class until next fall. "

The clinical students all looked over at Judy, who managed a smile and a wave while shifting uncomfortably in her seat. The Professor had never invited a visitor to the class before, and most of the students recognized Judy as the beauty everyone had been talking about. A 1L had never before been admitted to the class even as a visitor.

Putting Judy on the spot, Robin asked her, "Why don't you go ahead and tell us about the case you wanted to share?"

Judy smiled, but was flustered by all the eyes now upon her. "Well," she began hesitantly, "it's a case I saw in the Times about a man in Alabama who was arrested for distributing leaflets to potential jurors telling them that they had a right to..."

Javier immediately interrupted her. "Jury nullification. We already considered that case, Judy," he said, with more than a hint of condescension. "Professor Hammond decided not to take that case because it raises only a legal question for appeal, and not a factual one. And since none of us have law licenses to

27

argue appeals, we are mostly looking for evidence in cases that we can turn over to licensed attorneys in serious cases, like death penalty cases..."

"Thank you, Javier," Hammond said, cutting him off. He turned to Judy. "Yes, that's right. But I commend you for your interest and willingness to help. I do urge you to apply for the clinic next fall."

Judy turned red with embarrassment and rose from her chair, dropping her notebook in the process. "Oh, I'm sorry. Well, it was just something I read about. I should probably go, then..."

"Not at all, Ms. Alexander," Hammond reassured her, hoping to alleviate her discomfiture. "Please feel free to remain and hear what cases the others have found."

Judy looked around the room and sat.

"We've been studying for exams," offered Jerry Hill. "We really haven't had time to screen a lot of letters."

"I understand. So no one else has a case that might interest us?"

There was a long silence. Then Amy tentatively raised her hand.

"Yes, Amy? You've got something for us?"

Amy Yeager pulled out a newspaper clipping from her briefcase and handed it to Robin. "It's from last Thursday's Dallas Tribune. It about a man down in Appaloosa County, Texas, by the name of Roger Gardner who's been charged with first degree murder—killed his lover's husband they say."

"Has it gone to trial?"

"No, but..."

"Amy, you know we only look at cases where there's already been a conviction, and a final appeal. Then we investigate if we have reason to believe he's been unjustly convicted, especially if he's facing the death penalty. If this man's been charged in a capital case he'll either hire the best lawyer he can afford or the state will appoint him a lawyer. Any lawyer who represents him won't appreciate any of us..."

"But Professor, this case has a twist. He says he's willing to plead guilty..."

"We're even less interested in plea bargains..."

"He's offered to plead guilty in return for receiving the death penalty."

There was a long silence before Hammond said, "What?"

"There was a segment about that case on CNN last night," piped Jerry without raising his hand. "I saw it. One of the guests, an opponent of the death penalty, said it would be unethical for the state of Texas to accept such an offer, since the offer could only have been made by a disturbed individual who obviously only wanted the state to assist in his own suicide."

"And was there another guest who took the opposite view?" asked Hammond.

"A representative from the Appaloosa County District Attorney's office argued that if the offer were rejected, and the state had to hold a trial, it would cost the state millions of dollars, the family of the victim would be put through hell, and the evidence was so overwhelming that he was sure to be convicted at trial and almost certainly be given the death penalty anyway."

"Leave it to Texas!" said Jennifer. "It's already executed over five hundred prisoners since the Supreme Court reinstated the death penalty—more than any other state!"

"Hold on, everyone," said Hammond putting up his hands. "I'm wondering if the offer was made through his attorney." He paused to read the article. "It says he doesn't have an attorney."

"How is that possible, Professor?" asked Amy. "Isn't an attorney required in a death penalty case?"

Hammond shook his head. "Well, yes and no, a defendant charged with capital murder has a right to an attorney, and the state must provide one if he cannot afford one. But a defendant also has a constitutional right to represent himself unless the court finds that he is incompetent, and so unable to represent himself."

"Has there already been a competency hearing?" Amy asked.

"Look," said Hammond, "I don't know, but let's all slow down. It's an interesting case, I agree, but I think we all know it's not the kind of case we're equipped to look into. First of all, there's no conviction as yet, so there's no unjust conviction to look into. And even if there were, as I've explained, we're now limited to investigating local cases where there will be no need for transportation, lodging, D.N.A, or anything else that costs money. Is anyone here able and willing to put up maybe tens of thousands of dollars of their own money to go down to Appaloosa County, Texas, and find out what's going on down there?"

When no one raised their hand, Hammond continued. "OK then, let's drop it. This will be our last meeting before the winter break, so I suggest that you all devote your time now to studying for your exams. We'll plan to meet on the first Friday of the spring semester. I take it that, despite our lack of financial support from the law school that you'll all sign up for the second semester of the clinic. Reid?"

"Well, I guess I haven't really decided yet," said Reid reluctantly. "If we can't find a suitable case on a national level because of the lack of financial support, I'm not very optimistic that we'll find a suitable local one. We'll just be spinning our wheels."

"That's your decision, Reid, and I understand. It may very well be that by next year we'll have to close down the clinic entirely. But let me know. As you know I generally limit the size of the clinic to seven students, so if you decide not to take the clinic in the spring semester, tell me as soon as you can so I can open it up to another student."

Reid nodded. "Sure, Professor. I'll let you know by the end of the week."

"All right then, at least for the rest of you, good luck on your exams, have a good break, and I'll see you in January."

CHAPTER SEVEN

DECEMBER 19

Relaxing on the couch in his apartment, Robin Hammond put aside his stack of Civil Procedure exams and checked the email on his iPhone. As he rapidly deleted a stream of meaningless messages, he almost deleted one from "jalexander" but caught himself just in time. It read:

> *Dear Professor Hammond,*
>
> *I'm sorry I didn't have much to contribute at your last meeting of the Exoneration clinic, but I appreciate your letting me come to visit. I have finished taking my exams—including yours—and have some time now before the beginning of spring semester. I was wondering if you might have some time to talk with me about one of the cases that was brought up at the clinic meeting. If so, could you call me on my cell phone listed below and let me know a convenient time when I might meet with you?*
>
> *Judy Alexander*

Hammond sighed.

He rarely met with students during the holiday break, and was wary of such out of office approaches, especially by a female student, and even more by a very attractive one. He considered responding by email to tell Judy that he wouldn't be available until the beginning of spring classes, and to come see him in his office at that time. She wasn't a registered student in the clinic, so there was really no reason to meet with her. In any case, he had plans the following week to visit his on-and-off again, somewhat significant other, Adriana Snow, who lived in Honolulu. She had been his paralegal for eight years before he left his law firm to teach at Oliver Wendell Holmes School of Law. For the last several years they had spent Christmas together, and Hawaii was always a welcome respite from Manhattan winters. Nevertheless, he was tired of grading exams, and had no plans for the rest of the day. The weather had also turned nasty.

Despite himself, he found himself calling the cell number Judy had provided in her email. Maybe she wouldn't answer, and he could just leave a message.

The phone answered after one ring. "Hello?"

"Yes, hello. Is this Judy? This is Professor Hammond. I got your email asking me to call."

"Oh, thank you for calling, Professor. I was wondering if you might have some time to meet with me. I was very intrigued by the case one of your students brought up at the meeting, and was hoping I might talk to you about it."

"The one you brought up about jury nullification?"

"No, not that one, of course. I understand what you said about that one just involving the law and not requiring an investigation of alleged facts that may have resulted in an unjust conviction. But I was very intrigued by the case that—Amy, I think her name was—told us about the man in Texas who doesn't want a lawyer and who has offered to plead guilty to first degree murder as part of a plea bargain if in return the state would guarantee to impose the death penalty."

"Well, that case hasn't resulted in a conviction yet either, so that's why..."

"But it could, right? And very soon if the state agrees to that plea bargain—which is why the case really interests me. There could be so many different reasons why anyone would make such an offer, like..."

"Judy, listen. I appreciate your interest, but you aren't even registered for the clinic yet. As I told you before, why don't you apply to register for the spring—I think 1Ls are allowed one elective in the spring quarter—and we can talk about it then?"

There was a pause before Judy said, plaintively, "So you won't meet with me then?"

Hammond hesitated. He had to confess he was curious. Why would this beautiful woman—who surely could have the world at her feet—want to get involved in the grimy underworld of criminal law? Then he kicked himself for thinking like Cindy Leibowitz. He also had to admit that there must be a story there, and it might be a fascinating one.

"Well, I'm planning to go out of town next week, but I do have some time later today."

"Could we meet at the law school cafeteria?"

That would be the last place Hammond would want to meet Judy. The cafeteria was still open during the exam study period, and it would take only one student seeing him having an intimate lunch with the lovely Judy Alexander to set tongues wagging. Instead he suggested that they meet at his old haunt, the bar at the Mid-Town Hilton. Of course being seen with Judy in a dark corner of the bar would set even more tongues wagging, but it wasn't really a student haunt and he doubted if there would be any students there to see the two of them together.

"Do you know the Mid-town Hilton, across from the Museum of Modern Art?"

"I know the Museum, so I can find it."

"I'll meet you at the bar there at, say 7:00 P.M. this evening?"

"I'll find it."

"Right, see you there. Bye."

Not wanting to arrive at the Hilton in the jeans and sweatshirt she usually wore to class, Judy upgraded her ensemble to black knee-length skirt, white shirtwaist, navy blue blazer, long black cashmere coat, and black patent leather flat boots—which was more than enough to showcase her beauty as she entered the bar at the Hilton. Ignoring the admiring but not too subtle glances from prosperous looking businessmen as she walked by, she looked around until she saw Hammond in the corner booth. He saw her and waved.

"Well, this is nice," Judy said as she slid into the booth across from Hammond.

"Right on time. Any trouble finding the hotel?"

"No. I've visited the Museum several times since coming to New York, but to be honest I never noticed the hotel. Subway was more crowded than usual this time of day, what with the snow starting to fall, and cabs were impossible."

"Did you try an Uber?"

Judy shrugged. "Same problem."

"Can I get you something to drink?" Robin asked.

"Sure. A glass of red wine, maybe?"

"Cabernet Sauvignon? They should have it."

Hammond decided he could nurse some red wine himself and called over the waitress. "Two Cabernets please."

"How long have you lived in New York?" Hammond asked.

"Oh, I just came here to go to law school, so just since late August."

"And before that?"

"California mainly. My late husband was a Professor at UCLA and an archeologist, and we traveled quite a bit in the Middle East, especially Egypt..."

"Really? I'm sorry to hear about your husband—so young."

"He was forty-one actually, so eighteen years older than me."

Hammond was tempted to ask how long ago her husband had died so he could calculate Judy's exact age, but thought better of it—it must have been fairly recently. He guessed that she was in her early thirties, possibly as old as mid or even late thirties—in any case some several years older than the age of the average law student, though she certainly could pass for thirty. And she was, yes...stunning. But enough of the personal questions he told himself, much as he wanted to ask her "were you a student at UCLA when your met husband," and "how did he pass away?" He couldn't resist asking her just one more.

"And what made you decide to go to law school?"

Judy shifted uncomfortably. "Long story. To be honest I just wanted to do something different than what people thought I should or could be doing."

Not much of an answer, but that served him right.

Hammond put up his hands in apology. "Didn't mean to pry. So, you wanted to talk about the Texas case. Go ahead."

CHAPTER EIGHT

DECEMBER 19

Judy took a long sip of wine. "I've never heard anything like this Texas case. I guess I'm just intrigued about the story behind it."

Hammond put down his own glass. "It's probably just like Jerry said at the meeting. Gardner—that's his name?—committed a terrible crime, knows he's guilty and facing the death penalty, and would prefer a soft quiet death to ten brutal years on death row in Huntsville before finally being led down to the death chamber in front of gawking witnesses. Sounds kind of rational if you think about it. As a matter of fact, I'm surprised I haven't heard of death row inmates offering similar plea bargains. For all the other people in this country facing an imminent death, complete with a future of deprivation or agonizing pain, their only resort is to fly to Switzerland, check into one of the thanatoriums where they put you comfortably to bed, bring you your favorite dishes, play you some soothing Chopin *Nocturnes*, and then give you pleasant drugs to send you off to La-La land."

"They do that in Switzerland? Don't some states do that too—Washington?"

"Whole different deal there. You have to get two doctors to say you're terminal—lots of paperwork. Switzerland's the only place you can get it done with a minimum of hassle. They just need to know you're competent and know what you're doing. I recently read that a 104 year old man—a scientist from Australia—checked in at one of the thanatoriums in Switzerland. He had no terminal disease or anything, just said he'd led a good full life, and didn't want to wait to the bitter end before he finally got a debilitating disease, got hooked up to tubes in some hospital by those determined that he grind out his life in agony to the very last possible minute, or lose his mind along with his freedom to make his own choices. Doesn't sound all that irrational to me."

"Huh! I'll have to think about that, but..."

"Yes?"

"Well, I think there could be other reasons why this Gardner might want to demand his own death in return for a guilty plea."

"Really? Like what?"

"Maybe he's protecting someone. You know, dying for someone he's madly in love with. 'It is a far, far better thing I do, than I have ever done; it is a far, far better rest that I go to than I have ever known'—that sort of thing."

"Last line of A Tale of Two Cities, word for word. I'm impressed."

Not to be outdone, Hammond decided to throw his own allusion into her court. "Or perhaps like Richard Dudgeon in Shaw's play The Devil's Disciple, who went to the gallows to save the husband of the woman he loved?"

"Yes, exactly," said Judy. "Dudgeon took the place of the wife's husband whom the British General Burgoyne was looking for as a rebel leader in the Revolutionary War. Dudgeon was so in love with Judith—that was the wife's name—that he was willing to sacrifice his own life to save the life of her husband. That story line was repeated to much acclaim in the film Casablanca, with Humphrey Bogart and Ingrid Bergman.

"But according to the Times article," responded Robin, "this Gardner fellow down in Texas is accused of killing the husband, not saving him."

"Yes, that is a difference," she admitted. "I had to read The Tale of Two Cities in ninth grade English class. And in eleventh grade I played Judith, the wife of Richard Dudgeon in the school play."

"Interesting! So you didn't even have to change your name to play the role."

"Not really. My dad always insisted that my name was Judy—and definitely not Judith."

"Why was that?"

"I'm not sure. I always thought he named me after Judy Garland, and he said no one ever called her Judith."

"And your mother?"

At this, Judy looked down. Finally she said, "Could I have another glass? Would you mind?"

"Of course." Hammond waved to the waitress and then held up two fingers and pointed down.

There was another long silence as they waited for the waitress to appear with the glasses. He began to worry that the wine was beginning to affect both of them.

"So you're quite the romantic," Hammond finally said, though cringing inwardly as soon as he said it. It was a stupid thing to say, after all. But her reply was immediate.

"Maybe. Why don't you let me find out?"

Uh-oh thought Hammond. Maybe coming here wasn't such a good idea. Were they still talking about the case?

"And how could I do that?" he asked.

Judy now looked directly into her Professor's eyes and said: "Let me go down to Texas, Professor. I'll find out what the story is behind this case. I'm sure he's not guilty of anything."

"Judy, that's silly. How could you possibly arrive at such a conclusion based on a short article in the Times? You know nothing about this case."

"Exactly. That's why I want to go down there and find out."

"But as I've explained, it's not the kind of..."

"Yes, I know. The Exoneration Clinic only looks into cases after you find evidence that there has been an unjust conviction. But this is an unjust conviction just waiting to happen. If the Appaloosa D.A. decides to accept the offer, Gardner will be convicted. And like you said, unlike convictions after a trial, convictions after a guilty plea are almost never reversed except where there's a showing of an improvident plea. And in this case it's pretty obvious no one is urging or coercing him to plead guilty."

"Judy you're using words like 'provident plea,' and you haven't even taken criminal law yet. Is there something about your background I should know about?"

Judy ignored Robin's attempt to change the subject. "Professor Hammond, will you just let me go?"

Robin shook his head. "It's not up to me to tell you whether you can go. You can go anytime you want."

"No, I can't. I have to go as a student attorney attached to the Exoneration Clinic if I'm going to open the doors I need to get the information I need. Lots of D.A.s around the country know about the Exoneration Clinic. I've googled it. The clinic found D.N.A evidence in the Lawrenson case in Texas which resulted in a reversal of the murder conviction."

"I told you that you can apply for the spring semester."

"By that time he could have pled guilty and be on his way to the death chamber."

"I doubt it. In fact, I doubt the D.A. would ever accept a plea offer like that."

"So you won't sign me up now for the clinic?"

"Now?"

"You can, can't you? It's your course."

"You know there's no money for the clinic. You'd have to go down on your own dime—air fare, hotels, meals, the works."

"I can do that."

"Really? Then you're better off than most of the students here."

"So?"

Hammond took a deep breath. He would doubtless take some heat for admitting Judy to the clinic—who just happened to be the school beauty—without vetting other candidates. But Reid would probably not sign up as the seventh student, and there would be fewer students signing up for the clinic once the word got out that its funding was to be withdrawn.

Hammond surrendered. "OK. You'll have to sign up."

"Can you do that for me?"

"Sure. Happy now?"

"Yes." Judy rose abruptly from the table and picked up her purse.

"Where are you going?"

"Home to pack. I'm leaving for Houston tomorrow morning."

With that she was gone, leaving Hammond to wonder what had just happened. It occurred to him that there were over 250 counties in Texas, and Judy must already have scouted out the nearest city and airport to Appaloosa County, Texas.

CHAPTER NINE

DECEMBER 20

As the crow flies, Appaloosa County, Texas, was just about as many miles from Dallas as from Houston. But Judy had chosen to fly into Houston after checking by phone with the clerk of the Appaloosa County Court House. She learned that the original lawyer assigned to represent Roger Gardner was a junior partner in the Houston law firm of Crocker and Rutherford. She had decided that would be her first stop, and had packed a black suit and heels in a compact roller bag. She also sported a very lawyer-like distressed leather briefcase.

It was late afternoon by the time her plane landed and she picked up her rental car. She had already made a reservation at the Four Seasons Hotel on Lamar Street, but decided to drive straight to the law firm in hopes that it might still be open despite the late afternoon hour. Using her cell phone G.P.S she found the firm's location within the hour—a ten story building in Woodlands. After finding the glass doors to the eighth floor firm open, she walked in. She saw that there was no receptionist.

"Can I help you?" asked a young man in a dapper suit who was passing through the reception area.

"Yes, I was looking for Amber Hartman. Do you know if she's in?"

"She's probably gone for the day. Hold on and I'll check. Did you have an appointment?"

"Um, no. I was hoping I might catch her."

"Hold on." The man disappeared down the hall but returned to say that Amber Hartman was out.

"She should be in tomorrow morning. I'm not sure what her schedule is. I believe she has court in the afternoon, but you may be able to catch her if you come in early tomorrow morning. Say 8:00 A.M.? Would you like me to leave her a message?"

"No, no. I'll just come tomorrow morning. Thank you."

"Perhaps I could help you?" Judy was used to admiring male glances, and this young man's were fairly transparent.

"No, I'll just come back in the morning. But thank you."

Judy now drove to the hotel, had a light meal delivered to her room, and went to bed early. Her cell phone alarm wakened her at 6:00 A.M., and by 7:30 she was back at the law firm offices of Crockett and Rutherford. She was about to see if the glass doors would open when a harried young woman in tennis shoes, whom she took to be the receptionist, appeared and unlocked the glass doors.

"Traffic was terrible. Accident on the freeway! Don't you just hate that?" complained the harried young woman. "Whew! Come on in. Give me a minute, I'll have coffee ready in a jiff. Make yourself comfortable. Who are you here to see?"

The receptionist took her place behind the reception desk, took off her sneakers and pulled out a pair of heels from her bag.

"Amber Hartman," Judy replied. "I don't have an appointment, but was told that I might be able to catch her this morning."

"Just a minute. Actually she may already be in." said the receptionist. She pushed a button on the phone intercom.

"Ms. Hartman? I didn't know if you were already in. There's a young woman here who would like to see you. Can I send her down?" She listened, and then pointed down the hallway. "Fourth door on the right."

Judy appeared at the office door and introduced herself. "Hello, Ms. Hartman? I was told I might catch you this morning. Do you have a minute?"

Amber Hartman was busy shuffling some papers into a briefcase. She looked up.

"Actually I'm off to court very shortly, but I've got a minute. What can I help you with?"

"I wanted to know if you might have some time to talk about Roger Gardner."

Amber immediately stopped shuffling papers, put her briefcase down on her desk, and gave Judy her full attention. She seemed surprised, even stunned

"Roger Gardner?"

"Yes, I was told you represent him."

"Actually I don't. I mean I did. I was appointed by the court, but he dismissed me as soon as he heard I had been appointed. May I ask who you are? What do you have to do with his case?"

Judy held out her hand across the desk.

"Nothing, actually. My name is Judy Alexander. I'm a law student at the Oliver Wendell Holmes School of Law in New York. I'm a student in the Exoneration Clinic there, and we heard about this case. It's been on the national news."

Amber sat down. "Have a seat. Yes, I've heard of your clinic. An acquaintance of mine was counsel on the Lauridson case. Your clinic was instrumental in getting his murder conviction reversed. But this case hasn't even gone to trial. And he's insisting on being pro se."

"Pro se?"

"Representing himself. But he's not even doing that. He's saying nothing, doing nothing. When asked at his arraignment how he wished to plead, he stood mute."

"What happens now, then?"

"If a defendant refuses to plead, the judge ultimately has to enter a plea of Not Guilty in the defendant's behalf..."

"So that's when you were appointed to represent him?"

"Yes."

"Can't the judge force him to accept an attorney to represent him?"

"Not really. He has a constitutional right to represent himself if he so chooses—unless he's found to be incompetent."

"Is he? Incompetent I mean?"

"The court ordered a competency hearing, but he refused to talk to any doctor appointed by the court. Aside from that, there was no evidence that he was incompetent. In fact, he's a doctor himself, a very successful dermatologist. Prior to his arrest he had a thriving practice, working out of Dallas General. There was nothing in his background to suggest that he was in any way mentally disabled. Quite the opposite."

"But what, can you tell me..."

Amber got up from her chair and grabbed her briefcase. "Look, I have to go now—Judy is it?— and will probably be tied up most of the day. I should be available this evening. I'd be happy to talk to you about the case—always happy to help a law student—but I'm afraid there's really nothing you or your clinic can do, or be involved in for that matter. I should be free by 6:00 P.M. There's a nice little restaurant down the road from here—the Woodside Inn. Why don't you meet me there at 6:30?"

"Of course."

"Do you need directions?"

"No, I've got my G.P.S. I'll find it. I'll see you there at 6:30. And thank you."

CHAPTER TEN

DECEMBER 21

Judy chose a corner booth in the cozy Woodland Inn to wait for Amber. Although she was a half hour early, so was Amber who appeared only minutes later.

"What a day," said Amber as she collapsed in the booth. "I could use a Margarita." She waved for the waitress. "And what would you like—Judy isn't it? I know you told me, but..."

"Yes, and a Margarita is fine. Hard day in court?"

"Oh yeah. Bad domestic violence case. But let's relax first. I really need to unwind."

The two made small talk for a while until Amber finally relaxed and sat back.

"Now, what did you want to know about Mr. Gardner?"

"Well, just what he's charged with. I know its first degree murder, but what is the evidence?"

"Hard for a defense counsel to say this, but it's an 'open and shut' as far as I can see. Of course I only know what's in the police report, because Roger has refused to talk to me—other than to say he didn't want or need a lawyer. So I don't have to worry about client confidentiality in talking to you. I did bring a copy of the police report which was provided to me when I was first appointed."

"So what happened?"

"You can read the report yourself. I made a copy of it for you, but as I said, that's all I have or know about the evidence in this case. It really does seem pretty clear cut, though. Last August—the 28th at 11:00 P.M.—Doctor Gardner drove to the house of a Mr. Carl Otto, argued with him about something, and shot him—well, allegedly shot him—once in the head at point blank range in the living room. That's pretty much it. According to Madeleine, Carl Otto's wife, she was upstairs in her bedroom when she heard Gardner and her husband downstairs arguing and shouting at each other.

"Earlier that evening Carl had mentioned that Doctor Gardner would be coming over to discuss some financial matters relating to the finances of the Country Club in which they were both members—but she says she didn't hear Gardner come in. She said that she was in the shower, which explains why she didn't hear the doorbell. Then she heard a shot, and when she came downstairs, she saw Gardner still holding the gun, and Carl dead on the living room rug—which by that time was soaked with blood. Frantic, she said that she immediately called the police, who were there within fifteen minutes. When the police arrived, they found Doctor Gardner sitting down on a living room chair, looking down at the body, a blank look on his face. The gun, later determined to be the murder weapon, was resting next to him on the arm of the chair."

"So there's no question Gardner killed him?"

"The evidence is overwhelming. Gardner has never denied that he killed Otto, although he made no statement at all either at the crime scene when he was arrested or since then. He has been completely silent. But all the forensic evidence confirms Madeleine's story. The week before Gardner killed her husband, Gardner had bought a gun at a local gun store in his own name and signed the sales slip and background check form—the sales clerk also identified Doctor Gardner as the one who purchased the gun—and forensics later matched the bullet that killed Otto to that gun. Gardner also tested positive for gunshot residue consistent with him having fired the gun, but Madeleine's hands were clean."

"Wow. I take it you believe he's guilty?"

"Judy, if you ever become a criminal defense lawyer, you'll know that a good criminal defense lawyer never answers that question about a client. A good lawyer will always say that what the lawyer thinks about his client's guilt or innocence is irrelevant, so don't ask. If what the lawyer thinks were at all relevant, the whole long process of trial could be avoided—the judge would simply just ask the lawyer what she thinks, and take that answer as determinative of guilt or innocence. No need for a trial, cross examination of witnesses—no need for evidence at all. But, thank God, that's not the way our system works. It took over a thousand years of common law jurisprudence to develop the adversary system as the best process for determining guilt in a criminal case: two opposite sides presenting evidence, and an independent body—the jury, the conscience of the community—given the task of finding the truth."

Judy nodded. "But you said you thought Doctor Gardner was guilty."

"No, I said the evidence of guilt was overwhelming—which it is—especially when the defendant in this case refuses to assert any defense. I didn't say I thought he was guilty. But I will tell you this. There is something about this case that is not right. There is something about the evidence that we have now that does not reveal. And that's all I'll say. As far as the evidence goes, you can read the file as well as I can."

"But once you were appointed—before Doctor Gardner dismissed you, that is—were you able to get any background information? I mean about Doctor Gardner, Carl Otto, or about his wife Madeleine? What about the house where the crime was committed?"

Amber looked at her watch, but then nodded. "Yes, I did. And some of it is interesting. Maybe you can use it somehow to find a missing piece. I assume that's why you're here. First—about the house where the crime was committed. It's not so much a house as a palatial ranch estate. It's on forty acres, and looks much like the ranch on that old 1980s TV show, Dallas, of J.R. Ewing fame. Are you familiar with that show?"

"Sorry, no."

Amber smiled, aware now of the generation gap. "No matter. Carl Otto lived there for about eight years after the death of his first wife, Emma. Several years after her death, Carl met Madeleine Berger, a young woman—quite a beauty I'm told though I've never met her—who had recently emigrated from

Germany, and gotten a job as hostess of the Vista Hills Country Club where Carl Otto was a member. They must have hit it off, because they were married soon thereafter."

"Please. Go on."

"Would it surprise you to know that Doctor Gardner was also a member of the Vista Hills Club? Both Doctor Gardner and Carl Otto were on the Vista Hills executive committee. According to what Madeleine told the police, Gardner had come to Carl Otto's house to discuss committee matters on the evening of the murder."

"What was this Otto doing living on a Texas Ranch? Was he in oil?"

"Oh, no. He made his fortune—or his family did—in Germany before he ever came to Texas. His family owned some kind of construction and civil engineering company—salvage—in Germany after the war…"

"World War II, I assume you mean."

"Yes, but the firm is still a going concern in Germany. It was originally a subsidiary of I.G. Farben, which made poison gas during World War II. It became independent during the 1950s, and is now called Otto Wagner Koncept Konstucktion, or O.W.K.K. Group. I may not have that name exactly, but something like that. As one of the heirs of the original owner of the company, the rumor was that Otto got into some kind of dispute with some of the other heirs back in Germany, and decided to make a break, leave the country to live the life of a Texas rancher, bringing his wife with him. I have no idea where he got the idea for moving to Texas—I understand the TV show Dallas was quite popular in Germany in the 1980s, so maybe that's where he got the idea."
Judy made a mental note to look up the TV show Dallas on YouTube.

"His wife," Amber continued, "died from a stroke several years after he bought the Otto Ranch. As part of some kind of settlement with his Germany partners, he retained a passive partnership interest in the company, which apparently provided him with a good income. His ranch alone was appraised for property tax purposes—I checked—at twenty-four million. Not sure about his other assets, but I assume they were considerable."

"So Madeleine became a wealthy widow after the death of her husband. In Netflix murder dramas that's always supposed to be suspicious."

"Yes, but in this case the facts backed up her story. By the way, she no longer lives at the ranch, and recently put it up for sale. I think I heard she's moved to New York, but you'd have to check on that."

"I take it she was never a suspect in the murder of her husband?"

"Oh, no. Doctor Gardner is the only suspect."

"The police never considered Madeleine as a suspect?"

"Personally, I think they should have. But as I told you, there was never any reason to doubt her story, and all the facts backed her version of what happened."

Gardner never disputed any of it, then?"

"Actually, the good doctor never said anything one way or the other, but he never denied the story as Madeleine told it. As I said, he remained silent when the police questioned him at the scene and later at the police station."

"And he's never said anything since he's been incarcerated?"

"Nope. Nada. The only things he's said since the murder was to me—when they sent me to him as appointed counsel."

"And…?"

"When I went to the county jail to inform him of the judge's appointment of me as his counsel, he just looked at me through the bars and said that he didn't want counsel and would not meet with me. And then he turned away. And that was that."

"So he's been sitting alone in his cell since his arrest?"

"Yep, that's about the size of it. They did take him from his cell to his court arraignment where the charges against him were read, and he was advised of his rights. Again he was silent, thereby obliging the court to enter a Not Guilty plea."

"Unbelievable. And like you said, it just doesn't sound right."

"Well," said Amber as she rose from her seat, "that's about all I can tell you. I have to say I've never had a case like this, or even heard of one like this, but there's nothing anyone can do. There's certainly nothing you can do, either, so you've probably come on a wild goose chase. Maybe you can write a paper on this case back at your law school."

"Just one more question?" Judy pleaded.

Amber sighed, but sat down. "Sure, one more, but then I really need to get home and crash. I've got several court appearances in the morning."

"I understand. Thank you. OK, you said he's never said a word since the murder except to tell you that he didn't want you, or anyone, to represent him. But I read that he made an offer to the D.A.—to plead guilty to first degree murder in return for a death sentence.

"He made that offer in writing, not orally. He scribbled the offer on a note and put it in an envelope on which he wrote instructions to the corrections officer on duty to forward it to Eddie Matheson, the District Attorney for Appaloosa County."

"But can the D.A. even enter into such a plea bargain? I mean would it be legal?"

Amber shrugged here shoulders, and got up again from her seat. "Judy, I really have no idea, and since he's not my client I can't say that I am inclined to waste my time researching that question. Maybe you can write an article for your law school's law review on that question. But I really gotta go now."

As Amber walked away, Judy called out to her. "Could I talk to him? Do you think he would talk with me?"

Amber turned around with a puzzled look. "What?"

"I mean could I try to talk to him?"

Amber sat back down, and ordered another Margarita. "To Doctor Gardner? Are you serious?"

"Well, maybe he'd talk to a law student, you know, for educational purposes."

Amber suppressed an exasperated smile and shook her head. "You are kidding, right? He won't even talk to me, and I was appointed by the court to represent him."

"But if he wanted a lawyer, I assume he could afford to hire a lawyer of his choice, and not have to accept a court appointed one. He's a doctor, right? So, if he is guilty, are you thinking that maybe he's just decided to give up, seek a gentle death by lethal injection, and let the state accommodate him?"

Amber shrugged. "That's a possibility, I suppose, but so what? Where does that leave us? I think it's just as likely that its part of a perverse legal strategy—to come up with this ridiculous offer to discombobulate the court as a delaying tactic, with the idea of withdrawing his plea offer at a later date and accepting legal representation at the last minute before trial."

"I'd really like to try."

"Try what?"

"Try to talk to Doctor Gardner."

Amber was tempted to just tell this eager young law student that she was being naïve:

"And what exactly makes you think he'd talk to you if he won't talk to me?" said Amber with some exasperation in her voice.

"I don't know. The worst that could happen is that he would say no, right? So what's the harm in trying?"

"Well, it's a moot point. You'd never get the D.A.'s permission to get close enough to Gardner to even ask him if he'd talk to you. You're not his lawyer, you're not a relative, or even a friend, and the last thing Matheson would want is for some law student—he'd probably suspect that you were really a journalist masquerading as a law student—to get an interview. Matheson has already been deluged with requests from reporters whom he is pretty sure only want to turn this case into a cause celebre to push some political cause or another. Death penalty opponents are already using this case to try to discredit Texas' death penalty law, and Texas itself for executing so many murderers."

"Really? How so?"

"I don't know—by showing that the death penalty can be used by any nut to commit suicide and make the state complicit in his suicide? Who knows?"

"So I'd have to get this D.A. Matheson's permission to even gain access to Gardner just to ask him if he'd talk to me."

"As a practical matter, yes. Matheson rules that office with an iron hand, and has a reputation as the toughest prosecutor in the state. He has political ambitions, and never lets anyone forget he has never lost a capital case. He's notched eleven death penalty verdicts on his belt since he's been in office, and three have already been executed. I can assure you that he's not going to let anyone throw him off his stride in the Gardner case. He's already miffed that Gardner's written offer was leaked to the press. He's on the hunt now in his office to find the source of the leak."

"Now that the fact of the offer has been leaked, has he responded publicly in any way to Gardner's death penalty offer?"

"No, I think Matheson is just waiting for Gardner to crack, plead not guilty for real, hire a high profile lawyer—the better to gain media publicity for his political career—and give him the chance to rack up an easy death penalty conviction. The last thing Matheson wants is to rack up a death verdict only because a defendant offered it to him. No glory in that."

Judy looked resigned. "I see."

There was a long silence, but Amber didn't get up. Instead she ordered another Margarita and said, cautiously:

"It's a long shot, but I do have an idea."

Judy brightened. "To get an interview with Doctor Gardner?"

"Not to get the D.A.'s permission for an interview, but perhaps to gain access to Gardner so you can ask Gardner for an interview."

"So you're going to tell me, right?"

"You have no chance getting by Matheson, that's for sure. But I know for a fact that Matheson is scheduled for a three week fishing vacation in the Bahamas, and is due to leave tomorrow.

In his absence, his assistant D.A. Brett Hillman will be in charge of the office."

"And you think I'd have a better chance getting access to Gardner by going through this Hillman?"

In reply, Amber managed a mischievous smile. "Yes. Let's just say that Brett is a bit of a..."

"A bit of a..."

"Uh-huh. You got it. He's already been the subject of complaints from two of the female paralegals in the office—hushed up or paid off, not sure which. He's already hit on me several times—to no avail, of course. He's a scumbag."

Judy shifted uncomfortably. "And you think he'd..."

"Judy, I'll be honest here—woman to woman. With your face and figure, you'd have him eating out your hand in no time. You're a stunner, and don't tell me you don't know it."

Judy now turned crimson, and she wondered if it was the Margaritas that were talking now. "But I'd never..."

"I know you wouldn't, but with your looks you wouldn't have to, believe me."

For several moments the two woman simply looked at each other over the table.

"Well," Amber finally said. "You asked. Now I really do gotta go." She looked a little unstable.

Judy rose too and said, "Amber, you've had several of those Margaritas. Why don't you let me drive you home?"

Amber shook her head. "Can't leave my car here."

"I'll talk to the manager about leaving your car in the lot for the night. I'll take you home, and I can drive you back tomorrow morning to get your car."

Amber nodded. "Well, thanks. I guess you're right. The last thing I need is a DUI. "

******

Judy walked Amber up the sidewalk to her home and made sure she got in without falling. Before saying good night, she asked one more question:

"So as far as you know, this Brett Hillman will be in his office tomorrow, and Matheson will be on his way to the Bahamas?"

As Amber staggered into her townhouse, she turned to Judy and said:

"You go girl!"

CHAPTER ELEVEN

DECEMBER 23

The Appaloosa County District Attorney's office in the county seat of Lancaster was bright with Christmas decorations and holiday trees when Judy presented herself in the reception area.

She had tied her hair back in a ponytail and was dressed modestly in her knee-length black skirt, white blouse, and flats. Most of the desks in the outer lobby were vacant, due no doubt to the lax Christmas schedule during the holiday season. A receptionist looking very bored was on the phone and held up her hand to indicate the visitor should wait. It was obvious that her telephone conversation was a personal one, probably with a boyfriend.

Looking annoyed at having to cut her private conversation short, the receptionist finally hung up the phone and curtly asked the obligatory "may I help you?"

"Yes, good morning," said Judy. "I was wondering if I might see"—Judy took out a notepad from her purse and read it as if she had only been given the name of the person she came to see and couldn't remember it—"an Assistant District Attorney Brett Hillman. Is he in?"

"Your name please," came the short reply.

"Judy Alexander. Is he in?"

"Yes, I believe so. Do you have an appointment? Mr. Hillman is very busy today as it's his first day as Acting District Attorney while Mr. Matheson is on vacation. Can I ask what this is about?"

"It's about one of the cases that's being prosecuted by this office. It would just take a couple of minutes if I could see him."

"If you have information about a case, I'd suggest you go down to the Sheriff's office. It's just two blocks down on Main Street."

"No, I have no information. I'm a law student and am working on a law review article about a case, and was hoping..."

The receptionist cut her off. "No one in this office is allowed to talk to the media about an ongoing case. I suggest you write a letter. Now if you'll excuse me."

At that moment a hunky man in his mid-thirties sporting a well-appointed suit rushed up to the reception desk with a stack of papers in his hand.

"Angie, I need to get these subpoenas over to the Sheriff's office right away."

Angie took the papers. "Yes, Mr. Hillman. Right away." Hillman looked up as he handed Angie the papers, doing a double take as he sized up Judy, focusing transparently on her amazing legs. Suddenly smiling he asked, "And you are? May I help you?"

Angie cut in. "She's a law student wanting to talk to you about a case for some article she's writing. I told her we don't talk about ongoing cases."

"Oh, I think we can spare a few minutes for a law student," said Hillman. "All of us D.A.s were law students once."

Judy held out her hand. "Judy Alexander, sir. It would just take a few minutes. I'd really appreciate it."

"Of course," gushed Hillman. "Can I get you some coffee?"

"Oh that would be so nice, thank you," replied Judy, who really had missed her cup of coffee that morning, though she couldn't imagine that any office coffee would be up to her high standards for coffee.

"Angie," said Hillman, "two cups of coffee. Judy, cream and sugar?"

"Just a little cream, thanks."

"So, Judy, if you'll come with me."

Angie rolled her eyes as she watched Judy follow Hillman down the hall to his office.

"Come in and have a seat," said he. "Now what law school are you from?"

Hillman shut the door and took his place behind his desk.

"Oliver Wendell Holmes School of Law, sir."

"Oh yes, that's in..." He obviously had never heard of it.

"Manhattan, New York. It's a fairly new law school, established about thirty years ago."

"Oh yes, come to think of it, I think I have heard of it. Don't they have a clinic of some sort that tries to overturn convictions?"

"Yes sir, it does."

"Wait a minute, wasn't it someone from that clinic that convinced the Texas Supreme Court to reverse a murder conviction a couple of years ago?"

"I believe so. I wasn't at the school at that time."

Judy was thinking of how to direct the conversation away from that subject, since she was sure the subject of overturning convictions was not one that would endear her to most district attorneys.

There was a short pause in the conversation as there was a knock on the door and Angie brought in the coffee.

"Well," said Hillman after Angie had left. "You said that you were working on a law review article. How can I help you with that?"

Judy had thought for some time the night before how she might best broach the matter of the Gardner case. In the end, however, she couldn't think of any way to do so except to be up front.

"The topic came up in a criminal law class about whether it would be ethical—or legal for that matter—for a District Attorney to engage in a plea bargain with a murder defendant under which the defendant would agree to plead guilty in exchange for receiving the death penalty."

At this, Hillman's expression took on a look of exasperation as he sat back in his chair and looked up at the ceiling. If it was anyone other than a woman with Judy's spectacular looks he would have thrown her out of his office in an instant. Instead, he paused and forced a smile.

"Ms. Alexander, the whole story of that plea bargain is just fake news conjured up by the anti-death penalty lobby."

From her conversation with Amber, Judy knew that the Gardner had made precisely that offer—in writing—to the District Attorney. She also knew that the Appaloosa County District Attorney's office had made no public announcement either acknowledging that such an offer had been made, or, if it had been made, publicly rejecting it."

"So you have not received such an offer from Mr. Gardner?"

Hillman now looked distinctly uncomfortable. "I didn't say that. Mr. Gardner has refused counsel—presumably choosing to represent himself—so I have to consider that any communications between him and this office are privileged. As a law student, surely you understand that."

Judy didn't, but said: "I do! But the newspapers already know about it, and it's been on the news."

"That information was never released by this office to the public! There was a leak—a criminal act—by someone, either in this office, the sheriff's office, or the department of corrections, and we are currently conducting an investigation."

"I understand, and that's unfortunate, I agree. But now that it's out there, it does raise an interesting legal question, don't you think? Or at least an ethical question? And that's why I want to write an article on whether it would be ethical or legal for a prosecutor to agree to such a plea bargain, or even to entertain it. I was hoping you might have an opinion."

For a moment Judy worried that her attempt to stoke his ego had been too transparent. Apparently it hadn't.

"So purely hypothetical, then?"

"Yes...umh...hypothetical" Judy was now unsure if she was adequately laying the groundwork for the unusual request she planned to make.

Hillman sat back again and stared at the ceiling. Uncomfortable as he was about where the interview was leading, his feelings of vexation were trumped by his other more primeval instincts. If he were to engage Judy on some esoteric legal question fit for publication in a law review—too bad it had to be this particular one—there might be numerous opportunities for interfacing with her in the future.

"I'd really have to think about it. Of course, I'm not aware that these questions have ever arisen before in a court of law. As I see it, there would be a practical problem of enforcement of such a plea bargain. Assuming that a court would even approve it, what if the defendant later repudiated the bargain? Would a court—or the Supreme Court if it ever got that far—allow an execution to go forward under such circumstances? If not, then such a plea bargain is meaningless and virtually unenforceable. Personally, I think any D.A. would reject such a bargain out of hand, seeing it as a stunt made only for purposes of delay."

"Would you?"

"Would I what?"

"Reject such an offer if made by a defendant in a capital case?"

"I thought we were just talking hypothetically."

"We are, I'm just asking if, hypothetically, you would accept such a plea bargain offer. What if there were evidentiary problems in the case, and going to trial would risk an acquittal, on some legal technicality, of someone else whom you were sure had committed a murder? What if rejecting the defendant's plea bargain meant that the defendant would insist on going to trial, and thereby put the family of the victim through considerable trauma?"

At this, Hillman put up his hands and managed a smile. "Well, you've got something there. Really, I'd just have to think about it. It would depend on so many things."

Sensing that the interview had gone as far as it could on the purely legal question of the ethicality of death penalty plea bargains, Judy decided to cut to the chase.

"I understand, Mr. Hillman. But I'm also very much interested in why any defendant in a capital murder case would make such a plea bargain—the psychological aspect, that is."

"Now that I couldn't tell you, except to say that defendants who know they are caught and facing incarceration very often do choose suicide. 'Suicide by cop,' it's sometimes called, when a guilty defendant knows he cornered and facing such a fate anyway."

"So in our hypothetical case, this would be a 'suicide by court decree.'"

Hillman chortled. "Yes, I suppose you could call it that—-if it ever happened, which I doubt."

"Mr. Hillman, I wanted to ask you a very great favor."

"Well, of course, if I possibly can. I might be willing to help you with your article."

It was now or never to make her move.

"To write it, I think I really need to talk with Mr. Gardner—ask him why he made such an offer in the first place." Much as Hillman was inclined to ingratiate himself with the fascinating woman who sat before him, he could barely conceal his astonishment at this most surprising request. He responded:

"But that's impossible Ms. Alexander! Only his lawyer, family, and close friends can be permitted to see him. Plus he refuses to talk to anyone, even his appointed counsel!"

"Then if he refuses to talk to me there is no harm done, right? And if he does talk to me, I might find out something useful that would be helpful to understanding why he has refused the assistance of counsel."

"Even assuming that he would talk to you—which I strongly doubt—anything he said to you would be inadmissible in court. It would be known that any such interview was conducted with the cooperation of this office—after all, we're here talking with each other—and he would have to be advised of Miranda rights."

"Hasn't he already been so advised?"

"Yes, but that's not the point."

Judy now realized that Hillman was starting to not make sense, and probably just trying to be accommodating without making any real concession.

"So you won't let me try?" Judy asked with a puppy-like tilt of her head. "For the cause of legal education?"

Judy re-crossed her legs. Was she piling it on too thick, she worried?

"I...I don't know, "he stammered. "It's really not up to me. I mean, there's certainly nothing to stop you from just showing up at the County Jail, and asking to see Gardner. But I'm afraid the sheriff would just tell you that he's refused to see or talk with anyone."

"But if I went with your permission, the sheriff might let me try? I mean you're in charge now, right?"

Her final attempt to stroke his ego.

"I, I...don't know..."

Judy had promised herself that she wouldn't play this card—the one that all through her life had always worked—but she felt she was so close; and the alternative was to go back to Manhattan with nothing to show for it.

"Mr. Hillman, I would be so grateful if you could help me write this article, and to do so I need to at least try to talk to Mr. Gardner. If you let me go with your approval and just try, I'd really like to collaborate with you on this article. And if I do get to talk to him, perhaps afterwards we could get together to discuss what I found out?"

She hated herself for playing it, but she was sure the cause was just.

CHAPTER TWELVE

DECEMBER 23

"I'm here to see the prisoner Roger Gardner," Judy announced to the Deputy Sheriff on staff duty at the Appaloosa County Jail. She was dressed in jeans, sweatshirt, and wore a scarf over her head.

The deputy looked up from his pile of papers. "Sorry ma'am, its past visiting hours. And prisoner Gardner is not taking visitors."

Judy produced a signed letter from Deputy District Attorney Brett Hillman addressed to the Sheriff and said with as much authority as she could muster:

"Officer, as you can see, Mr. Hillman from the District Attorney's office has requested that I be taken to prisoner Gardner's cell—without first inquiring of Mr. Gardner whether he's accepting visitors. If after introducing myself to him at his cell, he says he will not talk to me, you are to escort me back here to the front desk and I will leave. If he will talk to me, you are to take him to a secure interview room and give me one hour in private with him."

"I see that," said the Deputy as he perused the letter.

"D.A. Matheson is on holiday," Judy pointed out, "so it is signed by the acting D.A.."

"We're aware that D.A. Matheson is on holiday, but this is a bit irregular. Please wait here while I check with the sheriff."

Judy smiled at the young staff officer who manned the reception desk while the Deputy disappeared behind a back office door. The officer smiled back.

"Can I get you anything while you wait? Water?"

"That would be nice," replied Judy. "I'm just wondering when the Deputy will be back."

"I'm sure he'll be back shortly."

The officer went to the water fountain and brought back a cup of water. It was a good quarter hour before the Deputy returned.

"Well, your request is a bit irregular," he said, clearly uncomfortable about the situation. "We'd prefer to get authorization for your request from Mr. Matheson, but we were not able to reach him."

"Yes, nor was I. That's why I went to Mr. Hillman for authorization, who is the acting D.A.."

"All right. Give us a few minutes. I'll have the prisoner taken to the interview room, and then I'll take you up, but I can tell you that he won't talk to you or anyone."

Roger Gardner, looked gaunt and frail in his prisoner attire which was at least two sizes too big, and there was at least several days' stubble on his face. After being introduced to Judy through the bars of his cell by the Deputy, he had reluctantly acquiesced in going to the interview room in return for being given a glass of fresh orange juice, and not being handcuffed. He sat stoically and impatiently in the interview room. A guard was posted outside the room.

"Who are you?" he asked sharply as the door opened and Judy appeared.

Judy took off her scarf, shook her head slightly, and managed a smile.

"Doctor, my name is Judy Alexander. I'm a law student, and I would be very grateful if I could have a few words with you. Would it be all right if I sat?"

Gardner shrugged and gestured for her to sit.

"You wouldn't know me," Judy said softly as she took the seat opposite him. "I'm not an attorney, or connected with your case in any way. I read about your case, and was hoping I might talk to you."

Gardner gazed at Judy for several moments in silence. If nothing else, the decorous young woman who sat before him was in radiant contrast to the miserable surroundings of the

Appaloosa County Jail. It was enough to break his self-imposed vow of silence.

He shook his head. "I have nothing to say about my case," he finally said.

"I understand that. But I haven't come to talk about your case."

At least he was talking, thought Judy, which was already more than he had done with all his previous visitors, including the attorney assigned to his case by the judge.

Gardner's voice softened. "And why would you come all the way from New York to talk to me if not about my case?"

"I'll be honest with you, Doctor. I am a student in the Exoneration Clinic at the Oliver Wendell Holmes School of Law in Manhattan. I was very intrigued about a newspaper article which came to our attention which reported that you had made an offer to the District Attorney to plead guilty to the murder charge which had been lodged against you in return for being given the death penalty. Is that true?"

It was a turning point in the interview—if Gardner was going to terminate the interview it would be after being asked this question—even after he had already insisted that he would not talk about his case.

Gardner folded his arms. "I told you, I won't talk about the facts of my case."

"And I fully respect that, doctor, but I'm not really asking about the facts of your case, am I? I'm just asking about whether you made an offer to plead guilty in return for being put to death. In my opinion, only an innocent man would make such an offer."

As Judy hoped, he felt compelled to respond—despite himself.

"And why on earth would you think that? Surely it must be obvious. It is the offer of a man with a guilty conscience, who cannot live with what he has done, who seeks death as just punishment for his sin."

"I suppose it could be that," said Judy, confident now that a real interview was underway. "But how many people have you heard of who have been convicted of murder, sentenced to life imprisonment, and on appeal pleaded that their sentence be commuted to death? Isn't it always the other way around—those who are guilty of murder and sentenced to death plead on appeal that their sentence be commuted to imprisonment as an act of mercy—mercy which they never gave their victim?"

For the first time since she had walked into the interview room, Judy noticed the faintest semblance of a willingness to interact with her. Having now apparently engaged him on a philosophical point, she decided to press her advantage:

"So are you saying that you did make such an offer? Since the reports of your offer were leaked to the press, I understand that the D.A.—and I think the Governor as well—have claimed that you are just grandstanding to get attention and sympathy, and that your real motive is to delay the proceedings, and perhaps make yourself a martyr to the cause of abolishing the death penalty by making the death penalty look ridiculous."

"So they think I'm willing to sacrifice my life for the purpose of advancing some social cause?"

"Yes, or perhaps just playing a game with the state since you know that such an offer could never be accepted."

"I don't know that at all. If the state has to go to trial because it refuses to accept my offer, it would take months of the court's time and appeals to convict me, perhaps years or even a decade or more, stretching state resources that could otherwise be used for much more worthwhile purposes."

"So you did make the offer? It's true?" Judy now had the confidence to interrupt her subject.

"Yes, I did, in writing, and in a confidential note to the D.A.. If I were grandstanding, I would have made the offer public, and through an attorney. It was the D.A.'s office who leaked the offer, not me."

There was now a long silence as each paused to size up the other. Judy now felt she had made some progress in achieving some rapport with Dr. Gardner and that he had opened up to her far beyond what she could have hoped for. Nevertheless, she decided not to press on by trying to get him to discuss the actual facts of the case—at least not now. She would respect his request to not talk about the facts of the case."

"Thank you doctor," she said as she rose from her chair and tied the scarf over her hair. Even though there was still at least another half hour of the allotted time remaining, she now thought it best to leave the good doctor perhaps wanting more.

"You are leaving so soon?" he said, looking almost disappointed. "Is that all? Have you no more questions?"

Judy turned before knocking on the door for the guard.

"Just one, Dr. Gardner. Are you willing to plead guilty because you really are guilty of the crime of which you are charged?"

He coughed in surprise at the question. "I am in full possession of my faculties, miss. Why else would any sane man offer to plead guilty to such a crime?"

Judy stood for a moment and gazed into the eyes of the man who reminded her of the countenance of a kindly Dr. Kilcare, or of a radiant Sydney Carton as he stood on the scaffolding before the guillotine in A Tale of Two Cities—and in whom she could see no guilt.

"For love," she said.

And then she was gone.

CHAPTER THIRTEEN

DECEMBER 25

Judy felt a tinge of loneliness as she woke up alone in her hotel room on Christmas morning, still feeling remorse over the card—or cards—she had played with Assistant D.A. Hillman. Since all offices and contacts would be closed, there was nothing she could do to further her mission. She thought about calling her on-and-off boyfriend in California, but thought better of it given that she had not contacted him since entering law school. She thought of calling her son, but remembering that he was on a discovery trip to Patagonia with a friend, and out of communication.

So was she to spend Christmas morning entirely alone, without any human communication whatsoever? Her thoughts turned to Professor Hammond. She recalled that in her last interview with him he had mentioned possibly spending Christmas in Hawaii, in which case she wouldn't want to disturb him. But since he had also said he hadn't made up his mind about going, she thought a call might be worth a shot.

"Hello," he answered promptly after one ring when she dialed.

"Merry Christmas, Professor. Is this a bad time? This is Judy."

"Well, it is Christmas."

"I know. I'm sorry. I didn't know if you were in Hawaii. I thought if you happened to be available I might give you a quick update on the Gardner matter. But if you're busy..."

"Not at all. Glad you called. No I decided to stay in town, finish grading the Civil Procedure exams, and just take it easy. I might go up to New Hampshire over New Years for some skiing, but hadn't decided on that either. So what's up?"

"Do you have a few minutes?"

"Umh...sure. Just working on Friday's crossword. Kind of stumped right now."

"Is that Chopin I hear in the background?"

"Yes, helps me think."

"My favorite composer as well. Any clue I can help you with?"

"As a matter of fact there is one. If I could just get this one clue, the whole bottom right of the puzzle would open up."

"Want to try me?"

"For one who isn't into crosswords, I must say you really helped with that 'yo-ho-ho' you came up with for 'refrain from piracy' last time. But this one is even harder, and even with google cheating I can't come up with a thing. The clue is 'anxious parent's plea to the school nurse'—thirteen down."

"Wow—that is a stumper. 'Anxious mother's plea to the school nurse.' I can't imagine. How many letters?"

"Let's see. Eleven. Wait—no twelve. So you can see how it would really open it up if I could get it."

"Any letters you already have?"

"I'm pretty sure the third letter is an 'L,' and the seventh letter is an 'N.' The eleventh letter might be a 'C,' but I'm not sure." Judy took out a piece of note paper and drew out twelve spaces, placing the three known letters on the indicated spaces.

"So with twelve letters it must be a run-on of several words. But I'm afraid you've got me, Professor. Is there any kind of theme to the puzzle?"

"Something about 'honesty is the best policy.' I did get four down—Diogenes—the Greek cynic philosopher who carried a lantern looking for a single honest man among all the faces of his fellow Athenians."

"Did you have to google that?"

Hammond chucked with embarrassment.

"Well, yes, but only after I tried everything else. As far as I can make out, the clue I gave you is google-proof. But I did google 'Everdingen,' one of the famous artists who painted or sculpted him. I must say, though that in my googling I did get some fascinating information about old Diogones. According to legend, Alexander the Great, who had been tutored by Socrates, went to visit the philosopher in Sinope and asked him what he desired, to which Diogones cheekily answered 'stay out of my light.'"

"I think I remember something about Everdingen in my art history class. But refresh my memory about Diogones."

"Diogones believed that manners were a form of dishonesty—lies used to hide a human's true nature. He believed in total honesty in action as well as in communication, and took to urinating or even pleasuring himself in public, contending that such activities were normal—that everyone performed those activities, but dishonestly hid in private what he did in public. No wonder that he was derided by his fellow philosophers as a 'Socrates run amuck.'"

"Yes, no wonder."

Hammond realized he was getting far off track and paused before continuing.

"But sorry, Judy, to get back to the reason for your call, tell me—any progress on your mission to get the information you were looking for in the Gardner matter?"

Judy, who had by now tuned out her Professor's exposition on Diogones, put down the pencil which she had been using to doodle letters on the twelve spaces on her note pad.

"Well, a little, I think."

"Tell me."

"I talked to Doctor Gardner in the County Jail."

"Really! I'm impressed! I can't imagine how you accomplished that. I understood that he wasn't even talking to his assigned lawyer. How did you manage it?"

Judy thought it best not to mention how she had manipulated Hillman.

"Well, I talked to Amber Hartman, the court assigned attorney for him. She gave me all the information she had about the case from the police files—which is quite interesting, by the way, and I'll tell you later—but she told me that, as reported, Dr. Gardner refused to talk to her."

"Did Hartman mention that she might have at least suggested to Gardner about entering an 'Alford Plea'?"

"I'm sorry, Professor, I don't know what that is."

This is what I get for not having taken criminal law before undertaking this business, Judy thought.

"This type of plea comes out of a 1970 Supreme Court case that came out of North Carolina: North Carolina v. Alford—1970 I believe. The law of North Carolina at that time provided that if a defendant charged with murder entered a guilty plea, he would retain the possibility of receiving a life sentence; but if he pleaded not guilty, and was found guilty of murder with a jury recommendation of death, he would thereupon be sentenced to death. So, on the advice of counsel, Alford then offered to plead guilty—since the evidence against him was overwhelming—in order to avoid the death penalty, but at the same time that he was pleading guilty, he also claimed on the record that he was in fact innocent."

"Can a defendant do that?"

"Well, the trial court accepted the guilty plea and sentenced him to life in prison. Alford later sought to withdraw the plea, however, claiming that 'I just pleaded guilty because they said if I didn't, they would gas me for it.'—or words to that effect. His petition to withdraw his plea eventually wound up in the U.S. Supreme Court, where Justice Bryon White wrote the majority opinion upholding the plea as provident, and thus not subject to withdrawal despite his protestations of innocence at the same time that he entered the guilty plea."

"So what does that mean?"

"It means that a court may in its discretion accept a plea of guilty from a defendant who states that he is pleading guilty only because, upon advice of counsel, the evidence is such as would likely convict him—even though the defendant at the time of entering his guilty plea proclaims his actual innocence."

"I still don't get it."

"It just means that if, in order to avoid a probable death sentence a defendant decides to plead guilty because he knows he will be convicted, he can still insist that he is in fact innocent. That plea will still be upheld as long as it was made with advice of competent counsel."

"So how would an Alford plea be relevant in the Gardner case?"

"Given that the evidence against Gardner is overwhelming and that he was likely to be convicted if he went to trial, it might make sense for him to plead guilty in return for a life sentence, even while proclaiming his actual innocence— which the Alford case allows him to do."

"But that's just it, Professor. First of all, Gardner refused to even talk to Hartman, so obviously she wouldn't have had the opportunity to even suggest that he enter an Alford plea. Second, Gardner gave me the distinct impression that he wants to plead guilty because...well, because it was only justice that he be sentenced to death. I assume also that he would prefer death to a life in prison where he would be vulnerable to sexual assault or worse."

"So he's representing himself pro se? That's not uncommon. "

"Pro se?"

"Representing himself."

Judy grimaced. Of course she knew that legal term. The Professor must have thought her a real dunce.

"Actually no. I got the impression from Amber that he doesn't want to be represented at all—by himself or otherwise."

"Well that is most unusual."

"As far as I could tell, he has done only one thing on behalf of himself since being arrested."

"Which is..."

"Apparently it is true, as reported, that he did make that offer to the D.A. to plead guilty in exchange for a guarantee that he would be given a prompt death sentence."

"You confirmed that? I know it was reported in the press, and was the basis for your interest in the case."

"Yes, Assistant D.A. Hillman did confirm that, though he expressed some anger that it had been leaked to the press."

"By someone in his own office, no doubt."

"I think Hillman realized that there was no other way it could have been leaked except by someone in this office."

"So why did you even have to meet with Hillman? I'm surprised old man Matheson—he's still the D.A. down there as far as I know—would let you do that."

"Matheson was on some fishing trip down in the Caribbean, and couldn't be reached—so Hillman was the acting D.A.. Amber told me that the County Sheriff would never let me see Gardner without the D.A.'s permission."

"I see. Well you were lucky then, because from what I know about Matheson—he's a legend down there because of his zealousness in seeking the death penalty—he would never have let you see Gardner. He hates the press—I know that—and he hates being manipulated by defense counsel, let alone by a defendant acting pro se. Did Hillman think you were a journalist?"

"Oh God no. No I told him the truth—that I was a student in the Exoneration Clinic at the Oliver Wendell Holmes School of Law, and that I was writing an article on the ethical ramifications of a plea bargain for death."

"Well, are you?"

"Am I what?"

"Writing an article?"

"I was thinking about it, yes."

"Huh. Well, ok. Can't argue with success. So Hillman gave you the heads up to see Gardner. That was an achievement in itself since he wouldn't even talk to his own assigned defense counsel. So did he tell you anything about why he made such an offer of a plea bargain?"

"He said he wouldn't talk about the case."

"So what did you talk about? The weather?"

72

"Actually, I take back a bit of what I just said. He said he wouldn't talk about the case itself—the facts, what happened at the Carl Otto house on the night of the shooting—but I convinced him that talking about the plea bargain offer wasn't the same as talking about the facts of the case. So I did at least get him to talk about the plea offer he made, and why he made it."

"So he bought your hair splitting on what constitutes talking about the case. That's interesting. And...?"

"I told him what Hillman thought about the offer—that Gardner was just grandstanding to the death penalty abolitionist lobby to get attention. And that seemed to get Gardner talking. He became quite upset—first that his offer had leaked to the press, and second that he was being censured for grandstanding rather than nobly taking responsibility for his actions."

"So where has all this gotten you?"

"Not very far, I fear. I was hoping you might have a suggestion."

"Well, it appears that Gardner had told you everything he's going to tell you—though I compliment you for getting him to talk at all—and he refuses counsel, so I don't see that there is anything else you can do. But you gave it a good shot, and you may have enough to get started on that article you said you would write. But you see, don't you, that as I told you, this is not really a case for the Exoneration Clinic. If I were you, I would come back and get ready to take your second semester of law school. "

There was a long pause as Judy returned to her doodles, and let her balloon deflate.

Finally, Hammond said, "well, if you're determined to pursue this case, I suppose you could ask Hartman if she knows of anyone who is close to Doctor Gardner—a relative, associate, friend, who might be able to shed light on his character and background, and who might know more about his relationship with the woman who was there in the house at the time of the shooting. What was her name?"

"Madeleine Berger. But there's nothing to indicate that there was any relationship at all. Gardner was just visiting her husband about a business matter relating to the country club to which they both belonged."

"Perhaps that's why there's so little information about any relationship. Anyway, it was just a thought. Let me know. And now, I should probably get back to my exams."

Judy laid down her pencil.

"Professor?"

"Yes?"

"'The clue was: 'mother's plea to the school nurse' you said?'

"Yes."

"And the theme of the puzzle was 'honesty is the best policy?"

"Yes."

"Tell me no lice."

"Say again?"

"TELL ME NO LICE."

There was short silence as Robin checked to see if it fit. It id. "Of course! You're amazing. Can't believe I didn't see it!"

"Goodbye, Professor. Happy Christmas. I'll follow your suggestion and let you know."

CHAPTER FOURTEEN

DECEMBER 26

Judy slept in late despite having gone to bed early the night before. Despite spending Christmas Day alone and having made very little progress in the Gardner matter, she did not regret having made the trip to Houston. In Appaloosa County she had found a world she would never have known existed if she had spent the time in a law school classroom.

But she also realized that her expectations had been too high. Professor Hammond had been right. What on earth had led her to expect that as a law student with but one semester of classes under her belt she would be equipped to investigate what promised to become a high profile murder case?

After ordering room service of coffee and fruit, she picked up her cell phone and called Southwest Airlines to make a reservation for a return flight to New York. She would return to her tiny apartment in Manhattan and begin work on that article on plea bargaining ethics she had told Assistant D.A. Hillman she would write—but without his assistance of course. And then she would sign up for her second semester courses which would begin in less than two weeks.

When she got a recording indicating that bad weather in major airports around the country had caused numerous delays and that she could expect a twenty minute wait before reaching a representative, Judy decided to just lie back in her king size bed and wait for room service to appear. As she did so, staring at the ceiling, she thought of Professor Hammond's suggestion.

To be sure, he had made the suggestion only after she had insisted that he make one. But as she now had nothing but time to waste, she again picked up her cell and dialed Amber Hartman.

She did not expect Amber to answer it on the day after Christmas, a Friday, which meant that it was most likely a holiday for the law firm and that Amber was probably taking some well-deserved time off. Planning to just leave a message thanking Amber for her help, she was surprised when Amber answered.

"Hello."

"Oh hello, Amber? This is Judy. I'm going back to York either today or tomorrow, and just wanted to thank you for your help and advice in getting the interview at the D.A.'s office."

"I was glad to help. Actually, I'm glad you called because I wanted to apologize for getting so blitzed the other night that you had to take me home. I don't think I've done that since college."

"Not at all, and I understand. You were very kind to see me and fill me in on what you knew about the case."

"Of course I didn't really expect you'd ever get permission to access Gardner at the County Jail. But Hillman really did see you, then? I knew he would be your only chance of getting permission to see Gardner in the County jail. I can tell you that Matheson would never have let you. So did Hillman agree to meet with you?"

"Yes, he did, and it was just as you predicted."

"I can imagine. But did it get you anywhere?"

"I'm a bit embarrassed to admit it, but yes."

"You don't mean he helped you get access to Gardner?"

"Yes, he did."

"Did you tell him you were a journalist?"

"No, just the truth that I was a law student from the Exoneration Clinic at Oliver Wendell Holmes Law School."

"I can't believe it! He actually agreed to call the sheriff and get you access to Gardner. I'll be honest. I'm amazed. Umh... don't know how to ask this, but did you have to do anything..."

"Not at all. Well, I did hint that I might like to collaborate with him on writing an article on the plea bargaining ethics..."

"I guess that was enough. What a pig. Well, like I told you, you go girl. I take it that Gardner wouldn't actually agree to talk to you, though."

"No, actually he did."

"You're kidding! You saw Gardner, and he sat down with you and talked?"

"Yes, but not about the facts of the case, or his side of it if he had one."

"But you did talk to him? That's more than I was able to do. He refused to even sit down with me, and I was his assigned counsel. But if he wouldn't talk about the case, what did you talk about?"

"I did get him to talk about his plea bargain offer after I told him about how it had been leaked to the press. He was mad about that. Then I convinced him that talking about the plea offer was not 'talking about the case,' or at least not the facts of the case."

"Well, whatever you said to get him to talk, you did more than anyone else has. So what did he say about his offer to plead guilty in return for a death sentence?"

"He just talked about it in general philosophical terms— that if a person was guilty of murder, justice demanded the death penalty."

"Well, that's a bunch of crap, but never mind. You got him talking, and that's a start. Did you mention that it might be in his interest to talk to me now?"

Judy was embarrassed that she had not thought of asking him that, and realized she had missed an opportunity to really help Gardner by suggesting that he agree to accept the legal help he obviously needed.

"No, I'm sorry. I should have."

"That's all right. I'll probably make one more attempt to see him now that you've gotten him talking at all. So you're going back to New York now?"

"Yes. I'm afraid so. I talked to my faculty advisor in the Exoneration Clinic yesterday, and he thought I'd done what I could and that I should just come back and get ready for spring classes—maybe try to write an article on the ethics of plea bargaining. The problem is that I don't really know anything

I didn't know before. I would have liked to talk to someone who could shed light on the circumstances of the case, and the character and background of Dr. Gardner.

"I know," said Amber. "There's not much in the police report about that."

"My faculty advisor did suggest that if I insisted on pursuing this case further I might ask you about any friends of Gardner, or relatives that might have useful background information."

"The doctor has a sister, Susan Gardner. She lives in Galveston. Before I made my first attempt to interview Gardner I did some preliminary research and found her name."

"Did you interview her?"

"No. I didn't feel I should do that until Gardner accepted me as his counsel. I couldn't really go to his sister and say 'I'd like to represent your brother, but he doesn't want me to represent him. I was hoping you could give me some information about him.'"

"Yes, I see. What about some of Gardner's medical associates, or his friends at that country club you were telling me about. I wrote their names down in my notes. Vista Hills, wasn't it?"

"Yes, but I didn't feel comfortable interviewing those people either. After all, if I'm not acting as counsel I wouldn't be compensated for my time, and I have plenty of paying cases at the office to keep me occupied—at $300 an hour I might add."

"I understand that too. But I wonder, do you think it might be worthwhile for me to try to interview the sister—Susan Gardner? I don't have to worry about billable hours after all."

"I could give you her name and address. But I don't have her number—it's unlisted. Still, I suppose it might be worth a try. If you do track her down, though, I would tell her the truth up front about your status as a law student and see if that carries any weight with her."

"Of course I would do that."

"And who knows? If you pulled off the miracle of getting her brother to talk, maybe she would be willing to talk to you too. If so, I'd appreciate you letting me know what she says. I'd still like one more shot at getting Gardner to let me represent him, or at least get him to agree to hire counsel of his own choice."

"How far is it to Galveston? I've never been there."

"About an hour and a half from here, depending on traffic." Amber paused to look through her notes. "She lives at an upscale historical home in Jamaica Beach. I'll text you her address."

"Thanks so much! And I'll keep you updated on any information I discover."

"You go girl!"

CHAPTER FIFTEEN

DECEMBER 27

It was a mildly chilly fifty-eight degrees at midmorning in Jamaica Beach when Judy's rental car drew up to a stately and historical three-story home of white wood, just one block from the beach.

Checking the address on her text message from Amber, she walked up a long wooden staircase to the front door and knocked.

A neatly uniformed chambermaid opened the door.

"May I help you?"

"Yes," said Judy as she again checked her iPhone. "Is this the residence of Ms. Susan Gardner?"

"Who's asking?"

"I'm a law student from New York, and I was wondering if Ms. Gardner might agree to talk to me about her brother, Dr. Roger Gardner."

The face of the somewhat dour chambermaid revealed skepticism. "All right. Wait right there," she said as she closed the door in Judy's face.

It was several minutes before the chambermaid returned. "You may come in now. Please follow me."

Judy followed her to a bright sitting room decorated with nautical memorabilia and a splendid view of the ocean.

"Please wait here," said the chambermaid. "Ms. Gardner will be here shortly. May I get you something, water perhaps?"

"No I'm fine. Thank you."

Judy sat for a few moments on the comfortable bamboo divan to which she had been guided. After a few minutes with no appearance of Ms. Gardner, she stood up and walked to the large picture window to take in the view. As she did so, there was a voice from behind her, and she turned to see an attractive middle-aged woman with luxuriant silver hair, dressed in a long white resort gown and deck shoes.

"You are a law student from what school?" the woman asked.

"The Oliver Wendell Holmes Law School in Manhattan, ma'am. I'm Judy Alexander."

"Please sit," came the reply, as Susan Gardner took her own seat by the far window. With what seemed to be a forced smile, she asked "and what have you to do with my brother Roger?"

"I am a student in a clinic at my law school," said Judy as she sat back in the divan. "It's called the Exoneration Clinic, which looks into cases in which we believe an injustice has been done, a wrongful conviction."

"But surely you know that there has been no conviction as yet in the case against my brother."

"Yes, I know. But we read accounts of the case in the media, and from those accounts several of our students in the clinic believed that there may be a risk of a wrongful conviction in that case."

Judy involuntarily bit her lip, as she realized she had told a little white lie: no other students in the clinic had thought any such thing. She was the only one who had gleaned any such risk from the sketchiest of reports in the press about the case.

"And what led these students to think any such thing?"

Judy cleared her throat as she realized she was facing something along the lines of a cross-examination. "Well, for one thing, it was reported that Dr. Gardner—your brother—has declined to give any defense to the charges against him."

"Surely your law courses have taught you that it is best for any criminal defendant to stay silent in the face of such a serious charge as murder. I do not see why staying silent should in any way lead one to believe that some grave injustice is about to occur."

"Yes, that is very true. But your brother has also declined to accept any legal representation, including the legal assistance of a lawyer assigned by the court to represent him."

"My brother is financially very well able to retain his own legal counsel. It was impertinent for the judge to presume to assign counsel for him. My brother is not an indigent."

"But your brother has declined to retain any counsel to represent him. I believe the court was concerned that declining all counsel was indicative of some kind of incompetency, since it is not rational to decline all counsel. So I believe the court assigned counsel to represent your brother at least with regards to the competency hearing."

"He was found to be competent by the court. That finding was based on interviews of my brother's associates at the hospital where he practices. There was no evidence whatsoever presented to the court as to any incompetency. And he has the right, so I have been told by my own lawyer, to represent himself."

"Yes, but he had declined to represent himself pro se as well."

Judy hoped that her use of a legal term was giving her some credibility with Ms. Gardner. "But what most aroused the concern of the students in the clinic, and our faculty advisor as well, was that your brother had made a written offer to the District Attorney to plead guilty in return for a prompt death sentence with no possibility of appeal. We felt that if such an offer were ever accepted by either the District Attorney or the court that a great injustice could occur."

"And why is that, Ms. Alexander?"

"Because no competent person charged with such a crime would ever refuse legal counsel or decline to make any legal defense unless he was sacrificing himself for someone else."

There was a long silence as Susan Gardner fixed her gaze on Judy, who shifted in her seat uncomfortably but decided to wait until Susan replied before saying anything further.

Finally Susan said, "You must forgive me. Ms. Alexander. I had to satisfy myself that you were, well...on the up and up. You have satisfied me that you are. I feel like I may confide in you."

There was another very long silence before Susan continued. "I agree in every respect with your analysis of the case against my brother. And I will tell you, without any doubt in my mind, who my brother is protecting."

"Madeleine Berger," replied Judy without hesitation, for after talking to Amber, studying the police file, and talking to Roger Gardner himself, she had already come to that conclusion.

"Madeleine Berger! Yes! You have it! That woman has beguiled my brother since the first day she came out of Germany and stepped into his life! There is no way that my brother would ever commit such a crime as that with which he has been charged. He is the most decent man I have ever known. The only other person who could have murdered poor, old, rich Carl Otto was his malicious and greedy wife—yes Madeline Berger!"

Judy waited for Susan to calm down a bit before asking, "But what actual evidence is there that your brother would have any reason for protecting Madeleine? What do you really know about any kind of relationship between your brother and Madeline?"

"I have made discreet inquiries. I know a number of Roger's friends at Vista Hills, including his partners in his dermatology practice. Of course none of them would come right out and say that Roger and Madeleine were in any kind of relationship, but there had been whispers. The two had been seen taking intimate walks together on the club grounds after hours, talking in hushed tones at a corner table in the bar late at night, going off together in his car..."

"Tell me honestly, Ms. Gardner. Based on what you know about your brother, can you really imagine that he would sacrifice his own life for such a woman?"

Susan sighed. "Yes, I'm afraid I can imagine it. He's never been particularly successful with women. He was an awkward student in school, bullied quite a bit, labeled as a nerd. In high school, and later in college he was quite the bookworm, didn't date, and to my knowledge never had a serious relationship with a woman."

"You don't think he was..."

"Gay? Absolutely not—never showed any propensity whatsoever in that direction. He often confided in me that he hoped to find the right woman, have children, a family. But in the end he found solace in his work. He graduated from Johns Hopkins Medical School with highest honors, and excelled both as an intern and residency in his chosen specialty of dermatology. He was a protégé of Doctor Frederick Mohs who pioneered a controlled procedure to treat skin cancer, and has written extensively on the subject in the medical journals."

"Do you know what Madeleine might gain by her husband's death?"

"Otto was a very rich man. And Madeleine lived like a queen in his mansion outside Houston. I know his family had interests in some German construction company prior to immigration to the United States, and his shares in that company would now go to Madeleine, but that's all I know..."

"Do you know where Madeleine is now?"

"No, since she's been cleared by the police I understand she's put the estate up for sale, and I heard she's moved to New York with her millions."

"So soon? Doesn't the estate have to be settled in probate?"

"Yes, I suppose. But I have no doubt she'll have access to all his assets in a very short time, especially if the murder case against Otto is resolved by my brother's guilty plea—death penalty imposed or not."

"Ms. Gardner, I'm just a law student, and I fear that nothing more can be done to save your brother unless he himself decides to tell us what really happened that night at the Otto Manor—or at least let's himself be represented by counsel. Will your brother at least talk to you?"

At this, Susan put her head down to try to hide what Judy could nevertheless see were tears.

"No, he won't see me or anyone. Like you said, he won't even talk to counsel."

Judy now considered whether she should tell Susan that she had actually talked with her brother. It might make her even more distressed to hear that he would talk with her and not with his own sister. On the other hand, if Susan later discovered that she had talked with Roger and not confided to her that she had, she might lose all the credibility she had thus far earned with her. And Judy had no doubt that she would need Susan's help if she was to make any further headway in the case.

"Ms. Gardner, I must tell you one thing, and I hope it won't distress you."

Susan looked up and dried her tears on a Kleenex she now held in her hand. "Please tell me anything you know!"

"Two days ago I was able to see and talk with your brother."

Susan looked up with astonishment. "He talked to you?"

"Yes, but not about the circumstances of the case—only about why, in general, one might offer to plead guilty in exchange for a death sentence."

"And what did he say?"

Judy struggled to find the right words. "Only that if one committed such a crime, it was only just that the death penalty be imposed."

"Oh dear God!" Susan now made no effort to hide her tears.

Judy stood up and walked toward Susan and held her hand. "Ms. Gardner, please know I will do anything I can do to save your brother, or at least convince him, if I get the chance again, to retain counsel for his defense."

Susan looked up, choking back her tears now. "Thank you, thank you, Ms. Alexander!"

"Please call me Judy. We're in this together now." She took out a card with her name and address. "Call me anytime."

"Thank you, thank you, Judy!"

And with that Judy took her leave.

CHAPTER SIXTEEN

DECEMBER 28

The long suffering but veteran receptionist for the Appaloosa County District Attorney's Office held the phone a foot away from her ear.

"Lucy! Get Brett on the phone! Now!"

The booming voice of Eddie Matheson was unmistakable.

"Of course, sir," replied Lucy, relieved that it was not she who was in trouble, but the dapper Brett Hillman whose Anthony DiNozzo flippant persona had long since gotten very old with her.

"Sir, I believe he stepped out a few minutes ago. I think he's off to Starbucks."

"Well get someone down there now to bring him back. Pronto!"

"Yes sir."

Lucy frantically waved over the paralegal who sat in the desk behind her.

"Jamie, can you go down to Starbucks and get Brett back here!" she whispered. "The boss is on the phone, and he's on the warpath!"

The paralegal grimaced. "Ok, I hope he's there! What if he's not?"

"Just go!"

Lucy composed herself and brought the phone back to her ear.

"Sir, Jamie's gone down to get him. Is there anything I can do? How is your holiday going?"

"Lucy, I'm sorry for shouting, it was uncalled for and I apologize. But I leave for just a couple of days, just a couple of days of some rest and relaxation. I sail back to Freeport after just a couple of days fishing out of cell phone range and get a text from

Sheriff Turner informing me that some journalist has gotten in to see Gardner. He says Brett called his deputy to authorize it. Lucy, what the hell is going on? I left deliberate instructions that no journalist was to be allowed to see the prisoner! Hell, he won't even see a lawyer for God's sake, or even his relatives! And the prisoner himself said he wouldn't talk to anyone! First the report of his death penalty plea bargain gets leaked to the press, and now this! Jesus, I can't leave for even a couple of days without the shit hitting the fan!"

"Sir, I don't believe it was a journalist. I think it was just a law student from up north. I think I heard her say that she was writing an article on the ethics of plea bargaining, or something like that."

In reply Lucy heard only a muffled obscenity, and then: "Heard? Heard? Who heard?"

"Sir, I'm not sure sir, just, you know, talk around the office. And I'm not sure who said it or overheard it somewhere."

"Unbelievable. Doesn't matter now. The damage's been done. Is Brett back yet?"

"No sir. I thought he was going to Starbucks like he usually does at this time in the morning, but I guess he could have gone somewhere else. Jamie should be back in a minute.

"All right. Lucy, now tell me the truth. You said it was a law student, and you said 'she.' So tell me the truth. Was she a looker?"

"Umh, well..."

"The truth, Lucy!"

"Well, yes, I guess you could say that."

"Of course!" Matheson sighed with disgust. "I knew it." He had bailed out his womanizing deputy many times, even at the risk of his own reputation. He had kept him on only because he was charismatic in the courtroom, and his Gentleman's Quarterly good looks had charmed many a jury, especially those with a fair number of females. In fact, Hillman's trial record of convictions was far better than his own, which is why he often appointed him to lead the prosecution team, even in high profile cases.

"Sir, if you can hold a minute, I'll go to the window and see if he's coming."

"Go ahead, Lucy. I'll wait."

Lucy looked out and hurried back. "Yes, sir. He's on his way up."

As Hillman entered, Lucy held out the phone with her left hand while pointing at it with her right and mouthing "boss!"

Hillman smiled, shook his head, and rolled his eyes before taking the phone.

"Hey boss, how are the fish biting?"

"Dammit, Brett! I can't leave the office for even a few days without you screwing things up! I couldn't believe it when I read Turner's text telling me you let some damn law student in to see Gardner! What the hell! You know damn well the prisoner is trying to grandstand this death plea bargain thing. And Gardner refused to even talk to the judge, or even the lawyer the judge tried to appoint for him! The death penalty abolition lobby is going to have a field day over this!"

"Eddie, come on, I couldn't see the harm in letting a law student see for herself that he wouldn't talk or make a statement. And what's he going to say, anyway? That he didn't do it? So what? The judge entered a not guilty plea for him when he refused to plead. End of story. "

"Yeah, well in the old days at the Old Baily London Yard they used to use an old fashioned crushing machine to slowly crush a prisoner until he entered a plea."

Hillman chuckled indulgently.

"Yeah boss. I know. And they used to dunk women in the river until they either confessed or drowned. Look, the case is a slam dunk. The bastard was caught with the smoking gun just a few feet from the victim—his finger prints all over it, and gun powder residue all over his hands. And it was his gun, for God's sake, and ballistics shows the bullet in Otto's head came from that gun. We've got an eye witness, or at least an ear witness, the victim's wife, who will testify that he was the only person in the house when she heard the gunshot and came downstairs. Plus we probably have a good motive too, if the gossip about his infatuation with the wife pans out. I've got Lewis tracking down all that now at his work and at the hospital where he practices. So we'll offer him a life sentence if he confesses and pleads guilty."

"For God's sake, Brett, as usual you're missing the point. First of all, he's not going to plead guilty in return for a life sentence. Yes, that's the usual way it works in these cases, but not in this one, and I'm pretty sure of that right now. He's trying to make a point. I haven't quite figured out what his point is exactly, but it puts us in a real bind. If we were to accept his offer to plead guilty in return for a death sentence, it would make us look like monsters. So we just can't do it. And if we go to trial and seek the death penalty against a respected medical doctor who refuses to even defend himself, we might look even worse..., and we'd still have to go the expense of a long drawn out trial. There'd be no problem if someone in our office hadn't leaked Gardner's plea bargain offer, but...have you found out who leaked it yet?

"No boss, sorry. But I'm asking around."

"Do more than ask around. Find the bastard."

"Boss, what makes you think Gardner even agreed to talk to this law student?"

"Brett, let me read you Turner's text:

"I was surprised when Deputy Jones showed me Brett's letter asking us to let the law student have access to the prisoner Gardner for the purpose of asking him if he would talk with her. Jones said the prisoner agreed to talk to her..."

"Well, it couldn't have been for more than a few minutes..."

"Shut up! Turner says she was in the interview room with Gardner for half an hour!"

"I didn't know that. But even if that's true, I don't know what they could have talked about. The law student wasn't his lawyer, so Jones could have sat in during the interview."

"Well, he didn't, so we don't know what they talked about. But they had to talk about something, and I doubt if it was about the Cowboys chances in the playoffs. I've gotta believe that they at least talked about the plea offer, and why he made it. If so, this 'student'—if she even is one—now has confirmation of the press reports about the plea offer, which up until now were not confirmed and could be chalked up to press speculation."

"Ok, boss, I guess I messed up, and I'm sorry. I just really didn't think it was a big deal, and didn't think there was any harm in helping out a law student."

"Uh-huh. I know you're always willing to help out students. So just how good looking was she?

"Not at all, boss. Didn't really notice. Just plain."

"Yeah, did she promise you anything? Suggest she might hook up with you later?"

"Boss!" Brett replied with a hurt voice. "You know me better than that."

"Uh-huh. Yes, I do. That's the problem. Look, Brett, I've put my ass on the line for you many times, and for one reason and one reason only—you get convictions. Don't know how you do it, but you do. OK, I'm sorry I yelled—and apologize to Lucy for me—but one more screw up like this, and I think you know what I'll have to do. I was only incommunicado for a few days. Next time you have to make any decision in my absence, wait, and call me first!"

"Got it boss. Won't happen again."

CHAPTER SEVENTEEN

DECEMBER 28

After her interview with Susan Gardner, Judy had procrastinated about making her plane reservation for New York. The more she thought about it, the more she considered what she might discover by talking to Roger Gardner's friends at the Vista Hills Country Club, and his medical associates at the hospital where he practiced. She was thinking about calling Amber Hartman to tell her about her interview with Susan and what she had told her about the possibility of an affair between Roger and Madeleine Berger. Perhaps Amber might also suggest the best way to get an entrée to both the club and the hospital.

She was about to pick up the phone and call when her cell rang. It was Amber.

"Hi Judy, it's Amber. Are you still in Houston or have you gone back to New York?"

"Hi Amber! So glad you called. I was just about to call you. No I'm still here. Yesterday I followed up on your suggestion to talk to Susan Gardner."

"Oh really?" Amber had not really expected that Judy would actually track down Susan in Galveston, and was surprised.

"Yes," said Judy excitedly, "she was very nice, a bit stiff at first, but then really opened up about her brother. She's convinced that Roger was having an affair Madeleine, and that he was refusing to talk about the murder in order to protect her."

There was a long silence as Amber considered how to respond to her enthusiastic young protégé without deflating her balloon.

"Sweetie, it was an open secret that Roger and Madeleine were having an affair. The D.A.'s office already knows that, and they've already sent their investigator to get numerous interviews with Roger's friends down at the country club and the hospital. There's nothing new there."

"Oh," said Judy, now realizing that her trip to Galveston had not resulted in any new information that might explain why Roger Gardner was refusing to talk to counsel, let alone why he made the extraordinary plea bargain offer to the District Attorney. She was also somewhat disappointed that Amber had not bothered to tell her all this before sending her off on a wild goose chase to Galveston. Was Amber just patronizing her by letting her think that she could actually make headway in the case?

"You see, don't you, that the fact Roger and Madeline were almost certainly having an affair doesn't explain anything about why Roger is refusing counsel, and it certainly doesn't help his defense if he finally decides to mount one."

"But if he's protecting her..."

"The fact that Gardner was having an affair with the victim's wife just plays into what will certainly be the prosecution's theory of the case if the case ever goes to trial—which I have come to believe it certainly will. The affair just provides the D.A. with the perfect motive for murder, and one of the oldest in the books: Roger Gardner was in love with Madeleine, and the only way he could have her was if her husband Carl was put out of the way. Madeleine may or may not have seduced Roger into committing the crime for her in order to inherit his fortune, but that in no way exonerates Roger who, according to the forensic evidence, actually pulled the trigger. If true, it might explain why Roger is covering for her and refusing to implicate her. He may figure that since he's sure to be convicted of murder in any case, there's no reason to bring the woman he loves down with him."

"And so he sacrifices himself?

"He sacrificed himself the moment he pulled the trigger. I do not find it irrational at all that a successful doctor who had it all would prefer a comfortable death to a brutal life in prison. And the D.A. is likely to leave it up to the jury which motive it finds most credible—that Roger murdered Otto without

Madeleine's knowledge or connivance to get him out of the way; or that Madeleine seduced Roger into killing Otto in order to inherit his estate. Matheson won't care which motive the jury adopts; he'll just care about getting the conviction."

"Amber, I know I'm just a first year law student, but I think something's missing in both those scenarios. Madeleine called the police shortly after Otto was shot, and Roger was still there when the police came. He did not attempt to get away. He was still just standing there when the police came, with the gun on the chair beside him. Madeleine made a statement to the police at the scene, and a more detailed one later at the police station. If Roger had immediately left, Madeleine could just have told the police when they arrived that an intruder had invaded the house for purposes of burglarizing it, was startled by Otto, and shot him. Unless someone actually saw Roger entering the house— and I saw nothing in the police report that there was—that story would have left both Madeleine and Roger off the hook. The police report shows that a gunshot residue test was conducted on Madeleine, and she was clean."

"Wow, you really read the police report in detail. But Judy, you might want to watch some of those real life murder shows on TV—stories about non-existent burglars almost never pass muster. The police inevitably discover holes in such stories, with convictions surely following."

"Maybe Madeleine never watched those shows. And there's something else that doesn't make sense to me. I learned something else from Susan about her brother. He was by all accounts, and for all his life, a kind, decent man, an excellent doctor and medical researcher. I find it hard to believe that he would allow himself to be manipulated by Madeleine to kill her husband."

"Have you ever watched the movie 'Body Heat'? That's exactly what happened in the film: a decent honest man is manipulated by a beautiful but scheming woman in to murdering her rich husband. The man, who actually commits the murder is caught and sent to prison for life. The last scene of the movie

93

shows the woman reclining on a beach in an exotic faraway land enjoying her millions—free as a bird."

"I think I have seen it once—on TCM. With Kathleen Turner? Maybe a good lesson for some men in this world."

"Yes, that's the one. But it's a common Hollywood plot, first brought to the big screen in "Double Indemnity" with Barbara Stanwyck playing the part of the woman who convinces Fred McMurray to kill her husband for her."

"You know your movies, Amber! Are you an old movie fan?"

"I guess you could say I am."

"But those old plots don't really fit what we know about this case. In both those films the idea is for the man to avoid being caught. In this case Gardner is just accepting his fate, even inviting it, without even attempting a defense. I know I have only Susan's word for it, but she knew Roger all his life, and I believe her when she says he could never have committed such a crime."

"I agree none of it makes any sense. I'm not sure we'll ever know the real story, especially if the case proceeds as I predict: the good doctor will persist in his silence and refuse all defense, for whatever unfathomable reason; the case will go to trial—because I do not believe the D.A. could ever accept his plea offer; Gardner will be convicted, and the jury may or may not impose the death penalty. End of story, as Hillman always says to me when I'm trying to plea bargain with him."

"OK, so you're saying it would be another exercise in futility for me to try interviewing his friends and associates."

"I have no doubt you could easily do so. You seem to have a knack for getting people to talk to you. But no, I don't see how doing that would help you in understanding this case—though I must confess I don't really understand why you'd want to. Is it really to just get material for a law review article? I recall that when I went to UT Law, first year students weren't even eligible to get on the law review until second year."

"No it's not that. I doubt if any law review would publish an article by a first year law student. It's just that…I'm intrigued I guess you could say. To be honest, I find law school to be a terrible bore, and I don't think I could continue without some real life experience to make it more interesting for me. Something in the real world. That's why I wormed my way into the Exoneration Clinic."

"Well good for you, honey. I'm sure there will be other interesting cases that come your way."

"I'm not sure. My faculty advisor in the clinic has told us that the law school is facing financial problems, and may have to limit the cases it takes—may even have to shut it down entirely."

"Sorry to hear that."

"Yeah, it stinks. But I really appreciate your giving me you time. Perhaps you could give me some updates as the case proceeds—if information comes your way."

"Sure."

"So I guess there's really no reason for me to stay here in Houston. I guess I should just return to New York because there's nothing I can do to that might lead us to what's going on with this case."

There was a long silence as Judy waited for a sign-off from Amber to say "yes, that's probably what you should do, so goodbye and good luck"

"Amber are you still there?"

"Yes, I'm just thinking if I should tell you something."

"Tell me what?"

"I don't know if I should, I really don't."

"Amber you've really got me curious, so now you've got to tell me. No fair saying there's something you know, and then saying you can't tell me. Please tell me!"

"To be honest, I had earlier made up my mind to tell you, which is why I called you in the first place. Now I'm not sure."

"Amber," said Judy with an air of a mock scolding, "you really should have told me about the rumors of the affair. "

"Yes, I guess so, and I'm sorry. I guess I should have. I guess I thought it might mean more to you if you got that information yourself."

"Well, you're forgiven if you just tell me what it is you were calling me about."

"All right, you've got me. But not on the phone."

"I can come meet you. At the Woodland Inn?"

"No, why don't you come to my house tonight? Say about seven? I'll make some de-caf coffee and fresh oatmeal muffins. You still have my address?"

"Absolutely! See you there at seven sharp!"

CHAPTER EIGHTEEN

DECEMBER 28

Still driving the Ford Focus rental car that she had not yet returned, Judy parked in front of Amber's charming little townhouse in the Woodlands Town Center. Amber met her at the door.

"Hey girl! Come on in!"

Amber led Judy into a sunroom adjacent to the kitchen from which Judy could smell the aroma of freshly baked muffins.

"I love your home!" said Judy.

"Thank you," said Amber as she took out a pan of muffins from the oven. "I like it, and it's within walking distance of lots of shops and cafes. In summer I love sitting out there in the sunroom in the evenings. I'm making de-caf, is that ok? I don't like to drink the real thing in the evenings."

"No, that's fine. Me neither."

"I can make tea if you prefer."

"No, the coffee is fine."

A regal looking white Persian cat came sauntering in to the sunroom and lay down next to Judy.

"Hope you like cats," said Amber.

"Of course. I've been wanting to get one since I moved to New York, but I've been so busy at school."

Amber brought in a basket of hot muffins and offered it to Judy, who took one. "Thank you. They look scrumptious."

"I'm reminded of the story of Winston Churchill," said Amber as she poured a cup of de-caf. "When one of his generals came into Winston's office only to find a cat sitting on the only available chair, Winston asked him if he liked cats. When the general hesitated, Winston reportedly said "Well, you'll like them while you're here."

Judy chuckled. "Well I do like cats, and this one is so beautiful."

"My Queen of Sheba. Twelve years old, and still my best friend. How's the muffin?"

"Good! And hot too!"

Both women settled down and took sips of coffee. Finally, Amber said "I know you're curious about what I want to tell you, but before I do I want to tell you about my godfather."

"Your godfather?" Judy couldn't imagine what Amber's godfather could possibly have to do with the Gardner case. She took another sip while she waited for an answer.

"Some background, first. I grew up in the town of Long Beach, California. You know it?"

"Oh yes. I've lived in San Francisco—Tiburon, actually, near Angel Island—and also in Santa Barbara. I've had occasion to visit Long Beach—pass through at any rate—though I've never stayed there for any length of time. I did stay for a weekend with a friend there in a very nice neighborhood there near the ocean."

"Yes, there are some very nice areas of Long Beach. Anyway, my father was the headmaster of a small but elite private school—the Long Beach School for Boys. One of the students in his school was a boy named Alec Hoxsey, the grandson of Earl Hoxsey, one of the pioneering Long Beach aviators. Earl Hoxsey had made something of a name for himself back in 1911, when he set a high altitude record of 12,000 feet—or something like that—at one of the perennial Long Beach air shows of the time. Later, he became quite wealthy when he became an early investor in the Douglas Aircraft factory which soon set up shop in Long Beach, and was instrumental in the creation of the Long Beach Airport at Cherry Avenue and Spring Street in 1923—one of the first established municipal airports in the United States. At that time it was far bigger than the Los Angeles Airport, and many thought it would be California's predominate airport for many years to come."

"Interesting!" Judy couldn't help interjecting. "I'm not a big fan of LAX today."

"Nor I. I avoid LAX whenever possible. Anyway, when Earl died in a plane crash in 1947, his only son Timothy Hoxsey then only fourteen, inherited his father's estate, though it was handled by trustees until he reached majority. I guess you could call him a billionaire today, maybe even an eccentric billionaire. Also by about this time, Tim had become good friends with my dad—mainly through various events at the school where Tim's son Alec was a student. Tim and my dad apparently really hit it off. Timothy used to take my dad up in his various airplanes, and his family and mine made a number of camping trips together when I was young. I called Timothy my 'Uncle Tim' when I was growing up.

Judy followed this narrative intently, becoming ever more curious about where it would lead.

"Then, when I was about fourteen, there were two untimely deaths. The first was that of my dad, who died of complications from a stroke—he was a heavy smoker. My mother had passed away some years before from ovarian cancer. The second was the death of Tim's son Alec, in an air race accident—a not unusual cause of death in the Hoxsey family. "

"I'm so sorry."

"You are kind. Yes, being an only child, and now an orphan—and my dad left me very little—I would have been consigned to some institution had it not been for my 'Uncle Timothy.' He most kindly took me in and cared for me as his own. I must confess to sometimes feeling that I was a substitute for his beloved son, for whom he grieved for many years and still does, though I don't now think it is fair to say that. "

"And Timothy is now your godfather?"

"Yes, 'Uncle Timothy' is now my godfather. He helped with my tuition and expenses at Stanford, and later with my law school expenses at the University of Texas Law School in Austin."

"Why did you decide to go to law school in Texas rather than in California?"

"Well, for one thing, I got a full scholarship, and wealthy as my godfather was, I wanted to spare him as much expense as I could. Plus a number of my mother's relatives live here in Houston."

"Does your godfather still live in Long Beach?"

"No, he has several homes around the world now, but is now somewhat of a recluse. In winter he prefers to live in his house on Catalina Island in the town of Avalon. Do you know the island?"

"Oh yes. I went to camp there for two summers as a child."

"Then you know it. As you entered the harbor in a ferry, looking to your left, do you recall seeing a large house on the hill overlooking the harbor—with large picture windows?"

"I'm not sure, I must have, but I was only about ten when I went to camp there."

"Catalina is a wonderful place. I visited Godfather often there while I was on holiday during my days at Stanford and U.T."

"I take it you are still very close to him."

"Very much so. We talk often, usually once or twice a week."

"That's nice. What do you usually talk about?"

"He doesn't much like to talk about his business interests, so I usually just talk to him about my work at the law firm, my career, my case..."

"About the Gardner case?"

"Yes, I have talked to him about it. When the judge in the case assigned our firm to represent Gardner during the competency hearings, I was hoping that if he was found competent—which he was, and without my input I might add, since he has always refused to talk to me—that Gardner might ask our firm to represent him. That would mean me, since I have the most experience with death penalty cases at the firm."

"Did you tell your godfather the umh...unusual facts of the case—that Gardner refused to talk to you or even retain other counsel for his defense."

"Yes, and he actually was not as surprised as I thought he might be. He thought it quite rational that if a person committed a horrible crime he would prefer a soft death to a life in prison—

especially if he had any kind of a conscience and felt that only by his own death could justice be done."

"That's what Professor Hammond thinks as well."

'Your faculty advisor?"

"Yes."

"But you don't?"

"No, like we discussed this morning, I think there's something missing in what you and I know about this case, and until we find out what it is, the idea of death as the only justice doesn't make sense to me."

"I can't really disagree with you."

"Have you talked to him more recently about the case?" Amber now shifted in her chair, and Judy sensed that she was getting close to what this evening's invitation was about.

"Judy, I talked to godfather last night. I was just filling him in with some details. I told him about you, a law student from New York coming down to talk to me because you had become interested in the Gardner case. I told him that I had suggested to you about going to the D.A.'s office and trying to persuade them to let you see Gardner."

"Really? What did he say?"

"I told him that I didn't think you'd have any chance of getting the D.A.'s permission to access Gardner. But I also told him about Matheson's absence, and how I suggested to you that you might take a crack at it with Hillman—and how you had—miraculously—gotten him to accommodate you when no one else had been able to do so."

"It really wasn't that hard."

Amber laughed out loud. "No I'm sure it wasn't. For you. And that's what seemed to interest my godfather. That you had gotten access when no one else could."

Judy shrugged. "Why would that interest him?"

"It wasn't until I told him about what I had told you the other night at the Woodland Inn that he began to press me on more details."

"Like what?"

"I told him what I had told you that night—that the victim in the case—Carl Otto—had a major financial stake in the Germany company Otto Wagner Koncept Konstucktion, or O.W.K.K.. Remember me telling you about that?"

"Yes...and..."

"Once I mentioned that name, he became very animated, pressed me for even more details—which I said I didn't have. That's when godfather issued forth with one of his very rare obscenities. He apologized profusely after uttering it, of course, but then when he had calmed down, asked me for a great favor."

"What?"

"To be honest, despite all he has done for me, I protested because I didn't want to do the favor he asked."

"Oh my God, Amber! What did he want you to do?"

Amber took a deep breath. "He asked me to persuade you to come see him in Catalina. Personally. He wants you to take on a task for him, and he is prepared to pay you whatever you ask if you will do it. He mentioned a ridiculous sum which I can only attribute to the fact that it may be indicative of the first onset of senility that I have not seen in him before—despite the fact that he is now in his eighties."

"Me!" Judy exclaimed. "Why on earth would he want me? He doesn't know anything about me? What could I possibly do for him that no one else could do far better?"

'I really have no idea, Judy, and he wouldn't tell me, though I pressed him several times to tell me."

"You have no idea at all?"

Amber pressed her lips. This was precisely why she had considered not performing the favor her godfather had asked, and instead just tell him that she had approached Judy but had been rebuffed.

"I do have one idea of what it's about."

Judy did not press, but waited for Amber to continue.

"There was one great tragedy in my godfather's life, one which I did not previously mention to you—a tragedy that went beyond the loss of his wife many years ago, and even the loss of his son Alec."

"Tell me," Judy asked gently.

"No, if you decide to go—and I would fervently advise you not to, I would advise you to return to New York as soon as you can—I think it better that he tell you of it in his own words."

Judy now shook her head in disbelief. "Amber, before I even consider taking on such request, I need to ask you one question. If the task your godfather has in mind for me does relate to the tragedy to which you referred, would it have any bearing on the Gardner case?"

Amber took a long sip of coffee before answering.

"Yes," she finally said, "I'm afraid it would."

CHAPTER NINETEEN

DECEMBER 29

After returning her rental car to Hertz at the Bush Intercontinental Airport, Judy stood on the off-ramp to await the arrival of the black Range Rover which she had been told would pick her up at noon sharp to take her to Sugar Land Municipal Airport where she would board Timothy Hoxsey's Gulfstream G500 jet to Long Beach, and thence to Avalon by boat.

She was still second-guessing the decision she had finally made the night before to go to Catalina—a decision she had made only after discussing the pros and cons with Amber into the wee hours.

The cons included Amber's concerns about Judy getting involved in a family matter with her godfather. Much as Amber loved her godfather and was grateful for all he had done for her, she also knew how overbearing and obsessive he could be once he had an objective in mind. She had also not been entirely forthright with Judy about the nature of the family tragedy which she was quite sure was behind her godfather's invitation to Judy to come see him. Amber knew very well what it was, and was concerned about how it might somehow rebound on her if Judy's involvement, should she choose to become involved, ended badly.

Another reason for Amber's reluctance to encourage Judy to accept the invitation was that Amber was as clueless as Judy was about why her godfather would choose Judy of all people for whatever task he had in mind for her. She knew he had hired and fired a small army of investigators, all to no avail, but that would hardly explain why he wanted a young woman he knew nothing about except the few off-hand references she had made about her during one of their recent phone conversations.

In the end, however, the "pro" which convinced Judy to accept the invitation was Amber's admission that whatever the reason was for the invitation, it likely did have something to do with the Gardner case—but this was only because the invitation had come on the heels of the phone conversation she had just had with her godfather. What the connection might actually be, however, Amber honestly had no idea.

As she waited, Judy thought about calling Hammond and discussing her decision with him. But it being only a few minutes before noon, she thought it better to concentrate on sighting the Range Rover. She could call later when she would have the privacy to discuss her decision without interruption. In any case, there might be little to discuss, since she would be presenting him with what amounted to a *fait accompli*. After all, there were still over ten days before the beginning of the second semester, and she had no plans until then. So why not take an executive jet to sunny Catalina and see what was up? She didn't see that she had anything to lose.

The chauffeur of the Range Rover saw Judy before she saw him driving up the ramp. He had already been advised through Amber as to what Judy would be wearing—blue jeans, a pink sweat shirt emblazed with "Texas Lone Star State" which she had purchased in her hotel's gift shop, and black and yellow running shoes, and pulling a small pink roller bag.

The burly driver who looked fresh out of a muscle workout, and himself dressed in blue jeans and sweatshirt, stopped the Rover in front of Judy and hopped out to open the rear passenger side door for her.

"Judy Alexander?"

"Yes. I am. You are..."

"Tyrone, Ma'am. I'm to take you to Sugar Land Municipal. May I take your bag?"

"Yes, thank you," Judy said as she gave him the bag. "Would you mind if I sat in front?"

"Not at all, Ma'am." Tyrone shut the rear door and opened the front one.

"Whew," said Judy as she settled in. "I was afraid I might miss you. How far to Sugar Land?'

"About thirty minutes, Miss, depending on traffic."

"You can call me Judy. Do you work for Mr. Hoxsey?"

"So I've been told, but I've only seen him once."

"Oh. And his plane is at this other airport?"

"Yes, and it's a beauty—a G500, top of its class. Sleeps eight, travels at .925 of the speed of sound, cruises at 51,000 feet, and has a range of 5,200 miles."

"Wow. You seem to know a lot about it. Have you been on it?"

"Yes, several times. As a matter of fact I flew on it early this morning from Long Beach."

"Thw plane that just came in this morning?"

"Yep. Got a call at 4:00 A.M. this morning telling me to get to the Long Beach Airport and be ready to fly with Mr. Chandler to Sugar Land."

"You came all this way just to pick me up at this airport?"

"Yep." Tyrone turned and smiled. "I guess you're some kind of VIP or something."

Judy laughed and shook her head. "Hardly. Will you be flying back too?"

"No, I wish. I've been assigned a number of errands to run here in Houston, so I'll be staying here for a week or so. Mr. Hoxsey doesn't keep a full time chauffeur at Sugar Land, just this car, which is why I came. You'll be flying back with Mr. Chandler, Mr. Hoxsey's personal secretary."

Judy reflected on when exactly she had told Amber the previous night that she would come to Avalon to see her godfather. It had been about 1:00 A.M. the previous night. That meant that Amber must have called her godfather very soon thereafter to tell him of her decision, and the jet had been immediately prepared to fly to Sugar Land. Judy had been surprised when Amber called her at 6:00 A.M. that morning to tell her to be ready at noon to be picked up at Houston International.

Well, Judy thought, Amber had warned her about her godfather's impulsive obsessiveness, but upon thinking this through she could only shake her head in amazement.

Tyrone drove the Rover right up to the waiting G500 warming up on the tarmac at Sugar Land. Jimmy Chandler, dressed to the nines in an Armani suit and looking like the master of ceremonies at the Academy Awards, greeted Judy as she emerged from the car.

"Welcome, Ms. Alexander. I am Jimmy Chandler, Mr. Hoxsey's personal assistant. He asked me to welcome you and thank you for responding so promptly to his invitation. Please call me Jimmy. Tyrone could you please take Ms. Alexander's bag to the rear bedroom."

"Yes sir," Tyrone replied and took the bag up the stairs to the cabin.

"Do you have any other bags?" Chandler asked.

"No, just the one," Judy replied. "I travel light."

"Very good. If there is anything else you require we can certainly obtain it for you once we arrive in Catalina."

"Thank you," said Judy still trying to take it all in. "I don't think I'll need anything."

"Of course. Now if you would follow me up the stairs I will get you settled."

The G500's interior was lavishly furnished with all manner of leather, teak, burnished nickel, glass, and cashmere carpets over marble floor. Emerging from a bar equipped with a wide variety of beverages and spirits came a comely hostess who looked like she had just walked off the catwalk of Victoria's Secret."

"Welcome Ms. Alexander. I'm Michelle," she said invitingly. "Please sit wherever you like. May I offer you a beverage?"

Judy looked around the cabin. There was an upholstered divan, several large leather chairs, a leather sofa, and an upright chair behind a burled walnut desk by the window. In the rear was a mahogany door which led to a spacious bedroom and private bath."

"Maybe a little later. Is this chair ok?" Judy asked as she motioned toward the desk chair.

"Of course, wherever you like."

"Are there any other passengers on this flight?"

"No, just you. And of course Mr. Chandler, and our pilot."

At this time Chandler, who had moments before entered the cockpit, emerged with the pilot. "Ms. Alexander, I would like you to meet Captain John Heath. He is a former Navy pilot, earned a silver star in the Gulf War. You are in good hands I assure you."

Heath nodded toward Judy. "Hope you enjoy the flight Ms. Alexander. We should have clear skies. Our flight time will be about two and a half hours.'

"It would take almost three and a half hours by commercial flight," Chandler couldn't help interjecting. "But we will be flying at .92 of the speed of sound, right captain?"

"Well, not quite, but certainly faster than a 737. We should be cleared for take-off shortly."

"I'm sure it will be fine," said Judy. "Thank you"

Within the hour the plane had reached cruising altitude. Judy remained in her desk chair looking serenely out at the thick clouds below, while Michelle prepared a mixed drink for Chandler and flavored sparkling water for Judy. Chandler ensconced himself on the divan and was reading documents he had spread out beside him.

Chandler looked up. "Everything OK, Ms. Alexander? Can I get you anything? "

"No, not at all. Thank you. The sparkling water is fine."

What Judy really wanted to do was to pump Chandler for anything he knew about why his boss was so eager to meet with her. Nevertheless, she resisted the urge, assuming that he probably knew nothing. If the boss had authorized him to say anything he would have already done so. She would just have to be patient, and content with small talk.

"This is certainly a beautiful airplane," Judy said, putting down her magazine.

"Yep top of the line. Unfortunately, it's too big to land at the Catalina airport, or at least, according to Captain Heath, it shouldn't be landed there because of the limited facilities there. Mostly only smaller private planes fly there. So we'll be taking his boat from Long Beach to Avalon. Have you ever been on a plane like this before?"

"Oh no, never. It's so luxurious."

"Have you ever been to Long Beach?"

"Yes, I've stayed there for a few days, but haven't really seen the city."

"The Long Beach Airport has an interesting history. It was the first municipal airport in California, and one of the first in the country. Charles Lindbergh flew here shortly after his trans-Atlantic flight. The story was that when his plane got near the airport he couldn't find the runway because the lights weren't turned on. When a pedestrian on the ground heard the drone of a plane above, he called the airport and told them to turn the lights on. Lindbergh later said that without that alert pedestrian's' phone call he would probably have run out of fuel and crashed. Another reason they call him Lucky Lindy, I guess."

"Oh my." Judy didn't want to sound bored, and it wasn't that she wasn't interested, but she was feeling drained and tired. Chandler continued with his history discourse.

"During World War II it was one of the most important airports in the country, with hundreds of bombers taking off and landing. And of course the Douglas company factory built many of those bombers here."

"Hmmm. Listen Mr. Chandler, I didn't get much sleep last night. I see there's a bedroom in the back. Do you think it would be all right if I lay down?"

Chandler stood up. "Of course. Please use the bedroom in the back. I'll wake you when we're about to land."

Judy slept soundly until wakened.

"Sorry I had to wake you," Chandler apologized, "but even on private planes we're supposed to make sure everyone on board puts on a seatbelt before landing."

After landing, the plane was met by another black Range Rover which was soon whisking both of them to the wharf just minutes away, where the boat—the "Princess Bonnie" was docked.

It was, of course, a yacht—a Cecilia 165 consisting of five cabins, a crew of eleven, and which sported a touch and go helipad, a submarine garage and accommodations for twelve guests. The "submarine garage" housed a Worx submarine and could be converted to a saltwater pool. The flush foredeck and fly bridge featured Jacuzzi pools, and the foredeck lounge converted to a nightclub. There were four large ensuite guest cabins on the lower deck, and a full-beam owner's suite which boasted a large marble finished bathroom with free standing bath tub. The main salon was topped by skylights and bathed with natural light. There was a drop-down television, and the décor was styled with polished oak, soft leather and copper.

Chandler ushered her into the owner's suite, where he invited her to rest if she wished. After splashing her face and hands, and now well refreshed from her hour's nap on the G500, she opted instead to go topside to feel the breeze and watch the looming shoreline of Catalina Harbor come into view. In the distance she scanned the hill above the harbor for the house which Amber had described to her.

The opulent surroundings, however, far from reassuring her, had left her on edge and anxious, asking herself what on earth she was doing here.

CHAPTER TWENTY

DECEMBER 29

As the Princess Bonnie slowly docked at the Hoxsey pier, Judy, perched on the bow with her hair blowing in the soft sea breeze, gazed up at the lovely homes upon the hill overlooking the Catalina harbor. Avalon was much as she remembered it as a young girl when she had gone to a sea camp some two miles down the coast of the island. She closed her eyes and let the breeze gently massage her face.

Up on the captain's deck, Chandler, who had been looking for Judy, saw her on the bow. Excusing himself to Captain Smith who was engaged in navigating the docking, he bounded down three decks to where Judy was standing at the bow.

"Hello Judy, hope you enjoyed our short voyage."

Judy was startled, as the shouts of the crew manhandling the landing ropes had prevented her from hearing Chandler's approach as she looked out toward the harbor. She turned around. "Oh!"

"Sorry, Judy," said Chandler. "Didn't mean to startle you. I see our car is waiting to take us up to see Mr. Hoxsey. Would you like to go down to your suite to freshen up before we go?"

"Yes, thank you. Perhaps I could go down for a few minutes. Back in fifteen minutes. Is that OK?"

"Take as much time as you need. I'll meet you at the forward gangplank when you're ready. "

It was now mid-afternoon, and she was as tired as she was apprehensive. Foregoing any attempt at make-up, she took a quick shower, brushed her teeth, rubbed some sun block on her face and hands, and changed into one of the two outfits she had brought with her—a short frock, flip flops, and floppy hat, and large sunglasses—and made up way up to the forward gangplank. A ship's' attendant waiting in the corridor took her bag.

"Well, I'm ready, sir!" Judy said with a broad smile that masked her nervousness.

"You look charming, Judy," said Chandler. "Now if you'll just follow me down to the dock."

The third black Range Rover she had seen that day awaited at the end of the pier. Very few residents of the island were permitted to have regular automobiles, and the few permits for such vehicles were rationed out to longtime and established residents and small businesses, mostly shops and restaurants. Obviously Mr. Hoxsey had one of the island's few permits. Tourists and other residents generally got about on small two, four, and some six seater buggies.

With Chandler taking the front passenger seat, Judy settled in the soft leather of the back seat and opened the window."

"To the house," Chandler said to the driver.

At the top of the hill the Rover came to a stop before a stately manor with white marble steps leading up to four white columns, between which were teak drums containing a variety of colorful flora.

Chandler opened the door for Judy. "If you'll just follow me. The driver will bring your bag up to your room."

For the first time, Judy realized that she was expected to spend the night—an event she had not assumed and had neglected to ask Amber about when she had called early that morning, but she had prepared for it just in case.

"If it's alright I'd like to take the bag myself" Judy said as she walked to the rear door where she took her small roller bag in hand.

"Of course," said Chandler. "As you wish."

With Judy pulling her bag up the marble steps and through the large mahogany door, Chandler led her into a large atrium. Its interior circumference was lined with bamboo couches and chairs, and decorated with a number of nautical artifacts, a large aquarium filled with salt water fish, and colorful paintings of the sea and ocean denizens. Dominating this spacious vault was a large picture window some twenty feet in height, which curved around the front part of the room and overlooked the harbor.

Somewhat in awe, Judy put down her bag by one of the bamboo chairs and walked toward the window. In the distance she could see all the pleasure boats anchored in the outer harbor, and below a small beach, but only a few hardy swimmers and sunbathers as it was the chilly season of the year. Further up the coast she could see the Hoxsey pier in the distance where seaman were still attending to the Princess Bonnie.

"What an amazing view!" she exclaimed.

Chandler came up beside her and pointed in the distance. "Right over there, about fifty yards or so beyond that red catamaran is where Natalie Wood's body was found after a night on the *Splendor* with her husband Robert Wagner."

"Oh."

At this moment the housekeeper came in, introduced herself to Judy, and asked if she would like anything to drink."

"Thank you. Perhaps some iced tea, if you have it?"

"Of course. Mr. Hoxsey asked me to tell you to make yourself comfortable. He should be down in a few minutes, as he is on a long distance call right now. Mr. Chandler, anything for you?"

"A Scotch and soda, please, Betty. Judy, would you like to see your room while we wait for Mr. Hoxsey?'

Judy nodded. "Sure."

She followed Chandler up a spiral staircase to a spacious upper floor room with sweeping canopy bed and another spectacular view of the harbor and hills beyond. A large marbled bathroom with a whirlpool bath and glass shower adjoined.

"So, Judy, I'll leave you here to get settled. Come down when you're ready. Dinner is generally served promptly at 7:00. Let me know if you need anything."

"Mr. Chandler..."

"Jimmy, please."

"Ok...Jimmy. Can I ask you a question?"

"Of course."

Judy paused to think how to ask the question.

"Yes?"

"Jimmy...do you have any idea why I'm here?"

'Jimmy' took a deep breath. "I'm sorry I really don't. Mr. Hoxsey confides in me on many things, as I take care of many of his appointments, arrange his schedule..."

"But not on why I'm here."

Jimmy shook his head. "No, on this...no, I'm afraid not."

"Aren't you even curious?"

Jimmy smiled. "I guess I'd be lying if I said I wasn't."

"But you have an idea; you could guess."

"Perhaps, but I don't think it's my place. You'll find out soon enough."

"Then let me ask you: am I the only mystery guest who's visited here."

"Mystery? Yes, I think so."

"Well, thank you, Jimmy. I'll be down shortly."

"Of course."

******

Judy was standing and gazing out through the window in the atrium when she heard footsteps and turned around.

"You must be Ms. Alexander!!" the man who entered said congenially, holding out his hand. "I am Timothy Hoxsey, Amber's godfather. I'm so glad you could come, especially on such short notice."

His appearance surprised her. The man whose appearance Amber had described only as being in his mid-eighties, was in fact strikingly handsome, with an ample mane of thick white hair, and a face which reminded her of an aging Cary Grant. His gait was tentative, as expected for a man of his age, but deliberate, and he looked fit and in glowing health—certainly not the doddering old man in a wheel chair she had imagined. Moreover, he was sportily dressed in white cotton trousers, white collared shirt, white and yellow running shoes, and sported an ample tan—an ensemble one might expect of a much younger man.

"I'm pleased to meet you," Judy said shyly, taking his hand. "Amber has told me so much about you."

Judy paused, as she realized that her last words were not quite true—Amber had filled her in on his 'overbearing and obsessive' persona, but not a word as to his appearance.

"Please sit," said Timothy. "I must say you are even more beautiful than Amber described to me."

"Thank you, sir," but I truly think not." Her face turned a soft crimson. She usually fielded the inevitable beauty compliments more gracefully, but this one had come from an octogenarian and out of the blue.

"And modest as well—not a common attribute of lawyers. I understand you are now a student of the law?"

"Well, yes sir..."

"Please call me Timothy. We're very informal around here."

"Well...umh...Timothy, I'm only a first year law student—actually first semester law student."

"Do you enjoy law school?"

"It's challenging, but I can't say I've really enjoyed it."

"Don't blame you. I took a year at Harvard many years ago—dreadfully dull."

"Oh, so you know."

"From what Amber has told me you prefer—how did she put it—'field work.'"

"Yes, I'm in a clinic—called the Exoneration Clinic at Oliver Wendell Holmes School of Law—we review cases in which we find that there may have been a miscarriage of justice, a wrongful conviction."

"An admirable mission."

Judy now hoped the obligatory small talk was over. She didn't want to be pushy, but knew that her anxiety would not be mitigated until she knew why she had been summoned.

"Sir..."

"Timothy."

"Timothy, this is a most beautiful place to which you have brought me, and I am truly in awe, but, but..."

"Ms. Alexander, I understand completely," he interjected. "And forgive me. I assure you that before the evening is out you will know why I am in great need of your services, and in a cause which I believe you will find equal to that which you pursue in your clinic."

"Sir...Timothy...I am only a first year law student and I cannot imagine what services I would be qualified to..."

"Ms. Alexander. At the present there is staff about, so we cannot talk in perfect privacy. Dinner will be served at seven. If you will join me, afterwards I will dismiss the day staff, including Chandler and my two secretaries—there will still be present in the house the housekeeper, parlor maid, and cook who will retire to their rooms on the third floor—and we can talk in my library with complete privacy. At that time I will tell you why I have had you come, and you can decide whether or not you are in a position to help me."

CHAPTER TWENTY-ONE

DECEMBER 29

When Mrs. Horrigan, Timothy's intrepid cook, had asked Judy what kind of meal she preferred, she responded that while she was mostly a vegetarian, she occasionally ate fish. It so happened that there had been a delivery of fresh fish caught that very morning, giving Mrs. Horrigan the opportunity to prepare her specialty dish of fresh Calico Bass for Timothy and his guest.

Mrs. Horrigan served a candlelight dinner in front of the window overlooking the harbor, now twinkling with lights.

"How is the Bass, Ms. Alexander? May I call you Judy?" Timothy asked.

"Of course."

"The dish is Mary's patented recipe. I hope you like it."

"It's delicious."

At that moment Mary entered to refill the wine glasses. Judy put up her hand to indicate that her one glass was enough. "Thank you," she said with a smile. "I fear I've had enough for this evening."

Mary nodded.

"You said that my goddaughter has told you something about me," said Timothy when Mary had returned to the kitchen.

"Yes, but I suppose not all that much, really—just that you came from a Long Beach family that was very active during the early years of aviation there."

"Yes, my father was one of the early aviation pioneers, and left me a legacy which I have endeavored to make the best of."

"Based on what I saw today, I can see that you have. I know Amber is very grateful for your help with her education."

"Yes, she was and is a fine girl, who did very well in all her studies, and has worked hard since. While I would not have chosen for her the profession she ultimately entered into, I have tried to support her in every way I can."

"You remain quite close to her, then."

"Very much so. We stay in touch regularly—by FaceTime, mainly in the evenings. I wish she could visit me more often, but her responsibilities at the law firm in Houston seem to keep her tied down most of the time."

"Do you live here all year round?"

"Mostly in the winter months. I also have a home in London, and apartments in Paris and Monte Carlo—mainly to be close to my business interests in Europe. But I consider Long Beach and Catalina to be my home territory."

"Catalina reminds me of the island of Capri," said Judy as she gazed out.

"So you have been to Capri often?"

"Oh, no, just once, on a student trip to Italy the summer of my third year in high school. I grew up in Tiburon, it's near..."

"Yes, I know it well—San Francisco, in the shadow of the Golden Gate. Well, before we retire to the library, Mrs. Horrigan makes a very fine cheesecake."

Judy, by now starting to feel exhausted—she regretted drinking a full glass of white wine—was anxious to get to the library where she could learn, before the evening was out, why she was there.

"No thank you. But perhaps if there is coffee..."

Judy usually eschewed coffee in the evenings as it tended to keep her up, but tonight keeping up was exactly what she wanted. Whatever Timothy was to propose to her that evening in the library, if she declined it, which she thought most probable, she wanted to return to New York before New Year's, get settled back in her apartment, register for the second semester, buy her law books, and start reading any advance assignments.

"Of course. I'll have Mary serve it in the library, and then let her go for the evening. Shall we go?"

Timothy led Judy to the library on the south wing of the house—a man cave if there ever was one, lined with shelves of

118

books of every kind and variety, and filled with all manner of nautical and electronic equipment and video screens. In one corner of the room there was a six foot high cylindrical aquarium filled with colorful, transparent, and gracefully floating jellyfish.

The two sat opposite each other in leather chairs, between which was a coffee table inlaid with topaz tiles. As Mary entered with a tray of coffee, Judy looked around and noticed a painting of a striking young woman on the wall behind an adjacent desk.

"Thank you, Mary" said Timothy. "You may go now."

"That painting..." said Judy when Mary had left.

"It's my daughter."

"Oh, Amber mentioned that you had a son, but she didn't mention..."

"She may have mentioned that my son Alec, by my first wife, died in an air race accident. My only other child, Bonnie, disappeared nineteen years ago, and was declared dead seven years later. The circumstances of her disappearance led to an official finding that she was murdered. Her murderer has never been found or brought to justice, nor has her body ever been found. She was only twenty-four years of age when she disappeared. She would be forty-three years if she were still living. "

"I'm so sorry. So Bonnie, the name of your boat..."

"The Princess Bonnie, the boat you arrived in this afternoon."

"I wondered. I can't imagine how it must have been to lose both of your children."

"You have seen the material things I have accumulated in my eighty-five years of life, much of which was made possible by the legacy of my father, though I built on it. But they mean nothing to me now, and I would relinquish everything I have in an instant to bring my only children back. My son died in an accident doing what he loved doing. Knowing that helped to minimize the pain. But somewhere out there is someone who murdered my daughter in cold blood. I have long given up hope that she is alive. Once I have told you the circumstances you will understand why there can be no hope of that. All that remains for me now is to obtain justice for Bonnie. If I can do that, I shall rest in peace when it is my time. But the time left to me to do that is diminishing even as I speak to you now. I have been told that I look fit, but I do not feel it, and my doctors will not assure me that I am good for more than one or two years—if that. My medical condition is slow-moving but relentless and essentially untreatable except for palliatives. "

From the intensity and emotion of Timothy's tragic story, it was now clear to Judy that this was the reason she was here. But she could still not imagine why he thought that she, of all people, could help him obtain the justice he so passionately sought for his daughter.

Timothy sat with his head bowed for several long minutes before he continued:

"When Bonnie graduated from Harvard Business School, she was eager to follow in my footsteps. Of course, I offered her a position in Hoxsey Industries, of which I was then chairman of the Board and majority shareholder. However, she would have none of it. She had always had a streak of independence ever since she was a child. 'Do dat myself', she would always say whenever I tried to help her with something. And so after graduation she circulated her resume to businesses and companies around the world. She definitely had a wanderlust, but not in any of my planes or boats. She wanted to make it on her own, and didn't even cite in her resume that she was my daughter."

"You didn't resent that?"

"Not at all. Although I would have done anything to help her in her career, I greatly admired her wish to make it on her own. Many a child of successful parents has gone to ruin trying to ride on their parents' coattails, or to live off their legacy rather than creating their own. I recently read that Jackie Onassis, when asked what was the greatest mistake she ever made, responded that it was naming her son after her husband, the president. The name was 'too much of a burden for her son to live up to', she said."

"I know Amber lives quite within her means as a lawyer."

120

"Since winning her job at that Houston law firm, Amber has never asked me for a dime, though I would gladly give it to her if she asked. And of course she has, by all accounts, done very well there. I did help her with her education, of course, and was happy to do so, but even then she insisted on going to law school out of state where she was awarded a full merit scholarship."

"It was only a few months after sending out Bonnie's resumes that she received an offer from a large German industrial conglomerate called Otto Wagner Koncept Konstrucktion."

A small lightbulb ignited in Judy's memory bank as she recalled her conversation with Amber that first night she had met with her at the Woodland Inn.

"O.W.K.K.?" She remembered the somewhat sinister acronym if not the full name.

"Yes. But it wasn't until Amber mentioned that name on the phone the other night on the phone as she filled me in on some of the details of the Gardner case that she was working on that it brought back the name."

Finally, thought Judy: a connection—albeit a slender one—between the Gardner case and Timothy's tragedy. "How so?"

"Several months after Bonnie began working at O.W.K.K., she met and began casually dating the son of one of the members of the Board of Directors of that company. His name was Hans Wagner, and his grandfather was one of the founders of the company. Although Bonnie had mentioned Hans a couple of times during my conversations with her—as with Amber now, we talked on the phone fairly regularly—she never gave me the impression that it was a serious relationship.

"Then, on a March weekend—which will be exactly nineteen years ago next March 17—Bonnie and Hans took a three day weekend trip together to Mont St. Michel off the coast of Normandy in France. On that Friday, they apparently travelled together by train from Frankfurt—where the main office of O.W.K.K. was located, and where Bonnie had an apartment—to Rennes, where Hans hired a private car which took them to the front gate of Mont St. Michel. Most visitors have to park their cars at a lot about a thousand meters away, buy a ticket and then take a shuttle bus to the gate. Later investigation by the French authorities revealed that Hans Wagner had legally obtained, through the auspices of O.W.K.K.'s internal travel department, a special pass that permitted any car hired by him to drop its passengers directly at the gate. It also included an entry pass for Bonnie's admission to Mont St. Michel. As a legal resident of the European Union, Hans was entitled to free entry."

"I'm sorry...Timothy..." Judy still did not feel comfortable addressing an eighty-five year old man whom she had just met as 'Timothy.' "I'm sure I've heard of Mont St. Michel, but don't really know what it is exactly."

"Ah," said Timothy, surprised that Judy did not know about Mont St. Michel. "You've never been there—on one of your high school student trips, perhaps?"

"No, I only went on one such trip, and that was to Italy."

"It's now one of the top tourist destinations in France, after the Eiffel tower and the Louvre. It's a very small island, just a few hundred meters from the Normandy coastline. Although for hundreds of years it has been accessible at low tide, most of those who tried to walk there were inevitably drowned when the swiftly returning tide carried them off at a speed in excess of forty miles an hour, making it as good as a moat."

Timothy went to a cabinet and returned with an iconic photograph of the Mont St. Michel and showed it to Judy.

"Oh, yes, I have seen pictures of it. I recognize it now."

"A monastery was first built on the Mont in the eighth century. For over one thousand years, the climb to the monastery on top was the end of a trail taken by pilgrims from all Europe. Attempts by various marauding armies to conquer the Mont were inevitably repulsed by its formidable defenses and deadly tides. By the time of the French Revolution, there were few monks left in the monastery. It was later closed and used as a prison for political undesirables. When the Germans attacked France in 1940, the quick collapse of the French army alarmed the entire world. Mont St. Michel immediately came under German occupation and control. A contingent of German soldiers soon set up an aircraft observation post and artillery battery on the courtyard to the upper entrance of the monastery, and S.S. soldiers later established a garrison there."

"Unbelievable. The S.S.?"

"The small local population living at the base of the Mont suffered the most. Deliverance didn't come until the allied invasion of Normandy in 1944 finally drove the Germans out. It has taken over three generations since then for the collective memories and trauma of those who lived under that occupation to be overcome."

Judy could see that Timothy was—albeit slowly— getting to the heart of what happened on the weekend of March 17, nineteen years before.

"Timothy, would you mind if I took a short break, and could I get a glass of water?"

"Of course," he said, taking a bottle of Voss water from his small refrigerator underneath his desk, and handing it to her. "I need a moment anyway to check for an email I'm expecting from Paris. Are you too tired to continue tonight? We could continue in the morning if you wish."

"No, I would like to hear the entire story before I go to bed tonight."

"Very well. Why don't you go out on the veranda and get a breath of fresh ocean air and return here, in say fifteen minutes?"

"That's fine. Fifteen minutes then."

CHAPTER TWENTY- TWO

DECEMBER 29-DECEMBER 30

"Feeling a bit refreshed?" Timothy asked. It was now well after midnight and he wanted to be sure that Judy would be up to hearing the rest of the tragic story he had to tell.

"Yes, the breeze has given me a second wind. Thank you."

"Care for anything else? Can I get you anything at all?"

"No, I'm fine. Please go on. I want to hear the rest."

Now holding a file with notes for reference he did so as follows:

"On Saturday, March 18 at about 9:30 P.M.—they eat later in Europe, especially in France and Spain—Hans and Bonnie went for dinner at the restaurant of the Sacre Mont Hotel, about halfway up the Mont. The room they had booked at the same hotel for the weekend overlooked the island's rocky coastline below. According to the staff at the restaurant, they each ordered a six course fixed Prix dinner—a main dish of fish for Bonnie, and a Filet Mignon for Hans. A little after 10:00 P.M., but definitely after 10:00 P.M.—between the fourth and fifth courses, Bonnie's phone rang. She usually turned off her cell when at dinner, but on this occasion apparently had not done so. In any case, she took the call, and two witnesses say she appeared quite distressed after taking the call. Excusing herself to Hans, she said something like 'Sorry Hans, I have to take this call, I'll be right back', then left the table, and walked out the front door. That was the last time Bonnie has ever been seen."

Judy sat silent as she took in what seemed to be an unbelievable story. "How was that possible? No one saw her? Could she have just left the island?"

"No. When Bonnie had not returned after about fifteen minutes, Hans became alarmed and went out to look for her. All the shops were closed by then. After canvassing all the narrow streets until midnight, and learning that there was no police officer on the island at that particular time, he demanded that the hotel manager call the police from the nearby town of Beauvoir with which Mont St. Michel shared a small police force.

"A Gendarmerie finally arrived about 1:00 A.M. on Sunday morning the 19th of March, but told Hans that there was nothing he could do at that hour, and to wait until morning. According to Hans, the Gendarmerie told him: 'You and she must have had an argument of some sort, sir, and she decided to leave without telling you where she was going.' Unsatisfied with this response, he was insistent that no such argument had occurred. Certain that she would have done no such thing, Hans says he heatedly pointed out to the Gendarmerie that not only was the tide up—which would have made leaving the island by foot impossible—but there was no transportation available of any kind at that hour either to or from the Mont across the bridge to the mainland; and even the reception station at the end of bridge was locked up for the night with no passage to walk through to the parking lot beyond.

Timothy paused to check his notes, and continued:

"Hans says he then insisted that the Gendarmerie check the closed circuit television monitors which recorded all persons entering and exiting the single gate through the stone wall around the Mont. To this the officer replied that review of the video recording would have to wait until the next morning when a technician could be summoned from the mainland to perform this task. He asked Hans to call the Beauvoir Station at 6:00 A.M. the next morning if Bonnie had not turned up by then.

"Hans then says he stayed up all night continuing to scour the island for any sign of Bonnie—every pathway, every ledge, every wall rampart—but to no avail. Although as instructed he called the Beauvoir station at 6:00 A.M. to report that Bonnie was still missing, it was not until the next day at noon that the promised technician arrived, now accompanied by a another uniformed police officer and an inspector—Inspector Jacques

Montague from the French Commune of Le Mont-Saint-Michel in the Department of Manche.

"Inspector Montague and the technician spent the afternoon in the guardhouse meticulously poring over the videotapes. They showed that not a single person had left the island between 10:00 P.M. on the evening of March 18 and 6:00 A.M. on the March 19—a fact confirmed by the night watchman at the gate. Checks were made of all the other hotels and restaurants. Nothing. All the shops were also closed during that time. The monastery itself was closed and locked down for the night. Video tapes of the time between when the gate was opened for deliveries to the hotels and restaurants at 7:00 A.M. and noon when Inspector Montague and the technician began reviewing the tapes showed no one meeting Bonnie's description either entering or leaving the island. For the next two weeks a Gendarmerie was posted at the gate to watch for any signs of anyone even remotely meeting Bonnie's description, and a technician was assigned to the guardhouse to watch the videotapes in real time. Bloodhounds were also called to scour the entire island to find a body that somehow might have been stashed in some unlikely location on the island. The mud and shallow waters surrounding the island were also searched by a small flotilla of patrol boats, and the tide was still coming in, not going out. A body would have been found if thrown over the ramparts. Again, nothing."

Now fully awake and absorbed, Judy could only say "Unbelievable. I take it there was a full police investigation thereafter."

"Oh yes. The investigation lasted for many months, but its factual findings were as puzzling as they were unsatisfactory:

"Bonnie had never left the island after she disappeared from the Sacre Mont restaurant on the late evening of March 18; no corpse was or could have been stashed anywhere on the island, and there was no possible burial site. The mud and shallow incoming tide surrounding the island were also searched. There was no place on the island where a body could have been buried without leaving a trace, every square foot of ground having been accounted for; and since the tide was coming in and not out, a body would have been found had a body been thrown from the ramparts. Even if the tide had been going out, a body would have been found. No one has seen or heard from Bonnie Hoxsey since the time of her disappearance. It has been almost nineteen years now with no sighting of her. A follow-up "cold case" investigation conducted seven years later confirmed no subsequent sightings, and made an official determination that Bonnie was dead.

"Its final factual finding was superfluous, though of course necessary—namely that Bonnie had indeed entered the island with Hans Wagner on the late afternoon of March 17, had taken a meal at the Sacre Mont Hotel restaurant at or around 9:30 on March 18, and had left the restaurant sometime before 10:45 P.M. after receiving a distressing phone call on her cell phone. This was confirmed by videotapes of Hans and Bonnie entering the Mont on the 17th, and the sworn statements of at least four employees of the Sacre Mont Hotel restaurant, including the waiter who served both Hans and Bonnie dinner on the evening of the 18th."

"So what was the conclusion, or explanation I should say?"

"That's just it, Judy. There was none. The final report had no final conclusion. As for an explanation, the report had none, except to speculate that either Bonnie had somehow found a way off the island while avoiding the video cameras and night watchman by jumping off a rampart and swimming against the deadly rising tide; or that she was killed on the island and buried there. As Bonnie used to say as a child: 'duh!' Of course that latter speculation is specious at best, since there was no evidence of any burial or stashing of a body in some nook or cranny of the island that could not be found by the bloodhounds, and no corpse was ever found in the waters surrounding the island despite a diligent sea search."

"Since one of those explanations must be true, which one do you think most likely?" Asked Judy.

"I do not think that the first speculation could be true. I do not believe for a minute that Bonnie would ever have left the island and then "gone underground" and never trying to communicate with me. If she had gotten in trouble in any way, she would have known that she could call me and I would have helped her in any way I could."

Judy hesitated to ask her next question, but reluctantly did so: "Did you and your daughter ever have any kind of falling out that would have led her to not communicate for so many years?"

"Of course I was asked that by Gendarmeries. But the answer is no. Never. We were always as close as a father and daughter could be. She would never have disappeared of her own volition."

"Then you believe that she is buried somewhere on the island?'

"No, I don't believe that, nor that she was somehow thrown over the ramparts into the shallow incoming tide. The island is very small, and every square foot of it is accounted for by pathways, shops, hotels and restaurants. A burial would have been impossible, and there is no ledge, rock, landing, or vantage point on the entire island from which a body could have been thrown—and in any case, no body was found despite the incoming tide."

"But one of those explanations must be true. I seem to recall a line from a Sherlock Holmes story to the effect that once all the possible explanations are dismissed, then what remains, no matter how improbable, must be true—or something like that."

"You are well read, Judy. Yes, I recall that line, but it does no good to us here because all the explanations are impossible."

"I recall something my physics Professor at UC told our class when talking about the big bang and the origins of the universe—namely that there are only two explanations for the existence of matter: first that matter has always existed; and second that there was nothing to begin with, and matter suddenly popped into existence all by itself from nothing. The first explanation simply begs the question, and therefore provides no explanation at all; and the second is also impossible on its face."

"An excellent analogy."

It was now three in the morning, and Timothy Hoxsey had still not answered the one question which she needed to have answered. And so she asked it:

"Timothy, why do you think I can help you in any way to find out what happened to your daughter?"

CHAPTER TWENTY-THREE

DECEMBER 29

By now even Timothy was looking worn and haggard after re-living the tragedy of his daughter. Although a longtime and confirmed night owl, it was late even for him. It was now apparent to him that Judy would not agree to retire for the evening until she had an answer to her question.

"Judy, over the last nineteen years I have used every resource at my disposal to find out what happened to Bonnie. I have hired the best detectives money can buy. I have called in chits from every influential person I know, including politicians across three continents—and I have gotten to know a number of them over the years, many of whom owe me favors. I have hired researchers from around the world to dig into the backgrounds of every person even remotely connected to the events of that night of March 18 at Mont St. Michel, almost nineteen years ago. I have presented myself in person to all the French authorities involved in any way with the investigation—all to no avail.

"I am ashamed to say that I have not always used—well, I will say it, completely legal methods—to obtain information, including cyber experts to gain access to documents, reports, emails, and the like, many of which are protected by various privacy laws. I am, as they say, at the end of my rope, and if what the doctors tell me is true, I am now facing going to my maker with no prospect of ever resting in peace."

"I understand," said Judy "I do. But how could you possibly believe I could find out anything that all those people you mentioned—experts in their field—could not find?"

"At the risk of possibly offending you I will tell you why I believe you are my last hope. But first I must tell you what has been the greatest obstacle to finding the truth that I have not yet been able to overcome. It is getting the people who may have answers to open up to me or my investigators about what they know. My detectives have interviewed these people, and I have done so in person. But everyone we have interviewed has had their own reason for not opening up to tell us what I'm sure they know—from the French *Inspecteur* General, to the Commissaire General de Police, to the Gendarmeries who I believe have bungled this investigation from the beginning, down to the waiters at the to the Sacre Mont Hotel."

"You mentioned before the Otto Wagner Koncept Konstrucktion Company."

Timothy's eyes narrowed. "Yes, especially them. They have stonewalled every attempt to get any information from them."

"And Hans Wagner? You say he was the last person to see Bonnie alive."

"Yes. He has consistently refused to talk to us. He always just refers us to the statement he made to the Gendarmeries and contained in their report. His statements are all self-serving. I believe very little of it."

"You didn't say 'especially' with regard to him."

"If you take on the task which I will present to you, I do not want to in any way perform it with any preconceptions that may bias you in any way."

"But haven't you already?"

"Let's say no more on that until you have agreed to my proposal."

"Very well. But I was concerned when you said that your proposal, whatever it might be, might in some way offend me. What did you mean by that?"

Timothy took a deep breath. "Have you ever read any of the writings of the Greek philosopher Aristotle? Any of his sayings?"

Judy thought this was an odd sequitur in response to her question, but answered: "Yes, perhaps a few of them I think."

"Can you recite one or two of them?"

131

Judy felt like she was being tested in some way. "Well, let me think."

"Take your time."

"Umh...how about 'the whole is more than the sum of its parts?' Is that one?"

"Go on."

"'The roots of education are bitter, but the fruit is sweet?'"

"I'm impressed. One more?"

"'Let's see: 'All human actions have one or more of these seven causes: chance, nature, compulsions, habit, reason...' I forget the last two."

"'Passion, and desire.'"

"Yes, OK."

"Now I have one for you, Judy."

"Yes?"

"'Beauty is a greater recommendation that any letter of introduction.'"

"Aristotle really said that?"

"He wrote it, yes."

"And what does that have to do with what we're talking about, and your proposal?"

"Several nights ago when I was talking to Amber, she was telling me about this Gardner case, and she happened to mention that the victim was a passive, but major partner in the O.W.K.K.. She also told me that his wife stood to inherit a lucrative interest in that company. It is a privately held company/partnership. I thought that an odd coincidence, since I believe that whatever the explanation may be for the disappearance of my daughter, that company had something to do with it, or at the least knows something about it."

"And Hans in particular? Couldn't it just be a coincidence that the wife of the victim in the Gardner case stands to inherit an interest in the same company you suspect of having information about the disappearance of your daughter?"

"That's what I thought too, of course, and still do for the most part. However, I do not wish to leave any stone unturned, and I believe that connection—thin as it may be—is worth pursuing. It was not until Amber told me about your success in gaining access to the prisoner Gardner that I thought of how you could be of help to me.

"Ever since Gardner was arrested and the judge in Appaloosa County appointed Amber's firm to represent him in competency hearings, Amber has expressed to me in our evening cell phone conversations her deep disappointment that the prisoner had refused to even talk to her. I think it affected her ego and her feelings of self-worth as a lawyer. In the last call I had with her just a few days ago, she related how you had somehow managed the impossible—getting Gardner to talk. Getting people to talk and tell what they know is exactly the kind of skill I need to employ if I am to ever get justice for Bonnie."

Judy now felt the same pangs of conscience she had felt when she had indeed played Hillman with suggestions that she might collaborate on a law review article with him. Understanding now why Timothy had expressed his concern that his coming proposal might offend her, she now defensively addressed that concern:

"I did nothing inappropriate to persuade Mr. Hillman to let me see Gardner! Are you saying that I seduced him or something to get what I wanted?"

"Not at all, Judy, and please forgive me if you took what I said to suggest any such thing. It's precisely because, according to Amber, you didn't have to do anything along those lines that I came to think that you would be the ideal person to pursue the avenues that have for so long been closed to me. If all I wanted was to use you as a honey trap, there are legions of young attractive women I could retain for the purpose—and they would all be seen for what they were, and thus useless. That's not what I want."

"Then what are we talking about..."

"What clinched my decision to call for your help was Amber's description of your..."

"My what?" she asked sharply.

"Your physical beauty, Judy. It is beyond extraordinary, of that you must be aware. You have surpassed all my expectations—tenfold."

All her life, Judy had been obliged to deal with the challenges that came from her beauty—the unwelcome and often obsessive attentions of men, the incessant come-ons heaped upon her no matter where she went, the jealousy of her female friends, particularly those who inevitably saw her as a threat to their relationships with their own male friends and husbands, and not least the threats and cruelties inflicted upon her by those whom she of necessity had to reject—no matter how conciliatory and gently she tried to couch those rejections.

"I hope you understand that what you're telling me now sounds like so many of the come-ons I've heard all my life."

"And for that I deeply apologize. I am an eighty-five year old man with very little time, and very little to live for except to find justice for my much beloved daughter. I can assure you that I feel strongly that you are now my last hope. I have no other motive than that. And in asking for your help, I would never ask you to do anything more than—say, suggest that you might be interested in some future collaboration."

At this Judy did smile and soften the sharpness of her voice. "Oh no, Amber told you that too?"

"Yes, I'm afraid so."

Judy shook her head. "I do feel bad about that. But I did think it was for a worthy cause. Since I heard about the Gardner case in the Exoneration Clinic I've instinctively felt that—I'm not sure why—that he must somehow be innocent."

"Some romantic notion about a man sacrificing himself for a woman he loved?"

"Don't tell me Amber told you that too?"

Timothy smiled and shrugged. "Could you bring yourself to believe that what I'm going to ask you to do is also a worthy cause?"

"Did Aristotle really say that—about beauty being a better recommendation that a letter of introduction."

"Yep. You can google it up if you wish. Just google up 'who said that,' and insert the quote. I didn't make it up, I assure you."

"And what if my 'beauty' does not give me the entrees you think it will?"

"Then so be it. But for the last nineteen years nothing else has worked in getting the information I need."

"I don't know, Timothy. I really don't. I'm due back in New York to register for my second semester. I don't want to jeopardize my law school career, such as it is."

"You know," he said, grasping now for an argument that might make his coming proposal more attractive to her, "getting information about my daughter could very well lead to a resolution in the Gardner case as well—and that, my dear, might very well put your Exoneration Clinic back on the map."

As arguments go, Judy felt this one a bit transparent, but let it go. "You know about it, then—the Exoneration Clinic, I mean, the trouble it might be in."

"Yes, and about your supervisor Professor Robin Hammond. Guilty as charged. I researched it last night before you came."

"You must have been pretty confident that I would come. Please don't tell me you researched me as well?"

Timothy turned slightly red. "Ok, I did, and I'm sorry. There wasn't enough time to do a full investigation of your background, so of course I had to be content with the very skimpy information to be found on the internet, including any criminal background, any liens, lawsuits against you, that sort of thing.

Judy frowned, the sharpness in her voice returning. "And?"

"You were clean as a whistle, I assure you. Surely you wouldn't blame me for doing a background check on someone to whom I was going to ask to do something for me. In any case, your background history seemed to abruptly stop at Tiberon, where you grew up with your father, a respected Egyptologist. "

"If I were even to consider your 'proposal'—which at this moment I very much doubt-—I would demand your promise that there would be no more investigation of me. I don't like it." Judy had no problem in speaking plainly and directly when she felt it was called for.

"I would promise that, absolutely."

"And would you tell me if you thought there was any danger to me in taking on this 'assignment' you have in mind?"

"I would. I don't believe there would be—at least not any that I could foresee. Of course I would give you ample warning if anything came up on the radar."

Judy stood up, took a last sip from her bottle of Voss, and looked at the nautical clock on the wall. It showed 4:30 A.M.., and she was about to keel over.

"Well, Mr. Hoxsey, I am going to bed."

"But you haven't heard my proposal."d

"I think I know enough of what you have in mind to think about it after I get a good night's sleep. It's been a long day"

"Of course. If you have a time in mind when you would like to get up, I can have Mary bring up breakfast to your room in the morning."

"No, if I get to sleep right away, I should be up by, say 10. We can talk then."

"You can find your way to your room upstairs, and you have everything you need?"

"Yes, and I brought an overnight bag. I'm fine. Good night."

CHAPTER TWENTY-FOUR

DECEMBER 29

After tossing and turning the rest of the night, Judy woke at 7:00. Still tired, she tried to go back to sleep, but couldn't. Instead she decided to lie back in bed and call Amber.

"Hi Amber, Judy. Are you at the office?"

"Nope, holiday hours, just puttering around the house. Are you in Avalon?"

"Yep, I sure am."

"I can't believe it! So you've met Timothy."

"I sure did."

"Oh my God, tell me. You went over on the Bonnie, I assume."

"Oh yes, and the G500 or whatever it is."

"Yes, all his toys are quite something. But tell me everything."

Judy summarized all the highlights of the previous day, including the substance of her night-long conference with Timothy, including everything that Timothy had told her about the disappearance of Bonnie. "I guess you know the whole story of Bonnie."

"I do, and I was afraid that's what this was all about. Of course, I had no idea when I last talked to him that my casual mention of O.W.K.K. would provide the link to his daughter that, apparently, has now set him off on renewing his search for answers."

"Yes, he made that pretty clear. But Amber, I do have a bone to pick with you. Why on earth did you have to mention to him about, you know, my physiognomy?"

"Physiognomy? You've been up north too long. Long time since I've heard that word. Sorry, I guess I did let it drop that my young law school protégé from up north was quite a beauty, and that she had somehow managed to get that bastard Hillman to let you in to see Gardner. But that was before I had accidentally got God-dad's mind racing about this O.W.K.K. connection."

"It's all right. But he did say something that got me concerned that...that he might be coming on to me. I wouldn't want to have anything to do with that."

"Oh, no, I know him, Judy, believe me. Don't' worry about that, please. He hasn't been frisky like that ever since Bonnie's mother passed away, and certainly not since Bonnie's disappearance. Since then he hasn't even dated anyone—not that there hasn't been a flock of gold diggers after him—and if he had even dated anyone he would have mentioned it during one of our frequent phone conversations. I mean he is eighty- five years old now for God's sake. And you're what—mid-twenties?"

"You're too kind. Older than that, I assure you."

"So what did he say?"

"Oh, you know, just that I was 'more beautiful' than you described—typical come on line."

"Well, if he had said 'you have such beautiful eyes' I might be more concerned. But no. I know him and have known him almost all my life. His interest in you is because he thinks you might be able to help him find out what happened to Bonnie. He's tried everything else, I know that. I guess it's like the patient who has incurable cancer and willing is to try any experimental treatment no matter how untested it is."

"So you're saying that anything I do to help him would be unlikely to achieve any results?"

"I didn't mean to say that. Well, maybe I did mean to say that. What has he asked you to do exactly?"

"Nothing yet, just implied. He's going to tell me today. Do you have any advice to give me?"

"Sweetie, you may remember that I advised not to go out there at all. But I promised Timothy I'd relay his invitation to you, so I did. That's all."

"He did tell me that anything we find out about Bonnie's disappearance might also resolve what is going on with Gardner and why he is refusing to defend himself."

"Really? I would take that with a grain of salt. It's such a thin connection—this O.W.K.K. thing."

"So you're saying I shouldn't agree to do anything for him?"

"I guess it depends. I certainly wouldn't enter into any kind of quid-pro-quo contract with him—you know, agree to do certain things in exchange for a fee, though I'm sure he'd offer you the moon. You can't take it with you, and money means very little to him."

"So what if anything do you think would be OK?"

"Look, you've got your law school career to think about. If you think you could skip a semester without any long term ramifications, I suppose there would be no harm in taking a pleasant sojourn to France, and talking to various people as long as you were careful not to let them know what your real agenda was."

"I think I could only justify doing that if I thought it might help me resolve the Gardner matter and give me material for my article—and that would help you, too, right?"

"There you go! But absolutely no contract—verbal, or God forbid, written."

"Definitely."

"But don't be surprised if he insists on rewarding you—with his yacht or something—if you do discover something, or even if you don't."

"I wouldn't be doing it for the money!" Judy said defensively.

"Just joking, sweetie."

"I still need to talk to Professor Hammond. I'm not sure what he'd say about all this."

"Better call him now before you reach any accommodation with Timothy."

Just then there was a soft knock on the door.

139

"Yes?" Judy called out.

It was Mary. "I have breakfast for you if you're up," she called out.

"Room service?" Amber asked.

Judy chuckled. "I guess so. I'll call you back after I've talked to Professor Hammond and Timothy. Bye."

"Come in!" Judy called out to Mary, who walked in with a tray of poached egg whites, dry toast, yogurt, fruit, and coffee."

"I had to guess what you'd like, ma'am."

"Well, you did an excellent job of guessing, Mary, it's perfect. Thank you!"

******

Judy enjoyed her perfect breakfast before calling Robin Hammond and telling him everything about the events of the past several days, including her interview with Timothy. Robin listened a good half hour without interrupting. He then gave her his opinion:

"Judy, I'll be honest. I don't like it. Not at all. You have made an excellent start to your legal education, and I think you'd be throwing it all away if you drop out of school now just to go on some goose chase across Europe for an elderly man you don't even know."

"I wouldn't be dropping out of school, Professor—just taking a semester off."

"Yes, but it's the second semester of your first year. The first year second semester courses are structured, and only taught during the second semester."

"But I could still take a semester off without dropping out, couldn't I?"

"Well, you'd have to get a waiver from the dean and registrar, but you still couldn't return until the second semester of next year."

"I didn't realize that."

"And for what, Judy? Whatever you agree to do over in France might not work out at all. And then you've wasted an entire year of your legal education."

"Well, I haven't made any commitment yet to Mr. Hoxsey, and I am not yet sure exactly what I would be expected to do. I'll find out later today. But it's not just for him and his wish to find out what happened to his daughter that I'd be going. I think I might also find something that would explain what is going on with regard to Doctor Gardner."

"It sounds like you're rationalizing."

Judy thought for a moment. "Maybe I am, but to be honest with you, I'm not that sure I want to be a lawyer."

"I'm surprised to hear you say that. We'll have to wait until you get all your exam grades back to determine how much real aptitude you have for the law, but I would be surprised if you did not do well. When I called on you in class, you gave the best recitation of a case I heard all semester."

"I was always prepared, that's true. Have you finished grading?" Judy knew she could ask this without suggesting any hope for favoritism in the grading of her exam because all law school exams were typed using laptops, and graded anonymously by student number.

"No, in fact I'm just bearing down now to finish my grading: twenty-two exams down, forty-two more to go."

"So no more crossword puzzles for a while."

"I'm afraid not. Not until I finish these last forty-two exams. I need to get them in by the first day of spring classes."

"Well, I'll let you get to them, Professor. I'll call you back when I know what this commission really involves, and let you know."

"Great. Keep me posted."

"Will do. Bye for now, Professor."

CHAPTER TWENTY-FIVE

DECEMBER 29

It was 8:30 A.M. when Judy, decked in a colorful sundress and white scandals, walked down the grand staircase to the atrium. Timothy was sitting on the bamboo divan looking over some documents that were spread out beside him.

"Good morning, Judy," said Timothy, as he swept up the documents to make room. "You slept well I trust. Come sit."

Judy sat. "'I've slept better to be honest. You gave me a lot to think about last night."

"I was thinking we might take a quiet walk around the island and we could talk—if you're up to it."

Judy smiled indulgently. She was pretty sure she was up to it despite not getting her full sleep allotment. And all power to Timothy if he was up to it.

"We could take one of my putt-putts up to that high cliff over there,' said he, pointing towards a precipice in the distance, "and take a walking trail from there."

"I could do that. Could I drive the putt-putt? They look like fun."

"Of course. I'll have one brought to the front. In the meantime you might want to take one of the sun hats we have lying around here." He called for Mary.

"Mary, could you see if we have one of those big sun beach hats in the hall closet. And maybe a sweater. It can turn a little cool this time of year. It will only get up to the fifties today."

"Actually I have a sweater I packed with me and a hat I wore on the boat," said Judy. "I'll go up and fetch them and meet you out front."

Judy took the driver's seat of the "tricked out" golf-cart that was waiting for them. She figured out the controls, and moments later was putt-putting through Avalon, past the

"Casino," and winding up past little houses and up a narrow road to the top of the high hill beyond. At the top she stopped to look at the view of the town below and the ocean beyond.

"Beautiful!" she said.

"Nice day, and you can see Long Beach clearly. Let's leave the cart here. The trail I have in mind in just over there."

They had not walked far when Judy spoke first. "Timothy, I talked to both Amber and my faculty supervisor this morning."

"Professor Robin Hammond?"

"Yes. He was quite adamant that I should not forego my second semester of law school. If I were to take the second semester off, I would necessarily have to take the first semester of next year off as well, which means I would miss an entire year of law school."

"You would be well compensated..."

"That is not my issue."

"I was going to propose..."

"Timothy, please don't think me discourteous, but rather than you making a proposal, I would like to tell first you what I might—and I underscore might—consider doing for you if I can."

"Of course. Please go on."

"First, I appreciate fully your need and desire to find out what happened to your daughter. I lost my father several years ago under tragic circumstances as well, so I can relate. You have also brought to my attention a possible connection between the disappearance of your daughter and a case which I became interested in while working with the Exoneration Clinic at my law school. I would have to be honest with you, and tell you that this latter case—the Gardner case—would be a major motivating factor in deciding whether to also pursue the matter of your daughter's disappearance."

"I appreciate that."

"Second, let me tell you what I might be prepared to do, and what I would definitely not be prepared to do. I assume that what you have in mind is that I make casual contacts with

143

those whom you believe may have some knowledge about what happened to your daughter. I would be willing to make those contacts on a casual basis, keeping in mind that if I do make contact with someone who has such knowledge, and they discovered the true purpose of my contact, that I could be placed in a vulnerable situation."

"I would take every precaution..."

"Please, let me finish. Also, know that under no circumstances would I ever allow any contact I make to go beyond a purely casual stage. I'm sure you know exactly what I mean."

"I do and agree absolutely, and that is exactly why I think you would be the best..."

Judy held up her finger to indicate that, again, he should let her finish. Like a chastened schoolboy he desisted.

"I know you think that my supposed 'beauty' is all that will be needed to extract information which by any other means could never be coughed up. For one thing I don't believe that for a minute, and for another, not everyone you might have in mind for me to contact is apt to be as easily manipulated as Mr. Hillman, who according to your goddaughter is..."

"An unethical scumbag."

"Amber used a different word, but yes, something like that. And I remind you, that I never promised him anything beyond the vague possibility of a future collaboration on a writing project."

Timothy nodded, but as ordered, said nothing.

"Finally it must be understood that if, at any time, I feel uncomfortable with any situation in which I find myself, I will be free to return home without any questions asked."

Judy now paused to indicate that Timothy was free to speak if he wished.

"I could not have said it better. You have taken the words of what I planned to propose right out of my mouth. But you have not indicated what you wish in terms of compensation for taking on such a commission, including, but certainly not limited to compensation for postponing your career in the law."

"I will not enter into any contract with you."

"Do I hear Amber's input here in that regard?"

Judy laughed. "You know your goddaughter well. Yes, Amber did advise me that if I were to accept this undertaking that I should not enter into any kind of contract with you, written, oral, or understood."

"Of course. And perhaps my goddaughter does not know me as completely as I know her. I would never have asked you to do so. Still, you must have some terms of compensation which I can oblige."

"I have very little money at the present time as I've used most of my money on this trip, so I would need all my expenses paid."

"That goes without saying. And of course all my resources would be at your disposal."

"As for compensation, I do not feel comfortable naming a sum. After I do whatever I feel comfortable doing—regardless of any success that I may or may not have—you can compensate me for whatever you think my efforts on your behalf have been worth to you."

"I think you can trust that I will take into account not only the sacrifice which you would be making in terms of your legal education, but also take into account what would be sufficient to express my deepest gratitude that you would accept this undertaking in any capacity whatsoever."

Timothy was still not sure if Judy had agreed to accept the undertaking.

"So you will go to France?"

"I still reserve my answer. I still need to talk to my Professor, and Amber as well."

"Of course. May I suggest that while you consider, you might take a look at what evidence I have accumulated over the past nineteen years. I have bound, catalogued, and indexed every document, interview, and official report that I have been able to obtain. You may have noticed the twenty-three bound volumes on my book shelves in the library."

"All those volumes are of evidence you have accumulated?"

"Many of them are also in digital form which you may access at any time on your computer or phone."

"There is so much. How long would it take for me to examine the documents available only in hard copy?"

"I will of course highlight and lay out for you in my library the most important and relevant pieces of evidence— the hard copies that because of their sensitive nature I would not dare download digitally to any computer. Those you would need to examine and digest in the confines of my library. I think you could digest those in, say, a week. The rest, mostly public documents and reports you could download later as the need arises."

"A week?"

"Perhaps less, depending on how fast you read, and how much time you need for rest and to clear your head. New Year is only the day after tomorrow. Hopefully you could take some time out to enjoy our festivities here on Catalina as we bring in the New Year."

"Wow. I will call the Professor and Amber and give you a firm answer."

"So now, let us return to our cart and see if Mary has some nice lunch for us."

CHAPTER TWENTY-SIX

DECEMBER 29

After a delightfully agreeable early light lunch prepared by Mary, Judy retired to her room to make calls to Hammond and Amber.

Hammond, whom she had no problem reaching because he still was holed up in his apartment grading exams, did not change his mind about whether she should accept the undertaking she described. He continued to urge her to finish her second semester, after which she could assess whether she truly wanted a legal career. He also stated again his concerns about the undertaking itself, fraught he believed with both uncertainty and possible danger. Nevertheless, he finally relented when Judy confided that she had already developed reservations about a legal career, and that a year off might give her time to consider them. In the end Hammond capitulated, assuring her that if, despite his misgivings she decided to go ahead, he would support her and be available to help in any way he could. If she wished, he would procure a waiver from the dean and registrar for her to take off the second and third semesters. This would allow her to retain the option of returning to Oliver Wendell Holmes School of Law in the spring of the following year. She said she did so wish and thanked him.

Amber too urged caution, but was relieved that Judy had not made, and would not make any binding commitment, and that if Judy did accept the undertaking she would only do so with the stipulation that she would be free at any time to withdraw. Amber also promised that she would do everything she could to oversee Judy's interests and keep her godfather in line—which she would have ample opportunity to do during her regular phone calls with him.

Taking a deep breath, Judy walked down the grand staircase to the library, and knocked. "Come in!" said Timothy, who was leaning over his big oak desk and organizing documents into different piles. She did so and stood by the door.

"Mr. Hoxsey"—she had decided that she couldn't get used to calling him 'Timothy,' especially now that she had decided to enter into the kind of semi-business relationship they had discussed—"I have decided to accept, with the conditions and stipulations you said you would agree to."

Timothy straightened and clapped his hands.

"Excellent! Then we must get started immediately. Please come over. I am making piles of those documents which cannot leave this room and which I do not wish to digitize or download to any computer. Did you bring a notebook with you by any chance?

"No, I usually use my iPad to take..."

"Never mind," said he delving into a lower desk drawer to retrieve a fresh lined notebook. "You can use this. I have organized these papers into several piles; the first contains the name, addresses, and in most cases the phone numbers, or at least the business phone numbers, of all those officially connected with the investigation itself, starting with the Commissaire General, down to Inspector Montague and the Gendarmeries under him."

"And this second pile?" It was the shortest, only half an inch high.

"Those are the names and last addresses of independent witnesses, not connected to the official investigators, though most, but not all, have given official statements to the investigators and police, and emails sent between them."

Judy pointed to the third pile—the highest, almost four inches high.

"Those are documents relating to those connected in any way with O.W.K.K.."

Judy started to leaf through them.

"And most of those are related to the backgrounds and activities of Otto Wagner, his father, and grandfather."

"Very impressive," said Judy as she picked up the top document on the third file and began perusing it.

Placing the document back on the pile she said, "Now I have a task for you, Mr. Hoxsey."

"Of course."

"You know I am studying for the law. And I should have made this much clearer. You intimated earlier that some of these documents may not have obtained by purely legal means— by which I take it that privacy laws may have been violated in obtaining them. If I am to have any future in the law—though I have not yet finally decided to pursue it further—I would not want to start it by being involved with, or making use of any such documents."

Timothy gave her a startled look.

"So, I am going to saunter, by myself, down to the city center and do a little shopping—start looking for a wardrobe suitable for various occasions in France. I only brought two outfits, and even back in my New York apartment I only have a couple of others. Until I return I would ask you to go through these three piles and withdraw any documents or papers that might—even possibly—have been obtained in violation of any law, either in French or American."

"But you would never have them in your possession..."

"It's a condition, Timothy," she said firmly, though by reverting to calling him by his preferred first name she thought she would soften what might otherwise sound like unreasonable goody-goody petulance.

"I will of course do as you request, though some of those documents you might find very useful..."

Judy shook her head. No..."

Timothy sighed. "Very well. But in return might I too make a request? It's an eminently reasonable one."

"Sure, Timothy, "she said, appreciative that he had so readily agreed to her latest terms of engagement,

"Completely legal, I assure you. I agree that you will need several ensembles depending on when and where you are in

France. I fear you will not find much of a selection in Avalon, however, which offers mostly tee-shirts and beach attire. The Princess Bonnie is available now to take you to Long Beach where you will find stores offering everything from formal designer clothes to the latest fashionable informal wear, and the Rover can whisk you quickly from store to store."

"Oh no, the ferry will be fine, Timothy, really."

"I promised to do as you ask, so you will not return the favor? There is also the matter of time. Waiting in line for the ferry, getting a ticket, trying to hook up with an Uber at the always chaotic Long Beach Terminal, would take all day, most of the evening, and leave you little time for shopping. You will return exhausted even if you don't miss the last ferry back to Avalon. It will take me most of the afternoon to perform the task you gave me to withdraw some of the documents from my three piles, but if you return in time for dinner this evening you will still have plenty of time to get started on reading and taking your notes of the Sanitized files that will await you on your return."

Judy sighed. "You're very persuasive. All right. I'm sure you'll want to see me off to France as soon as possible, so OK. But I still want to do a little shopping downtown here first. I haven't walked through Avalon since I came here to summer camp."

"That's fine. If an hour would be enough time for that, I'll have Chandler pick you up in the Rover at the Buccaneer Shop on Duke Street—say at 2:00 P.M.?"

"Chandler? Do I really need a chaperone?"

"It would be best if he goes as he needs to give directions to Captain Harper, make sure you are settled on the Bonnie, and make arrangements for the Rover to pick you up at the other end in Long Beach."

"Well, OK, but I don't want to get used to all this. Can he make it 2:30? I'd like a little more time."

"Sure, 2:30, then. Have a good shopping trip. Do you want to drive the putt-putt down the hill?"

"You mean you don't have a helicopter to drop me down in the center of town?"

150

"Now you've hit a sore point. I have a perfectly good helipad on the roof, and one on the Bonnie as well, but the town elders in their infinite wisdom refuse to let me…"

"I was kidding!"

CHAPTER TWENTY-SEVEN

DECEMBER 29

Judy stood up on the bow railing of the Princess Bonnie, closed her eyes, and let her deep dark hair flow gently behind her in the gentle evening breeze.

"I'm flying!" she whispered into the wind as she held her arms out to each side.

Her Rose DeWitt reverie was broken by the unwelcome voice of her chaperone behind her. This was the second time in as many days that he had startled her from behind.

"Ms. Alexander, the captain thinks you should come down now. It's getting a little choppy!" It was his attempt at a diplomatic way of telling her that neither he nor the captain wanted to risk returning to Avalon Sans the Princess Bonnie's only passenger.

Judy stepped down, turned and gave Chandler a guilty look. But Chandler was no Jack Dawson and it was starting to get nippy. "Sorry! I didn't mean to alarm the captain."

She looked back up to the bridge where Captain Harper smiled and waved to her. She returned both the smile and the wave.

"We're about fifteen minutes out, if you'd like to have a nightcap in the salon," Chandler suggested. "I texted Mr. Hoxsey, and he's holding dinner until you arrive.

""Oh, I'd like to stay on the deck if that's all right. I promise not to stand on the railing."

"That's fine. I'll bring your new coat to wear if you wish." Judy did not refuse. "Thank you. It's in the salon." The evening had cooled rapidly, and she had bought a bright red woolen coat at Nordstrom, one of only a few items she had actually purchased after shopping for several hours in Long Beach. Her only other purchases were a sturdy pair of black walking shoes from Macy's, black cotton trousers from Anthropologie, Lululemon yoga pants and top, and—her only luxury purchase—a red cashmere scarf from Neiman Marcus. The bags were in the salon.

******

"Ah, you're back! Excellent! Mary has dinner waiting. How was the trip back on the Bonnie?" Timothy asked enthusiastically when Judy and Chandler entered the atrium.

Judy was wearing her new red coat, scarf, and walking shoes; and Chandler carried only the one shopping bag from Anthropologie into which had been placed the two items Judy had bought earlier in Avalon.

"I have to admit, it was enjoyable," said Judy as she took off her coat and plopped herself on the divan. "I'm afraid I could get used to all this."

Chandler put down the shopping bag. "Will you need me for anything more this evening, sir?"

"No, you may go Chandler. And thank you for watching over our precious cargo here."

"Of course, sir. I'll say goodnight, then."

"So," asked Timothy. "Is that all you bought today?"

"Yes, I didn't really see that much that I liked. I did buy two other things in Avalon, though." She pulled out from the shopping bag a Catalina Island sweatshirt and a Catalina blouse.

"Well, never mind. You would probably do well anyway to travel light when you fly to France and you can then purchase what you need when you get there."

"Would you mind if I went up to my room for a few minutes before dinner?"

"Not at all. But before you do, I would like you to meet someone."

Entering the atrium from the north wing was a middle-aged, attractive woman wearing a textured tencel crepe skirt and low-heeled boots, and sporting a messy French Twist hair style streaked with silver highlights.

153

"Judy, I'd like to meet Sophie Dorleac. She has taught French at UCLA for many years, and has served as my translator for many years when I conduct business in France. She is now available for tutoring. Sophie, this is Judy Alexander."

Sophie held out her hand. "Good evening, Judy. Mr. Hoxsey tells me that you will soon be travelling to France on some business for him, and that I might be helpful to you in learning a little French before you go."

Judy was a little taken aback as she had not thought about the need for brushing up on her French, and she had not discussed this with Timothy.

"Do you speak any French now?" asked Sophie.

"I took it for two years in high school, but that was some time ago, and I fear I remember very little of it now."

"Well, you have taken basic grammar, and that's good. We won't have to start completely from scratch."

Sophie turned to Timothy. "If she will give me four hours a day for the next week, and she applies herself, I should have her speaking passable colloquial French by the time she leaves for France. Is this one week deadline before she leaves at all flexible?"

Judy and Timothy looked at each other. "Not absolutely," said he. "But we had both decided that one week would be sufficient time for her to review certain documents in preparation for the business she will be conducting on my behalf in France, so we would like to stick to that time frame span if at all possible.

"I understand. Well, we shall do the best we can. But she will have her work cut out for her to undertake those preparations as well as study and practice her French."

At that moment Mary appeared to ask if everyone was ready for dinner.

"Give us fifteen minutes, Mary. Judy will that be enough time for you to freshen up?"

"Actually, ten will do. Would it be alright if I wore what I have on?" asked Judy.

"Of course. We never require formal attire for dinner here in Avalon."

"My trip was only finalized this morning, Ms. Dorleac. However did you manage to get here so quickly?" Judy asked. Do you live here in Avalon?"

"*Mon dieu*, not at all. Not that I wouldn't' love to live here. It's so lovely. I live in LA, but Timothy and I are old friends, so when he called me early this afternoon of course I was happy to oblige. I took the first ferry. "

And he probably made it well worth your while, Judy thought, but did not say it.

"Timothy, if it's all right, I'd like to skip dessert, and start reviewing the materials you laid out for me in the library. Ms. Dorleac..."

"Please, Judy, call me Sophie."

"Of course...Sophie, if I'm to leave in a week, I was thinking we could have our lessons in the morning from eight until noon. Would that work for you? I could then concentrate on my business preparations in the afternoon. That would still leave me time to do my homework in the evening."

"*Il n'y a pas que le travail dans la vie?*"

"I'm afraid so, Sophie," Timothy answered for Judy. "I'm quite anxious that Judy will be ready to leave no later than a week from today. But it will not be all work and no play. Tomorrow you will settle in for your lessons and review, but the night after I invite you both to join me for the annual gala New Year's celebrations at the Catalina Casino—dinner and dancing until the fireworks at midnight. I buy eight tickets every year, and I would be honored to be joined by both you lovely ladies.

Timothy rose from his chair to point out the Casino across the harbor.

"I saw it as we passed it in our putt-putt this morning. I didn't know they had gambling on the island." said Judy.

"Oh no. There's no gambling there. The name 'Casino' on Sugarloaf point just means 'gathering place.' The new building there was built in 1929. Wrigley—you know, the chewing gum guy. He built it to be the first movie theater specifically designed to show the new 'talkies.'"

"Is it formal?" asked Sophie. "*Mon dieu*, I have not the *robe du soir* for such an occasion!"

"And I too have nothing to wear either," Judy protested. I was not looking for a formal gown, or high heel evening shoes when I was shopping this afternoon."

"Not to worry, ladies. Chandler will be going to Long Beach first thing in the morning to purchase gowns for both of us. You have only to give him your sizes before he goes. Sophie?"

"I wear something between a four and a six and size six shoes."

"That is my size as well. Perhaps closer to a four and I wear size five shoes," said Judy.

"That's all he will need, then. We can draw on Mary's sewing skills if size adjustments need to be made."

"So, Judy, you are off to the library?"

"Yes, just for an hour. It's been a long day, and I need to be up bright and early for my French lesson with"—Judy turned to Sophie and smiled—"Ms. Sophie. In the evenings, will you be available to help me with any homework you give me in the morning?"

"Of course, *mon char*. I will be staying here for the entire week, so I will be available should you have any questions at all. In fact, since we will be having dinner together every night, let us make a rule that only French can be spoken between us."

"Yes, then you too can have your little secrets," said Timothy, "as I speak little French myself—just enough to get around in Paris when I am there."

"Good night, then all. See you in the morning."

CHAPTER TWENTY-EIGHT

JANUARY 7

The sun was barely up on a very cool and foggy Catalina morning when the black Rover rolled up the pier to the waiting Princess Bonnie.

Chandler opened the back door for Judy, while Timothy got out from his side. Two sailors from the Bonnie took Judy's two suitcases up the gang plank.

Judy wore her new red woolen coat, black trousers, and sturdy walking shoes, and her hair was tied in a ponytail. She had brought her one small roller bag she had brought from New York, and another roller bag she had purchased in Avalon to accommodate her few additional clothing purchases. Much as she loved the gown she had worn at the New Year's gala, she could not bear to have it squashed into one of her suitcases. Both she and Timothy had agreed that she should travel light.

"Well, this is it Judy," said Timothy, taking her hand. "I'm sure we've forgotten something, as travelers always do, but if so you can purchase what you need in Paris."

It had been an intense week—early morning French lessons every day followed by a light lunch, afternoon document review in the library, light dinner, homework, and conversational French sessions in the evenings. There had been only two breaks from this concentrated regimen during the week: a short putt-putt drive—she loved driving them—to the Catalina airport from which Timothy took her for a helicopter tour of the other side of the island; and of course the New Year's gala at the Casino where she been the object of much admiration in her resplendent empire-waist gown. The few Catalina denizens who didn't know Hoxsey—many of the guests were from the mainland—asked if she was his granddaughter, while others asked if she was his goddaughter, Amber. Many of Timothy's neighbors on the island had heard of him speak of Amber, but had never seen her. Arthur Hensley, an old friend of Timothy's who was at the gala with his wife, remarked to him that she was truly exquisite and asked if he had perhaps been playing the part of Professor Higgins to Eliza Doolittle's *My Fair Lady* at the royal ball.

"Let me take a minute," said Judy nervously. "It has all been so overwhelming." She looked in the large shoulder purse she had slung over her shoulders. "I have my notebook, with the list of all my contacts—that's the most important—which I will guard with my life. My iPhone, of course—my iPad is in my case—my wallet..."

"You have all the history and guide books on Mont St. Michel which I gave you?

"Yep, in my bag."

"Check to see if you have the Amex card. You can't do much without that. And you have the francs I gave you?"

"Yes, though I promise not to spend anything more than I need to."

"That's fine but spend whatever you need to make progress. Now we've been over your itinerary before, but just to be sure: you should be in Paris by this evening. From the Bonnie, Jimmy will take you to the G500 which is waiting for you at the Long Beach airport. You are familiar with it. It will take about four hours to arrive at Teterboro airport in New Jersey. You will have an hour or so to disembark there, if you wish, as it will take that long to re-fuel, and conduct final flight checks. Captain Heath will take on another co-pilot there as well. From there you will fly to Le Bourget airport in Paris, which is situated next to Charles de Gaulle Airport."

"Let me guess. There's a Rover at Le Bourget as well."

"Jimmy will still be with you and will accompany you to the Mandarin Oriental in Paris. And from there..."

"I will be on my own."

"Yes, very much so. And you have no problems with your persona—I prefer that word rather than 'cover story.' We have discussed it at length, but let's go over it a final time."

"I will tell the truth about my background and the reason for being in France as much as possible. I am a law student from the Oliver Wendell Holmes School of Law in Manhattan, New York City. I am also a student in the Exoneration Clinic at the law school, and taking a year off to do a research project on how, in countries outside the U.S., criminal cases are resolved without going to court."

"Go on..."

"Yes, research on how plea bargaining is handled around the world. I've yet to learn what it's called in European countries. That's what I'm going to find out."

"There you go. It's important that you stick to that story, because if it's checked, it will turn out to be true. If anyone called Professor Hammond at the law school, he would back up that story, right?'

"Yes, I'm sure he would. I'll have to call him to make sure, though."

"The more difficult decision you will have to make is whether to disclose that your research involved looking at the Gardner case in Texas. Apparently the Gardner case has started to show up in the European media. All European countries, including France, have abolished the death penalty, and some commentators there have noted the Gardner case in Texas as an example of how senseless the death penalty in America has become. But bringing up the Gardner case with a contact will be tricky because there is always the chance that contact may pick up on the fact that the victim had an interest in O.W.K.K., and that Bonnie vanished while on an outing with the son of a top O.W.K.K. executive."

"I'm thinking that I would only disclose my connection to the Gardner case if a contact insisted in knowing more about my research, and it was the only way to convince him that my research was real."

"Or maybe that's the one situation in which you would want to avoid all reference to the Gardner matter entirely. But that's a decision you'll have to make off the cuff and at the time."

"I'm sorry, Timothy, but I'm nervous." Judy felt herself shaking in the cold morning breeze.

"Of course you are. You are my last hope. I know better than anyone, including you, how much of a long shot this is. So please come back immediately if you have feel the slightest hint of danger. If you find nothing, I will put a close to all my efforts, and accept that I will never know."

Chandler was at the top of the gang plank looking inpatient.

"She coming, Jimmy!" Timothy called out to him.

He held out his hand. He was not the hugging type. "Well goodbye Judy, for now. Please give me updates whenever you can."

She took his hand. "I will. Goodbye, sir."

CHAPTER TWENTY-NINE

JANUARY 7-8

After a quick hot shower, Judy looked out the bedroom window of the G500 at the stark arctic landscape below as she dried her hair. It would be another several hours before they would arrive at Le Bourget. She cracked open the cabin door to take a peek at Chandler. He was out cold on the couch. The co-pilot was just leaving the forward bathroom to return to the flight deck and did not notice her. She quickly shut the door before he did.

Curling up on the bed and sipping a glass of white wine, she returned to the book she had started reading, *History of Mont St. Michel*. The iconic picture of the Mont illuminated in the lights of Christmas Eve on the front cover fascinated her. Timothy's brief history had been interesting, but she wanted to know more. It was a good place to start before trying to make contacts in France. She learned that the island is located about a half mile from the northwestern coast of France, and is only about seventeen acres in total area. Very few people—only about fifty as of 2015, the book's publication date—actually live on the island fulltime. Most of those seen during the daytime are either tourists, or employees of the restaurants, hotels and shops. Most of the hotels are clustered around the base of the Mount, but a few are situated mid-way to the top, with panoramic views of the surrounding sea.

One of these was the Sacre Mont Hotel.

Judy made a note of this. This hotel—and the room in which Han Wagner and Bonnie had stayed together the night before her disappearance—would be one of her first stops.

She continued reading:

The island's natural fortification consisting of a steep central hill, a natural moat and treacherous tides surrounding had it, created the perfect defensive position. There was evidence of additional fortifications being built as far back as Roman times. By the eighth century, the feudal society which had evolved by that time was reflected in the composition and construction on the island. At the top was the House of God in the form of a monastery; in the middle were the houses and interior walls and fortifications, and at the bottom lived the farmers and fishermen. The very appearance of the Mont was enough to give pause to any army contemplating its assault. With its high manmade walls of stone complementing its natural fortifications, a small number of defenders could hold off entire armies foolish enough to brave it deadly tides just to get to its base.

According to legend, in 1708 the archangel Michael appeared before the bishop of the nearby town of Avranches and instructed him to build a church at the very top of the Mont. After work began, the king of the Franks found he could not defend his kingdom from the Vikings, so in 867 in the Treaty of Compiegne, he handed over the Mont to the Bretons. A hundred years later, William Longsword annexed the entire Cotentin Peninsula from the Bretons, making the Mont become an irretrievably part of Normandy.

In 1433, a contingent of soldiers held off the entire English army during the Hundred Years War between France and England. The same natural hazards that made the Mont virtually unassailable also made it an ideal location for an escape-proof prison—a feature that Louis XV1 took advantage of when he turned the holy place into the Ancient Regime's version of Alcatraz.

As part of the French commune of Manche, which extends to the mainland, over sixty of the buildings in the commune have been designated as historical monuments.

******

Judy put down the book, rose from her bed, and looked out the window to see a landscape shimmering in green in the twilight which she took to be Ireland. Deciding to catch some shut-eye before landing, she lay back and closed her eyes until awakened by a knock at her door by Chandler.

"Seat belt alert, Judy! Arriving in fifteen minutes."

"OK, be out in a few!"

******

One of the advantages of private air service from California to Paris was that it was not necessary to arrive in the morning after losing a night's good sleep. Nevertheless, the evening drive from Le Bourget to the Mandarin Oriental and then checking in to her room and bed was somewhat of a blur, and she slept soundly until 10:00 A.M. the next morning.

Quickly showering, dressing, and packing an overnight bag—leaving her other luggage with the concierge until she would return within the week—her first task was to take the subway to the Gare du Nord to purchase a coach rail ticket to Rennes. From there she would take a tourist bus to Mont St. Michel.

Despite Timothy's generous offer to use his Amex card for any expenses she might incur, she had decided that her role as an impecunious law student taking a year off to do some empirical legal research would carry more credibility if she traveled and maintained herself frugally. Much as she could get used to the incredible luxury of the Mandarin, she planned to spend only one more night there before deciding where next to set up shop—she guessed that would probably be in Frankfurt— and then play it by ear.

In taking the subway, she found that Sophie's intense refresher course in French had enabled her to easily navigate what would otherwise have been confusing signs and ticket machines. At the Gare du Nord ticket counter, she was delighted that the clerk listened to her ticket request in French without batting an eye—it would be a two hour trip costing only sixteen Euros.

Reading the guidebook on the rail journey, she learned that she was most fortunate to visit Mont St. Michel in January because it was the low season and visitors could therefore avoid the monstrous tourist crowds that besieged the Mont in the summer months. She learned from an elderly French woman sitting next to her that there would be no snow when she arrived—that snow rarely fell until February, and often no snow fell even then. She would probably be able to procure a hotel room on the island itself without a reservation. A middle aged couple from New Zealand sitting across from her told her that they were vising the Mont for the first time, and excited to mark it off their bucket list.

The tour bus from Rennes brought her to within a forty-five minute walk to the Mont. She could have taken one of the shuttle buses even closer, but, since she had been wise enough to bring only her very light overnight roller, chose instead to walk—the better to take in the air and scenery of the Mont at a distance. Before taking the walk across the bridge, she stopped to make a call to the Hotel Sacre Mont. She had written in her notes that Hans and Bonnie had slept together in room 201 the night before her disappearance, and was hoping the same room was available for the next couple of night.

It was, for a modest price due to the low season.

The walk across the bridge was an experience in itself. Several years before this 2,100 foot long bridge had been built at great expense to replace the causeway. This bridge allowed water to flow freely around the Mont, whereas the causeway had allowed the buildup of silt.

With the temperature in the 40s, Judy was glad she had come bundled in her new red coat, the cashmere scarf, and especially her sturdy walking shoes. It was drizzly and overcast as she pulled her roller up along the winding cobblestone path—called the "Grand Rue," though the width of it hardly exceeded ten feet—to the entrance of the Sacre Mont. The desk was unattended, and there was no one about. Rather than ring the bell, she decided to sit on a comfortable chair until a clerk appeared, and review her notes.

When the clerk appeared to welcome her and ask for her reservation, she responded in French—again being understood, much to her satisfaction. She learned that her room would not be in the main hotel building, but at the end of a secondary pathway that led up to a small house which featured both her room 201, and one other.

After surveying her small but cozy accommodations— including one full-sized bed—she noticed that there was a small courtyard beyond two glass doors facing the bed. As she stepped out to take in the view, she was disappointed that the light fog obstructed her view of the vast ocean beyond, but could only imagine how spectacular it would be on a sunny day.

Nineteen years after Bonnie's disappearance she did not expect to find anything of consequence still in the room. Nevertheless, she took careful notes of the layout of the room. Then, after freshening up and unpacking, she stepped outside to explore the surroundings.

Upon hiking up the small path to the house her attention had been focused on finding her room. Now, however, she noticed that only a few yards up the path was a small iron-gated cemetery, not more than forty feet long and twenty-five feet wide which enclosed some thirty to forty gravesites. Each of the graves was topped by granite or other stone sepulchers. Several were filled with fresh flowers. Most impressive were the elaborately decorated and carved metal crosses mounted on many of them. The gate was not locked, and Judy entered.

She had long been fascinated by cemeteries, and now stood spellbound at the sight of this one. There was no human being in sight, and a light fog was now descending on this ancient grave site which made it only that more enchanting. She took pictures of the various shrines and tombs, and made notes of some of those who had found their final resting place there.

Searching for a reference to this little cemetery in her guidebook, she came across an allusion to it in a picture and paragraph on the Church of Eglise Paroissale Saint-Pierre dedicated to Saint Pierre, the patron Saint of fishermen. At the far end of the cemetery were some fifteen stone steps that led up to the small church. Off the beaten tourist track that led up to the great monastery at the top of the Mont, this small church was as charming and beguiling as the cemetery to which it was attached.

Judy walked up the steps to the church entrance which was guarded by a statute of Joan of Arc. Her history book told her that the valiant defense of Mont St. Michel against the English was what had inspired Joan of Arc to lead the French army to victories against the English.

Venturing inside—for the doors were unlocked—she was mesmerized first by the light from the exquisite stained glass windows, and then enthralled by the statute of Saint Michel slaying the dragon. To the side in an apse was a statute of the Madonna and child. Arrays of candles lit the inner Sanctum of the chapel, which she was later to learn was the parish church for fifty or sixty residents who lived on the island. She later learned that because this little chapel was accessible only by a side path splitting off from the Grand Rue, most tourists missed it entirely.

Judy put some francs into a small alms box and lit a candle. Then she took a seat in one of the pews and sat there in mystical contemplation for at least an hour before returning to her room—and wondered, "could there be any significance to the fact that this little out-of–the-way church was nestled just yards from Room 201 of the Sacre Mont Hotel, and to the truth of what happened nineteen years before?"

CHAPTER THIRTY

JANUARY 8

Upon returning to her room, Judy reviewed her notes of all the details that were known about the night before Bonnie's disappearance: Hans and Bonnie had entered the restaurant of the Sacre Mont at 9:30 P.M. The primary server of their dinner was a man named Achille Bernard. The manager of the restaurant was Victor Dubois. All gave the same story to the police—that between the fourth and fifth served courses, Bonnie had received a call on her cell phone, said something to her dinner companion, and then left by the front door. She was not seen again in the hotel or restaurant. Hans gave essentially the same story to the police, but after doing so declined to volunteer any additional information.

Judy planned to wait until 9:30 to enter the restaurant, hoping to re-create the same scenario. She realized, however, that it would be impossible to do so inasmuch as she had no dinner companion. She therefore decided to enter the bar adjoining the restaurant an hour or so earlier. Perhaps she would test Aristotle on the off chance that a dinner companion might appear, or at least a local who might provide her with some of the local color. It was a silly idea, but she had plenty of time and the surroundings were benign enough.

Not wanting to attract the wrong kind of potential dinner companion, she dressed only in her black cotton trousers, sturdy black walking shoes, and white sweatshirt.

Taking a seat at the bar, it was not long before a young Frenchman in his twenties with three day stubble and dressed in Chinos and tee, sat beside her.

"*Puis-je vous offir un verrre?*" he asked with a slur in his speech which suggested that he was already well on his way to inebriation.

Judy made an instant decision that he was not what she had in mind for either a dinner companion, or someone who could fill her in on the local color.

"*J'attends quelqu'un*" she said with a polite but firm shake of her head.

"Okayyyyyyyy," he said, with a long drawl before downing whatever he was drinking in a broad gesture and staggering out to the rue. "*Je recois le message!*"

Judy returned to slow-sipping the Chartreuse she had ordered when she heard a voice behind her say in slightly accented English:

"Sorry about that. There's a ski team from the Sorbonne staying here on their way to a competition in the Alps this coming weekend, and they can get a little brazen when they've had a few."

She turned to see at the corner table a clean-shaven man with silver sleeked hair and dressed in a dark button down shirt and blazer. He was the only other person in the bar.

"Was my French that bad?' she asked.

"Not at all. Very good, in fact. But I've visited California many times, and I'm making a wild guess that you are from there."

"And where are you from, may I ask?"

"In a way, I am from here, Mont St. Michel."

"In a way? Do you live here?"

The man walked over to where Judy was sitting.

"No, but I grew up here on the Mont. I live now in Beauvoir which is near here and part of the Mont St. Michel Commune. My father still lives here—one of the fifty or so who still do."

"You still live here—in Beauvoir, that is?"

The man took a seat next to Judy.

"No, I went to university in Paris, and after graduation worked for the E.F.G. Construction Group. I retired two years ago, and after my wife passed away I decided to come back to the Mont St. Michel commune—Beauvoir, to be near my father. And what about you?"

"I am a law student from a law school in New York."

"How interesting! So I guessed wrong."

"Actually you didn't. I'm originally from California, near San Francisco. But I chose to go to law school out of state in New York—Oliver Wendell Holmes School of Law. Have you heard of it?"

"No, sorry, I can't say that I have. I've heard of Oliver Homes—a great American jurist, n'est ce pas?"

"Yes. But the school was only opened about thirty years ago."

"And what brings you to Mont St. Michel in the middle of the low tourist season?"

"I've taken a year off to do a research project on the ethics of plea bargaining in criminal cases."

"Plea bargaining?"

"Yes, as when a prosecutor and defendant enter into a deal under which the defendant agrees to plead guilty to a lesser charge in exchange for a lesser sentence. Do you have that in France?"

"Well, I'm not a lawyer, but I did have occasion as a construction manager with E.F.G. Group to deal with lawyers. My understanding is that some kind of what you call 'plea bargaining' is permitted here in France, but only in minor cases, and no proposed sentence in the bargain can exceed one year. I believe I heard that the law may have changed on that recently, or is being proposed, but do not know the details. I do know that much of our legal profession is very opposed to more extensive plea bargaining—thinking that justice should not be the subject of such base bargaining, but rather what the evidence is in a case."

"That is interesting! I didn't know any of that. Perhaps you could advise me as to how I can get more information on French procedures—which I can use in my research."

Judy now considered whether she should bring up the Gardner case in which a defendant had proposed a bargain to plead guilty in exchange for a death sentence. But not sure

169

whether this would risk connecting her to that case, she decided instead to change the subject.

"Perhaps I should introduce myself. My name is Judy. Judy Alexander." She held out her hand.

The man took it. "And mine is Jules. Jules Armand. I am very pleased to meet you."

"You speak very good English, Jules."

"But still with an accent you can detect, I presume."

"Perhaps, but only barely, I assure you."

"I studied four years of English at university, but also was obliged to speak it regularly during my twenty-five years at E.F.G.. We had a number of joint construction projects working with American engineers, so my knowledge of English was valued by my employers. It is probably possible to speak a foreign language without accent only if one grows up speaking it, and I did not."

There was a pause as Judy finished her Chartreuse and began to rise.

"Umh...Judy, I was planning to have dinner this evening at the restaurant here this evening. "Would you care to join me?""

"You were dining alone?"

"Yes, I fear so. I am a widower, and my father, who lives down the hill, turned in early, though I did invite him."

"Sure. Why not?"

"Splendid. The restaurant here is one of the best on the Mont. Shall we go?"

******

Jules and Judy both ordered the six course dinner, and Jules insisted on choosing a vintage wine for both of them.

"Are you fully retired, Jules, or do you have some work on the side?" Judy asked to make conversation.

"Well, yes, actually I do. I give guided tours of the Abbey three times a week—one in French in the morning, and one in English in the afternoon. In a pinch I give one in German if they're shorthanded, though my German is not as good as I would like. It's basically a volunteer job, but they do pay me a small stipend, pay for my parking, gas, and so on."

"How interesting! I imagine you know more about the Mont than just about anyone."

"That could be! I love giving the tours. I meet a wide variety of people, and some of them become quite interested in the history of this sacred place when I tell it to them. Of course we also get the tourists who are only interested in taking their selfies or marking it off their places to go in France, and could care less about the history."

"Americans?"

"I shouldn't say that. We have tourists from all over the world."

"You're being diplomatic, I fear."

"Not at all, and by and large most are well-behaved and ask good questions. It's why I enjoy being a guide here. As I said, I grew up here, and I have wonderful memories of my childhood. But there are few jobs or opportunities for young people here, and most leave here for the big cities when they are able. My father is one of the old guard who remain here and live on the Mont full-time. He still lives in the same stone house on the south side of the island in which I grew up. I sometimes stay with him on days when I have a late tour. I've urged him to come live with me in my home in Beauvoir, but he insists on staying here—which is fine. He's happy here."

"I can tell you I am very much interested in the history. I've been reading an excellent book on Mont St. Michel."

"Oh yes? Which one?"

"*The History of Mont St. Michel* by Jacques..."

"Jacques Girard. Yes, that's a good introductory history. I have a few other books which I'd be happy to lend you."

"I'd like that. I'm only staying for a few days, though."

"Then I have a few extra copies I could part with. Have you had a chance to see much on the Mont yet?"

"I just arrived this afternoon, so I haven't yet taken the tour of the Abbey."

171

"Then you must come tomorrow and join my 3:00 P.M. tour."

"The one in English. You don't think I'd be up to your tour in French in the morning?"

"Well..."

"It's OK," said Judy with a laugh. "I'm just teasing, and you're right I would get more from the afternoon tour. So I'll come, absolutely."

"Inquietant! I will look for you."

"But I can't imagine the Abbey could be more amazing than the little church I saw this afternoon right next to my hotel room."

"The Church of St. Pierre! So you must have one of those two rooms of the Sacre Mont situated next to the cemetery."

"Yes, the one closest to the cemetery—just a few steps away in fact."

"You are fortunate indeed to have that room. It is much in demand because of the view. Summer visitors must make reservations for that room many months in advance. And I must tell you that there is far more to gaze upon in that little church than in the Abbey."

"Really? Why is that?"

"A tragic story. After the Germans blitzkrieg began to overrun France in June of 1940, the Minister of Culture became concerned that the Germans would consider the Mont to be a defensive fortress and bomb it, or just as bad, occupy the Mont and loot it of all its treasures—as of course they did with many other of France's art and treasures. So he ordered that all the Abbey treasures—art, statues, furnishings, archives, precious historical documents, everything—should be quickly packed away and hidden away in the little town of St. Lo which he believed would not be a target of bombing."

"So what happened?"

"It turned out that St. Lo became a critically strategic town during the allies' Normandy invasion in 1944. The allies completely flattened St. Lo. Virtually all the Abbey treasures that had been stored there for safekeeping were destroyed. Much of its history was also destroyed forever."

"How terrible!"

"As a result the Abbey is basically as empty now as a tomb. It is still an unforgettable sight from the outside, of course, even from a great distance, and remains today as the most beautiful example of medieval religious and military architecture. The irony is that the Germans never bombed, looted, or defaced the Mont in any way; there was nothing left in the Abbey for the Germans to loot. They did later set up a military observation post and a small anti-aircraft battery in the courtyard of the Abbey entrance, but the Abbey itself was spared the ravages of war. During the German occupation of France it became a major tourist destination for German soldiers, and many thousands of them visited it during their furloughs."

"And the Church of St. Pierre?"

"Thankfully, none of its treasures were disturbed. Its religious artwork, statutes, and stained glass windows remain untouched. It's a shame that so many tourists come just to see the Abbey, where there is virtually nothing to see except the inside of its walls, and yet miss the treasure that is the Church of St. Pierre."

"And its cemetery."

"Effectivement. It is the most beautiful cemetery in the world. My mother is buried there."

"Oh, I shall look for it. What is her name?"

"Louise Armand."

"Do you recommend to the visitors in your tour groups that they should visit the church?"

"I did when I first started conducting the tours. But now I no longer do so. I'm content to leave it and the cemetery as a hidden treasure to be visited only by those who can find it on their own. It is easy to overlook. You were fortunate that the Sacre Mont gave you one of the two rooms that are adjacent to it at the end of the path that splits off from the Grand Rue and dead-ends at the cemetery."

At this moment Judy looked at her watch and noted that it was ten minutes after ten and remembered her silly idea that at that time she would exit the restaurant and recreate the tragedy that had taken place nineteen years before. Of course, she wouldn't now dream of creating another scene by leaving without telling her dinner companion that she needed to leave for several moments, and unlike Bonnie, she fully intended to return—alive.

"Jules, it will be a few minutes before the final course. Would you excuse me for just a moment? I forgot something in my room and would like to fetch it. I'll be right back."

"Of course," Jules replied. "If the waiter comes by I'll ask him to wait until your return. Can I fill your glass?" He had the tact to not ask what it was that she had left in the room.

"Thank you. Maybe just a quarter of the glass."

Judy picked up her purse and exited out to the Grand Rue. For several moments she looked both up and down the Grand Rue. It was deserted. It was absolutely quiet. Finally, she decided to go up to where the small path leading to her room—and the cemetery—split off from the Rue. Arriving at her room, she did not go in, but instead turned around to look at the cemetery. The faint glow of light from the Abbey lighting above gave all the gravesites and iron crosses a mystical sheen.

She stood standing there for several minutes before returning to the restaurant below. She found that waiter standing next to their table chatting with Jules.

"Ah, you have returned," said Jules. "Have you retrieved what you left in your room?"

"Yes, I forgot my wallet of all things."

"I would have been most pleased to take care of our dinner."

"Oh, don't be silly."

"Oscar here was just about to serve the final course." Turning to Oscar he said in English, "May I introduce you to my new friend Judy? She is a law student from America who is visiting us to learn about our legal system here."

Oscar seemed to understand. "*Bonsoir, Madame,*" he said, bowing his head.

"*Bonsoir,*" returned Judy.

"Oscar is an old friend of mine. He has been working here for a long time—how long has it been? *Onze Ans, non?*"

"*Oui.Presque douze,* Monsieur Armand."

Jules turned to Judy. "Almost twelve years. His father was a fisherman, and knew my father."

Judy then had a thought. "Oscar, could I ask you a question?"

Jules translated for Judy.

"*Bien sur. N'importe quoi.*"

"Oscar says ask him anything."

"Well, I'm not sure how to ask this in French, so I'll just ask him in English—if you can help me, Jules."

"Oscar, before I came here, a classmate of mine at school told me that she had visited this restaurant several years ago, and was impressed by the service of her waiter here, a man named Achille? Is he still working here?"

Jules translated, and Oscar answered in French—much too fast for Judy to understand.

"He says there is no one by that name currently working at the Sacre Mont. However, he seems to remember one of his fellow waiters mentioning someone by that name who had worked here many years before."

"Oh, no worry, just thought if he was still here I'd tell him that my friend Tiffany said 'hi.'"

"*Merci*, Oscar," said Jules.

As Oscar left to bring the final course, Jules said, "you know, I seem to remember a waiter by that name some years ago when I came to visit my dad."

"Really? Do you happen to remember another employee of the hotel—perhaps a manager—by the name of Victor Dubois?"

Judy regretted asking the question almost immediately. It would be a stretch to explain to Jules that her friend Tiffany had also asked her to say "hi" to the restaurant manager.

Jules did seem a little surprised by the question, and Judy wondered if perhaps he was wondering if there was more to her presence in Mont St. Michel than she had let him believe.

"Oh, I did know Victor quite well. He left for a manager's position in Lyons some time ago."

Judy decided not to go further, and changed the subject.

After finishing the final course, Jules said, "I think they're ready to close shop here tonight. In lieu of dessert, would you like to retire to the wine bar? They will be closing soon too, but perhaps we could nurse a liqueur?"

It was well past 2:00 A.M. when Judy decided to risk going further—albeit in the most casual way as she could muster.

"Jules, in your time at the construction company, E.G..."

"E.F.G. Group."

"Yes. Did you happen to ever have contact with a German construction company by the name of O.W.K.K.?"

"Why yes, several times. Why do you ask?"

"Oh, no reason. Another classmate of mine, a German exchange student, happened to mention to me that his father worked at a company by that name—a construction company."

Judy's heart pounded as she wondered if she had now gone too far. She had no doubts about Jules—he seemed legitimate enough, and hardly likely to have any questionable affiliation—but who knows to whom he might innocently talk to at some later about her odd interest in a German construction company."

"It's interesting that you would ask. I have worked with several of the engineers with that company and have always worked well with them. But..."

Judy waited for him to continue.

"Well, for many years there have been rumors about that company.

"Oh, how so?"

"The rumors? They had to do with one of the founders of the company in the years after the war—Otto Wagner. It was rumored that he had previously either worked at, or had some kind of position with the I.G. Farben Company. He was investigated by the allied commission after the war—how diligently many now question—but nothing could be definitely proved."

"I.G. Farben?"

"It was founded in 1925 and soon became the world's largest chemical cartel. During World War II it established a rubber plant and synthetic oil program at Auschwitz, using slave labor. After the war, the Allied occupation authority took over the company with a view toward dismantling its industries in order to render impossible 'any future threat to Germany's neighbors or to world peace.' I think those were the exact words of the allied authority. Several of the company's officials were later convicted of war crimes, but the charges against Otto Wagner were eventually dropped for lack of evidence. Moreover, as the cold war with the Soviet Union got more heated, the process toward dissolution slowed. Eventually it was broken up into three independent units. I think Hoechst might be one of them. O.W.K.K. was formed from another remnant of I.G. Farben, but I don't really know the details."

"Is this Otto Wagner still living?"

"Oh no. He died years ago in the mid-1950s. His son, Helmut Wagner ran the company for years thereafter. He's retired now, and I think his son Kurt now runs the company; but he has several siblings who have major positions in the firm."

Judy wanted to ask: is Hans Wagner one of those siblings? But she now feared she had already overplayed her hand, and now thought she should call it an evening. She began to gather her purse and coat.

"You know, Judy, it is interesting that you should ask about O.W.K.K., though," said Jules before she could rise.

Judy froze. "Yes?"

"About the time I was retiring from E.F.G., the firm was considering an invitation by the French Minister of Culture to bid on a project here at Mont St. Michel."

"Really? What kind of project?"

"For some years the plaza at the entrance to the Abbey has suffered from some deterioration of its foundation. It is the place where tourists now gather as they wait their turn to join a tour in the Abbey. It has a magnificent view, and in the summer it is filled with the tourists taking pictures and selfies. The commission to be bid on was to partially demolish and then rebuild the foundation of the plaza. It was to be a fairly big project, and my firm was anxious to win the commission."

"So your firm bid on it?"

"Oh yes. I in particular urged our Board to make a low bid. I felt it would give us a high profile in the industry if we could win it."

"And did you?"

"No. We were outbid by O.W.K.K.. Every bidding firm was required to make a sealed bid. But somehow O.W.K.K. outbid us by a very narrow margin. It got the commission."

"So has work begun?"

"Not yet, but perhaps soon I understand. Several preparatory engineering studies had first to be conducted, but I have heard that those are now close to completion. The last I heard is that work is to begin within the next few months. Work has already begun on providing a temporary alternative entrance to the Abbey, and notices have been sent to the various travel agencies and guide book publishers to advise visitors to expect some inconvenience while the re-construction of the plaza takes place."

"Well," said Judy trying to feign only slight interest, "I'm glad that I came when I did. How long is the construction to last once it starts?"

"At least six months, I've heard."

"Well it's past my bedtime, I'm afraid," said Judy holding out her hand. "Thank you so much for the dinner. I enjoyed it!"

"Good night then. Could I walk you to your room?"

"Oh, it's just a little up the path. I'll be fine but thank you again."

"I'll see you at my tour tomorrow?"

"Absolutely. I'm looking forward to it."

CHAPTER THIRTY-ONE

JUNE 29, 1940

The line of bedraggled refugees—carrying their few possessions on their backs or in flimsy carts—stretched as far as the eye could see on the road from Paris. The faces of each of them—men, women, and children—manifested the shock, dismay, and desperation each felt. Most had no idea where they were going. They only wanted to get away as far as possible from the enemy at the gates of Paris.

In the previous war France had kept the enemy at bay for over four years at the cost of a million and a half killed, and many thousands more disabled, blinded, and disfigured for life. During those years, French soldiers had repeatedly launched mass charges into the teeth of murderous machine gun fire to save or retrieve a few yards—sometimes only inches—of sacred ground. On the single day of August 22, 1914, over 27,000 Frenchmen were killed outright, leaving behind destitute widows and children. In the previous war, over twenty million people suffered agonizing deaths fighting for a few clods of sod.

Now, in the six weeks since Germany had invaded France on May 20, 1940, the unthinkable had occurred. The allied generals, both French and British, had been determined to fight this second war as they had fought the first—sitting in trenches behind machine guns for defense and making suicidal charges into enemy trenches for offense. Since that previous war, the French military had learned the wrong lessons from the war and had convinced the politicians to expend the national treasure on building a "super trench"—a wall they called the Maginot Line, built under millions of tons of concrete and bristling with artillery and machine guns.

Unfortunately, this heavily fortified wall did not reach all the way around France. It stopped at the border of Belgium.

All the Germans had to do was go around it. This they did by dashing through the barely defended Ardennes Forest—which allied generals thought was impenetrable by vehicles—with fast moving armored vehicles led by generals well trained in the art of 'blitzkrieg.' In but 150 hours the Panzers had swept all the way to the English Channel, completely surrounding the entire British army in Belgium. Although much of the shell-shocked British army was able to evacuate at Dunkirk, it left the French army's entire northern flank exposed. It remained only for the Germans to 'mop up', and on June 22, scarcely twenty-eight days after the Germans invaded, France capitulated.

The mopping up process involved seizing defensive strongpoints, and nothing loomed larger as a defensive position than Mont St. Michel along the Normandy coast. Since there was little threat to the German army from the sea—what remained of the British army was in shambles—the German General Staff did not deem it necessary to heavily fortify the Mont. A small contingent of ten to fifteen observation and communication personnel would be sufficient as an occupation force.

It was in the lead of this contingent that Unteroffizier Gerhard Richter commanded a convoy consisting of one SD7 armored personnel carrier, and three Maultier halftrack trucks. Richer and his two top aides, Obergefreiter Klaus Berger, and Gefreiter Dieter Jager, along with seven Gemeiners rode in the half track. The remaining Gemeiners in the contingent followed in the three trucks—two of them loaded with the observation and communication equipment, and the third containing supplies, including extra fuel containers, food, and a crate of champagne they had appropriated from a storehouse on the outskirts of Paris.

"*Aus den weg!*" Richter shouted at the pitiful refugees lining the road. As exhausted women and children scampered to the side of the road, some falling headlong into a muddy ditch as they did so, the convoy raced ahead.

Klaus, seated beside his superior in the half track, spread his map out across his lap as he gave the driver directions.

181

"How much further until the turnoff to Normandy?" Richter demanded to know.

"In four miles, Unteroffizier," came the reply. "If we don't have any more delays caused by all these derelicts clogging the road, we should arrive at Mont, Mont..."

"Mont St. Michel, Obergefreiter! You will know it when you see it. There is a picture of it in the order file."

"We should arrive there by nightfall."

"*Ausgezeichnet!* We will stop just past the turnoff. Most of these stragglers will be turning south, so the road should be clear by then. We'll refuel at that time from our fuel containers."

The soldiers were in the jubilant mood, laughing and singing. They were part of an army that had just won a military campaign that had astounded the world, and they had not only come out of it unscathed, but were being assigned light duty at France's great cultural icons. They were arriving conquerors and the world would be at their feet.

"When we stop to refuel tell the men that they are not to touch the champagne until we arrive and set up shop at the Mont. We can celebrate then, but not before!" barked the Unteroffizier.

"*Jawohl.*"

******

It was well past 2:00 A.M. when the Mont came into view— its silhouette far in the distance outlined by a three-quarter moon. It was another hour before they arrived at the shore, where they stopped and stood in awe at the Mont and Abbey above in the moonlight.

On the lookout for any hostile activity, the convoy slowly rolled up the causeway to the front gate of the Mont, only to find the front gate locked and no one about.

"All right. No use roiling the natives until morning," Richter said. "We'll stay here until morning. Get some sleep. Dieter, assign one of your men for lookout duty."

Being in charge of the operation, Unteroffizier slept fitfully. With sunrise at 6:30 A.M., he roused his men and stationed them in formation on his flank. He then fired his Luger into the air while Klaus banged on the gate with the butt of his rifle.

"Open up in the name of the occupation forces of the German Reich!"

When no one appeared immediately to open the gate, he ordered that a machine gun be set up. Before it was ready to fire, an elderly man with a white beard appeared at the gate and with trembling hands began to unlock it.

"*Schnell!*" Richter shouted.

The gate opened and the man stood shaking, obviously in a state of terror.

Richter turned around to his men. "Who speaks some French? Dieter, I heard you speaking some French on the way here."

"*Yawohl*", said Dieter, saluting. 'I speak a little, sir."

"Tell this man that we are here in the name of the occupation forces of the German Wehrmacht and the German Reich, and he is under our authority. If he follows our instructions we will have no wish to harm him."

Richter waited as Dieter translated his German into halting French. Though the man did not seem to fully understand what was happening, he nodded continuously.

"Tell him that we will need someone to guide us up the lane to the Abbey"

After some translation and a muttered response from the Frenchman, Dieter said, "he says that we cannot bring all these vehicles to the top, as there is but a narrow path to the church and our heavy vehicles would damage the cobblestones."

Richter considered. "All right, we will leave the half-track here at the gate. But all the trucks must go up as far as they can. If there is damage he can make a claim later to the occupation forces. I will pull the half-track to the side, but I want all three trucks to come through the gate and follow the path up to the abbey as far as they can go. I am told that there is a plaza at the top where we can set up our equipment."

Richter started directing the vehicles, which only narrowly fit through the front gate before making the trek to the top. Along the way, a few Mont residents stepped outside their houses to watch this parade, while others only cautiously watched from their windows. Leaving two men in charge of the half-track below, Richter followed the trucks up the Grand Rue to the base of the 350 stone steps known as the Grande Degre which led up to the church entrance. After laying down all of his gear except for his rifle, he climbed the steps and began banging on the imposing iron doors at the top of the stairs. It was several minutes before a monk in long brown robes opened one of the doors just wide enough to peer outside.

Richter roughly pulled open the door, and called back to Dieter.

"Tell him that we are here on authority of the German Force of Occupation, and that I and several of my men will be entering now to inspect the chambers and accommodations of this abbey. I also want him to guide me through the church to the higher levels of the abbey and to the terrace which lies at the top. Then he and any other monks still in the building must vacate these premises within one hour"

Dieter translated in his halting French, and then translated the monk's reply. "He says to follow him and he will show you. He says there are only four other monks in the church, and none at the present time in the abbey above. He says none of them live in either the church or the abbey, and reside in their huts below the Mont."

"All right. Tell Klaus to come with me while I inspect the premises."

Klaus and Richter followed the monk up to the first level which housed a spacious hall called the Aumonerie. From there they walked up to the second level known as the Knight's Hall, which opened up to the Cloisters and the Refractory. The final

184

staircase led to the third level which opened up to the Grand Terrace.

"*So, das ist es!*" Richter exclaimed with excitement when he emerged from the dark halls and chambers of the abbey into the glittering sunshine that cascaded over the spectacular Grand Terrace. "*Was fur eine herriccht Aussicht!*"

Richter could not have imagined a better observation and communications post than this spectacular viewing platform at the top of the world. It was also spacious enough to accommodate all the equipment that they had brought. Even without binoculars one could see planes or tanks coming from fifty kilometers or more in all directions.

He told Klaus to go down and tell the men to start unloading the equipment from the trucks and bring them up to the Terrace.

By the next morning he had set up shop, looking forward not only to a peaceful and safe tour of duty atop the great French icon that was Mont St. Michel, but also to the magnificent views that would greet him and his men every morning.

CHAPTER THIRTY-TWO

JANUARY 9

"Please gather around, everyone who is here for the four o'clock tour of the abbey!" Jules called out to all those who stood about on the Grand Terrace waiting for the tour.

It was to be a relatively small group of only about twelve or thirteen on this chilly January afternoon, unlike the groups of forty or more which formed for this tour in the summer. When Jules didn't see Judy in the group, he scanned the Terrace for her. He saw her at the east end looking out over one of the ramparts at the sea below.

As the group gathered, Jules said, "Please stay right here. We will begin in just a few minutes." He walked over to Judy.

"Are you coming?" he asked.

"Oh, yes! Sorry! I guess I was just mesmerized by this view. It's amazing! I'm coming!"

Jules guided the group through the doors and waited until all had entered the narthex.

"Welcome to the Abbey of Mont St. Michel," Jules intoned. "We are about to take a spiritual journey into the Middle Ages. You see around you a marvel of medieval construction. All of you came to the Mont by simply walking across our amazing bridge which was just completed a few years ago, and replaced the causeway which had prevented the free circulation of water around the Mont. But imagine, if you will, how each and every stone you see around you, including the ones that hold up the gothic spires above you, was carried by hand across the Bay of Mont-Michel at low tide. Many of those who carried the stones were simple pilgrims. Neither carts nor horses could be used, as they would become mired in the quicksand. A large number of those who dared to walk across with the stones on their back didn't make it, carried away by treacherous and unexpected riptides and quicksand, giving up their precious stone blocks to the sea.

Every head was turned up to gaze at the vault above. The narthex led into the Eglise Saint-Michel Abbey Church itself. Construction had begun in 1020 A.D. and featured a Romanesque nave. Later, 15th century architecture was added. So magnificent was this structure that maps of the Mont labeled it as "*La Merveille*" ("The Marvel").

"The pilgrims called this site 'The Heavenly Jerusalem,' and 'the Pyramid of the Seas.' I'm sure you know by now that it was Saint Michel who in 708 A.D. appeared in a dream to the local abbot and directed him to build an Abbey on this Mont."

Jules continued with the history until he noticed that several in the group were wandering off. This often happened because many of the tourists were less interested in history than in just getting through the tour so that they could mark it off their list of places to see.

"Now, if you'll follow me, we shall go down to the 'Crypt des Gros Pillars' which adjoins the 'Salle de Chevaliers.' This is where visiting noble knights were received and given accommodations in return for hoped for silver that would supplement the coins of the pilgrims."

The mention of "knights" seemed to perk up everyone's interest a bit, and all followed him down to a great hall below.

"As many of you may have heard, most of the stained glass windows were removed from the Abbey during the war—for safe keeping in St. Lo. Unfortunately, they were destroyed during the war. However, since that time, stained glass replacements have been made and installed to replace the ones that were destroyed."

Jules pointed up at a series of three stained glass windows—a large circular window interlocked with two smaller circular windows on each upper side.

"You may notice how this creates an image of Mickey Mouse. This set of interlocking circular windows was inspired by Mr. Walt Disney himself, who visited the Mont here in 1952, and offered to finance the creation of these windows if built to his specifications."

There were oohs and ahs as everyone in the group looked up. "Yes, I see it!" said one elderly gentleman. Now, finally something interesting to look at in this old tomb of an Abbey!

Next on the tour was the Cloisters, a meticulously groomed green lawn surrounded by Ionian columns on all four sides.

The final stop on Jules' medieval journey was the "*Aumonerie*," a spacious hall used as a dormitory for 13th century the pilgrims, and lined with luxuriant gardens.

Trying not to look bored himself—he had after all conducted this tour many hundreds of times since his retirement to the Mont St. Michel Commune—he finished up the tour early, much to the relief of several in the group who seemed anxious to get back to their rooms and prepare for a good dinner at one of the great French restaurants on the Mont. Not Judy, however, whom he was pleased to see was hanging on his every word and writing feverishly in her little notebook.

Tips were not permitted—being considered an insult to a professional and highly educated guide.

"Goodbye everyone," said Jules, "and thank you for interest in our magnificent Abbey on the Mont!"

The group dispersed until Jules and Judy were standing alone.

"Did you enjoy the tour?" Jules asked.

"Yes, very much so. Thank you. It was wonderful."

"I see you took notes."

"Yes, I did. You told us a lot things that I didn't get from the books I've been reading. And of course, it means so much more when you can see the things you're reading about."

"Quite so. And that reminds me. I promised to give you a few of my books on the Mont."

"Oh no, I doubt if I'll be back to return..."

"Not at all. I want you to have them. I know you will get the most out of them. When will you be leaving? Not tonight, I hope."

"No, it's too late to return to Paris tonight. I have my room here for another night, but was planning to leave first thing in the morning."

"So back to Paris, then?"

"Yes, I think so."

"To continue your research on—what did you say—'plea bargaining?'"

"Yes. I have a list of people I would like to interview there."

"You must tell me all about it, and let me deliver the books. Do you already have plans for dinner tonight?"

"No, I thought I'd just get a little..."

"Nonsense. You must join me for your last night on the Mont. If you can, I will take you to La Mere Poulard. It is legendary institution on Mont St. Michel, begun in 1888 by Annette and Victor Poulard. She was only twenty at the time, but her food was so good that the pilgrims who came always came to sample her famous cooking..."

Judy smiled.

"Sorry. You have had enough history for one day, Judy?"

Judy laughed. "Not at all. I find it fascinating. It's just that I have a lot to do. But I'd be glad to join you for a light supper, Jules, just not a six courser. Perhaps an appetizer, and a glass of wine? I need to get back early tonight—you know, check my mail from the states, calls, and collate my notes. Would that be all right?"

"But of course. It's a little after five now. Would six be too early to meet at La Mere Poulard?"

"That's fine. I can be ready then. Where is it?"

"Just a two minute walk from your room, Number 18 on the Grand Rue. There a big sign in front with an image of Madame Poulard holding her cooking pan with a long handle."

"I'll see you there!"

189

CHAPTER THIRTY-THREE

JANUARY 9

As promised, the iconic image of Madame Poulard at the front of the stone building on the Grand Rue left Judy no doubt that she had come to the right restaurant.

A smiling young dark-haired hostess, decked in the same long apron worn by the original Madame Poulard, seemed to be expecting Judy and greeted her at the entrance.

"You are Judy? Monsieur Armand is waiting for you."

"Yes," replied Judy tentatively, somewhat taken aback that the hostess seemed to recognize her.

"If you will follow me, I will take you to your table."

Judy followed the hostess to a small side room with but two candle-lit tables clad in white linen, at one of which sat Jules who rose when she entered.

"I hope I'm not late, "said Judy.

"Not at all," said Jules as he came to her side of the table to pull out her chair. "It is I who am early. I am delighted you have come."

"What a charming little place," said Judy as she took in her surroundings. "Thank you. But I was a little surprised the hostess seemed to know me."

"It is the oldest restaurant on the Mont, and serves the best French cuisine. Their butter biscuits are world famous, and made with the finest butter in all of Normandy. And yes, I described you to Marie as the most beautiful woman who would be visiting tonight."

Judy laughed. "You are too kind, but isn't that what Frenchmen always say to the woman they are with?"

Jules held out his hands as if to show his innocence. "*Je plaide coupable.* But no, it is not true what they say."

"Well, Jules, I hope you didn't expect that I would dress up in anything other than what I wore at your tour this afternoon. I only had forty-five minutes to get ready, after all."

"*Je n'ai pas non plus.* Of course I too had no time to go back to Beauvoir to change and return in time."

"Yes, I'm sorry that we have to eat so early. I really do have so much to do tonight before bed, and I will be leaving at 6:00 A.M. in the morning to catch the bus to Rennes for the early train to Paris. I'm also afraid that jet lag has finally caught up with me, but I didn't really feel it until I was taking the tour this afternoon.

"*Je comprends*, and I promise to get you back early. You had said you will only have time for an appetizer? I think that is what we call a hors d'oeuvre."

"Is there a difference?"

"*Mais oui. Hor d'oeures* literally means 'out of work' but translates as 'outside the meal', and is served separate from a meal. An 'appetizer' is the first course of a meal, *n'es pas?*"

"I didn't know that! Well, I've learned a lot today. So what would you recommend for our 'outside the meal' this evening?"

Jules handed her the *hor d'oevre* menu.

"I can recommend Madame Poulard's chicken-liver Mouse with Raspberry Jelly. Also, Lemon-Parsley Gougeres. Plateau de fruits de Mer with Two Sauces is excellent. My favorite is the escargot."

"I don't know..."

"Perhaps the Peach and Goat Cheese Tartine, or the Baked Brie in Puff Pastry?"

"How about this Phyllo-Wrapped Brie with Fig Preserves and Toasted Walnuts?" Judy asked.

"I've never had it, but I can assure you it too would be excellent. Shall we order it? I'll have the escargot."

Jules ordered the *hor d'oevres* and a bottle of Chateau Mouton Rothschild Paulillac.

"*Alors*, Judy. What did you do today while you waited for the tour?"

"Well, I woke up at 4:30 A.M.—jet lag I guess—so after lying in bed and unable to get back to sleep, I decided to take a run around the Mont."

"You ran around the Chemin des Remparts?"

"The ramparts? Yes, it was wonderful, the scenic views were amazing. I ran around twice, which according to my fitness watch was over two miles. Stopped to take a look at the Chapel of Saint Albert. Then, let's see. Just came back to the room and freshened up. There was a coffee-maker in the room, so after I came back I brewed my coffee, and went out to the veranda to watch the sun come up."

"No wonder you were a little tired by the time you came to the tour."

"Not really. I usually do try to run at least a mile every morning—in Central Park when I'm in New York—though I must confess I've missed my runs all this past week. No excuses, just haven't. Anyway, after having a muffin down in the Sacre Mont lobby, I went down to the Tourist Office..."

"Ah yes, now housed in the old Burgher's Guardroom..."

"But they weren't open yet, so I went back up to the Saint Pierre parish church. I found your mother's grave at the little cemetery..."

"Oh, you did. I'm glad you found it. Her birthday is coming up next week and I must remember to lay flowers on her sarcophagus."

"Then I entered into the church—so nice that they keep it open all night—lit a candle, and just sat in the pew and, well, meditated, I guess..."

"There is no more peaceful place to do so on earth."

"After some time I heard the bustle coming up from the Rue, and decided to see what was opening up. By that time it was ten, and I saw the sign for the Arch...Arche..."

"The Archeoscope. Yes, my cousin owns it—the only multi-media show on the Mont."

"It was so interesting, describing the construction and history of the Mont. But I did have one question. A map of the

Abbey shows the area labeled as 'Merveille.' What is that and what does it mean?"

"It simply means—in English—a 'marvel,' or 'wonder.'"

"Oh, I see. It is a wonder."

"But the word does carry a secondary meaning in an entirely different context, which you will find in the urban dictionary: the 'merveille' is described as 'the most beautiful woman in the world. Everyone wants her, but one person in particular can't live without her, and regrets them ever breaking up with each other.'"

"Hmm. Not sure I get that one, so I'll stick with the merveille that is the Abbey. That's the marvel I can understand."

There was a short pause in the conversation, until Jules said, "I'm sure you took many notes today."

"I did! I took a lot at the History Museum..."

"The Logis Tiphaine—just recently turned into a museum. It was built in 1365 by the Knight Bertrand du Guesclin, the leader of the King's army. He built it for his wife Tiphaine. Not exactly the Taj Mahal, but quite a bit older."

"I took pictures of all the medieval furniture and artifacts—so interesting. Then I went back to the room, and took a little nap before getting my tour ticket and coming up to the Grand Terrace to meet you for the tour. Did I miss anything on my little self-guided tour this morning?"

"I think you saw most everything. Maybe next time you visit you could venture down to the Porte Eshausette or the Musee Grevin."

Judy took out her notebook. "Could you spell those? I wish I could stay longer, but you've given me something to come back for."

"What did you think the highlights of my tour were, if I might ask?"

"Oh, everything! It was all so fascinating. And that's so amazing about Walk Disney coming to visit and commissioning the windows of Mickey Mouse."

Jules looked at Judy and gave her a mischievous smile, as if you say "you really believed that?"

"What!"

Jules shook his head.

"It's not true?" asked Judy in disbelief. "Oh my God, you made that up?"

Jules laughed. "Come now, Judy. Surely you don't think that our stained glass artisans would create a Mickey Mouse window to install in our most cherished cultural icon?"

"Jules!" Judy exclaimed before joining in his laughter. "You're terrible!"

"Well, you must admit it does look like a representation of that venerated mouse."

"You must think we Americans are so gullible!"

"You weren't all Americans on the tour today. There was an Australian couple..."

Judy just shook her head. "Are you the only guide that tells that story about Walk Disney?"

"We all do. It's just a blague—a joke. So many of the tourists told us that the windows looked like Mickey Mouse, that we just decided to go with it."

"Well, I can't believe I fell for it. But I guess it is funny. You probably should tell people, though."

At just that moment Judy's iPhone beeped. She glanced at the screen. "I'm so sorry, Jules. I have a text from my supervising Professor. Probably wants an update on the law review article I'm writing under his supervision. I've had some difficulty getting texts, so would you mind terribly if you excusing me for just a moment?"

"*Bien sur que non.* Not at all. I'll wait outside."

"No, no. I'll step outside. I'll be back in a minute."

Judy went out to the lobby and read. The text was not from Professor Hammond. It was from Timothy:

INFORMATION THAT FRENCH INSPECTEUR GENERAL PHILLIPPE DURAND ATTENDING RECEPTION AT THE D.A.NISH EMBAS.S.Y IN PARIS ON TUESD.A.Y, JANUARY 12. MEET AS.S.ISTANT ATTACHE FRANK HOLDER AT U.S. EMBAS.S.Y WHO WILL ACCOMPANY YOU. MEASUREMENTS FOR DRES.S. HAVE BEEN SENT TO BEAUMENAY JOANNET AT 17 BOULEVARD ST DENIS. PICK UP TOMORROW BY FIVE. DO NOT REPLY. THIS MES.S.AGE ENCRYPTED, BUT DELETE IMMEDIATELY.

Judy quickly wrote the information in her notebook, deleted the text, and returned to the table. Her Phyllo-wrapped Brie was waiting for her.

"*Est-ce que tout a bien?*" asked Jules as he poured her a glass of wine.

"Oh yes, everything is fine. My Professor just wanted an update, but I do need to get back to call him. What time is it in New York?"

Jules checked his watch. "I would say it is about...a little after noon or so?"

"Oh, that's fine then. Let me finish this delicious looking Brie, but then I'm afraid I must go."

"*Je comprends.* But, Judy, it is not necessary that you take the bus so early. I would be glad to drive you to Rennes and you would not have to leave so early."

"You are kind, Jules, but I already have my bus ticket, and I'm fine. But thank you."

Jules seemed disappointed, but it could not be helped. Judy picked at her brie but unfortunately it was not to her liking. Nevertheless, she realized she had already hurt her dinner mate's feelings, and so ate as much as she could, washing it down with the wine.

"Oh, I almost forgot, before you go," said Jules as he picked up a briefcase, withdrew several books, and laid them on the table.

"Oh, thank you!" said Judy. Welcoming the opportunity to set aside the brie, she picked up the book on top of the stack, and began leafing through it. "These look amazing! Thank you so much! If you give me your address I will send them to you as soon as I have read them."

"They are for you to keep Judy. I have several copies of them. But perhaps we could exchange emails if you would like to remain in touch. If you are able to return, I would be happy to show you the places you missed on the Mont."

"Of course. Do you have some paper?"

Jules patted his chest. "No, I'm afraid..."

"Here," said Judy, tearing a small strip from the notebook and writing down her unsecured email address. And here, you can write yours down at the bottom of this page."

"And now you must go so early?"

"I'm so sorry Jules, but yes, I do need to go now. Thank you again for all your help. Please stay and finish your meal." She held out her hand, which Jules took and kissed in the French fashion.

"Goodbye, then, Judy. *Fais attention.*"

"I will. Goodbye, Jules."

Jules stood standing until Judy was out of sight. Then he whispered to himself: "*merveille*" before sitting down to down to finish his wine.

******

Back in her room, Judy spread out the books on her bed and wondered how she would fit them into her roller bag. Keeping her coat on and wrapping her cashmere scarf over her head, she walked out to the room's veranda to take in and breathe the ocean breeze.

She felt bad about Jules, who had obviously become enamored of her. Although he had enjoyed a most successful career in which he held a high and responsible position in a major company before his retirement, his life had now become somewhat empty, no children, his wife having recently passed away, and now having little to do in his retirement but to care for his ailing father and cater to irritating and often ignorant tourists. In different circumstances she might have let things go further on the basis of friendship alone. He was most kind and attentive, well-educated, and not unattractive, though the age difference was significant, but surely he could see that there could be no future beyond friendship with her. She could recall so many prior occasions in which, allowing sympathy and compassion to overcome her judgment honed in past relationships, she had allowed a friendship to progress— only to discover that the "friend" had become obsessed, infatuated to the point of madness, and even suicidal. Bitterness and recriminations inevitably followed, some of which caused her to fear for her own safety, and she could not count how many "friends" she had lost in that way.

In any case, she was well aware that she had taken on a mission—a good cause, she reminded herself—which could not be compromised by any such distractions. She felt a twinge of guilt because—well, it could be said, she supposed—that she had indeed "used" Jules to get information and make a contact that might be helpful to her in succeeding in her mission. But she also remembered that she had made a promise to herself before agreeing to undertake the mission, that she would never—even in this good cause—allow any such consociation to progress beyond what she had just allowed with Jules. She wanted to save Doctor Gardner from what she was sure was a grave injustice, and she also wanted to give a dying man the peace of mind that no amount of money or superficial toys could ever give him. Finally she wanted justice for Bonnie. But she was determined that in doing so she would inflict an absolute minimum of harm— hopefully none to any innocent person—and this included not allowing any such consociation to develop to the point of anyone throwing themselves in front of a truck for love of her.

Before retiring to her bed, she would have liked to call Timothy to tell him the contact she had made. The only piece of information that she thought worthy of report at this point was Jules' experience with dealing with O.W.K.K., his suspicions of its connections to I.G. Farben and the Nazi regime, and the fact that Hans Wagner, Bonnie's companion on the night she disappeared, was closely connected to the family which controlled O.W.K.K.. There was also the connection to Gardner's case, since the widow of the man Gardner was accused of murdering now stood to inherit a substantial interest in O.W.K.K.. But most of this Timothy already knew, though Judy now had confirmation of these connections from an independent source.

Timothy had made clear in his text that she was not to reply. So instead she spent the next two hours reviewing her notes. Suddenly, an idea popped into her head. She read the same notes again. The idea wouldn't go away. Instead her idea got stronger. Though it was based far more on speculation than on verifiable facts, it presented a solution—not to the question of who had murdered Bonnie, or why; nor to the question of why Doctor Gardner was insisting on death in return for a guilty plea. She had a long way to go before she could find a solution to those questions. But it was a first step.

She believed that she now knew what had happened to Bonnie on the night she disappeared, and where Bonnie was at that very moment. But until she had more facts and could confirm her speculations, she dared not risk calling Timothy and giving him false hope.

She recalled the passage from Arthur Conan Doyle's celebrated sleuth: "Once you eliminate the impossible, whatever remains, no matter how improbable, must be the truth."

CHAPTER THIRTY-FOUR

JUNE 6, 1944

Unteroffizier Gerhard Richter stood on the north side of the Grand Terrace and scanned the horizon with his oversized Leica binoculars which were attached to a sturdy tripod. He thought he could hear gunfire in the distance, but it was too faint for him to be sure, and too far to see even with the binoculars.

It was 7:45 A.M., so a haze was still blocking much of the morning sun; yet from his perch high atop the Mont he could still see for many kilometers in every direction. The rough weather had improved since the previous morning, but he could see that the waves were still choppy.

In the four years since his small observation and communications Kolonne had occupied Mont St. Michel, Gerhard Richter had enjoyed the kind of soft duty that many of his compatriots fighting to the death on the frozen steppes of Russia would have envied. Although he was only an Unteroffizier—the equivalent in rank of what the American army called a "warrant officer," higher in rank than noncommissioned officers and enlisted men, but below commissioned officers—he had held absolute sway and authority over his domain on the Mont.

During his four year regime he had enjoyed the status of King of the Mont, receiving and providing hospitality to over 350,000 off-duty German troops who had visited the Mont during those years. The Mont was second only to the Eiffel Tower as the occupiers' favorite tourist attraction, and at an admission price of only fifty pfennig was a cheap outing.

Among the visitors were a number of high-ranking officers, including several Schutzstaffel Generals—"Protection Squadron" or S.S.. A frequent visitor was S.S. Major Hermann Schneider, whom Richter got to know well, and who seemed to appear on the Mont almost every other weekend. On several occasions Richter had surreptitiously allowed Schneider to stay overnight on the Mont, a privilege he granted to very few visitors, even to some of the S.S. generals.

It was shortly after one of those visits in December of 1943, that Richter had ordered his men to dig a large hole in the east section of the Grand Terrace. Through his connections with Schneider, he had even arranged for special earth digging equipment to be delivered to the Mont—equipment which was much needed along the Normandy Coast to build Rommel's "Atlantic Wall." How Schneider had managed to get this equipment delivered, Richter did not know, and did not ask.

The hole to be dug was to be three feet long and two and a half feet wide. But it was not these dimensions which caused grumbling among the Gemeiners who were assigned to dig it, but the depth. It was to be ten feet deep, which would first require carving out the cobblestones that overlay the Terrace, then chiseling through several feet of the stone blocks which provided the flat foundation for the Terrace, and finally hewing into the bedrock below. Even with the special digging equipment, it was a daunting task. The cobblestones were to be delicately chiseled out by hand so as not to damage them, and then placed in neat stacks next to the nearby rampart. So too were the stone blocks to be carved out with a minimum of damage to each stone and likewise neatly stacked next to the cobblestones. The digging equipment was to be used mainly to cut deep into the bedrock that underlay the stone. All the residue from the rock fill from the bedrock was to be placed in canisters and stored next to the cobblestones and stone blocks.

The task had taken two weeks to accomplish, and was much resented by the Gemeiners who had become used to the leisurely manning of the observation and communications equipment, followed by evenings of drinking and listening to the German radio and British music on the B.B.C.—a practice frowned upon by the High Command, but in Richter's little kingdom, soft duty gave way to boredom.

After only the first few days of this digging, Obergefreiter Berger had come to Richter to let him know that the men were resentful of the task assigned to them because they could not understand what it could possibly be good for.

"*Geh mir aus Augen, Klaus!*" Richter had responded with vehemence. "This is none of the men's concern! Gemeiners are not privy to orders from the high command regarding installation of special weapons and machinery that will be assigned to us very shortly. Tell the men that if they mention anything about this project that they will be put on report.Verstehen?!"

"*Jawohol Unteroffizier!*" Klaus had replied, and nothing more was heard again from the men about the hole.

Part of the problem in digging the hole had been that only three of the original Kolonne contingent were still on the Mont, and the total number of personnel under Richter's direct command had dwindled to but eleven, including Obergefreiter Klaus Berger and Gefreiter Dieter Jager.

Meanwhile observation and communications equipment was scattered all across the Grand Terrace. In the previous weeks High Command had alerted him to an imminent invasion by American, British, and Canadian forces—somewhere on the French Coast, but no one knew exactly where. However, few of the officers and men Richter had talked to during their recent visits to the Mont thought that the invasion would come in Normandy. It was much more likely that the invasion would take place at Calais, which was only twenty-one miles across the channel from England.

Now on this early blustery morning of June 6, 1944, it was considered even less likely that an invasion of Normandy would occur, or even that an invasion would occur anywhere on the coast of France. This was because the weather was seen as unsuitable for invasion. Surely no one would attempt an invasion in such weather. So sure of this was the German High Command, that it gave General Rommel, who was to command the German forces against any invasion, leave to go home to visit his wife back in Germany for her birthday.

Never in world history had a wife's birthday played such a pivotal role in the annals of human warfare. Unbeknown to the German High Command was that General Eisenhower's meteorological advisor, Captain James Stagg, had discovered during his meticulous scrutiny of the meteorological data, a narrow sliver of a break in the horrendous June weather which, in combination with tolerable moon and tides, would occur on just one day: June 6.

With the High Command convinced that any invasion would occur at Calais, and the Commander of the Atlantic Wall defenses out of communication with his forces, the invasion had a slim chance to actually succeed.

But one more thing had to happen in order to give the allies an even chance: the 21st Panzer Corps—bristling with tanks and armor, which allied intelligence had failed to discover, and which, being only meters away from the beaches could easily slaughter the floundering, seasick, half-drowned and disoriented Americans soldiers staggering half-dead on to Omaha Beach under heavy machine gun fire—had to stand down and not attack for at least five hours in order to allow enough American soldiers to solidify their hold on the beach and establish command and control.

Without that critical delay, the invasion would be crushed, the men thrown back into the sea to be drowned and machine-gunned as they screamed for their mothers and flailed about under the waves. With this massive loss of men and equipment, it would be another year, or more, before the allies could recover enough to even try again. In the meantime, the Third Reich would survive, and the fate of millions still barely surviving in the camps sealed forever.

And so fate intervened. The Fuhrer, who had insisted that only he could unleash the 21st Panzer Corps, had left strict instructions that his sleep was not to be disturbed until noon. He liked to sleep in. It was a luxurious late morning snooze that would change the world forever. The panzers never budged.

******

The radio message which Unteroffizier Gerhard Richter received at 8:05 A.M. was garbled. Paratroopers had been sighted during the night, ships had been observed north of Mont St. Michel approaching Normandy beaches, and men were staggering ashore. But with no central command, confusion reigned. No one knew what was happening. It was probably a diversionary attack, one message claimed. The real attack would come later at Calais, so troops and units should stay where they were.

When Richter asked what action he should take, there was no answer. A message later that morning from a nameless radio operator calling from the 352nd infantry division asked if he had any men to spare, and if so to send them to Vierville-surmer.

This last call Richter dismissed as a joke. He had only a handful of men under his command, and no combat arms to speak of. All he could do was hunker down, hope for the best, and await orders once the situation had been stabilized.

He called his men together, and relayed the garbled messages he had received. He gave only one specific order:

"Cover the hole with metal plate, and cover the cobblestones and stones with tarp. Tie them down. Then man the ramparts and radios and report any sightings to me."

CHAPTER THIRTY- FIVE

JANUARY 10

The bus to Rennes was delayed by a traffic accident, with the result that Judy missed the train connection to Paris which she had planned to make. After waiting several irritating hours for the next train at the very crowded Rennes station and finding only unappetizing fast food available, she was exhausted even before she finally boarded the next train to Paris—and it was not an Express.

It being a late Sunday afternoon, all the seats in the coach section were taken, and it was not until after three stops that she finally found a seat, offered to her by a young man in cycling attire who apparently thought his offer entitled him to a flirt.

Politely shaking her head—*"je ne comprends pas"*— she at first tried to review her notebook, but the constant jostling and loud conversations from the returning weekend revelers surrounding her made that impossible. A family of five had asked her to exchange seats so that they could sit together. Another passenger behind her was shouting French into his cell phone at such a decibel that she could not, despite herself, help but understand a few words of it.

She put the notebook back in her purse, laid back in her seat, and shut her eyes—not to sleep, but to try to think. She replayed in her mind the notebook entries she had studied the night before. She focused on the three entries from which she had deduced what had happened to Bonnie on the night she disappeared some nineteen years before. Though improbable, it seemed the only possible explanation of what had happened to her. She knew she would have to gather more information before she dared to reveal her theory to Timothy, or at least request the means to confirm it.

After a dozen replays of those critical three entries in her head, she decided to give her mind a rest and let it wander. Half asleep by now, she began thinking, for no particular reason, of something early that morning which had struck her as odd. She hadn't given it a second thought at that time since she was preoccupied with quickly packing, showering, and dressing to get ready to catch the 6:00 A.M. shuttle bus across the bridge to the tour bus to Rennes.

It was simply this: when she returned to her room the night before, after her dinner with Jules, she had noticed that the inside compartment of her roller bag which held some of her tourist brochures, tickets, hotel reservations and the like—but not any documents relating to her mission which Timothy had insisted she should on no account keep in any of her suitcases—was zipped up. She was sure that when she left her room to meet Jules at La Mere Poulard she had left it unzipped. Now as she thought about it, she did not recall zipping it either after she returned from dinner, or that morning when she was packing.

It was probably nothing. She must have just forgotten that she had zipped it. Of course all of Timothy's important information and documents were carefully ensconced in either her iPhone or notebook, both of which she kept on her person at all times.

Then, despite herself, she fell asleep in her very cramped seat amidst the chaos of loud talking, revelry, and passengers, including a large group of cyclists, getting on and off at each of the local stops. She had not worried about missing a stop if she nodded off, since the last stop of the train would be Paris.

She did not awaken until the train arrived at Gare du Nord shortly after dark. Deciding that it would be less hassle to simply take the subway from the station to within walking distance of the Mandarin Oriental rather than going outside to try to summon an Uber or taxi in the traffic chaos in front of the station, she finally arrived at the Mandarin.

Although she had planned to vacate the Mandarin and look for an apartment or B&B the day after returning to Paris, she had also taken the precaution of reserving a room for the evening in which she arrived back in Paris.

"I have a reservation," Judy announced to the well-appointed clerk behind the alabaster hotel desk. "Also, I would like to retrieve two bags I left with the concierge."

"Of course Madame," said the clerk in crystal English as he motioned for the bell boy. "Your name?"

"Judy Alexander."

"Yes, of course. Your same room is still available if that would be satisfactory."

"Yes, that's fine."

"There are two messages for you." The clerk handed her two sealed white envelopes.

******

Back in her room, Judy kicked of her shoes, plopped herself on the silk cushions of the plush king size bed and read the first message. It was from the manager of the fashion house of Beaumenay Joannet. It advised her that her dress was finished, and asked whether she would prefer to come the next day for a final fitting and pick it up, or have it delivered tomorrow at her convenience. They would also be happy to deliver her black patent leather Manolo Blahnik pumps and Cartier pearl necklace. Phone numbers were provided.

Judy could not help but roll her eyes. She had no complaint about Timothy helping to set up a potential meeting with a personage who might be able to provide her with information about Bonnie, but surely he didn't have to choose all her accoutrements as well. Although she was sure that the fashion house was closed for the evening, she was tempted to call and leave a message telling them to forget the dress, shoes, and necklace. She would go out in the morning and buy her own ensemble suitable for an embassy reception.

But then she reconsidered when she thought of the Manolo Blahniks, a designer brand she had never even come close to affording—and thought, well she might just take a look at them after all. She might even take a look at the dress. But she would draw the line at the pearls. Didn't Timothy understand that her cover would never pass muster if she wore Cartier pearls costing God knows how much?

Putting aside the first message, she tore into the second. On U.S. Embassy letterhead it was a note from Assistant Attaché Frank Holder, advising her that he would pick her up in an Embassy car at 7:30 P.M., Tuesday evening, January 12. He inquired whether she would prefer to meet him in the Mandarin Lobby, or if he should come to her room. His cell phone number was provided.

Checking her watch to see that it was only 8:30 P.M., she decided it wasn't too late to call.

"Frank Holder," came the prompt pick-up.

"Hello, Mr. Holder, this is Judy Alexander. I just received your note about Tuesday night."

"Oh yes, Ms. Alexander. Would you prefer to meet me in the lobby there at the Mandarin, or I could come to your room."

"The lobby would be fine. I believe there are some divans around the fountain. I can wait there."

"Excellent. I shall see you there, then."

"Umh, Mr. Holder?"

"Yes?"

"This reception is at the Danish embassy?"

"Yes, it is a reception for the new Danish Ambassador, Noah Svendsen. Unfortunately our U.S. Ambassador—my boss Keith Hendrickson—is in Washington this week, and could not attend, so I am attending in his absence."

"I see. Do you know why I've have been invited?"

"Not a clue. Just got a note from Ambassador Hendrickson on my desk last Saturday morning saying I'm to accompany you to this reception—or you're to accompany me. I'm not sure which."

"Well, then, I will see you Tuesday, at 7:30, in the lobby."

"I'll look forward to it. How will I recognize you?"

"Hmm. I haven't decided what I'll be wearing yet. How formal is it?"

"Oh, I don't know. I don't think it will be a ballroom type of event, so formal gowns would be out of place. I can check if you like."

"No, that's all right. But maybe something like a 'little black dress'? They seem to work for most formal occasions."

"I'm sure that would be fine. Shall I look for you in one when I come?"

"Let's say yes for now. If it's something else I'll let you know. How will I recognize you?"

"Black tie, penguin suit. Tall, dark, handsome."

Oh brother. It could be a long night. "Right. Until Tuesday evening then."

"Yep, see you then."

Judy threw the notes to the side, lay back and stared at the ceiling. Maybe she would be lucky, and the dress from Beaumenay would be a little black one, or something like it. If not, she'd go out and find one. She had the whole day tomorrow to look for one.

She looked at her watch and estimated it was about 3:00 P.M. in New York, and noon in California. She would have liked to call Timothy in California, but she was afraid that if she did so she'd end up scolding him for messing with her wardrobe, and he'd end up scolding her for contacting him when she had nothing of substance to report. So instead she called Robin Hammond—but not before drinking a glass of the Mandarin's complimentary Louis Jadot Puligny-Montrac to relax.

"Hello? Professor?"

"You're lucky I answered your call," said Robin, recognizing Judy's voice. "I'm not answering calls this week."

"Really Professor, that's not very nice."

"Kidding. I'm actually very glad you called. I've been worried about you. Where are you?"

"Paris. Why not answering calls? Have you finished your exams?"

"Actually I turned them in on Saturday."

"And?"

"And what?"

"How did the class do?"

"About average, I'd say. Not spectacular."

"I don't suppose you could tell me how I did."

"You know better than that. I only grade numbers."

"I know. If I gave you my number could you look it up for me?"

Nope. Not allowed either. You have to do it. But you could look it up yourself. You have internet access on your phone, don't you?"

"Yes."

"Just log in to the law school website, follow the prompts, and enter your exam number. You'll have to wait a few days, though. They usually take three or four days to check the exams for complying with the mandatory grade median and mean. After that you can download your grades."

"I can wait. So what are you doing? Crossword I can help you with?"

"Actually just finished one, but thanks, though I could have used your help. Now tell me what's happening with your ...umh, commission. Is that what you call it?"

"Does it matter? I know you don't approve, but I had a wonderful time yesterday exploring Mont St. Michel. Have you been there?"

"Years ago, on a college trip. Don't remember much."

"I took a lot of notes. I think I have an idea what happened to Bonnie."

"Oh, come on. Have you been drinking?"

"Well, maybe glass of...Louis Jadot..."

"That explains it. Now tell me something seriously."

"Just an idea. Several things I've got to do before I can confirm it."

"So can you tell me this idea of yours?"

"Of course not. I have zero evidence."

"Of course."

Judy tried to decide whether she should tell him about the closed zipper, but decided against it.

"How about the Exoneration Clinic? Have you had any more meetings?"

"Nope—not until the semester starts next Monday."

"Have you talked to the registrar or Dean about my taking a semester off?"

"No. and I told you it would have to be the whole year. The school is deserted. I'll talk to them later this week."

"Before the semester begins, though."

"Yes, I said I would. Now tell me what's next on your agenda?"

"Well, it seems I'm going to a reception at the Danish Embassy Tuesday evening."

"Really! How did you manage that?"

"Timothy set it up, of course. I think I'm supposed to try to get an interview with the French *Inspecteur* General of the Police who will be at the reception. Some young man, an attaché of the US. Ambassador is going to accompany me."

There was a long pause.

"Are you there, Professor?"

"Yes, I'm here. You know, Judy, it is one thing to go traipsing around Mont St. Michel, or wherever you were or are, but getting involved with the Chief of Police of France is something else."

Judy wondered if she felt a twinge of jealousy in his voice.

"I'm not getting involved, Professor. I'm just trying to get an interview with him to get his thoughts on the ethics of plea bargaining."

"Uh-huh. For the paper you're going to write."

"Yes, for the paper I'm going to write."

"You know my feelings about all this. And please stop calling me Professor. If you're really going to drop out of school, you can start calling me Robin."

"Ok, Robin. But I've told you I haven't made a final decision about dropping out."

"I think you'd be making a mistake. Promise you'll call me if anything weird starts happening."

"I promise."

"Good. Just please be careful, and please don't worry me. Because you are worrying me."

"I will be careful, and I won't do anything that might worry you. But I'm flattered you care. You wouldn't be jealous, would you?"

At this, Robin wondered if he had allowed himself to enter the forbidden world of transatlantic flirting with a student, and just maybe she with him. In any case, she was definitely getting to him. He couldn't think of what to say.

"What? Don't be silly! Of course not...I...I..."

Judy laughed at his new found awkwardness. "It's OK, Robin. Gotta go. Errands to do tomorrow. Good night!"

Judy lay back on the comforter, sipped another glass of Louis Jadot, and then another. She smiled inwardly. She had to admit that her passing reference to the "young attaché" who would accompany her to the embassy reception had been gratuitous, and perhaps a little mischievous. For Judy, Robin's single most attractive trait was that he had always seemed immune—even oblivious—to her charms. It was refreshing. But now she wondered if she had aroused the good Professor into abandoning the one trait which most endeared him to her.

She curled up and either went to sleep—or passed out. The next morning she wasn't sure which.

CHAPTER THIRTY-SIX

JANUARY 12

Judy had to admit she felt a bit like Eliza Doolittle out of the pages of *Pygmalion* as she sat, elegant legs crossed, on the silken divan in front of the sprinkling fountain in the Mandarin Oriental's lobby. Occasional droplets made it all the way to the tips of her Manolo Blahniks.

As she had hoped, Timothy had made the right choice in ordering a classic little black dress from his favorite fashion house, Beaumenay Joanett. Although it was "littler" than she would have chosen—it was in fact a mini-dress—she reluctantly decided to keep it because it fit perfectly and gave the impression that it had been poured on rather than put on.

Nor had she been able to decline the paradisiacal Manolo Blahniks, although they were so delicate she could not imagine ever wearing them again, let alone walk in the four inch heels.

She had drawn the line, however, at the Cartier pearls after seeing the price, which she thought obscene. She could not deny that they were the perfect complement to her classic black ensemble, but sending them back had given her the perfect excuse to spend the previous day exploring the shopping venues of Paris to look for a reasonably priced necklace of simulated pearls.

She had found what she was looking for at Abercrombie and Fitch on the Rue Saint-Honore—a necklace of simulated white pearls on sale for half price at 175 euros. She was sure that none but a master jeweler could tell the difference between her simulated necklace, and the real one which had the price of a Land Rover—at least not from a distance of five paces.

Just for fun, she had finished the day window shopping on the Les Champs—Elysees, shaking her head in amusement at the 37,000 Euro price of the crocodile boots in the window of the "original" Louis Vuitton Store. What kind of woman would buy boots priced at over $40,000, she wondered.

She had spent the morning at the Mandarin salons having her hair luxuriantly coifed in an open style. In the afternoon she had returned to her room to study the background information on *Inspecteur* General de Police Phillippe Duran which Timothy had sent on her secure email. It read:

The Inspecteur General is fifty-eight years old, a thirty-three year veteran of the Police Nationale. He is a widower, a family man with three grown children, of impeccable reputation, has no known vices—including with women, drugs, or sobriety—and is due to retire sometime in the next two years. It is doubtful if he has any direct knowledge of Bonnie's disappearance or the case surrounding it inasmuch as he was only a commandant divisionnaire at the time and not in the direct line of the investigation, though he is and was surely aware of it. However, if you can get an interview with him and he is willing to help you, he may be able to authorize, or even direct those within the organization to talk to you. He rarely if ever gives interviews to the press, and tightly controls what is released to the press. Neither I nor any of my agents have had any success in interviewing him. If you are able to gain an interview, the most difficult decision you will have to make is when, or even if, you should go beyond your cover of just being a law student wanting to learn about French and European plea bargaining rules and ethics, and risk divulging your interest in Bonnie's disappearance. If you do so, it would obviously be helpful to our mutual cause if you can proceed in your commission without divulging you ties to me, or to the Gardner matter in Texas. Please delete this message as soon as you have read it. Contact me only if you find something solid. I have endured too many false hopes.

The appearance of the young man in exquisitely pressed penguin attire who entered the Mandarin Oriental Lobby was much as Judy expected. As he had so immodestly advertised, he could easily grace the cover of Gentleman's Quarterly. Reminding her of the persona and looks of the actor Tyrone Power of the 1940s films she had watched on TCM, she guessed that he was in his early forties and had the air and confidence of a male who knew he was attractive to women.

His face brightened considerably when he saw sitting on the divan by the fountain the woman whom he could only hope would be his charge for the evening. What had promised to be a boring diplomatic chore now seemed to offer most unexpected possibilities.

"Ms. Alexander, I presume?" said he.

"Mr. Holder, I presume?" replied Judy.

"I believe I am, Madame. Your chariot awaits. Are you ready?"

Judy nodded.

"Just follow me."

A black Lincoln SUV was waiting at the Mandarin entrance. The embassy driver came around to open the rear door for Judy.

"Raymond," said Frank to the driver after taking the back seat next to Judy, "this is Judy Alexander, who is the ambassador's guest this evening. To the Danish Embassy, 77 Avenue Marceau."

"Yes, sir"

"So," he said turning to Judy, "you look lovely this evening. May I call you Judy?"

"Of course. And thank you."

"I'm afraid I haven't been told much about the purpose of our visit to the Danish Embassy this evening. As I mentioned, Ambassador Hendrickson is out of town this week and so unable to represent the United States at the reception for the new Danish Ambassador. He has asked me to go in his place. I just got the note about you accompanying me a couple of days ago."

"I too received a similar note a couple of days ago. Apparently my Professor at the Oliver Wendell Holmes Law School in New York was a classmate of Mr. Hendrickson at Princeton—or some school like that—and asked him if he might help introduce me to some people in Paris who can help me in writing a study with him on the law and ethics of plea-bargaining in the criminal justice systems of the European Community."

"And he suggested that the new Danish ambassador might be the one to interview?"

"Oh, no. But apparently he had information that the French *Inspecteur* General de Police would be attending the reception, and thought he would be a good person to interview. I'm not sure how he knew that."

"Well, your Professor must be a very good friend of the ambassador, because I'm afraid that it's very unlikely that the *Inspecteur* would be receptive to an interview, particularly at such a venue. Have you tried calling his office for an appointment?"

"I guess Professor Hammond—he's my Professor doing the study with me—thought I'd have a better chance of getting an interview if I approached him in a social setting."

"I suppose that may be true, as I don't believe the *Inspecteur* gives very many interviews. But I wouldn't get your hopes up."

"We both knew it was a longshot, but, you know, I'm in Paris trying to get background for the study, Professor Hammond knows the Ambassador, maybe called in a favor, so..."

"Well, I'm glad he did."

The car turned on to the Champs-Elysees.

"There's the Eiffel Tower," said Frank. "Have you been up it yet?"

"No, I had a chance yesterday when I took a walk in this area, but didn't have time to visit it. It looked like there were long lines."

"Not as bad as in the summer, when you can wait several hours at a number of security checkpoints."

"Yes, I've heard."

Not wanting to be caught ogling Judy's spectacular legs without saying something, he said: "I like your shoes."

"Oh you do? Thanks. I bought them yesterday because I really didn't have anything suitable for an embassy reception. It's my one extravagant purchase since coming to Paris, though I'm having second thoughts now. I hope I can make it through the evening without tripping."

"I'm sure you'll be fine."

The car turned on to the Avenue Marceau.

"We're just about there," said Frank. "It's that building up ahead on the right."

The embassy was part of a large city block, and somewhat nondescript, recognizable only by the white cross on red background flag that hung over its entryway.

"Denmark is not a large country, so it can't be compared to our embassy. Its reception hall is small by large embassy standards, but intimate and well-appointed on the inside. I've only been there once before."

******

Judy held on to Frank's arm as they approached the embassy entrance where the two of them were announced and discreetly screened by security.

After entering, Frank began to introduce Judy to the distinguished guests who had already arrived—first introducing himself as the U.S. Ambassador's representative, and then introducing Judy as a young American law student who was conducting a study of plea bargaining procedures in France and in the European Union.

This topic proved to be an entrée into conservations with a number of guests, especially a cadre of young French lawyers who began to hover around Judy. All seemed to be impressed by Judy's charming attempts to converse in French, though as the conversations got more in depth they tended to morph into English.

By ten o'clock the Champagne generously offered on silver platters by crisply uniformed waiters and attendants had served to animate the intercourse. Shortly thereafter, glasses were clinked, and attention asked for invocations by the French Ambassador who welcomed the incoming Danish Ambassador. Speeches by various French dignitaries followed.

Judy took advantage of the clinking glasses to migrate over to Frank who was standing by the liquor bar. She whispered to him:

"Which one is the *Inspecteur* General?"

"Third from the left of the microphone. The bald-headed one with the mustache. Are you ready for me to introduce you?"

"Have you introduced yourself to him yet?"

"No, I was going to wait and introduce you at the same time as I introduced myself."

"Can you come out to the hallway for a moment?"

Both stepped out.

"So what's up?" he asked.

"I'm not sure that directly introducing me is the best way to go about it," said Judy.

"What do you mean?" he said in a louder whisper.

"It just seems so obvious."

"I don't see why. It's pretty straightforward. I just introduce myself on behalf of Ambassador Hendrickson, and then casually introduce you as a visiting friend of the ambassador, a young American law student studying the French legal system. How else are you going to talk to him?"

"I don't want to talk to him tonight."

"What? I though that's what we were here for."

"After the speeches, you could just go and introduce yourself—you know on behalf Ambassador Hendrickson. Try to engage him in conversation for as long as you can. Then, almost as an afterthought, you ask him if he happened to hear about the Texas case of a man who offered to plead guilty to murder in return for being given the death penalty. I know it's been in the papers here, because I've just been talking to some French lawyers who told me that the case has been in the news here."

"I don't see how..."

"Let me finish. If this sparks a response or interest on the inspecteur's part—I'm hoping it will because the E.U. has abolished the death penalty and plea bargaining is strictly regulated—then you can, you know, casually mention that a friend of Ambassador Hendrickson just happens to be accompanying you here tonight, a young American law student here in France conducting a study of how plea bargains are regulated in the E.U. That's when you can point me out to him. I'll be over by the open bar. Then you just wave to me, and I'll wave back. That way he'll know who I am. If he wants to talk to me he can come to me, rather than me going to him."

"There a lot of 'ifs' in that scenario, Judy. What if he doesn't bite?"

"Then I guess you'll have to introduce me directly, and hope for the best. That can be our Plan B. But I think my way has a better chance of success."

"You must know something I don't."

"Maybe I do."

"You know I only signed up to introduce you to the *Inspecteur*, not to engage in this kind of..."

"But you'll try?" She touched his wrist. "For me?"

Frank knew he was being manipulated, but as he looked into her big brown eyes he felt like he was melting into a warm puddle at her Manolo Blahniks—despite himself. It was a situation in which he had never found himself when interacting with women, and he wasn't sure he liked it. In fact, he was sure he didn't. At any rate his confidence was shot.

"All right," he relented helplessly, "but if your plan doesn't work, and you lose the chance to interact with him at all, you won't blame me."

"Agreed. I think the speeches are over. Now you'd better go."

Judy watched as Frank weaved through the crowd of guests toward *Inspecteur* General Durand. It was some minutes before those engaged in conversation with the *Inspecteur* wandered away and gave Frank his opening. As Frank and the *Inspecteur* talked, Judy broke away from the young lawyers who had gathered around her again, sauntered over to the liquor bar, and waited.

There were several people waiting in the wings around the *Inspecteur*, obviously waiting for their chance to get into the conversation with him. It was now or never.

She was about to give up her plan as a failure, when Frank turned to wave at her, and the *Inspecteur* looked in her direction. Judy waved back.

It was after midnight when Frank and Judy said their final goodbyes to the guests amidst much revelry, laughing, hugging, and exchange of email addresses. A French law student from the Sorbonne Law School and nephew of the French Ambassador had been following Judy around like a French poodle all evening, but had failed to cut her from the herd to get her phone number. He made one final try before Frank and Judy escaped to the waiting Embassy Lincoln.

"Whew! Tired?" asked Frank.

Judy lay her head back on the headrest. "Yes, very. And my feet are killing me. These shoes are insufferable. I wasn't sure if I'd make it through the evening."

"You can take them off if you wish."

"No, it will take me too long to put them back on."

"I could help you with that."

Judy rolled her eyes and gave him a shake of her head.

Frank shrugged. Not much was working for him tonight, as Judy had been monopolized by the assemblage of young French lawyers who hovered about her most of the evening.

"Not much traffic on a Tuesday night at this hour. We should have you back at the Mandarin in about ten minutes."

"Great," said Judy as she looked out at the light of the shops and monuments of Paris."

"Listen, I'm sorry your plan didn't work out, "said Frank sympathetically. "We knew it was a long shot, and like I feared, I didn't get a chance to introduce you to the *Inspecteur*. But say, if you're free tomorrow, I'd love to take you to Eiffel Tower. The Embassy has some VIP passes so you wouldn't have to wait in line. Tomorrow night you might enjoy the show at the Moulin Rouge and a late dinner at the Dragons Elysees—best restaurant in Paris."

"You are kind, Frank, and I'd love to. But some other time. I have an engagement tomorrow afternoon."

"Oh," said Frank, his once confident demeanor now crestfallen. "May I ask where?"

"The Prefecture de Police in the Place Louis Lepine on the lle de la Cite."

"The Prefecture? But how..."

"About an hour after our mutual wave, a waiter came to offer me a glass of Champagne. As I took it, he also gave me a sealed note."

"From..."

Judy opened her purse and handed it to Frank.

"You read French, don't you?

"Enough, yes."

The note read:

I understand you are engaged in a study of how we in France regulate and control what you Americans call 'plea bargaining.' I would be pleased to assist you in any way I can. Please call my office in the morning at the number below if you can meet with me in my office at the Prefecture de Police tomorrow afternoon at four o'clock at the address below.
Inspecteur General de Police
Phillippe Durand

CHAPTER THIRTY-SEVEN

JULY 28, 1944

Schutzstaffel Major Hermann Schneider had his orders. In the aftermath of the failed July 20 attempt by Clause von Stauffenberg to assassinate Hitler, the allies were poised to break out of Normandy and sweep across France to liberate Paris.

Reichsfuhrer Heinrich Himmler had given orders that the only concentration camp in France—Natzweiller-Struthof—was to be closed down, and its inmates gassed, burned, or buried alive; or if that was not possible in the time required, to be transferred to camps inside Germany to be killed there.

The camp had originally held over 52,000 inmates, but 22,000 still remained, including 6,000 children. If the allies were to overrun this camp and see for themselves the dying and burned men, women, and children, it would be difficult to maintain the fiction after the war that the camps never existed, and were mere fictions of allied propaganda. Those responsible for this horror would surely be held accountable.

The Natzweiller-Struthof camp was located in the Vosges Mountains outside the Alsatian French village of Schirmeck, thirty-one miles southwest of the French city of Strasbourg. Major Schneider was on his way to the camp with orders to meet with the commandant and insure that all inmates were killed or transferred by the end of the month. He was then to insure that the camp was then to be razed to the ground and all traces of it buried deep in the ground. When he had heard that orders were to be issued for this task, he had volunteered.

Rumors had already spread and been widely disseminated that over five thousand of the alleged conspirators to the assassination attempt had been rounded up and strangled slowly by piano wire, which took almost an hour for the wire to cut through the neck and kill the victim as he dangled, kicked, and choked. Hitler had all the hangings meticulously filmed to provide evening entertainment, and watched them night after night with glee and satisfaction.

Hitler's revenge on the alleged conspirators had accomplished it purpose: there would be no more assassination attempts, and the war would end only when Hitler himself was surrounded and cornered in his underground bunker in Berlin. Many thousands would have to die before this took place, and it would take almost another year.

Yet there were a number of high ranking Nazi officers who, though they dared not engage in any conspiracy, nevertheless saw the handwriting on the wall and recognized that it was only a matter of time before the war would be over. The allies were on the verge of breakout in the west, and the Russians were grinding down the remnants of the German army in the east. For them, the primary objective was first, to survive the war, and second to provide for their future after the war if possible.

Major Hermann Schneider was one of those Nazi officers. His rank and authority might help him survive the war; but he knew that securing his future after the war would depend on having the money and means to do so.

He had a plan. The first part of his plan he hoped to accomplish when he arrived at Natzweiller-Struthof with his cavalcade of three SD7 armored personnel carriers, two Maultier halftrack trucks, and four Einheits-Diesel trucks. His personnel included fourteen Schutzstaffel soldiers, all armed to the teeth.

The second part of his plan depended upon the cooperation and help of the friend he had made during his visits to Mont St. Michel over the past four years—Unteroffizier Gerhard Richter.

As the S.S. Cavalcade stopped on the outskirts of Strasbourg to re-fuel, Schneider barked to his radio operator:

"*Funktioniert das radio?*"

"*Ja, Major.*"

"*Gib es mir.*"

After several attempts, Schneider made contact with Gerhard Richter.

"Gerard, are you there? Can you hear me?"

"Yes, but speak louder."

"Is the hole ready?"

"Yes, but you must come quickly. We are ordered to evacuate within three days."

"The Americans are close?"

"Yes, but they are not coming this way yet."

You must stay for five more days. Can you do that? How many men are still left with you?"

"I have only seven men to fill the hole. I can stay for five more days, but you must hurry, Hermann!"

"I will be there."

"*Auf Wiedersehen,* Hermann."

CHAPTER THIRTY-EIGHT

JANUARY 13

Having now mastered how to navigate the Paris subway system, Judy found it not only more convenient but faster than calling an Uber in the middle of rush hour. She arrived at the security entrance to the Prefecture a half hour before her four o'clock appointment. As instructed on the note presented to her at the Danish Embassy, she had called that morning to confirm her appointment with the *Inspecteur de Police.*

Wearing the same black trousers, blouse, red coat, black walking shoes, and cashmere scarf she had purchased in Long Beach, she carried only her small Baggallini hand bag containing her iPhone, passport, and notepad. Nevertheless, it was closely scrutinized by the security personnel as she passed through the metal detectors.

"*Votre enterprise, Madame?*" the security guard asked.

"*J'ai randez-vous avec Inspecteur General de Police,*" she replied as the guard closely examined her iPhone.

"*Avec Inspecteur General Durand?*" The guard seemed skeptical, and asked her to open up her bag.

"*Oui,*" she replied as she opened her bag for inspection. She was pleased that at least up to this point, her French had been passable enough to be understood.

"*Votre nom at votre passeport.*"

"Judy Alexander." She presented her passport.

He scrutinized it as well. Finally he said, "*Un instant s'il vous plait,*" picked up his phone and made a call.

After several long minutes, the guard said, "*Proceder,*" and gave her instructions to the *Inspecteur's* reception desk on the fourth floor.

There she was met by a receptionist who seemed as doubtful as the guard. Apparently, it was unusual for the

Inspecteur General to meet with young women alone in his office. If she were a witness, she would be meeting with the *Inspecteur*'s subordinates, not the *Inspecteur* General himself, and if she were a journalist she would not have gotten this far.

Judy repeated to the receptionist that she had an appointment with the *Inspecteur* General at four o'clock. It was now 3:50 P.M.

"*Assey-vous s'il vous plait,*" said the receptionist as she too picked up the intercom.

Judy sat on the reception couch, but waited less than five minutes before the *Inspecteur Durand* emerged from the double doors behind the reception desk.

"*Tu es Judy Alexander?*" he said effusively as he held out his hand.

"*Oui, Inspecteur.*" She recognized him instantly from the Danish Embassy reception.

"*Entrez s'il vous plait.*" He led her to his office down the hall. It was a large office decorated with small artifacts, statuettes, and French paintings. A large floor to ceiling window presented a panoramic view of the lle de la Cite.

The *Inspecteur General,* not yet aware of Judy's limitations in speaking French, welcomed her in French:

"Last night, Ambassador Hendrickson's attaché told me that you were a guest of the Ambassador, and that you were a law student in New York and were working on a study of our plea bargaining system here in France. I'm sorry that we didn't get a chance to talk, but since you were there you know that it was difficult for me to get away."

"*Pardon, Inspecteur...*" Judy replied tentatively. Although she had gotten the gist of the *Inspecteur*'s welcome, she thought it best not to try to get through the whole interview in French.

"I understand," said he, in English, "my English is only passable, and I commend your efforts to speak our language. So many Americans come to France and make no such efforts, expecting us to speak English. When we visit the U.S., we do not expect everyone to speak French. So I commend you. But you must excuse my English, as my American and English friends tell me that my accent is very strong. Now, how can I help you? What would you like to know about plea bargaining in the French system of justice?"

"I understand that it is very much different than how plea bargaining is done in my country."

"Very much so, though I do not presume to know much about how it is conducted in the United States. What you call 'plea bargaining' we simply call a pre-trial guilty plea procedure. Such a procedure is only permitted in minor cases, and any sentence proposed by the prosecution cannot exceed one year. I understand that there is no such limit on plea bargaining in the United States—that even life sentences without parole can be the subject of such plea bargaining."

"That is true. Perhaps you've read about the plea bargain offer made by a murder suspect in Texas recently, offering to plead guilty in exchange for the death penalty."

"I have. *Barbare!* Personally, I believe that all 'plea bargaining' is a dishonorable practice, and I have always discouraged the practice. Punishments, in my view, should not be bargained for in the manner of merchants haggling for the best price. I suppose there is no great harm in it as a means of disposing of the great number of minor infractions, which might otherwise clog the system. But very serious offenses—certainly rape or murder—should not be the subject of such back room haggling. No! It is not justice. Non!"

Durand continued giving Judy a long and detailed exposition of plea bargaining in the French system. Since most of what he was telling her she already knew, she considered now whether she should attempt to turn the conversation to the case of Bonnie's disappearance.

In deciding that this was neither the time nor place to do so, she considered several factors.

First, she was sure that the *Inspecteur* would see through her if she attempted to do so. For one thing, there was simply not time to casually introduce the subject into the conversation.

The *Inspecteur* had graciously offered to assist her on a legal issue that was of interest to him; and while her "beauty"—he was a "Frenchman" after all, for whom the keeping of a mistress on the side was not considered a high crime or misdemeanor—may have been a factor in sending her the note offering an interview, she doubted if he expected any more diversion than having an attractive American law student hang on his every word, and perhaps convey his strong feelings about plea bargains to his counterparts in the United States.

Second, he struck her as a man of honor, confirming Timothy's background research of him as a man of impeccable reputation. If the *Inspecteur* was looking for some sweetness on the side, he would have proposed that he meet her at some out-of-the-way bistro in the manner of an assignation—not in his office in full view of his staff. He had offered her this one interview, and she felt it would be a betrayal of his good faith if she now revealed an alternative motive. If she did so, she would not blame him if he then treated her in the same way as any other journalist trying to extract information from him.

Lost also would be her chance to gain the trust she needed before asking for his assistance in gaining access to those of his subordinates who would have the information she needed to find out what happened to Bonnie. If Bonnie's disappearance was to be raised in conversation, it would have to be in the form of an aside—an 'afterthought'—and not as the driving purpose of her investigation. Simply put, a single one hour interview would not provide the time that she would need to drop such an afterthought into the conversation.

Sensing that the time allotted for her interview was about to expire, she waited for a pause in his exposition to say:

"*Inspecteur,* I know how busy you must be. I was wondering if any of your subordinates might have time to meet with me on how guilty plea procedures are administered in practice..."

"I think that could be arranged..."

"Also, perhaps you could recommend someone who dealt with guilty plea procedures in important cases in France before the present plea bargaining procedure was introduced in 2004. I think you mentioned that it was codified in a statute"—Judy referred to the notes she had been taking—"CRPC 495-7, I think is the statute?"

"That is correct..."

"Before I came to France to work on this study, several of my fellow clinical students at my law school googled names of several of your best detectives—preferably retired now so that they would have the time to consult with me. Do you happen to recall a detective by the name of *Inspecteur Jacques Montagne?*"

Durand's face showed immediate recognition of the name. "Why yes, I knew him well. A most competent and resourceful detective. And, of course, he is retired now. I might be able to give you his address and number if you like. I think he and his wife retired to the south about five years ago."

"That would be wonderful! *Merci!*"

Durand picked up his intercom and called an assistant.

"My secretary will give you his address and number before you leave, though I cannot guarantee that it is up to date. You understand, of course, that this personal information must be kept confidential."

"Of course."

"Please give my regard to Jacques. Of course you will respect his wishes if he is not inclined to discuss such matters, or even to meet with you at all. That will be entirely at his discretion. But I would be happy to write you a note of introduction if you wish."

"I would be so grateful. Thank you again. And just maybe what I learn will be of use in reforming the plea bargain procedures in the U.S. I agree with you that they are barbaric."

Durand took out some note paper and wrote a short note, which he handed to Judy.

"And here is my card. Please call anytime if I can be of any assistance to you. And give my regards to the Ambassador if you see him again. It was a pleasure talking with you. Please feel free to call me if I can be of any further assistance in your study."

Both rose to say goodbye. Judy held out her hand, which Durand took and kissed—in the French custom.

CHAPTER THIRTY-NINE

JANUARY 14

After an early morning checkout from the Mandarin Oriental, Judy arrived by Uber at Paris Europocar to rent a compact Renault Sedan. While waiting for the car to be readied for her, she scrutinized the G.P.S map which would guide her to the home of Jacques Montagne.

According to the address, the retired *Inspecteur* and his wife now resided in a farmhouse near the village of Saint Jeannet, about forty-four kilometers northeast of Monte Carlo in Southern France.

The iPhone G.P.S estimated that if she left Paris by 10:00 A.M., and allowed only one hour for lunch and refueling she could expect to arrive in the medieval town of Saint Jeannet by eight o'clock that evening. That gave her an hour before she left Paris to get a quick breakfast cappuccino and roll at a bistro next to the rental office. She would also have time to reserve by iPhone a Bed and Breakfast in the village. A quick google search of Saint Jeannet revealed that it was a medieval residential village overlooking Nice with a panoramic view of the Mediterranean.

Despite being a most charming medieval village, it was, according to the google page she downloaded, 'blessed by the Gods' by virtue of having somehow escaped the attention of tourists, of which there were few. This may have accounted for the ease with which she found an available Bed and Breakfast for that evening in the home of a Madame Lara Bisset, who told her that she would wait up for her arrival that evening.

Although she was able to begin her journey before 10:00 A.M., it took a good hour to escape the confines of Paris and start making good time on both the A6 and A7. Making only a rest stop for refueling along the A7 where she grabbed a baguette, cheese, and bottle of Evian, she arrived in the general vicinity of Saint Jeannet before eight o'clock. Hampered by the dark and some narrow mountainous roads, she did not find Madame Bisset's Bed and Breakfast until almost nine. She called the establishment before approaching the door to be sure she was at the right place.

Judy's conversational French proved most useful as Madame Bisset apparently spoke no English at all. Ushering Judy to her bedroom with little fanfare—it was obvious that it was past her usual bedtime—the Madame asked only what time she would be up for breakfast and said they could discuss her future plans in Saint Jeannet at that time.

Judy's tentative plan was to call Jacques late the next morning—hopefully he would not be on holiday somewhere outside the village—and let him know that she had a letter of introduction from the *Inspecteur* General. She would then follow up and ask if she might visit him at his convenience sometime during the day.

******

For breakfast the next morning at seven, Madame Bisset offered Tartine with butter and jam, fruit, and an exquisite café crème. With her host now in a talkative mood, Judy asked—in French—if Madame knew of a M. and Mme. Montagne who lived in the area. By her animated response, it was clear that she did, though she spoke so fast that Judy grasped only a few words.

"*Merci,*" replied Judy, though if her host had given directions, there was no way she could have understood them. Judy would instead have to rely on her G.P.S. directions. Before making her call to M. Montagne, she wanted to explore the village on foot and take her morning run.

"*Je reviendrai,*" said Judy, "*dans une heure. Est-ce que tout va bien?*"

"*Mais bien sur,*" came Madame Bisset's prompt reply.

231

Although Judy could not understand Madame Bisset's rapid delivery, she was pleased that at least her host understood her.

After wandering through a maze of shady alleyways, she picked up a well-marked hiking trail, stopping only to look at the medieval chapel of Saint Bernardin before running up the trail to the base of an immense *'baou'*—a towering cliff that overlooked the village. After an exhilarating climb, she ran down to the town square where she stopped to rest at the terrace of the Fontaine du Bouef, from which there was a wonderful view of the countryside and sea in the distance.

Since she carried her phone in her side pack, she decided to sit by the fountain and make her call from there before returning to Madame Bisset's.

"*Allo?*" It was a woman's voice.

"*Bonjour. Mon nom est Judy Alexander. J'ai une lettre de introduction de Inspecteur Durand.*"

"*Un moment.*"

It was a full minute before a man's voice came on the phone.

"*Puis-je vous aider?*"

"*Tu es Monsieur Jazques Montagne?*"

"*Oui, oui, je suis Jazques Montagne. Puis-je vous aider?*"

Judy continued in halting French, and wondered how long it would take for *Monsieur Montagne* to suggest that she continue in her native tongue.

"Hello, *Inspecteur*. My name is Judy Alexander. I am an American law student from the United States visiting France to study several aspects of the French legal system. I recently had occasion to meet with *Inspecteur General de Police Gerard Durand*, and he kindly suggested you as someone who might be able to help me."

M. Montagne now understood that he would have to speak slowly, but did not yet suggest that Judy continue in English. Out of courtesy he would wait until the caller asked if she could continue in English.

"I would be most pleased to answer any questions you might have about our system of justice. And you say you have a letter of introduction from my old friend Gerard Durant?"

"Yes, I do. That would be wonderful if you could help."

"Where are you now?"

"I am here in Saint Jeannet. I am staying with Madame Bisset. Do you know her?"

"But of course. She is a cousin as a matter of fact."

"Is there any chance that you might be available today sometime—at your convenience?"

"But of course. We are doing nothing in particular today, though my wife Clara is making some jams."

"What would be a good time today?"

"I think Clara has some ham in mind for lunch if you would like to join us at around noon?"

"I would love to. Can you give me directions? I have your address and a G.P.S., but..."

"I'm afraid your G.P.S. might not help you. Our farmhouse is a bit off the beaten track."

"If you could give me directions..."

So far, Judy had understood most of what Jacques had said, but was concerned that she might not understand directions.

"Could you tell me in...I mean do you speak...?"

Jacques understood.

"Of course. It will give me a chance to practice. But you will forgive Clara, as she speaks very little."

"Of course."

Jacques proceeded to give Judy very detailed directions in English. Like all the polite Frenchmen she had met, he was happy to speak English once an American had shown an earnest attempt to speak in French. Until then, many would not give you the time of day.

******

233

Although Jacques had said that it would take only fifteen minutes to drive to his farmhouse from where she was, she thought she should allow at least a half hour to find it in case she made any wrong turns. That still gave her time to return to Madame Bisset's, shower, and change.

After informing her host that she expected to be back that afternoon—she wasn't sure how long she would be welcome at the Montagne farmhouse—Judy began her drive to the farmhouse.

Despite her concerns about getting lost in the narrow mountain roads, she arrived at the farmhouse in less than twenty minutes. The directions had been so precise—even as to the type of tree to be found at a turn off, of which there were a number, many without street signs—that she made not a single wrong turn.

Judy could not help but smile when the forest trees opened up to a picturesque farmhouse that was both rustic and charming. It had a wood column porch made of resawn barn beams, multiple gables, assorted arches, and a steep roof.

Jacques, wearing overalls, flannel shirt, and Chore Jacket, was raking a small garden in front of the farmhouse when he heard Judy's car and turned to greet her.

"*Monsieur Montagne,*" said Judy as she emerged from the Renault.

"You are Judy? Welcome," he said.

They shook hands as Judy looked over at the house.

"What a lovely house."

"You had no problems finding us?"

"Your directions were very precise. Thank you."

"Won't you please come in and meet my wife Clara."

Clara was sitting at the kitchen table with her jars of jam when Jacques and Judy entered.

"*Bonjour,*" said she as she rose to greet her visitor.

"*Bonjour,*" replied Judy.

"Please, come sit," said Jacques as he ushered Judy into the living room.

Judy was entranced by the décor—mismatched and distressed furniture pieces which nevertheless fit elegantly together when combined. There was a bright airiness to the entire interior, which made it most inviting.

Jacques and Clara sat on a well-worn tufted sofa, while Judy sat in an equally worn peacock chair.

"Tell me about yourself," began Jacques. "We don't receive many visitors out here. How is my good comrade-in-arms, Gerard, doing these days?"

He spoke in English, though it was apparent that Clara understood none of it.

Judy took Garrard's letter from her purse and handed it to Jacques, who read it with nostalgic delight. Judy waited for him to finish reading it before saying:

"I am in my first year of law school in New York. I am working on a project concerning comparative legal systems, and my Professor suggested I take a semester off to visit your lovely country to compare the legal systems of our two countries."

"You are quite right to come in person, as most of what there is to learn about our French system of justice is not to be found in books or treatises."

"It is so interesting that you would say so, for I have learned that since arriving here."

"How so, may I ask?"

"I was most fortunate to meet your *Inspecteur* General de Police at an embassy reception a few nights ago—you have his letter. He was most kind and invited me for an interview the very next day."

"*Extraordinaire!*" exclaimed Jacques. "I am most flattered that my old friend thought to recommend me as someone who could help you. You were most fortunate indeed. Even as my subordinate in my division many years ago, he had an—'aversion'...?"

"Yes, aversion."

"*Merci*, I have said it correctly. He had an aversion to journalists. They were always nosing into our investigations, trying to get information, which if released would undermine our investigations."

"But I am not a journalist, *Inspecteur.*"

"*Assure, pardon.* If you were, Gerard would never have granted you an interview. And you can be sure that he would have checked your background as well before granting an interview."

At this, Judy held her breath, though hoping it did not show. She had assumed that Frank had told Gerard that she was a law student from the Oliver Wendell Holmes School of Law conducting empirical research on the French legal system. It did not occur to her that he would "check her out" before inviting her for the interview. But of course, being the chief of police, it would have been unprofessional for him not to do so. Timothy's insistence that she not diverge from her 'story' that she was just a law student conducting research on the French legal system—a fact that could be easily checked—had been sound.

At that moment, Clara excused herself to finish preparations for lunch.

"Were there any particular aspects of our system that you are focusing on?" Jacques asked.

"Yes, in the matter of how guilty pleas are administered. As I am sure you are aware, in the United States legal system over 97% of cases are resolved by the bargaining of their guilty pleas."

"*Mon Dieu!* I had no idea! Trading people's lives in such fashion!"

"That is why both my Professor and I thought we should write an article advocating reform. But first we thought we should examine how other civilized countries engage in this practice."

"I would be most happy to help you with such a study."

"Have you heard, or read in any of your newspapers here about the case in Texas, in which a man charged with murder offered to plead guilty in return for being put to death?"

"I believe I did read something about that! *Incroyalbe!*"

Clara emerged from the kitchen to announce lunch.

"Come, Mille Alexander, please join us for lunch."

"Call me Judy, please."

"*Mais Oui,* Judy. Please join us."

******

Clara had prepared a lunch of ham, potatoes, vegetables from their garden, and a variety of cheeses—and of course, wine.

"Your house is so charming," said Judy. "Right out of a fairy tale picture book."

Knowing that his wife spoke no English, Jacques translated for her.

"*Merci,*" said Clara. *Nous aimons ca.*"

Clara continued in French which Judy did not fully understand. Judy turned to Jacques to translate.

"She says you are very beautiful," said Jacques.

Judy blushed. "*Merci, mais non...*"

"She wants to know if you are a fashion model or actress, and says you remind her of Catherine Deneuve."

"Catherine Deneuve?"

Judy vaguely recognized the name of the French actress, trying to remember if she was the actress in the film Indochine she recalled seeing some years before.

"It is a great compliment, Judy. Catherine Deneuve is one of our most cherished French actresses. Some years ago she succeeded Mireille Mathieu as the official face of Marianne, our French national symbol of 'Liberte.'"

"*Vous etes gentil,*" said Judy with a smile as she tried to imagine herself as the image of France.

Dessert was a delicious raspberry macaroon.

"It is Clara's special recipe," said Jacques, obviously proud of his wife's cooking and baking skills.

"Delicious, *merci.*"

"Now," said Jacques, "perhaps you would enjoy a tour of our little farm."

"I would, very much."

While Clara excused herself to retire to the kitchen, Jacques showed Judy the environs—a stable with two stout horses, a coop with a small flock of chickens, and a garden growing a variety of vegetables.

The two then retired to the study where Judy explained her interest in France's plea bargaining system, and Jacques elaborated in great detail the way in which guilty pleas were administered in France. Judy took meticulous notes, although many were a repetition of the notes she had already made from what she had learned from Jules, Frank, the assemblage of young French lawyers who had hung about her at the embassy reception, and, not least the *Inspecteur General*.

"Of course," he said, "there may be more recent legislation in this regard, which I have not kept up with. You may also wish to consult CRCP 495."

"Yes, I definitely plan to do that."

"May I ask what your plans are now? How much time do you have before you must return to your law studies?"

"I have taken this semester off to work on this project. So far I have only interviewed you and the *Inspecteur General*. Perhaps you know of some others who might help with my study?'

"Most of the people I might recommend live back in Paris or its environs. I will look up some of my files and notes for some more names of people who might assist you. Until then, since you are here in Le Midi, or as we call it PACA—the Provence-Alpes-Cote-d'Azur—perhaps you would care to stay for a few days to visit. You are staying at Madame Bisset's are you not?"

"Yes, she provides a very nice room for me there."

"Judy, would you excuse me for a moment? I'll be right back."

Judy nodded. "Of course. I'll finish my notes."

Jacques returned several moments later and said:

"Judy, Clara and I would be very honored if you might stay with us for a few days. We don't get many visitors down here, and we would be delighted to show you some of the beautiful places that are only a short distance from Saint Jeannet."

"You and Clara are so kind! But I have already arranged with Madame Bisset to stay..."

"Lara is my cousin. Why don't Clara and I take you back to your room and we can fetch your bags. It's almost dark and you can easily get lost on these mountain roads. I will talk to Clara, and I'm sure she will have no problem with you coming back with us. We have a nice guestroom which you should find comfortable."

"I don't know what to say..."

"Then say no more. I will bring around our little Peugeot and we shall go."

"Then I would love to. Thank you!"

CHAPTER FORTY

JANUARY 15

After a brief nightcap and evening conversation, Jacques and Clara bid goodnight to their guest, who retired to her room. It was even more comfortable than Jacques had advertised. Its antique bed had a half canopy of lightweight cotton trimmed with tassel along the openings.

Judy thought of calling Robin—their last conversation had ended on something of a sour note—but thought better of it when she realized that any conversation was likely to carry through walls and disturb her hosts.

Instead, she texted him, telling him where she was, and telling him how delighted she was to be staying in an idyllic French farmhouse with such a kind couple as hosts. More important, however, she informed him that she was staying in the home of *Inspecteur Montagne*, who nineteen years before had led the French investigation into the death of Bonnie Hoxsey.

She thought also of texting Timothy to report her contact with the investigating *Inspecteur*, but realized that until she had found a way to actually engage him on the matter of that investigation, there would be little of substance to report.

Timothy had also made clear that he preferred that any reporting be done through their secure iPhone audio link rather than by texting since it was as likely to be recorded if hacked.

After lying in bed for a half hour cruising the internet on her iPhone, she fell gently to sleep.

******

It was sometime in the dead of night that she was awakened by a tinkling sound. It was coming from the kitchen. She was at first alarmed until she walked into the hallway and saw that it was Jacques preparing some warm milk on the stove. When he saw her, he motioned for her to come in.

"Would you care for some warm milk?" he asked in a low voice.

"I'm afraid I'm not much of a milk drinker. But perhaps a cup of tea if you have it?"

"*Bien sur!* Please sit. I have tea. I will make it. Is herbal all right?"

"Yes, thank you. I prefer it."

"I hope I didn't wake you," said he as he heated the kettle.

"Not at all. I'm still having a bit of a problem kicking my jet lag, I think."

"It can easily take a week or more. I know from experience."

Judy blinked her eyes. "What time is it?" she asked as she sat down at the kitchen table.

Jacques took out a timepiece from his pocket. "Almost two o'clock, though my watch can be off by five minutes either way. One nice thing about retirement is that time does not create the stress that catching criminals did when I was with the Force." The three of them had retired at about nine o'clock, and Judy had fallen to sleep about eleven, so she had slept for three hours.

"And how do you happen to be up at this hour, *Inspecteur*?"

"I'm afraid I've always been a bit of a…*insomniaque*…how do you say in English?"

"Pretty much the same—'insomniac.'"

"Yes, I only need about four to five hours of sleep. That's proven to be both a blessing and a curse. It helped me during my detective days, when time was often of the essence, but at home Clara still needs at least seven hours. So over the years we have reached an accommodation."

"I hope we're not disturbing her now."

"*Cieux non.* Clara sleeps the slumber of the dead. She also snores—as you can hear—but so do I, so we've gotten used to each other. We still sleep in the same bedroom and the same bed. Many of my contemporaries do not."

Jacques served Judy her tea and she took a sip.

"It's butterfly pea flower. Do you like it?"

"It's different, but yes I like it."

"Clara is something of a tea connoisseur, and that is one of her favorites."

"I want to thank you for your help this afternoon helping me understand plea bargaining in the French legal system."

"*Vous etes le bienvenu.* We don't call it that, of course. It's simply a procedure for the entering of guilty pleas. We didn't have such a procedure like the plea bargaining you're talking about —certainly not a formal procedure—for most of the time I was active on the Force. C.R.C.P. only came into effect in the last several years of my tenure, and applied only to minor cases. All my investigations were for serious crimes—felonies you call it—and the C.R.C.P. did not apply to those."

There was a brief pause in the conversation as he sipped his warm milk.

Judy was thinking: it might now be the best time to steer the conversation to Jacques' investigation of Bonnie's disappearance. But how to do so without raising suspicion? Timothy and his agents had spent years trying to interview the key players in the investigation, only to be told to butt out, with threats to complain to the American ambassador if they persisted. If she did not proceed delicately, and if her true mission was suspected, she imagined that the up-to-now kindly former investigator might feel his hospitality abused, and usher her from his premises with great indignation.

"How many years were you with the police?" she asked in a manner which suggested she was just trying to make conversation with a fellow night owl over tea and milk.

Jacques rubbed his chin as he considered. "Thirty-two years if you consider my first two years in training."

"I imagine you must have had a number of big cases in that time."

"*Oui*, including a number of cases I would just as soon forget. I had to learn very early on not to let the horrible crime scenes I saw affect me when I came home to Clara. I was not always successful, and many a night was filled with nightmares. But Clara has always been by my side and supported me. Without her I doubt if I could ever have continued what I was doing."

"You are most fortunate in that respect. What would you say was your biggest success?"

Jacques put down his glass of milk and sighed. "Well, twenty-four years ago—or maybe it was twenty-three—as one of the youngest detectives on the Force, I tracked down a serial killer and rapist that had been terrorizing a small town in Provence. I followed leads that my superior at the time told me would be futile. But against my superiors' orders I followed those leads anyway. When I was successful in finding the perpetrator I received the *Medaille d'Honneur de la Police Nationale*—the highest award of the French National Police."

"You must be very proud."

"Yes, but there was a serious downside. In receiving the medal I incurred the enmity of many of my superiors. They later did everything they could to hinder my career. It was largely because of their interventions that I never rose above the rank I held at that time."

"I'm so sorry."

"Don't be. In fact I much preferred what I was doing as a detective to pushing paper at a higher administrative level."

Judy swallowed hard before she asked her next question:

"Were there any failures that you now regret in which you failed to find the perpetrator?"

Jacques looked directly into Judy's eyes and squinted. After a long moment he finally said:

"Yes, there was one, nineteen years ago."

Judy hoped Jacques would continue, but instead he picked up his empty milk glass and put it in the sink.

"I think we'd better be back to our beds," he said brusquely.

"Yes, of course," said Judy. "I'm sorry if...*Bon Soir, Inspecteur.*"

******

As Judy returned to her room she was sure that she had over stepped and lost any chance of fulfilling the task that a desperate and dying father back on Catalina had assigned to her with so much hope.

She had gotten three hours sleep, but that was all she was going to get that night.

She could only think: "He knows."

CHAPTER FORTY-ONE

JULY 29, 1944

The cavalcade of Schutzstaffel vehicles had traveled back roads all through the night, and now, in the early morning hours, stopped in a forest clearing just a few miles from their destination. All of Major Schneider's men were tired and in need of sleep.

His second in command of the contingent, Lieutenant Otto Wagner, asked his superior if he wanted to stop in the clearing and allow the men an hour or so of sleep.

"*Ja*, Lieutenant . But just one hour. Time is of the essence now. We will have only the rest of the day to complete our work at Natzweiller-Struthof. Post a sentry and then join me over there."

Schneider pointed to a clump of trees about twenty meters away. As the sentry was posted and the men stretched out in the trucks, Schneider and Wagner found a private cove out of earshot of the men.

"Are you still with me, Otto?" asked Schneider with a hushed whisper. "Because if you are not, say so now!"

"Yes, Hermann. We have discussed it many times. I am with you."

"If we are caught, you know the consequences."

"I know. The piano wire."

"Even if we are caught by the Americans, it would be hanging at the very least."

"I understand, Hermann. But what choice do we have? Even our superiors know it is only a matter of time before the Americans and Russians join up. When the time comes there will be no way out if we don't have money. And lots of it."

"I already know two of our superiors—those who have access to it—who are sneaking away with what they can carry, stashing away gold and jewels from the camps—taking little bags of it here and there, hiding it, burying it so that only they know where it is, so that only they can retrieve it after the dust settles."

"Have you seen any of this—with your own eyes, I mean?"

"Yes, I have, Otto. I have personally seen the Merkers Salt Mine outside Frankfurt. I have seen it with my own eyes! I went there on an inspection tour with the Reichsfuhrer last February. It's over fifty meters deep in the ground.

"You saw gold?"

I have never seen so much gold, Otto. There were hundreds of bags of foreign currency, thousands of gold bars, ten thousand at least, hundreds of boxes of gold bullion, thousands more bags of gold coins, dozens of bags of platinum. Unbelievable, Otto! And diamonds—huge bags of them! And the artworks! Renoir, Rembrandt, hundreds of the most valuable paintings by the great masters!"

"And who will inherit this windfall of treasure after the war?"

"Whoever occupies Germany after the war—Russians or Americans. Since the mine is near Frankfurt and the Rhine, probably the Americans or the British. It will be impossible to hide it for long. Our generals who know the location and are captured will trade away its location return for their lives."

"How many of these hordes of gold are there?"

"I have only seen the one in the Merkers Mine, but I know that there are many more. You remember that I have been at headquarters for the past year and I have seen the documents. We document everything."

"Why hasn't this gold already been sent out of the country—to Switzerland, or Portugal after the gold is laundered in Switzerland—in return for raw materials to build our war machine?"

"Much of it has, but there is more gold than even those two neutral countries can absorb. There is no way to hide these huge caches of gold and jewels, and there is no way to get them out of out of Germany while the war is still going on. Only the smaller troves, in places where no one would look and to which no more than one or two men are privy, can escape detection."

"But you have still not told me, Hermann, where we are to get our hands on some of this gold—and where we are to hide it once we get it."

"The trove I have in mind is small only in comparison to places like the Merkers Mine—but enough to make us both millionaires in any country we choose to go to after the war. But I need your help, Otto."

"You have it. You have it! Is that why we're going to Natzweiller-Struthof?"

"Of course, Otto. I have seen the documents at headquarters. The last shipment of gold and jewels to Berlin from that camp was October 23 of 1943. It went to the Reich bank in Berlin. Since that time over 50,000 inmates have passed through the camp, and of course all of them were stripped of their valuables. The gold teeth of those burned in the ovens would alone be worth millions. Most of it is still there, Otto. It has to be."

"But the camp is to be closed, you said."

"Precisely, Otto. I volunteered for this assignment so we could get there before any further transfers of the gold could be made."

"How do we know there haven't been recent transfers to Berlin?"

"I told you, Otto. I have had access to the transfer orders. The gold is still there."

"Do you expect that there are any Schutzstaffel still at the camp?"

"I know the commandant—Fritz Hartjenstaf—is still there. I saw the order commanding him to stay at the camp until we arrive and I certify that the camp is ready for final destruction. I have a copy of that order with me. There may be a few Schutzstaffel staff there as well, but no more than a skeleton crew."

"Will there still be prisoners there?"

247

"There shouldn't be. They should all be burned by now, or shipped back to camps in Germany or Poland. But that is one thing we must be sure of before certifying the camp for final destruction. There must be no bodies lying around by the time the Americans overrun it."

"Is the Commandant part of your plan?"

"No, Otto. He is what you call a 'true believer.' He's been with the S.S. since the days of Ernst Rohm. He would never go along with it. In fact, he'd probably report us to Himmler."

"So how will you...I mean..."

"Leave that to me, and follow my lead."

"How will we know where the gold is buried?"

"The commandant, will know and will lead us to it. Who do you think was responsible for storing it?"

"But won't the Reichsfuhrer be suspicious if a shipment of gold is not made to Berlin after the camp is closed?"

"There will be a shipment, Otto. A shipment of gold—minus the gold, diamonds, and jewels that we retrieve first. All the rest of our contingent will return to Berlin with the remaining gold, jewels, and paintings. The paintings of course we will not be able to take. You and I will then alone go with our stash to our next assignment—to close down another place in imminent danger of being overrun by the Americans. That is why we have very little time. I should tell you also that here is something even more valuable than gold or diamonds that we will retrieve at what is left of the camp."

"What?"

"You will find out soon enough. You know enough already. Just follow my lead and don't ask questions."

Otto nodded. He had only one more question: "Where is our next assignment, then?"

"That I can tell you, Otto."

Otto leaned forward to hear what Hermann's guttural whisper in his ear:

"Mont St. Michel, Otto. Mont St. Michel."

CHAPTER FORTY-TWO

JANUARY 16

Judy slept fitfully, but was wide awake by 6:00 A.M., waiting to hear the sounds of her hosts in the kitchen preparing breakfast.

After Jacques' curt dismissal of her during the night before, she was sure now that she had not only undermined her mission and failed both Gardner and Timothy, but more to the immediate point—insulted her generous hosts and betrayed their hospitality.

Nevertheless, she did not want to sneak out of the house by the back door. She would instead wait until they rose, and then apologize to them in person before leaving.

She would now have to face the fact that her mission was over, and it was time to return to the U.S.—first to Catalina to apologize to Timothy for her failure, then to Appaloosa County in Texas to apologize to Amber, and possibly to Doctor Gardner, if he would even agree to see her, and finally back to New York to apologize to Robin Hammond who had tried to persuade her not to give up a promising legal career in favor of going on a fool's errand.

While she waited, she packed her bags tightly. Once she made her apologies to her hosts, she would not linger and impose her presence on them any further.

It was not until two hours later that she heard the first tinkling of dishes in the kitchen. As she entered the kitchen, she saw Clara cooking some eggs.

"*Bonjour*, Clara."

Clara turned to Judy with a smile.

"*Bonjour*, Judy! *Entre dans!*"

Clara's demeanor was not that of an insulted host. Was it possible that Jacques had not told his wife of their guest's insult to their hospitality?

Judy smiled in return. "Jacques?"

"*Oui, oui!*" Clara pointed out the window to the courtyard where Jacques was sitting in a lawn chair facing away from the house.

"*Merci, une moment.*"

Keeping her smile, Judy withdrew from the kitchen and went out the back door to the courtyard.

"Jacques?" said she as she approached him from behind.

"*Asseoir,*" he said without turning around and pointing to the lawn chair next to him.

Judy took a deep breath and sat.

There was a long silence as the two faced toward the forest below.

Finally Jacques said," You did not come to see me because you were interested in the French system for administering guilty pleas." He said it with the inflection of a statement, and not a question.

"That's not entirely true, *Inspecteur.* That was part of the reason for contacting both you and the *Inspecteur General.*"

"How so, Mille Alexander? Tell me please."

Judy answered in detail, staring with her involvement as a law student in the Exoneration Clinic at Oliver Wendell Holmes School of Law, and then explaining her interest in the Gardner case in Texas, her subsequent association with Gardner's appointed counsel, Amber Hartman, the interview with Gardner's sister in Galveston, her intent to write an article on plea bargaining, and finally her interview with Gardner himself.

She left out only her later involvement with Timothy Hoxsey, and her subsequent acceptance of his commission to find out what happened to his daughter, Bonnie.

When Jacques did not immediately respond, she added: "I believe Roger Gardner is innocent."

"I see. Very admirable of you to go to all this trouble on behalf of someone you did not even know."

Judy was not sure how to respond to this, and waited.

"You said, Mille Alexander that your interest in studying the French plea bargaining system was only part of the reason why you went to such trouble to contact me. What is the other part?"

"I fear you already know, *Inspecteur.*"

"Tell me about Timothy Hoxsey, Judy."

Judy was gratified that Jacques had reverted to calling her by her first name, but was taken aback by his direct reference to the man who had given her the assignment of finding out what happened to his daughter.

Before she had a chance to answer, Jacques continued:

"For the last nineteen years, Mr. Hoxsey has been sending his agents to this country to extract information from those who investigated his daughter's disappearance. And I was the original investigator assigned to the case. I filed the report of our investigation. "

"And you have stood behind that report for all this time?"

"No, Judy. I did not stand behind my report, and do not stand behind it to this day."

"But what...why...It was your report..."

"My report was rubbish. *Ordures!*"

Judy could now only listen in stunned silence and wait for Jacques to explain.

"I told you last night that in my early days as a young detective I was awarded the Medal of Honor of the National Police for tracking down a most notorious serial killer in Provence. I was the youngest person on the force to ever receive this honor. But in doing so I incurred the enmity of my superiors who had ordered me not to follow several of the leads which ultimately led me to the killer. When I received the award they could not very well say that they had ordered me not to follow the very leads the led me to the killer. But they never forgave me, and did everything in their power to prevent me from advancing in my career."

"Yes, I remember what you told me."

"I am ashamed to say that when I was assigned to the case of Bonnie Hoxsey's disappearance, I was determined not to make the same mistake again. I had just married Clara, wanted to raise a family, and was living off the bottom rung of a detective's salary. I could not afford to alienate a whole new group of superiors who had by that time risen above me."

"Are you saying that you were again told not to follow certain leads in that investigation?"

"Judy, I am reluctant to answer that question, but not because of myself. My career is over. I live on a fixed pension, which is not going to change, whatever I tell you now. But I am concerned about Clara. And I am concerned about you."

"Me? But..."

"If it were just me, I would like nothing more than to clear my own conscience before I face my maker. Like your Mr. Hoxsey, I too do not have so many years left to me."

"I understand you concern about your wife, though perhaps you have overstated it out of your love and concern for her. But surely you can let me judge for myself whether it is worth some risk to myself to help a dying man find out who, and why his most beloved daughter disappeared from this earth; and why a man sitting in a prison in Texas is asking to be put to death so that he can, I believe, answer for the sins of another."

"You are most persuasive, Judy. You would make a good lawyer, which is why I would urge you most strenuously to return to the study of law."

"But you will tell me what you know?'

Just then Clara appeared at the door to the courtyard and called out that breakfast was ready. Jacques waved.

"Let us go to breakfast, Judy. Clara has plans to visit her sister in Saint Jeannet today and will be there most of the day. That will give us the entire afternoon alone to talk. Perhaps you can also tell me what connection the case in Texas has to do with our investigation of the disappearance of Bonnie Hoxsey. If you still want me to tell you everything I know, I will do so, but only after I have apprised you of the risks of acting on what I do tell you."

"So I have not abused your hospitality?"

"*Au Contraire*, Judy. *Pas du tout*. Clara and I are both delighted that you have come to visit. "

"I am so relieved, *Inspecteur*. I was so sure this morning that you would ask me to leave forthwith."

"Clara would be devastated if you could not stay awhile. She is quite taken with you, you know. Nothing would please her more than to have the girl with the goddess face of Marianne, the French symbol of '*Liberte*' grace us with an extended visit."

CHAPTER FORTY-THREE

JANUARY 16

Jacques called out from the kitchen:

"Can I offer you some coffee and one of Clara's raspberry macaroons? There are still several left, and if you don't help me eat them, I fear that I would eat them all and that would not be good for me."

It was mid-morning, and Clara had already left in the Peugeot to visit her sister in Saint Jeannet. Before Clara left, Judy had taken a short jog through a nearby forest path trying to clear her mind. After freshening up and changing into jeans and her Catalina sweatshirt and trainers, she had taken her place in the peacock chair, waiting for Jacques to join her. Now that she was close to getting some real information, she was apprehensive about what Jacques might confide about the Bonnie investigation—if he was still willing to do so. She wondered if she was really ready to hear it, or if she even wanted to hear it.

Up until now it had all been rather fun and exhilarating—travelling on yachts and private jets, going to embassy balls, shopping, meeting interesting and important people, and seeing interesting places. Now, she wondered whether Jacques' revelations would inspire her to carry on with her quest for justice—which Robin was sure was quixotic—or alarm her to the point where she would finally recognize the reality that she was just a first year law student with no particular investigative skills, and give up. What was she really doing here? If nothing else, she now told herself, she hoped to at least get information that might either confirm or refute the idea which she nursed since leaving Mont St. Michel: where Bonnie's body would be found.

Jacques emerged from the kitchen.

"Judy?"

"Oh, sorry, *Inspecteur*," replied Judy, awakened from her deep thoughts. "Actually, instead of coffee, do you still have any of that herbal tea—what was it?—butterfly pea..."

"Butterfly pea flower. *Mais oui*, I will bring it for you."

"And as for the macaroons—perhaps we could share one? They are delicious, but perhaps that way neither of us would feel too guilty."

"An excellent idea. I will be right back."

Jacques retreated back to the kitchen and returned with two small plates, on each of which was a half a macaroon.

"The tea will be ready in a few minutes," said Jacques, handing Judy one of the plates, and taking his plate back to the couch where he sat.

"*Inspecteur*, before we begin, I just have one question."

"*Bien sur.*"

"It's about Clara. I have to ask. Does she know anything at all about the Bonnie investigation that you undertook nineteen years ago? I mean did you talk about it when you were investigating, or have you talked to her about it since then?"

Jacques shook his head and said:

"The answer is no. From the first day of our marriage I promised myself that I would never burden her with my work. Much of what I saw was much too horrible to bring home. I loved her too much, and still do. And it has worked out better that way. I learned—I tried, anyway—to let my home be my sanctuary, to leave my cares, my apprehensions, my misgivings at the office and on the field. Without preserving my home as my sanctuary, I would never have preserved my sanity—or my job for that matter, such as it was."

"But you said you needed her support..."

"*Effectivement*, I did. She could always tell when I was distressed, and in the early days of our marriage would ask if I wanted to talk about it. I would always tell her 'no', and she understood. Since those days she has never asked."

"It must have been difficult to not have someone to talk to, to confide in, and to help relieve your stress."

"To burden her with my cares would only have increased my stress and anxiety. I had plenty of other matters to confide in with her. Aside from the horrors of my work, we have kept no secrets from each other. She did not need to hear about the bloody bodies I saw at grisly crime scenes, nor of the pressures that came down upon me from my superiors to do things which I thought were wrong."

"She is very fortunate. As are you, *Inspecteur*."

"I am, *effectivement*. And you are kind to say so. I cannot tell you how many of my colleagues have suffered divorce and estrangement from their spouses. I believe Clara and I found the proper way—I did not bring my problems home, and she provided me with the support, sanctuary, and respite I needed to keep doing what I was doing."

"The police force did not provide some kind of counseling services where you could at least talk to someone about the stresses created by your job?"

Jacques shook his head and stifled a cynical-laden laugh as he said:

"There were services. But there was never a guarantee of confidentiality, or at least any that I could completely trust. And on my salary in the early days, and even after, I could not afford a private counsellor."

"I cannot imagine how difficult it must have been."

"It still is."

There was a long cause before Jacques continued:

"I must apologize to you, Judy. I did not mean to be abrupt last night, or this morning. It was not until we talked a little that I realized that you might just be the one person in whom I might, after all these years, confide."

"*Inspecteur*, I am flattered that you might think so, but I would not want you to...I mean I am just..."

"After you went on your run this morning after breakfast, I confess that I did have second thoughts about confiding with you about the Hoxsey investigation. But after watching you scamper down our path through the woods, I thought about it further. I finally realized that perhaps you were really were the God-send I have needed for a very long time. My concern now is that if I now un-burden myself, I may be simply transferring that burden to you."

Judy nervously took a bite of the macaroon as she considered how to respond. From the kitchen came the whistle of the boiling water for her tea, giving her a few extra moments to think what to say.

"Just a minute," said Jacques. "I will get your tea."

When he returned with the tea, Judy said:

"*Inspecteur*, I need to know. Not just me, but two other people who have suffered greatly also need to know. I can promise you that anything you tell me I will keep in confidence."

As if to underscore her words, she took the notebook which she had carried with her when she took her seat on the peacock chair, put it in her tiny Baggallini bag and zipped it up.

"No notes," she said.

CHAPTER FORTY-FOUR

JULY 31, 1944

The lone Schutzaffel truck sped west along the only paved roads that ran from Strasbourg to Normandy. It was the dead of night, as few Germany military vehicles dared to travel on the roads near Normandy during the day when allied fighters and bombers strafed anything that moved with a hundred miles of the beaches. General Rommel himself had learned that the hard way when his halftrack was attacked and he was seriously injured.

Major Schneider and Lieutenant Wagner were the only passengers in the truck. The chaos in occupied France was only now getting started, and would soon reach a crescendo. Both men knew that time was critical. It would be only days, perhaps only hours before American troops arrived at Mont St. Michel.

Schneider's S.S. rank, and his orders signed by no less than the Reichsfuhrer himself would guarantee him safe passage to Mont St. Michel as long as he travelled only by night and with his headlights off. German soldiers and sentries stopped him at numerous checkpoints, but all waved the S.S. Major and his adjutant through. Civilians were not even allowed on the roads at night.

"Stop here, Otto," said Schneider. "Call Richter on the radio. Make sure he will be there when we come, and tell him to expect us no later than 4:00 A.M. I'm going to check in the back."

While Otto made his call, Schneider got out of the passenger seat and opened the back of the truck. He knew the large metal ammunition box was still there, but he wanted to see it again for himself.

He unlatched the box, and there it was: fifty-two of the thirteen kilogram gold bars, four bags of rare gold coins, three large bags of diamonds, another two bags of precious stones, emeralds, sapphire, and rubies, and one bag of platinum bars—all untraceable. By the time Otto's grandson Hans Wagner was forty years old, this trove would be worth between 200 and 250 million dollars.

But there also was a leather file which contained documents which Schneider was sure would someday be worth far more. He leafed through them once more to be sure they too were all there.

Satisfied that all the treasure was accounted for, he tied the rear truck flaps, shut the rear door, and climbed back into the cabin.

"Is Richter there and ready?"

"Yes, he is there. But if you can't be there well before dawn, he says he will have to leave."

"Then step on it, Lieutenant."

"Yes, Major."

There was a long silence as the truck sped on.

"Is there something the matter, Otto?" Richter asked.

"Was it necessary to shoot Commandant Hartjenstaf?"

"Of course it was. He showed us the entire stash in the underground bunker. Like our men, he saw us load everything into all the trucks, except this one. Commandant Hartjenstaf and the men knew that you and I had orders to continue on the next day to the Mont in the empty truck. But after I sent the men to the barracks on the other side of the camp, the Commandant saw you and me loading this truck with our selected treasures from the other trucks. He would have later learned that we took that truck to the Mont. He would have notified S.S. Headquarters immediately."

"How can you be sure that none of the men will notice the lightened loads in their trucks?"

"Because in terms of volume, our treasure was a very small percentage of the total volume to be sent to Berlin. As you know, we were careful to redistribute the gold bars into the other empty ammunition boxes, then cover them with a tarp and seal them. I also unloaded the full and heavy ammunition boxes in our truck into the other trucks."

"But the inventory. When the trucks arrive at the Reich bank won't it be noticed that the contents of the other trucks do not match the documented inventory of valuables taken from the camp bunker?"

"You forget that I am the one who prepared the inventory. The inventory will reveal no discrepancy."

"But to shoot the Commandant..."

"You will recall that I did so only after all the men and other trucks had left the camp. The three remaining camp staff left with the men in the other trucks. It was then just the three of us. We held a court martial in the Commandant's office. We committed no murder. You read the charges: failure to secure the camp as ordered; failure to raze it and insure that no bodies were left for the allies to find when they overran the camp; and corruption. Have you forgotten that we found a bag of gold coins in the Commandant's desk?"

"But surely the Commandant will be missed."

"Of course he will. But I remind you that I have had access to documents at Headquarters, including a document charging the Commandant with corruption. I have in my file the authorization to hold a court martial and to execute the Commandant if corruption could be proven. It was, and the execution was carried out. Even if a discrepancy in the inventory is ever found, it will be attributed to the Commandant."

"But if we are stopped, if our truck is searched before we get to the Mont..."

"Then, my dear Otto, we are screwed. If that happens I have my pistol, and as agreed, I will shoot you and then myself. But we have gotten this far without being stopped or searched. No sentry or orderly is going to stop two S.S. officers carrying out their orders. I am more worried that if we do not arrive at the Mont before dawn, an allied aircraft will see and strafe or bomb us on the road."

There was another long silence.

"Otto, now is the time to be strong. It is a matter of days now before the Americans and British break out of the Cotentin Peninsula. Our intelligence informs us that thousands of allied planes are preparing a massive bombardment of our front lines. Once they break through, the allied armies will spread out all over France. Paris will fall quickly. I know the Americans. If they catch us it will be the noose. You think we are the only ones looting these treasures? I have word that Hermann Goering has plans to raze his mansion—Karinhall—and hide his looted treasures in secret forest bunkers to retrieve after the war. It's every man for himself now."

"But why do we have to bury this stash at Mont St. Michel? Can't we just bury it in some secret place in the forest or dump it into a big lake somewhere? Then come back and find it after the war is over?"

"No, Otto. First of all, you'll never find it. It won't ever be safe. If people find you dredging a lake, it will be reported to the allied occupation forces. This way, we—and only we will always know exactly where it is."

"But how will we ever get access to it?"

"Now you know why I chose you to be part of this plan. Isn't your uncle the head of a large salvage and construction firm associated with I.G. Farben?"

"Yes, but..."

"The day will come, perhaps years after the war, when re-construction will be necessary on the Mont. The Grand Terrace will someday need shoring up. Some Construction company will be commissioned to undertake the task. Until them, Otto, only we will know exactly where this treasure is."

"Just us? What about Richter?"

"He will know. He is trustworthy and part of this plan. He and I have been planning this for many months."

"So just the three of us? What about Richter's three men who are still on the Mont and who will help us carry and bury the box?"

"They will not see inside the box. They will not know what is in it."

"But surely they will suspect."

"You are right, Otto. It may then be necessary to conduct another court-martial."

The truck arrived at the causeway well before dawn. Unteroffizier Richter and his three remaining men were waiting at the gate. Richter led the truck up the Grand Rue to the Abbey entrance.

"Do you have the ropes and cart?" Schneider asked

"*Yawohl, Major!*"

From there it took the efforts of all six men to pull and carry the ammunition box to the Grand Terrace.

Minutes before the rising sun, the ammunition box was lowered into the waiting hole, and covered with rubble, stones, and tile—where it would stay for many years to come.

CHAPTER FORTY-FIVE

JANUARY 17

Jacques brought out a file.

"Let us go into the kitchen, so I can lay out these documents."

Judy followed him to the kitchen table.

"Let's see. This is my report. I was called to the Mont on March 18..."

"*Inspecteur*, I actually have a copy of your report."

"Oh yes. Of course. Courtesy of Mr. Hoxsey I presume. But that is only the official report which was approved by the *Inspecteur* General. Here is the part which was exorcised from my report."

He handed Judy several pages which Judy had never seen before, and which she was sure Timothy hadn't either, or he would have provided her with them. Jacques waited while Judy perused it.

"As you can see, my investigation led directly to Hans Wagner—and not just because he accompanied Bonnie Hoxsey to the Mont on the evening in which she disappeared."

"What other evidence did you have, then?"

"For over a year I had been investigating the O.W.K.K. Construction firm on suspicion of bid-rigging, and connections to organized crime. They had been outbidding competitors, some bids by only small margins, and several competing firms asked the Inspector General to look into it."

"And he assigned you to the investigation?"

"Yes. I began investigating the backgrounds of several of the owners of O.W.K.K., and what I found was disturbing. Hans Wagner's grandfather, Otto Wagner, founded O.W.K.K. in 1948 in collaboration with several people he knew who worked at I. G. Farben during the war. As you know, I. G. Farben produced much of the poison gas that was used to kill inmates of the concentration camps. One of those camps, Natzweiller-Struthof, was, I am ashamed to say, located on French soil, near Strasbourg. In investigating the background of Otto Wagner—he died in 1959—I found documents linking him to membership in the S.S. Of course, this did not necessarily implicate his grandson, but I followed these links to several of the officials in our own organization here in France."

"The French National Police?"

"Yes, and also to owners and C.E.O.'s of other construction firms—some in France, and some in Germany. I also discovered that there had been a number of previous complaints about O.W.K.K., all of which had been cut short or quashed on order of higher ups in the police."

"Do you think some of them were...were..."

"On the take? I suspected it, yes. But when I filed a confidential internal report linking members of the Wagner family to these important people, I was ordered, without explanation, to drop my investigations. At the time, I was in no position to question my orders, and despite my suspicions, I complied and thought no more of it."

"Until..."

"Until the disappearance of the American girl Bonnie Hoxsey."

"Why? What did she have to do with your bid-rigging investigations?"

"Up until her disappearance, I had no reason to question my own actions. The truth is that I hold myself partly responsible for Bonnie Hoxsey's death."

"How, *Inspecteur?*" Judy could hardly believe what he was saying.

Jacques took a deep breath before continuing. "I have never told anyone this. Bonnie Hoxsey came to my attention through an informant whom I had placed in the offices of O.W.K.K.. He was a small time criminal, a drug user who occasionally dealt heroine, and was facing a number of years in prison. In exchange for dropping the charges, he agreed to apply for a job—a filing clerk—at O.W.K.K. and inform me of anything that might assist me in my bid-rigging investigation. He was hired. In the course of that job he did not find any incriminating documents or letters, but he did report to me in passing that an attractive young American girl had been hired as an assistant to Hans Wagner, and that Hans seemed to be enamored of the girl. My informant said he often saw the two of them leaving the offices together. On other occasions he saw the two of them holding hands, kissing out in the parking lot, going off together in Hans' B.M.W."

"How long did that go on?"

"For some time, and I asked my informant to give me regular reports. After some time, it occurred to me that if anyone would be in a position to come across incriminating evidence against O.W.K.K., it would be this young girl. So I arranged for one of my officers to intercept her one morning on the way to work, and ask if she would consider helping the police on an important investigation. She had no way of knowing at that point that the investigation had anything to do..."

"With her boyfriend."

"Of course I never thought she would agree, and I was surprised that she agreed to meet with me. She was an amazing young woman, and actually excited about doing something adventuresome for the French police. She was appalled, of course, when I told her that we suspected Hans and his family of ties to organized crime, and even more appalled when I told her of the Wagner family's association with former Nazis and collaborators."

"So she agreed to help you?"

"*Dieu aide moi!*" I am now ashamed to say that she did. I should never have involved this beautiful, innocent, young woman. I told her she would be doing a great service to France. I was so eager to further my career and break open this bid-rigging scheme that I accepted her help. I did not seek approval from my superiors, because I was sure they would never approve.

I also did not know which of my superiors were involved in the previous cover-ups of my original bid-rigging investigation. ”

“What did you ask her to do, exactly?”

“Only to keep her eyes open, especially when she went to his house and stayed for the weekend, which she often did—to be on the lookout for any letters, documents that she might see lying around, or telephone conversations she might overhear.”

“And did she ever find anything?”

“Not for several months. Then the night before she and Hans went to Mont St. Michel, she called me at the unlisted number I gave her. She said that she had been staying at Hans' house during the previous week and that Hans had a visitor in his study. She was watching television in the downstairs living room when she heard shouting upstairs. She took this opportunity to go upstairs and listen outside the study door. She couldn't understand everything they were saying, but she did distinctly hear the words '*das ist erpressung!*' and a reference to some letter.”

“That was all?”

“When she heard them approaching the study door, she hurried back downstairs. Both men then came down the staircase, rushed passed the living room, and took their argument outside. She looked out the window and saw that they were still arguing next to the visitor's car. She then quickly scampered upstairs to see if the letter the men had been shouting about was lying around or on the desk.”

“And was it?”

“She said there was a letter on the desk, just lying open. It seemed to be a very old letter, written in German. Fortunately Bonnie had a conversational knowledge of German, and also an excellent memory. She knew she wouldn't have time to find a pen and paper to copy the letter before Hans returned, so she tried to quickly memorize as much of contents of the letter as she could before he returned. It consisted of a list of names, and a location where could be found a trove that would enable the entire family, and its future generations, to live in comfort for the rest of their lives if it could somehow be accessed.”

"What does '*erpressung*' mean?"

"It is the German word for 'blackmail.' Bonnie knew the word. She said she tried to leave the study before he came up the stairs, but he intercepted her at the top of the stairs. She had closed the study door when she exited, but had forgotten that the door was open when she entered. She was sure he noticed. At first he was angry, and asked her what she was doing. She made some excuse about wanting to find a pen to write down a recipe that had been on the television, but she doubted if he believed her. He then went over to the desk and looked at the letter, and then looked at her suspiciously. She felt like he wanted to ask her if she had read it, but then he didn't, so she felt like she had gotten away with it."

"Did she give you the names she could remember from the letter?"

"Yes, I wrote them down. I made a memo of everything she told me." Jacques leafed through his file to look for the memo.

"And the location of the 'trove.' Did she tell you that?"

"Let me see. I don't remember. Yes, here it is. I had completely forgotten it. The 'trove' was at Mont St. Michel."

"And you did not think that reference was significant, given that it was at Mont St. Michel that Bonnie disappeared?"

"At the time, not at all. There were many treasures on Mont St. Michel, and all except a few in the Chapel of St. Pierre— some silver crosses and statues—had all been relocated off the Mont before the Germans came to occupy it. So the reference didn't make any sense to me, and to be honest, I thought she had just misread the location on the letter."

"There is nothing more specific about the location other than 'Mont St. Michel?'"

"I don't think so. No, wait a minute. I did write down the 'Grand Terrace', as well, but of course that made no sense at all, and still doesn't. There are no treasures on the Grand Terrace."

"Did you write down who signed the letter?"

Again, Jaquez examined the memo. "Yes, she remembered that as well—Otto Wagner."

"Wasn't that the name of Hans' grandfather?

"Yes, as a matter of fact it is—though it is not an uncommon name."

"And the date of the letter? Was that on the letter, and did she tell it to you?"

"Yes, I did write it down. 1948."

"*Inspecteur*, I don't suppose you could let me have that memo?"

Jacques hesitated. "I'd better not, Judy. You can copy it if you wish."

"I will. Thanks. But, *Inspecteur*, do you know what this memo means—especially the list of names? It means that Hans Wagner not only had the opportunity to murder Bonnie, but he also had a motive."

"I thought it might, and reported the contents of the memo internal report to the *Inspecteur General*. But the opportunity was not so clear. You will recall from the official that all the witnesses at the Sacre Mont said that Hans had remained in the restaurant for almost an hour before leaving to look for Bonnie."

"So he could have had a confederate, who first called her to draw her out of the restaurant and held her, and then Hans went out and killed her."

"But as you know, a body has never been found. There is no place on the Mont where a body could be hidden. And the video-tapes of people leaving the Mont in the hours and days after Bonnie's disappearance showed no indication that the body was taken off the Mont."

"But why was the motive never mentioned in the report?"

"The *Inspecteur General* excised it from the official report. He said that Bonnie's call to me was insufficient to establish a motive. In fact, he admonished me most strenuously for using a young innocent American girl as an informant, and told me that if it ever got out that I did so, it would have serious diplomatic repercussions—not only with the United States, but with our

European allies. He also warned that if I said one word about it, that he would have me fired and prosecuted."

"For what?"

"It doesn't matter. I was in the wrong and I knew it."

Judy tried to manage a smile, but it was difficult. She now understood the burden that Jacques had suffered for the past nineteen years.

"*Inspecteur*, I need to make several calls and texts. Have you heard that there was a recent bidding competition for the reconstruction of the Grand Terrace at Mont St. Michel?"

"I did hear of it, but as you know I'm retired now. I don't know the details."

"So you wouldn't know have information that O.W.K.K. won the bid, and by a narrowly higher bid."

"I've been out of the loop for years, Judy. Is that important?"

"Would you know, or have you heard that there was any investigation of that bidding competition?"

Jacques shook his head. "I wouldn't know. As I said, I've been out of the loop for years. Do you think that's important?"

"I believe it may be. *Inspecteur*. I need to get going making my calls. But first, what can you tell me about this Hans character?"

"I remember he was good looking, but arrogant and young when I interviewed him during my investigation. I recall that his age was twenty-five or six—so that would make him about forty-five or so now. "

"What more do you know about him?"

"I learned that he was a rather notorious..."

"Womanizer?"

"Yes, I think that's what you Americans call men like that. Always want to be seen with the most attractive and beautiful women to feed their ego as movers and shakers."

"I thought as much. OK, if I'm lucky I will get responses to all of my calls and texts—hopefully within the hour. When does Clara get back?

"I think she may be staying with her sister until after dinner, so a couple of hours."

"Perhaps you could rest awhile while you wait for her. I will need to talk to you very shortly."

Jacques nodded.

Judy returned to her room and sent two text messages. The first was to Timothy:

> *YOU DID A WONDERFUL JOB CONNECTING ME WITH THE INSPECTOR GENERAL IN PARIS, WHO IN TURN LED ME TO RETIRED INSPECTOR MONTAGNE. I MAY BE GETTING CLOSE, BUT NEED YOU TO PERFORM ANOTHER MIRACLE: WHERE CAN I "ACCIDENTALLY" RUN INTO HANS WAGNER AT SOME MAJOR EVENT—VERY SOON.*

To her admirer Jules, whose number she had been careful to keep in her notes, she texted:

> *JULES, PLEASE CALL ME AT THE NUMBER BELOW AS SOON AS YOU CAN. I NEED TO KNOW WHAT THE PROTOCOL WAS FOR BURYING YOUR MOTHER AT THE CEMETERY OF THE CHAPEL OF ST. PIERRE. ALSO, I NEED YOU TO CONDUCT A METICULOUS INSPECTION OF THE TILE, SURFACING AND REPAIR RECORDS OF THE GRAND TERRACE. PLEASE CALL ME AS SOON AS YOU CAN. YOUR FRIEND, JUDY*

Her final text was to Amber:

> *AMBER, I'M GETTING CLOSE. COULD YOU TELL ME AS SOON AS YOU CAN WHAT THE PENALTY IS IN TEXAS FOR ACCES.S.ORY AFTER THE FACT, AND ALSO THE RESULTS OF GARDNER'S MOST RECENT PHYSICAL EXAMINATION. ALSO, PLEASE HAVE POLICE CHECK IF THERE IS AN EXTRA BULLET*

HOLE IN THE HOUSE AT THE CRIME SCENE.
THANKS, JUDY

CHAPTER FORTY-SIX

JANUARY 17-18

Clara returned home a little after eight o'clock from her sister's. After a half hour or so of conversation in the salon in which neither Judy or Jacques brought up the matter of the Bonnie investigation, "good nights" were said and Clara retired to the bedroom. Before Jacques followed her, Judy whispered to Jacques:

"*Inspecteur*, one moment before you retire? I am still waiting on answers to some of the texts I sent a few hours ago, and one return phone call. Depending on those answers, if I receive them tonight, I will need to leave here immediately."

"Tonight? *Vraiment?* But...Clara will be most disappointed..."

"I don't have time to explain, but after what you told me this afternoon, everything fits into place—not only with what happened to Bonnie, but also why there is a man in Texas willing to be put to death."

"What do you mean? I mean how could you possibly ..."

"I wrote everything down," she said as she thrust a sealed envelope into his hand. But I still need one more piece of the puzzle, and to get it I will need your help."

"I don't know what I can do..."

"You still have some contacts with people in the police force whom you can trust, do you not? Maybe a favor or two you can call in?"

Jacques thought for a moment. "*Peut-etre*, but I would need more information..."

"It's all in the letter. For one thing I know where Bonnie is buried and I need it to be confirmed right away."

"*Quoi?*

"I will tap lightly on your door before I leave to say goodbye. You said Clara is not a light sleeper?"

"*Oui, mais...*"

"I could be leaving even within the hour. Don't read the letter until I leave."

It was 3:00 A.M. when Judy tapped on her hosts' bedroom door. Jacques immediately appeared at the bedroom door.

"You are leaving?' he whispered.

"Yes, I must be at the Nice Cote d'Azur Airport by 7:00 A.M., so I must go. Can you help me with my bags?"

"*Bien Sur,*" said Jacques as he carried Judy's two large bags to the Renault and placed them in the trunk.

Judy rolled down the window. "Please text me the information I asked for in the letter as soon as you obtain it. Then...please, *Inspecteur*, use those results to do everything you can to obtain an exhumation order as soon as you possibly can and text me the results."

Jacques shook his head. "Such things take time..."

Judy touched his hand which rested on the car door window. "I know. But I have faith in you. It will be your chance to clear your mind of this case that has been such a burden on you all these years."

"I will do everything I can."

"Please give Clara my apologies for leaving like this, and give her my thanks for her kind hospitality.'

"I will. Goodbye, Judy."

CHAPTER FORTY-SEVEN

JANUARY 18-19

Judy sat in the VIP Lounge of the Business Terminal of the Cote d'Azur airport and looked out to the tarmac at the morning arrival of private jets.

While she waited, she re-read Timothy's reply to the text she had sent him the night before:

SORRY FOR DELAY, BUT IT TOOK TIME. INFORMATION IS THAT WAGNER WILL BE ARRIVING IN SANTA BARBARA FROM SAN DIEGO ON HIS YACHT ON JANUARY 20 FOR THE INTERNATIONAL FILM FESTIVAL. THERE WILL BE A GRAND GALA AND RECEPTION AT THE RITZ-CARLTON BACARA ON HOLLISTER IN GOLETA ON THE 20th. CHANDLER WILL MEET YOU AT THE AZUR D'COTE AIRPORT AT 7:00A.M. THIS MORNING, COMING FROM PARIS. REFUEL AT TETERBORO. ARRIVE SANTA BARBARA AIRPORT AT 6:00 OR 7:00 P.M.. I AM ON MY WAY FROM LONG BEACH TO MEET YOU IN SANTA BARBARA.

It was only minutes after she recognized the G500 gleaming in the morning sun on the Tarmac that Chandler appeared at the lounge doors and looked about.

Judy waved to attract his attention.

"Good morning, Judy," said Chandler. "Are you ready?"

"Yes, I'm ready. I will need to make some calls from the satellite phone on the plane after we're in the air. I don't think my cell phone will work over the Atlantic."

"No problem. G500's come equipped with satellite navigation and telephones."

"Then let's go!"

CHAPTER FORTY-EIGHT

JANUARY 19

Due to delays in refueling in Teterboro, the G500 did not touch down at Santa Barbara until dusk.

Timothy was there to meet Judy as she clambered into the waiting Black Land Rover. Chandler followed with bags.

"Welcome back, Judy," said Timothy, kissing her hand. "I trust you were able to get a good rest on the way back."

"Thankfully, yes. I didn't get any sleep last night, but thankfully I slept soundly on the plane most of today. We were delayed in Teterboro, but I was able to make a number of calls from there while we waited. It was easier that way..."

"I trust you have good news for me, then..."

"None that I can report right now, Timothy. But based on the information I received from my phone calls this afternoon, I hope I shall very soon."

"I don't suppose you can enlighten me now?"

"I'd like to wait. I have to be sure. Please be patient. It's possible I am wrong, but I don't think so. I'm waiting on some information I hope to receive tonight. I will need your help on several things, though."

"You know that all my resources are at your disposal. But is it really necessary to face-off with Hans Wagner? I think it could be dangerous."

"I may not be able to. Just because I'll be at the Gala..."

"You've already accomplished more than all my private investigators and researchers have done in the past nineteen years. I told you before that you are my last hope."

"What danger would Hans pose to me personally, here in the U.S.A.? I mean there will be thousands of people around here in the next week."

"Like me, he has his own agents, and I have not been able to track them all. There is one piece of information that might interest you, not with regards to Bonnie, but in regards to that Texas case you were telling me about."

"Really!" exclaimed Judy. "You must tell me! It could be one of the remaining pieces I'm looking for!"

"I don't know if it is true or not. I wouldn't even have discovered it had you not asked me to track the whereabouts of Hans Wagner, and I came across her as I was doing so."

"It's about the woman who is accompanying Hans on his yacht."

"Yes?"

"Would you believe it's...?"

"Timothy, it's not..."

"Yep. Mrs. Madeleine Otto, formerly Madeleine Berger."

"Jesus!"

"Does that little piece of information fit into your puzzle?"

"It certainly does. But I'm going to have to re-arrange some of my notes to take this in. So they're coming together, in his yacht? They're romantically involved?"

"That I'm afraid I couldn't tell you. But except for some of the female kitchen and cabin help on board, she's the only female on board. So yes, I would guess it's either a romantic or business relationship—more than likely some of both."

The Range Rover now drew up to the Bacara entrance.

"I will only be a few doors down from you," said Timothy. Chandler will get you to your room. Once you're settled in, you can come join me in my suite and let me know what else you need."

"Actually, I've written it all down." She handed him another sealed envelope she had prepared while waiting on the tarmac in Teterboro. "I think I'll turn in tonight and maybe head off the jet lag I know is coming. How about breakfast tomorrow morning?"

"Sure. I'll text you my suite number."

"Great. And you'll be going to the reception tomorrow night?"

"Yes, that's why I did everything I could to get here tonight. Even so, I have only tomorrow afternoon to get ready. You have my invitation?"

"I'll have it for you when I see you in the morning."

"Do you think Madeleine might be there with Wagner at the reception? That might make things more difficult."

"Probably. Just be careful. Do you know what you'll be wearing?"

Judy resisted the inclination to scold him about his concern about her clothes. "Well, I don't have time to go shopping, so the black dress I wore at the Danish Embassy will have to do."

"No doubt it will. Tomorrow morning, then."

Judy retired to her room, but wanted to make one more phone call before sleeping off her jet leg.

"Professor?" she asked when Robin Hammond answered the phone after the second ring. "I'm sorry it's so late. Were you sleeping?"

"Yes, but not very well. Where are you?"

"I'm in Santa Barbara, California, if you believe it."

"Back in the good old U.S.A. Thank God!"

Judy spent the next hour filling him in on everything that had happened since they last talked and what information she had received.

"And on that information alone you believe that you know why Gardner has asked for the death penalty, where Bonnie's body is, who killed her, and why?"

"Yes I do. All of that. But I'm not saying anything until I get three texts—I'm hoping to get them tonight. I have my phone on peak volume so I won't sleep through them if they come through."

There was a long pause before Robin said, "Judy, have I ever told you that you are...quite extraordinary?"

"Why, because I came up with 'tell me no lice'?"

"Partly, yes. But you never cease to amaze me."

"And...?"

"What will you do now?"

"There also one more thing I need to do."

"Yes?"

"I'm almost afraid to tell you for fear that you will scold me."

"I know better now. Please tell me."

"I'm going to a reception at the Bacara resort. I'm going to confront Hans Wagner."

"Judy, based on everything you've told me, do you think that's wise? If he's as dangerous as you suspect..."

"See, that's why I didn't want to tell you."

"Sorry, it's just that, well, you're almost home now. At this point can't you just tell Hoxsey what you've found out, and if you've discovered criminal activity just report it to the police."

"What the French police? Professor—sorry, I guess I can't get used to not calling you that—I'll be all right. And if I am right about everything, I just may be able to get back to school for this semester."

"You've already missed two weeks."

"If I could register, I could get the books and notes..."

"Forget about that. You're staying at the Bacara in Santa Barbara, right?"

"Yes."

"I'm coming out there."

"What? Professor—Robin—that's crazy. Besides, by the time you get here tomorrow night, I'll already be at the reception."

"Until I get there, please be careful. I'll see you when I see you!" Click.

Judy shook her head, pulled up the covers, and went instantly to sleep.

CHAPTER FORTY-NINE

JANUARY 20

Judy woke at 5:30 the next morning. She had not gotten any of the phone or text replies she was expecting, but hoped that she would receive them during the day before the reception that evening. After throwing on her jeans and t-shirt, she walked down the hall and knocked on Timothy's door. After several moments, Timothy appeared at the door looking bleary-eyed.

"Morning, Timothy. Sorry to wake you so early, but I have a lot to do before the reception tonight."

"Come in. Won't you come in for breakfast? You were going to fill me in."

"I can only stay for a minute. I need to collate my notes and field a number of calls and texts I'm expecting during the day. I'll be able to fill you in a lot more after I receive them."

"And you really think you need to interface with Wagner? I'm not sure that's a good idea. If you could just tell me what you had in mind..."

"Timothy, "she said firmly. "We talked about this. You signed me up for all this, and now you have to let me do it my way." If you only knew, you wouldn't let me out of this room.

"I haven't had a chance to line up an escort for you. I guess Chandler could..."

Judy chuckled at the suggestion. "No thanks."

"I've got several men close by in the area who will be watching over you—a couple of them will be at the reception, in case anything happens...maybe one of them could..."

"I'm going to have to go this one alone. Your men need to keep their distance."

"I'm in awe of your confidence."

"Don't be. If I fail tonight, I'm afraid all I have is just speculation, which is why I need confirmation."

"And you think only Wagner can provide it?"

"I should be getting some confirmation today from other sources, but I really need Wagner's confirmation."

"And if you don't get it..."

"What's that they say in all the movies? Failure is..."

"Yeah...not an option."

"Something like that."

"OK, Judy, now you're scaring me. Look, I know I dragged you into this. I practically made you an offer you couldn't refuse. I was so desperate to find my daughter's killer. But I'll be honest. I'm having second thoughts now. If something happens to you..."

"Timothy, stop! Now will you be at the reception?"

"Yes, of course. But I'll keep my distance. What will you wear tonight?

"I have no time to shop for clothes today."

"I could have someone..."

"No. Your little black dress will do just fine."

"I'm sure it will. All right. Looks like you're calling the shots tonight—against my better judgment."

"Good. And oh, I almost forgot. Did you get me that little item I asked you for?"

"Yes, I have it. My top security man delivered it to me last night. Hold on, I'll get it."

Judy tapped her feet impatiently as she waited.

Timothy returned from the bedroom with a small velveteen bag about the size of a cigarette case. Judy slipped it into her little Baggallini.

"I'm not sure if I'll need it", said she, "but I want to have it in case."

"I won't even ask. The directions are inside the bag. You should probably have a gun too."

"Don't need it. I have my handy..." She pulled out her tiny pepper spray canister.

"I thought you might say that. But I insist you also take this." He handed her a tiny earphone. "Insert this in your ear when you want to communicate with me. It also has a very sensitive microphone so that I can hear what anyone is saying to you within ten feet or so—unless there is a lot of crowd noise in which case I may not understand what is being said."

"Well, its' very small. I guess my little bag can fit it in."

"Until tonight, then."

CHAPTER FIFTY

JANUARY 20

Wanting to arrive at the reception with as much anonymity as possible, Judy took two Ubers—one late that afternoon which took her high up to the Belmond El Canto, where she sat on the veranda sipping a Voss and gazing out at the sea beyond; and the second back to the Bacara, fashionably late for the film festival reception.

As she had hoped, all her anticipated texts and return calls had come through to her by noon. Much to her satisfaction, though not to her surprise, all of them served to confirm what had previously been only speculations on her part. It remained now only to bring everything to a final conclusion.

Once you eliminate the impossible, whatever remains, no matter how improbable, must be the truth.

Dressed in her little black dress, Manolo Blahniks, and simulated pearl necklace, Judy stepped out into the reception hall and showed her invitation. Struggling not to totter in her four inch heels—only the second time she had ever worn them—she began to weave her way through the crowd of elegantly turned out guests. Without the benefit of a consort to make introductions, she wandered between various guest clusters, striking up conversations where she could and pretending to sip the champagne offered by the roving servers in white coats and black ties.

It did not take long before she attracted the attentions of would-be producers, unattached males, and agents who, gathering around her after cutting her from a conversation cluster, inquired if she was in any of the films on the festival lineup, and if she was not, inevitably offering their cards.

Feigning a touch of tipsiness, she took the cards with a flirtatious smile, and returned the flattery by thanking them and gushing how impressed she was by the titles on the cards.

After an hour of this, however, she realized that she was no closer to Hans Wagner, and in fact was not sure she would recognize him if she saw him. There was a picture of him in one of Timothy's files which she had tried to memorize, but it was not a recent one and not of high quality. She began to worry that for some reason he wasn't even at the reception.

Escaping from one such coterie with the excuse of needing to powder her nose, she retired to the foyer of the resort's ladies' room and inserted into her right ear the tiny earphone Timothy had given her.

"Timothy, can you hear me?" she whispered loudly.

After some static came, "Yes, where are you?"

"Second floor ladies' room. Is he here?"

"Yes. Go downstairs and cross over to the fountain. He's standing in the far corner beyond the fountain about ten feet from the bar."

"Is Madeleine with him?"

"She was, but I don't see her now. Right now there's a couple standing next to him—the woman is in a red dress—and another tall man with silver hair."

"Got it. Bye."

"Wait..." Too late.

On her way to the fountain, Judy looked for a group of mostly men who would be in sight of the bar. Just at the time she needed to find one such grouping, there was suddenly just open space.

Judy stood in the middle of this momentary clearing, took a glass of champagne from a passing server, and turned around as if looking for someone. It was not long before a small late twenties man with shoulder length black hair approached her. His name tag read: "Arthur Lash, Aurora Horizons Entertainment."

"Looking for someone?" he asked.

"Hi, yes, I'm afraid I've lost my date."

"I'm sure he'll show up. Can I get anything for you?"

"Oh, thank you. I'm afraid I've already had too much champagne."

At this point, young Arthur was joined by two more men, older and more impressive looking, each with name tags indicating high positions in the entertainment business.

As a coterie began forming around her, Judy looked beyond them toward the bar. And then she saw him—standing next to him was the woman in the red dress, confirming her identification. The woman was elderly, definitely not Madeleine. Shifting slightly to the left of one of the men in her coterie, she came into Hans Wagner's direct line of sight, now only about fifteen steps away.

Hans looked at her, smiled, and raised his glass.

Eye contact was made when Judy returned both the smile and raised her champagne glass.

Judy realized now that her immediate challenge was to retain the attention of the men around her. She knew that it was not enough that she be alluring; Hans must see her as being desired by other men—the better to both inflame his ego and arouse his competitive and predatory instincts. There was also the added complication that, unlike the Danish Embassy reception, this film festival gala was filled with a flotilla of beautiful young starlets with whom she would have to compete.

With a laugh, Judy began to tease the men around her: "Now which handsome man is the owner of that big bad beast of a yacht I saw anchored in the harbor this afternoon?"

No doubt all the men at that moment would have been only too happy to claim ownership.

"Oh, the Lady M?" said one, eager to at least show off his knowledge, if not ownership, of yachts. "Yes, built by Lurrssen. I've read about it. At least fifty meters long, four decks—based in Flensburg, Germany I believe, but more recently sails out of San Diego. Or at least I'm told."

"A beauty!" gushed Judy. "Who owns it, does anybody know?"

Arthur Lash, up to this point outgunned by the others, now piped in. "It's owned by the O.W.K.K. Company. We wanted to use it as a set for a film we produced last year."

"Did you?" asked the taller man.

"What?"

"Use it as a set?"

"Oh no. They wanted 100K for four hours. Can you believe that? But I can tell you who the C.E.O. of the company is. He's right over there."

"Where?" asked Judy.

Arthur nodded to where Hans and the matronly woman in the red gown were talking to several other men.

At this, Judy looked up to see if she could re-establish eye contact with Hans. She did, and this time she waved. He motioned for her to come over.

"Oh gentleman, would you excuse me for a moment?"

Judy turned toward Hans and his party, noticing that their conservation had lapsed, and the four of them were momentarily looking out on the gala floor.

At this, the deserted men were left to sigh.

Well, I guess if you have a yacht," one said as the coterie retreated for better hunting grounds.

******

"Hello sir, "said Judy as she tentatively approached and held out her hand to Hans. "Please forgive me. My name is Judy Alexander, and my friends over there were just telling me that you are the proud owner of that beautiful boat out in the harbor, so I just had to meet you."

Hans took her hand. "I regret that the boat is not mine, Ms. Alexander, but since you ask, it is the property of a German Construction Company with which I am connected. And I must

285

say that the boat is not half a beautiful as you *mein liebling*. I am Hans Wagner, and very pleased to make your acquaintance."

Hans turned to his guests. "May I introduce you to my very good friends, Mr. Karl Becker, and his lovely wife Maria? And this is Roger Kennedy. You may know him as he is the coordinator of this very fine film festival here in Santa Barbara."

"So nice to meet all of you," said Judy. "I didn't mean to interrupt. I'm just a movie buff, and I hear there are some fine films that will be shown here, which I would very much like to see. Anyway, so glad to meet all of you."

Judy turned to go and held her breath before Hans said. "Won't you stay awhile? As a film buff, perhaps you could advise me on which films I should be sure to see."

Fortunately, Judy had anticipated this possible mode of entre and had googled the films offered by the festival while sipping her Voss earlier in the day at El Canto.

"I would love to," said Judy. "Are you with someone here who might like to join us?"

"Yes, but I see that for the time being she is occupied with some other of our friends here. And do you also have someone with you?"

"Actually no, I'm afraid. Just all by my lonesome this trip."

"You must tell me more. It's a bit noisy down here. Perhaps you could join me in the lounge upstairs where we can talk about the films?"

Hans turned towards his other guests. "Karl, Maria, Roger, would you care to join us?"

"Thank you, Hans," said Roger, "but I should probably mingle with our other guests."

Karl and Maria too also begged off. They knew Hans well, and knew better than to intrude on his quest to make a new conquest.

Upstairs in the lounge, the orchestra music from below was well muted, and a piano player, seeing the two in hushed conversation in candlelight, set a romantic mood. Judy talked authoritatively about the films, explained how she was taking

286

some time off from law school to "find herself" for a year before returning to her studies. Hans told of his life as the head of one of Germany's biggest construction companies, and how his family had struggled to build it from the ashes of the war.

It was after midnight when Judy stifled a yawn.

"This has been so interesting talking to you, Hans, but I fear that I am fading. I should probably go now. Perhaps I will see you again during the festival."

"Are you staying here at the Bacara?"

"Actually no. I could hardly afford it. There is a Comfort Inn not too far from here."

"Judy, you said before you were interested in the Lady M. My friend and I are the only passengers on it this week, and I have six unused staterooms in which you are welcome to stay in tonight if you wish."

"Oh dear, Hans, that is such a kind invitation, but I don't know. Of course I'd love to. Would your friend mind you taking on a guest?"

"Well, let me see? Hold on." He took his cellphone from his pocket and called a number. He did not try to keep his conversation private.

"Hello, Madeleine? Where are you...I'm just up here in the lounge talking with friends...Were you planning to come aboard this evening, or stay here at the resort tonight...yes, I thought you might...uh-huh...you had mentioned perhaps staying for the entire week during the festival...so if you're still planning to do that...I know, the boat can't dock here in the basin so we have to take the dinghy...I understand...but I think I'd better get back tonight...a lot of cables...faxes, business I need to take care of...uh-huh...yeah, I'll be back to the resort tomorrow, probably in early afternoon...OK...have a good time...bye."

Hans turned to Judy. "So, no problem, *Liebling!* My friend won't even be coming aboard tonight, or for the rest of the week probably..."

Judy put on her best act in hesitating. "I don't know..."

"Look, if you're concerned about Madeleine, she's just a family friend, I assure you. But if you wouldn't feel comfortable... we wouldn't be alone, you know. The captain's on board, six of the crew, and, let's see, at least seven cabin and kitchen..."

"It is tempting—more exciting than the Comfort Inn I'm sure...but I'll need my things, my suitcases."

"You'll have everything you need for tonight on the boat. We can retrieve your things tomorrow from your hotel."

"Well..."

"Then it's settled. I'll tell you what. Follow me down to the back entrance, and I'll have my car brought around. My people are very discreet. They'll take us to our tender, which will take us out to the Lady M. You'll enjoy yourself. *Ich verspreche.*"

"I can't believe I'm doing this."

Hans stood up and held out his hand. "*Lass uns gehen Liebling.* It might be a little breezy out in the harbor. Do you need to get a coat?"

"Yes, I'll go fetch it from the coatroom and meet you at the back entrance. Give me fifteen minutes?"

"Of course. I'll have a car waiting."

CHAPTER FIFTY-ONE

JANUARY 21

As the Lady M was anchored well beyond the yacht basin, it was not until after 2 A.M. that the tender approached the boarding steps of the vessel.

Although there had been a driver of the car that took them from the back exit of the Bacara to the tender, Judy noted with some concern that Hans alone had taken the helm of the tender. Nor was there a crew member of the Lady M to greet them at its boarding steps. Only the ship's navigation lights were on, and the portholes were dark.

"I guess everyone is asleep?" Judy asked as Hans helped her up the stairs to the main deck.

"I'm sure Ship Master Graf is tucked away at this hour, but of course there is a crew member on the bridge twenty-four hours, even at anchor. Our Stewardess, Victoria, may be up, but we won't disturb her but I know you're tired, so let me show you to your cabin."

Is he really going to let me retire to my own stateroom tonight without putting the moves on me? Judy wondered. If so, that would make her task more challenging, as she had no intention of ever going to sleep on this boat.

"Actually," said Judy, "I was tired, but the breeze on the way here gave me a bit of a second wind. I'd love to see the ship if you have time to show me."

"But, of course." Hans said. "Follow me to the Grand Saloon." He pushed a switch which lit up the entire second deck, including the saloon, dining room and galley."

"Oh my!" Judy gushed.

Hans next took her to the upper decks, and after lighting up the entire upper deck and proudly showed off the sky lounge, sun deck, and a floor to ceiling glass enclosed gym with a panoramic ocean view.

"We won't disturb whoever is on the bridge. Perhaps with your second wind we can enjoy a final nightcap in the saloon below?"

"You know, I think I might really enjoy a glass of wine right now. This boat is amazing!"

In fact, Judy had been careful all evening not to consume more than the tiniest sips of champagne, as she knew she would need the full use of her faculties if she was ever to fulfill the mission she had assigned herself on the Lady M.

"But of course! Shall we lay below?"

"Lay below?"

Hans laughed. "No, *Liebling*, the term is not what you think, I assure you. It is just the nautical term for 'going downstairs.'"

"Ah, of course," said Judy. "I should know that."

As they 'lay below' to the foyer which separated the saloon from another compartment, Judy asked what the door across from the saloon led to.

Hans seemed to hesitate, but then said, "Come I shall show you." He opened the mystery door—to his study.

"Wow," said Judy as she took in the large teak-paneled study, grandly furnished with nautical fixtures, a Daum crystal vase atop a long console next to a variety of electronic equipment, an overhead with dark wenge inlays, gold inlays in foliated Kozmus granite on the floor, and desk and cabinetry in mahogany burl.

But what she noted most particularly was the very sturdy safe wedged underneath the cabinet behind the desk. It had, as Timothy had promised it would have, a Protaxtite digital keypad. But that promise, premised on information Timothy had gathered from an informant who had secured employment as a steward the previous year on the O.W.K.K. yacht, came with a caution: the code on the digital lock, or even the kind of digital lock itself, may have been changed since then.

"Please, feel free to kick off your shoes and make yourself comfortable," said Hans as he poured a glass of wine and handed it to Judy.

"Donnhoff Oberhausen Brucke Riesling, 2003," he said. "I hope you like it."

"Thank you! I think I shall," said Judy as she kicked off here shoes, took the glass and smiled flirtatiously. "It's divine, Hans. I think I may be in heaven right now."

"Glad you like it. It is my favorite. Now, where were we?"

After another half hour of rather mindless conversation about the features of the Lady M, as well as the consumption of the glass of Riesling, Judy realized she could not maintain sobriety if she drank another full glass.

"Hans, if I drink another glass I shall expire right here all over your Corinthian leather chair. Perhaps I should take you up on letting me crash in one of your staterooms tonight."

Something was wrong. Her Plan A had been to romantically ingratiate herself with Hans to the point that, like Bonnie had done nineteen years before, she would be able to gain his confidence and get information. But he wasn't reacting as she expected. He should be all over her by now. She would have to go to Plan B, and she would have to implement it very soon.

"Of course, *Liebling*, let me show you to your stateroom. Come, take my hand."

"Ok, Mr. Hans Wagner, if you say so," she said with a feigned inebriated drawl. She picked up her shoes and with an affected stagger followed him to the stateroom below. Then she sloppily kissed him on the cheek.

"Good night Hans! Thank you so much for everything! And I love your boat!" She shut the door.

"You will find nightclothes and shirts in the closet!" Hans called from outside the door.

"Thank you Hans! See you in the morning! Good night!" Judy waited for several minutes to see if he might open the door and have his way with her while she was—he surely must think— very drunk.

When fifteen minutes passed without hearing anything further from outside her stateroom door, she began to look through the drawers and cabinets for some clothes to replace her little black dress, which was far too tight for easy maneuvering in tight spaces. She did find some nightclothes, but instead picked out a bikini bathing suit—no doubt left in the drawers for guests—and a t-shirt cover. She looked for some jeans and sneakers, but found none. She would have to go barefoot.

Grabbing her Baggallini, she slowly opened the door, looked down the passageway, and quietly made her way up to the study.

CHAPTER FIFTY-TWO

JANUARY 21

Using her penlight, Judy found her way to the safe behind the study desk. Withdrawing the cigarette case sized electronic device that Timothy had given her, she punched in the numbers that she had previously memorized.

Nothing happened. She tried again, with no different result.

She did not expect to find the original of the letter that Otto Wagner had written to his son in 1948, and who had in turn handed it down to grandson. No doubt his son had never been able to arrange access to the trove during his time at O.W.K.K. lifetime, but now with his grandson Hans' corrupt winning of the construction contract to reconstruct the crumbling Grand Terrace at the top of Mont St. Michel, family access to the trove was finally assured.

More important than the trove, however, which would solve all of the financial problems now facing both O.W.K.K. and the Wagner family, were the names listed on the letter. These were names of those who had profited from their access to other Nazi treasures and who were complicit in the producing of poison gas at I. G. Farben. The living children and grandchildren were now enjoying the fruits of that legacy, including gold, diamonds, and precious stones stolen from concentration camp inmates, and which now lay safely protected in numbered Swiss bank accounts. Others with links to those on the list now enjoyed stolen wealth in secret Swiss accounts, or occupied high positions in both the French police and the German government—making them all subject to blackmail.

She was now quite sure that Hans had used that letter to blackmail the visitor to his home on the night that Bonnie had stumbled on the letter in Hans' study just days before Bonnie had disappeared on the Mont. Hans would hardly risk removing the original letter which must now surely reside in his numbered safety deposit box in a Swiss bank. That letter—with its blackmail potential—would now be more valuable to Hans than the trove itself. She had therefore deduced that Hans would very likely have a copy of the letter in his safe in the Lady M study. There were a number of Germany dignitaries at the film festival, and he would need that copy to carry out his blackmail.

With the hand held device unable to provide her with access to the safe, Judy decided her best course was to quietly creep back to her assigned stateroom and get off the Lady M the next morning as soon as possible. She had taken a chance—a longshot at that—and lost.

It would be more difficult to confirm her conclusions without the Otto letter, though she was sure her conclusions were correct. Based on the responses to the emails and texts which she had received in the last twenty-four hours, she believed that even without the Otto letter in hand, she might still bring down Hans—if she could just get off the boat.

Once safely back in Santa Barbara, she could resolve the mystery of what happened to Bonnie, why Gardner had asked for the death penalty, and be able to lead authorities to the trove on the Mont. Such a trove, if recovered, could then be used to provide compensation to victims of the Holocaust and their families.

Still on her knees as she put the digital device back into her Baggallini, Judy heard the sound of the study door opening. She turned off her penlight, and quickly retrieved the pepper spray canister, cupping it in her left hand. It was too late.

The study lights came on, and standing at the door was Hans Wagner, smirking, and holding a SIG Sauer P238 handgun aimed at her head.

"Please, feel free to kick off your shoes and make yourself comfortable," said Hans as he poured a glass of wine and handed it to Judy.

"Donnhoff Oberhausen Brucke Riesling, 2003," he said. "I hope you like it."

"Thank you! I think I shall," said Judy as she kicked off her shoes, took the glass, and smiled flirtatiously. "It's divine, Hans. I think I may be in heaven right now."

"Glad you like it. It is my favorite. Now, where were we?"

After another half hour of rather mindless conversation about the features of the Lady M, as well as the consumption of the glass of Riesling, Judy realized she could not maintain sobriety if she drank another full glass.

"Hans, if I drink another glass I shall expire right here all over your Corinthian leather chair. Perhaps I should take you up on letting me crash in one of your staterooms tonight."

Something was wrong. Her "Plan A" had been to romantically ingratiate herself with Hans to the point that, like Bonnie had done nineteen years before, she would be able to gain his confidence and get information. But he wasn't reacting as she expected. He should be all over her by now. She would have to go to Plan B, and she would have to implement it very soon.

"Of course, *Liebling*, let me show you to your stateroom. Come, take my hand."

"Ok, Mr. Hans Wagner, if you say so," she said with a feigned inebriated drawl. She picked up her shoes and with an affected stagger followed him to the stateroom below. Then she sloppily kissed him on the cheek.

"Good night Hans! Thank you so much for everything! And I love your boat!" She shut the door.

"You will find nightclothes and shirts in the closet!" Hans called from outside the door.

"Thank you Hans! See you in the morning! Good night!"

Judy waited for several minutes to see if he might open the door and have his way with her while she was—he surely must think—very drunk.

When fifteen minutes passed without hearing anything further from outside her stateroom door, she began to look through the drawers and cabinets for some clothes to replace her little black dress, which was far too tight for easy maneuvering in tight spaces. She did find some nightclothes, but instead picked out a bikini bathing suit—no doubt left in the drawers for guests—and a t-shirt cover. She looked for some jeans and sneakers, but found none. She would have to go barefoot.

Grabbing her Baggallini, she slowly opened the door, looked down the passageway, and quietly made her way up to the study.

CHAPTER FIFTY-THREE

JANUARY 21

"Well, *Liebling*," said Hans Wagner, "it seems that you have recovered quite remarkably from your state of inebriation. May I help you find something?"

For a moment Judy was frozen. She realized that there was little she could say to explain why she was on her knees in front of the safe wearing a bikini and holding a digital safe cracker in one hand and a small canister of pepper spray in the other.

She stood up. "Oh, there you are, Hans. I didn't want to wake you. I was just looking for a pen to write down a recipe I saw on the internet."

The ingratiating smile of the man with the gun dissolved almost imperceptibly into a glare.

"Did you really think you were going to come here to this film festival, lure me into your bewitching net, spy on me, and steal my little secrets? *Zum schamen, Liebling*."

"You mean like Bonnie did?"

"*Eine schlampe!* Your employer, Mr. Hoxsey, has been hounding me for nineteen years! Did he really think that I was not aware of all the agents whom he sent to spy on me? My own agents tracked every one of his operatives—including you, *Liebling*. We knew about you from the day you set foot in his lair at that island—what do they call it, Catalina? He tried every artifice at his disposal to spy on me with his detectives and researchers. We knew it was only a matter of time before he tried the honey trap—how predictable! Though I confess you were not what we expected."

Judy now realized that the zipped compartment in her suitcase had not been a figment of her imagination. She scolded herself: how could she have been so complacent, so unobservant—so unsuspicious?

"You have me there, Herr Wagner. I'm just a naïve first year law student. But how do you account for your one big mistake that even I was able to discover? It was not difficult for me to check the burial records of the Saint Pierre cemetery which showed that there was an official burial scheduled for the morning after you had Bonnie killed. You had it all arranged, didn't you? You knew in advance the exact time that the gravediggers would begin their digging on the day on which you and Bonnie arrived on the Mont...so you also knew in advance that there wouldn't be enough time to conduct the burial itself before dark...that the coffin would have to be placed in the chapel for the night, and that until the next morning the open gravesite would be left unattended. It was a simple matter in the middle of the night for your henchman—whoever he was—to dig the grave a little deeper, place the body of Bonnie within it, fill it with enough dirt to bring it up to the previous level, knowing that the next morning the coffin would be lowered into the grave above Bonnie's body without anyone being the wiser."

"You have quite the imagination, *Liebling*, and I must applaud you for that. In fact I am impressed. But since you must know I have no intention of letting you leave this boat alive, I'm afraid your speculations must remain just that –speculations."

"What was the call your henchman made to Bonnie in the restaurant? Did the caller claim that *Inspecteur Montagne* was on the island and urgently needed to meet her in her hotel room, which conveniently was only a few meters from the Saint Pierre Cemetery? And was it there that he strangled her?"

Judy's mind now raced. All she knew was that as long as she kept him talking, the longer the time she would have to figure out something, anything.

"You know that Timothy knows where I am," she continued, "that I'm on your boat."

"That will make no difference. We will be weighing anchor in a few minutes. After we chain you up we will be out to sea, and you, my *Liebling*, will disappear beneath the waves. Whatever your intention was, whatever you might or might not have told your employer—and I doubt you told him anything about coming on board this boat tonight—there will be no confirmation that you ever arrived on board, and I will simply deny that you did."

Judy had a sinking feeling as she realized that the only person who could possibly verify that she ever arrived on the Lady M was the driver—obviously one of Hans' henchmen— who met them at the back entrance of the Bacara and drove them to the tender. No one on board had seen either of them since they boarded.

"You know," said Judy, trying not to show her panic, "we know the content of the letter your grandfather wrote and put in the family safe deposit box in your Swiss bank. Bonnie saw that letter the night you tried to blackmail the man who visited at your home, and she told *Inspecteur* Montagne of the contents of that letter."

Hans shook his head in amusement. "*Inspecteur Jacques Montagne.* We were fortunate he was so incompetent—or corrupt. I don't know which—probably both. But it doesn't matter. If *Inspecteur Clouseau* knew anything about the contents of that letter, I wonder how he would explain to the authorities why he said nothing of what he knew to his superiors nineteen years ago. You would have me believe that now, all of a sudden, he remembers what some slut told him. Surely you can do better than that, *Liebling.*"

"Then how would we know that not only is your grandfather's trove of Nazi gold buried on the Grand Terrace of the Mont, but also buried there are documents that show the complicity of those named in the letter—complicity with the murder of thousands in the only concentration camp on French soil...and how the children and grandchildren of those men continue to enjoy the fruits of that complicity? And how would we know that O.W.K.K. rigged the bidding for the reconstruction project for the Grand Terrace?"

"Ah the royal 'we.' But if you had anything more than your wild speculations, you would never have risked coming on board this boat with me to try to find this letter you talk about. I wonder if you realize that every word you utter serves only to confirm the necessity of insuring that you do not leave this ship. And so, *Liebling*, if you will be so kind as to leave this room and go below, I will follow you."

"Before we go, there's one thing I don't understand."

"Really. Something you haven't figured out? Surely not."

"How does Madeleine fit into all this?"

For the first time since Hans had shown his true colors, he looked surprised.

"You know, Hans, Madeleine of the Lady M. "

To buy precious minutes, Judy knew she had to keep up her outward appearance of passive resignation to her fate, but her mind was racing. Keep him talking, wait for an opening—any opening.

"It makes no difference now *Liebling*, but I must confess that I am curious what you know about her."

"I know that she killed her husband Carl. I just don't know why."

Hans smirked. "Carl was my cousin, the bad sheep of the family—or you would probably say the good sheep. Through inheritance, he held a major ownership position in O.W.K.K., but we knew he would never go along with our bid-rigging plans. He began pressing the family to sell the company."

"But you had no intention of selling the company when its greatest potential asset was yet to be realized."

"You mean the half billion dollars now lying in the ground ten feet below the Grand Terrace on Mont St. Michel?"

"You weren't about to share that trove with him. So you had to get rid of him."

"It was just a matter of time before he discovered what we were doing and—how do you say it—let the cat out of the bag.

So we made him an offer he couldn't refuse: if he would leave the country, retire, stop pressing to sell the company and leave us alone, we would send him regular and generous dividends, and he could have the good life in retirement clipping his coupons."

"But since he was older, you couldn't risk that he would pass away and leave his ownership interest to some honest relative who would discover your dirty secrets. You needed to make sure that his interest in your miserable company would go to his wife—and thus to you—and that's where Madeleine came in."

"Yes, and you are correct this ship bears her name. A remarkable woman. I met her in San Moritz while skiing there with my father. Most beautiful woman I'd ever seen. No man could resist her, including me. And certainly not Crazy Otto as we used to call him—putty in her hands. Almost as beautiful as you, *Liebling*. It is such a shame that you now leave me no choice."

"So Madeline tracks down poor Carl down in Houston, and seduces him into marriage."

Hans shrugged. "Carl can't believe his luck! He's the envy of all the hen-pecked husbands at the Country Club."

"So your Madeleine turns to seducing an honest hard working doctor who has never found love. Convinces him that Carl is abusing her. One night she kills Otto with a clean shot to the head while he is sitting in his favorite living room chair. Then she calls poor love-sick Roger, tells him that she killed him in self-defense and asks him to set the scene and confirm her story with the police. I'm guessing that he wipes Madeleine's fingerprints from the murder weapon and then fires a second shot in order to put gunshot residue on his own hand. All for Madeleine."

"And he wouldn't be the only one who would die for the woman he loved. You're guessing now, but close enough. And ah yes, we know all about the good Doctor Gardner as well. When tracing your movements before you went to Catalina Island—our agents found out all about that. We had to know what connections there were and how you happened to go see Hoxsey. We never did really find out why you went or what the connection was, but I guess we know now. But we did find out that Doctor Gardner has nothing to lose. Pancreatic cancer. When he found out he was a goner, of course he didn't want anyone to know. He'll be dead long before they ever stick a needle in him. Your death will be much less painful. I can promise it will be quick, *Liebling*. You needn't worry about drowning with chains still wrapped around you. One quick shot and it will be over before you ever hit the water with the chains wrapped around you. You're too beautiful to suffer needlessly, *Liebling*. "

"You're too kind, Hans. I wonder what the besotted doctor would say if he knew that he was sacrificing his life to save a woman who never loved him—who killed her husband only to get her share of Nazi gold that belongs to the families of victims of the concentration camps...who..."

"It is a hypothetical question, since he will never know."

Hans looked at his watch. It is time, I'm afraid. Now go below." He motioned with his gun.

"Don't want blood on your Persian carpets I take it. Hard to explain to the police who will surely search this boat after I disappear. Much easier to clean up down in the engine room. No, Hans, I think you'll have to shoot me right here! I'm not going down."

Hans waved his handgun toward the door. "Enough! Go!"

At that moment, the ship's engine began to roar and vibrate, and there was a jerk as the anchor chain clanked against the side of the ship. Judy took advantage of this momentary distraction and movement to throw the digital device at Hans' head, causing him to duck and fire his Sig Sauer wildly. In an instant she rushed past him, releasing the pepper spray in the general direction of his face as she did so.

Momentarily disabled, Hans turned and blindly fired three more shots from his SIG Sauer in Judy's direction. Two bullets narrowly missed her and lodged in the teak door frame, but a third found its mark in Judy's left arm, causing her to drop the pepper spray canister.

Judy made a mad dash for the stairs topside where she frantically climbed the steps. Hans followed, firing two shots up at her which made sharp clinking sounds as they hit the inlaid gold on the Egyptian artifact on the staircase landing.

Leaving a trail of blood behind as bullets whizzed past her, and running as fast as her adrenalin could power her, she made it to the aft railing, over which she catapulted herself in a spiral dive into the dark cold water below.

CHAPTER FIFTY-FOUR

JANUARY 25

Robin Hammond sipped his coffee in the breakfast room of the Holiday Inn Express, Santa Barbara, and checked both his email and texts on his iPhone. He had arrived in Santa Barbara three days before, and had immediately tried to call Judy. Getting no response, he had then tried to track down Timothy Hoxsey. During his previous iPhone conversations with Judy, she had only given him Timothy's name and home on Catalina Island, but not his phone number, which was unlisted.

The day before he had finally been able to google a number for Hoxsey Aviation and leave a message for Timothy Hoxsey. He was still waiting for an answer when the phone rang.

"Mr. Hammond?"

"Yes, this is Mr. Hammond."

"Mr. Robin Hammond?"

"Yes."

"This is Brian, Mr. Hoxsey's secretary. You left a message for him yesterday?"

"Yes, I did. Is he available?"

"Yes, Sir. Please hold for Mr. Hoxsey. I'll patch you through to his cell."

"Hello. This is Timothy Hoxsey. You left a message inquiring about Judy Alexander and said it was urgent. "

"Yes. My name is Robin Hammond. I am one of Ms. Alexander's Professors at the Oliver Wendell Holmes School of Law in Manhattan, and her faculty advisor in the Exoneration Clinic."

"Oh yes, Judy has mentioned you to me."

"And she has mentioned that she was working on a project for you, and has told me something about it. I have not been able to reach her, and was hoping you could help me."

"Where are you now?"

"Holiday Inn, on...hold on...West Haley Street. Where are you now? I need to know if Judy is all right."

"I think we should talk. I am staying at the Bacara, here in Santa Barbara, not too far from where you are. I could have my car come by to pick you up."

"I could get an Uber...please tell me..."

"It would be faster and more convenient for me if you permit me to have my car pick you up. Can you be ready outside the front of your hotel in, say, fifteen minutes? We will talk as soon as you get here."

"Yes. I will be there."

******

The black Rover pulled up to the Bacara entrance.

"Mr. Hoxsey is waiting for you in suite 201," said the driver.

"Thank you, "said Robin. He rushed as fast as he could to the suite to which he was directed and knocked impatiently.

"Mr. Hammond?" said Timothy as he answered the door.

"Yes."

"Please come in and have a seat, Professor Hammond."

Robin entered and took a seat on the sofa. "I need to know about Judy."

Timothy sat on the chair opposite. "First, Professor, I need you to tell me what you know about what Judy has been doing for me."

Robin didn't like this answer, but saw he had no choice if he was to get any news about Judy. He summarized the content of his conversations with Judy. Timothy noted that he covered only what Judy had been doing up until Judy's arrival in Santa Barbara. Robin knew nothing about what had happened thereafter, her meeting with Hans at the reception, or what she did with him after that.

"I see. She has kept you well informed."

"I would like to be up front with you, Mr. Hoxsey. From the beginning I disapproved of her working for you. As the faculty advisor to the Exoneration Clinic I reluctantly gave her permission to go to Houston to investigate, on behalf of the clinic, an extraordinary case of a man who offered to plead guilty to a crime of murder in return for receiving the death penalty. Somehow she got sidetracked from that task. I understand that you had something to do with that."

"That is true, but as you just acknowledged in your summary of what she told you, only half the story. As you know, it turned out that her investigation in Houston, during which she made contact with my Goddaughter, Amber, had a number of connections to my long search to find out what happened to my daughter nineteen years ago when she disappeared on the small island of Mont St. Michel off the coast of France."

"That may be, but I understand you have immense resources. It was irresponsible for you to commission a young law student just starting her legal education for such a dangerous task—for what reason I cannot imagine, and if because of that..."

"I am quite deserving of your censure, Professor, and I can only say on my own behalf that both Judy and I were aware of the dangers that could ensue with both her investigations—and yes, especially the one with which I was most concerned. As to why I believed that only she could find answers that had long eluded all my own investigators, I can only answer that I discussed those reasons with her, and I believe that only she should divulge them to you."

"Enough of this! If you don't tell me about Judy, and where she is, I will go to the police. I insist that you tell me now!"

Timothy sat back in his chair.

"She is alive, Professor."

"And she is alive and well?"

"I regret to say that she is in the hospital."

"Jesus! I knew this would happen!"

"Please calm yourself, Professor. Her prognosis is good."

"No thanks to you! Now tell me what has happened to her!"

"She took it upon herself to go with Hans Wagner to his boat, the Lady M, which was anchored out beyond the Santa Barbara yacht basin..."

"You let her go alone with him to his boat?"

"I would never have agreed had she asked me, but she did not. Fortunately, however, I had provided her with an internal earpiece, allowing me not only to hear everything that was said by her and to her on the boat, but also to record it. As soon as I was aware that she as going with Mr. Wagner to the boat, I became concerned and, through my contacts, alerted the Coast Guard to be in the vicinity should they be needed. It turns out that the Lady M was already under surveillance based on Interpol alerts. When I heard Hans threaten to kill her, we called the Coast Guard to immediately converge on the Lady M."

"Jesus!"

While one Cutter raced toward the Lady M to board her, the other launched a helicopter with searchlights to scan the water around it. Even so, it took almost fifteen minutes to find her.

"The waters around Santa Barbara in winter must be very cold!"

"About fifty-five degrees at this time of year. Under such conditions hypothermia can cause death in ten to fifteen minutes. When the searchlights found her, she was barely able to stay above water, almost comatose, and losing blood from a wound from her upper arm where Hans had shot her."

Robin could only shake his head. "Unbelievable."

"The Coast Guard frogman immediately went in, pulled her up to the chopper, an gave her emergency hypothermia treatment. She was only wearing a bathing suit and a t-shirt, if you can believe it. They warmed her with warm towels, and covered her with warm blankets and dry compresses. Of course they also stopped her bleeding. The chopper then rushed her to Santa Barbara Cottage Hospital where she received further treatment in the emergency room. It was nip and tuck. A few minutes longer in the water and she wouldn't have made it."

"And she's recovering? Will she have any long term effects?"

"The doctors say she should make a full recovery, but want to keep her a few more days."

"Have you been able to see her?"

"I met the chopper at the hospital when she came in. She was still almost comatose when I saw her, but she did manage to say one thing to me before they made me leave the premises."

"And...?"

"She asked me to call Amber and ask her if they found the second bullet. Do you know what she was talking about?"

Robin thought for a moment. "I think I do."

"Well you can tell me about it this afternoon. I called the hospital this morning, and they say we can visit with her this evening from seven until nine. She's already talked to the police and the Interpol agents. Will you come?"

"Of course."

"I'll tell you what. Why don't you meet me out by the large pool in about an hour? We'll take a walk around the environs, and I can fill you in. I'll tell you this now, though. She found out what happened to my daughter, and who did it. And much more. And she can prove all of it.

CHAPTER FIFTY-FIVE

JANUARY 25

There was a slight breeze from the sea as Timothy Hoxsey and Robin Hammond walked together along the foot path surrounding the Bacara.

"I have a lot to fill you in on," said Timothy. "As I told you, we have a complete tape of everything Hans confessed to Judy about his part in the murder of my daughter, where she was interned on Mont St. Michel, and where the stolen Nazi gold was hidden on the Grand Terrace. But first, tell me what you make of the question she posed to me as she was brought in to the emergency room after being fished out of the sea by the Coast Guard."

Very well, "replied Robin. "I understand that your goddaughter has already related to you why it was that Judy came to Houston in the first place."

"Yes—as a student in your Exoneration Clinic at Oliver Wendell Holmes School of Law she became intrigued by the story of the man charged with murder who had offered to plead guilty in exchange for being sentenced to death."

"Judy had developed a romantic theory as to why any man charged with murder—Dr. Roger Gardner—would make such an offer to the prosecutor. After reading the police report, talking to the witnesses, including the doctor's sister, and talking with the prisoner himself, and learning as much as she could about the wife of the man he was accused of killing, she concluded that the good doctor may not have been capable of either committing the murder or conspiring to do so—even for the love of a woman for whom he would do almost anything."

"The key word there being "almost.""

"Precisely. He would not kill for her. But, in Judy's romantic notion, such a man might be willing to sacrifice himself to save the woman he loved if he was convinced that she had already killed an abusive husband in self-defense in the belief that she would be in great danger if she did not act preemptively."

"This woman would have to be fairly confident in advance that he would do so after she told him that she had killed her husband."

"She would probably have to go to Plan B if he had not been willing to do so—just stick to the story that she had killed him in self-defense and hope that she could convince the police of that. But she did not have to go that route, with the risks that would entail, when, as she expected, Gardner agreed to help her cover up the crime, and even take the blame himself."

"But I understand that the evidence showed that Gardner had not only purchased the murder weapon himself, but was tested at the crime scene for gunshot residue and tested positive."

"Yes, he had indeed purchased the gun several weeks before the murder, and had given it to Madeleine so she would have it available if her husband should attempt to abuse her. Of course that played into Madeline's hands. Gardner was by then well plied with her stories of Carl's relentless abuse."

"But what about the gunshot residue..."

"That's where the second bullet comes in. Judy surmised that after Gardner came to the house to find Carl dead on the floor from a gunshot wound to the head, the only way he could make his story credible was if he fired the gun himself. He probably did not want to go outside to fire the gun, since that might have alerted the neighbors and called in the police before the two were ready to receive them, and so he probably fired it somewhere in the house—preferably in an obscure location where the police would not be likely to look."

"Given Madeline's story to the police that she had been upstairs when she heard just one shot and came down to find her husband dead on the floor, and Gardner's refusal to say anything to deny it, I suppose the police had no reason to go looking for a second bullet."

"Precisely. And I assume that's why Judy asked if the police had found the second bullet. I know Judy has been communicating with a number of people over the past several days, and I assume that one of those communications was to your goddaughter Amber asking her to have the police look for the second bullet in the house."

"Do you think they found it?"

"I don't know. Perhaps Judy herself can tell us this evening when we visit her at the hospital. I know she did not have her cellphone or bag when she was fished out of the sea—presumably she dropped it when running from Hans or if not, when she thrashed in the water—but I'm sure she would have had time by now to use a hospital phone to contact Amber."

"On the recording of what Hans said to Judy before she managed to dive overboard to save herself, Hans said that Gardner had pancreatic cancer."

"Well, hopefully we shall soon find out. Now, Timothy, it's your turn to tell me what Judy found out about your daughter."

"Judy took detailed notes of everything she saw on Mont St. Michel. In one of her few communications to me, I learned that she was able to arrange to spend two nights in the very room in which Bonnie and Hans had stayed on the night Bonnie disappeared. While there, she noticed that a gravesite was being prepared in the nearby cemetery of St. Pierre. The hole had already been dug, and the soil was sitting in a pile, but the internment was not actually to take place until the following morning.

"Later she met a retired engineer—named Jules, she said—who had worked for a construction company. From him she learned about the burial protocol for the St. Pierre cemetery. The gravesite, he told her, were family plots, but due to severe space restrictions, more recently deceased family members had to be buried below or above previous family members. Later Judy learned from retired *Inspecteur* Montagne that a similar gravesite had been similarly prepared on the very evening of Bonnie's disappearance. From that she concluded that the only place Bonnie's body could have been placed that evening was in that gravesite. It would have been a simple matter for one of Hans' goons to dig the gravesite a little deeper during the night, place Bonnie's body in it, and then cover it up to the previously level. On her way to Santa Barbara, she contacted Montagne and asked him to arrange the exhumation."

"When did Judy tell you all that?"

"A few hours before she went to the film gala reception. She called and told me."

"But has her deduction been confirmed? Have they found your daughter's body in the gravesite that was prepared that night? Did they find her body there?"

Timothy's eyes moistened. "I called my contacts in Paris. They found her exactly where Judy said she would be. We still have to do a D.N.A. test for confirmation, but her clothes, a description of her ring, her bag and identification—were all found with her body."

"One more thing that Judy discovered, and I'm not sure you know anything about it."

"I'm trying to take this all in."

"In the course of investigating Bonnie's disappearance, she also came across evidence that there might be a huge cache of Nazi gold buried under the Grand Terrace of Mont St. Michel."

"Whaaaat?"

"It was a deduction she made from clues she obtained from several sources. From her friend, and apparent admirer, Jules, she learned that O.W.K.K. had recently won a bidding contract to excavate and rebuild the Grand Terrace at Mont St. Michel, and that the circumstances of that bid were suspicious. Just a few days ago, she also learned from Jules that there was indeed a plot of tiles which had a slightly different hue from tiles on the rest of the Terrace. From Montagne she learned that O.W.K.K. had been investigated for bid rigging for many years. And from the information that my own daughter Bonnie had given to Montagne, she learned that a letter in Hans' possession had referred to a treasure of Nazi gold on the Grand Terrace."

"But that's hardly enough to..."

"It was confirmed by Hans himself on the night he tried to kill Judy. We have it all on tape. I called the French authorities immediately after we heard the tape."

"So is the treasure there? Have the authorities found it?"

"That too has been confirmed. The news will break in the French press tomorrow morning, just a few hours from now—and from there it is sure to be a big story in media around the world. Preliminary reports suggest that it is one of the largest Nazi gold hoards that has been in the last thirty years. I have been assured that once the treasure is accounted for, the proceeds will be distributed to the families of the victims of the concentration camps, and particularly to the victims of the concentration camp at Natzweiller-Struthof."

"I need to sit down", said Robin, pointing to a stone wall along the path.

For some time Timothy and Robin sat on the wall, saying nothing, and looking out at the sea.

Finally Robin said, "I am very happy to hear that you have some closure about your daughter. And I am sorry for what I said about your taking advantage of Judy, although I can still not completely condone the danger you put her in."

"I understand, and hope you can too. I could not bear the thought of passing on without knowing what happened to my only daughter. Judy has given me a gift I can never repay. Already I am informed that Hans Wagner has been arrested by Interpol, and will face all kinds of charges in France, and not least charges of attempted murder here in the U.S."

"From what I know of Judy, she will not expect or want any payment. She went to Houston to right a wrong, and did so at her own expense. She agreed to help you for the same reasons."

There was another long pause before Timothy said, "You know, no one but Judy could have found Bonnie—not all my investigators, not all my researchers, none of them. Only Judy could have pulled this off."

Robin sighed. "She is incredibly brilliant and resourceful. With only a couple of clues she was able to come up with a crossword that I would never have gotten in a million years. I guess she translated that skill—compiling clues to find a solution—into her investigation of your daughter's disappearance. I regret that she now has second thoughts about using that skill in the law."

Timothy looked at Robin and shook his head. "Professor, I don't mind telling you that I like you. I also don't mind telling you that I do not have many days left in me. But in those days that I do have, I hope we can be friends and stay in touch. And I hope that in time you can forgive me."

Robin nodded. "I do, but if anything had happened to her...I do thank you for taking me into your confidence."

Timothy's demeanor now turned harsh. "But I don't mind telling you that you are an idiot!"

"What?" Robin replied before he realized that Timothy was scolding him in good humor as a friend.

"Do you really think I invited Judy to take on this investigation because I thought she was so brilliant and resourceful?"

"But she is!"

"Absolutely she is. I wouldn't deny it for a moment! But I didn't know that when I hired her—that was the bonus I got, though I had no reason to expect it from her."

"I don't think she could have accomplished what she did without both..."

"Beauty and brains, yes. I agree she needed both to find my daughter. Quite so. Are you a student of the classics, Professor?'

"Not really, but I have a feeling you're going to enlighten me."

"You've heard of Socrates."

Robin smiled indulgently. "Yes, my good friend, I have heard of Socrates."

"And his sayings?"

Robin shrugged.

314

"It was one of those aphorisms that led me to invite Judy to help me find Bonnie: 'Beauty is a greater recommendation than any letter of reference'"

"Socrates really said that?"

"Google it. I hope you do not think me politically incorrect. But do you really think Judy could have done what she did without it—get the information she needed to know about O.W.K.K. and its link to Mont St. Michel without it? Could she have gotten an interview with the Chief of Police of France without it? Or in the matter of Doctor Gardner, win an interview with him, when no one else could?"

At this, Robin felt compelled to reveal a twinge of offense. "She is not, absolutely not..."

"I know that, Professor! And that's why, when Amber told me what Judy had accomplished, I knew Judy would be my only hope. I didn't want a Mata Hari, a honey trap, or a seductress! I wanted someone who could find my Bonnie without being any of those things! Just being herself. Do you understand?"

'I'm not sure."

"She is very beautiful, you know."

"Of course. Anyone can see that."

"Devastatingly beautiful, Professor! I'm not sure she even realizes the power of her beauty, which is well-nigh absolute. A Helen of Troy with a goddess face that could launch a thousand ships! A Nefertiti!"

Robin shook his head. "Yes, she's very beautiful. I get it. Do I detect that perhaps you have fallen in love with her yourself?"

"Not at all, Professor. If I were forty years younger, who can say? I do very much admire her, and am now very much indebted to her. I had only one motive in inviting her to help me, and that was finding my daughter. I hope you believe that."

"I do believe that, my friend. I believe that."

"But what about you, Professor?"

"Me? What do you mean?"

"You came all the way from New York just to see her. Why did you do that?"

"I was concerned about her. I feared she was in danger, and I was right."

"Be honest, Professor."

"If you mean, am I in love with her? Of course not! She could have anyone she wanted. Falling in love with her would bring only heartbreak, as I'm sure it has been for many others." "So you are saying you are not good enough for her, and that's what keeps you from falling in love with her."

"No, I mean...well, maybe...I mean I'm just..."

"You must have some very energetic cat to tie up your tongue so tightly."

"Mr. Hoxsey! Enough! Can we talk about something else? Like what is going to happen to this Madeleine Berger person now..."

"So, if not you," said Timothy, ignoring his plea to change the subject, "who do you think would be worthy of her? A millionaire, like me for that matter? A celebrity, a senator, a..."

"Please stop!"

"As you wish. But when you talk to Judy tonight—I will talk to her alone for the first hour, and leave you alone with her to talk for the next hour—don't talk to her about her travails of the last month. I have already left a message telling her that due to her excellent work I have found Bonnie, and also the treasure. She will be feted around the world for what she has accomplished. But more important, she has performed the one task to which I entrusted her. I will talk to her of all these things. But when you talk to her, just listen to what she says to you and ask no questions—listen between the lines. Watch how she reacts to the fact that you are here for her."

Robin stood up and held out his hand to Timothy to help him rise from the stone wall. "Sure Timothy, sure. Shall we go now? I will meet you at the hospital at seven."

"Professor," said Timothy as he let Robin pull him up, "this could be the beginning of a great friendship."

CHAPTER FIFTY-SIX

JANUARY 25

Robin arrived at the Santa Barbara Cottage Hospital at fifteen minutes before seven and sat in the first floor lounge to wait for Timothy. He placed his bouquet of roses on the couch beside him. He had to wait only another five minutes before Timothy arrived with Chandler in tow.

"Good evening, Professor," said Timothy. "I see you arrived early. Shall we go on up?"

Robin stood and said, "I just asked the staff and they're pretty strict. They won't let us go up to her floor until visiting hours begin at seven."

"Nonsense! We shall go up now." Timothy turned to Chandler. "Wait down here. I shall be back in less than an hour." Then he said to Robin, "Very nice flowers!"

"You're not going to wait until after I've talked to her?" Robin asked.

"No, Professor, and I won't take up my whole hour. I intend to tell her the wonderful news that all her conclusions have been confirmed—that they have found Bonnie, and the Nazi gold as well. And of course I will express my profound thanks for all she has done. After that I want you to have the remaining time with her alone. I don't intend to wait around and hover."

Up on the sixth floor the hospital staff succumbed to Timothy's authoritarian air and agreed to let them sign in early for visiting hours.

"You are friends of Judy Alexander?" asked the nurse.

Timothy and Robin looked at each other before Timothy replied, "Yes we are very good friends. I am Timothy Hoxsey and this is Robin Hammond. We left her a message letting her know we would be visiting this evening. Do you know if she received it?"

"I'm not sure sir, but if you sent a message to our day staff I'm sure they gave her the message."

"How is she?"

"She is almost fully recovered from her hypothermia treatment, but is still a little groggy from the anesthesia she received this morning after additional surgery on her arm. She may still be suffering from pain. She has declined to take any pain pills."

"That sounds like our Judy, all right," piped Robin.

"Nurse, "said Timothy, "we are going to see her separately, if that is all right. I will see her now, and Mr. Hammond will see her after I leave. Is that all right?"

"That's fine. But both of you must leave by nine."

"Understood."

Timothy turned to Robin. "I shouldn't be more than a half hour."

It was forty-five minutes later when Timothy returned to the waiting room.

Robin put down his vending machine coffee. "How is she?"

"She's fine. I gave her all the news."

"She must have been very happy to hear it."

"She was, of course but I do think she wants to see you. Go on down. She's waiting for you—third room on the left."

Robin knocked on the door.

"Come in."

Despite the ordeal which she had just recently sustained, she looked radiant, though her arm was heavily bandaged and in a sling. All around her, and indeed all around the room were flowers of every kind, giving the hospital room the ambience of an Amazon jungle.

"Well, Professor," she said with a mischievous smile, "I see you have tracked me down all the way to beautiful downtown Santa Barbara."

"Wow," said Robin, "You must have a lot of admirers. It's like the Botanical Gardens in here."

"Just Timothy's work, of course. The nurses are already complaining about it."

"I see. Well, its's not every day that one of my students pulls out all the stops to be admitted to my Exoneration Clinic, and then immediately disappears across the world. The other students have been asking about you."

"I'm not sure my original mission has as yet been fulfilled."

"We shall see about that. But Timothy warned me not to ask you about any of your exploits, and instead just come and listen to you. I'm sure you've already had to answer all kinds of questions."

"Oh yes. Yesterday morning I talked to the FBI, an agent from Interpol, and some French detectives. I'm talked out, I'm afraid. But please sit down, Professor."

He handed her his flowers and sat. "I brought these for you, but I'm not sure they compare to Timothy's, and I'm not sure there's any more room for them."

"Don't be silly. I'll find a place." She held them with her good arm. "Thank you."

There was an awkward silence.

"So why did you come?" she asked.

"I was...you know..."

"I know. You were worried about me. You were concerned about my safety, you were..."

"I was!" he interrupted defensively.

"That's sweet, Professor."

Professor! She was still addressing him that way. It was not a good sign, and he had long since given up trying to persuade her to call him by his first name.

"How long before they let you out of here?"

"Probably another three or four days. Maybe a few days longer than that. But I'll need some help with my bandages for several weeks after that."

"I'm sure I could help you with that."

Oh what a dumb transparent thing to say. Robin kicked himself for saying it.

"That would be nice."

Maybe not so dumb after all? Robin consoled himself.

Judy sat up, suppressing a grimace of pain in her left arm. "But don't you have to get back to the Law School. You have classes, don't you?"

Robin took a deep breath. "Actually no. I had a bit of a —disagreement, shall we say—with our illustrious dean over the future of the Exoneration Clinic. He had decided to cut off all funding for it, though he would let me continue the clinic as a simulation course. He wants to allocate all available funding to teaching courses which prepare the students to pass the bar—teaching to the test, in other words. Not my idea of sound pedagogical policy."

"Simulation course? So no more actual clients or victims of injustice? Just hypothetical scenarios?"

"That's about the size of it, and that's not what I signed up for when I left private practice to teach there."

"But don't you teach a class in Evidence in the second semester? Haven't classes already started?"

"Yes, but one of my colleagues at the law school has been hankering to teach that course for years. Because I've only taught two classes so far this semester, the Dean and I reached an agreement that my colleague would take over that course, and I would then be free to..."

"Take care of me?"

Are you teasing me, Judy? Robin asked himself as he sat back to take in what she really meant.

Finally, he said with no hint of jocularity in his voice, "I would consider it a privilege. And in return, every Saturday you would agree to help me solve the Saturday *New York Times* crossword—preferably in less than twenty minutes."

"I could do that."

"You mean..."

"But first you need to take me to Houston."

"To Houston?"

Judy shook her head. "You have no idea why I need to go there? Really?"

"I'm sorry. Of course I do."

"I just received a text from Amber. She got the police to conduct a thorough search of Carl Otto's home. They found the second bullet."

"Really? That's a big house, I understand."

"They found the bullet exactly where Doctor Gardner said it would be—which confirms his story."

"His story? I thought he wasn't talking to anyone."

"Amber sent him a letter outlining how Madeleine Berger had used him to get her hands on the Nazi gold buried at Mont St. Michel—gold that should be used to compensate the families of Nazi concentration camp victims, and not to line the pockets of a manipulative woman who never loved him, and who lied to him about the abuse she claimed to have suffered from her husband."

"So she got him to open up about what really happened?"

"Yep. And the District Attorney now claims that they suspected all along that she had murdered her husband, but that their hands were tied when Gardner refused to rebut her story."

"What about the fact the Madeleine didn't test positive for gunshot residue?

"He explained that too—when she shot her husband, she simply wore heavy gloves and coat which she later disposed of."

"So Gardner admitted that he was an accessory after the fact?"

"Yes, because it's apparently the truth. And finding the second bullet in the wall behind a picture on the third floor of the mansion confirmed it to the D.A.'s satisfaction."

"But he's still on the hook for accessory after the fact?"

"Yes, but he's agreed to let Amber represent him on that charge. She says she's negotiating a deal now with the D.A. under which the charges against him will be reduced to a misdemeanor and a suspended jail sentence if he agrees to testify against Madeleine."

321

"Where is Madeleine now?"

"I'm told that the night after Hans was arrested, Madeleine high tailed it to Europe—Germany they think—but they're looking for her. Texas will seek extradition if they find her. Hans of course will be prosecuted here in California for my attempted murder, based on my testimony and his admissions in the recording. After that, it is hoped that Germany will seek his extradition to stand trial for the murder of Bonnie—and for bid rigging. One thing is for sure—O.W.K.K. is out of business."

"So, whenever you're ready to go to Houston, I'll pick you up. Three or four days you said?"

Judy smiled and nodded. "Hopefully."

CHAPTER FIFTY-SEVEN

FEBRUARY 2

Robin and Judy, her left arm still bandaged and in a sling, stood on the upper arrival level at Houston International Airport.

"What kind of car does Amber have?" Robin asked.

"A blue RAV-4, I think. The traffic is terrible this afternoon, especially with this rain. "

"She should be by any minute. Keep looking."

"You know, "said Robin, "Timothy did offer us the use of his jet."

If he only knew what Timothy in his gratitude had really wanted to give her, which included title to the jet and yacht.

"I told you. No more of that, Professor. Right now all I want is to get back to normalcy, with no Chandler hovering over me. Keep looking."

Robin sighed. "I'm looking!"

"Wait, there she is!" Judy waved and Amber found an open spot in front of them. Amber got out to help Robin with the bags.

"Hello, Amber, I'm Robin Hammond," said Robin as he and Amber plowed their bags into the rear of the RAV-4.

"Yes, hi. Judy has told me all about you. Welcome to Houston."

Robin insisted that Judy take the front seat with Amber, though Judy had protested that Robin should sit up front.

"You've got the bad arm," said Robin, "and you'll need extra room. Besides, I think you and Amber have a lot to talk about."

Amber and Judy exchanged a delicate hug—with due care taken not to touch Judy's left arm.

"So where are you taking us?" asked Judy when they had gotten underway.

"Galveston," Amber replied.

"Really? Why so?"

"There are two very grateful people who want to see you, and I think you can guess who they are."

"Really? I think I can. I would very much like to see them too."

It was three hours in difficult traffic and rain before they arrived at Jamaica Beach before the stately old historical home of white wood.

Roger Gardner and his sister Susan were at the door to greet them.

"Thank you so much for coming!" gushed Susan as she gave Amber a hug. "And I'd give you a hug too Judy, but and I shall wait until your arm heals before I give you the hug you deserve."

The five retired to the living room as Susan served tea, sandwiches and cakes.

Judy walked over to Doctor Gardner and offered her good hand. "I am so glad to see you, Doctor, and under more happy circumstances than the last time we met."

The doctor still looked haggard after his ordeal in the Appaloosa County Jail, but was in better shape than when Judy had last seen him.

"We're so grateful to Amber, said Susan "She got the D.A. to release him from jail on his own recognizance, and I've been fattening him up since he came home."

"It's Judy you should be thanking," said Amber.

Everyone was silent as the Doctor began to speak. "Judy," he said with obvious emotion, "there is no way I can thank you enough. Words are not sufficient to express my gratitude."

"I know the three of you have much to talk about" Susan said to her brother, Judy, and Amber.

Susan turned to Robin. "Professor, I see the rain has stopped. I was wondering if you might take a walk with me along the beach and leave these three to talk among themselves for a while."

Robin looked at Judy, who nodded.

"I'd be happy to," said Robin. 'I've never been to Galveston, but have heard much about it, and would love to see it."

"We'll be back in an hour," said Susan. "I have a roast in the oven which will be ready when I return. I trust all will join us for dinner. Roger, would you mind taking a look at the roast until we return?"

"Of course, Susan. Enjoy your walk."

Susan led Robin down the path to the sea.

"Beautiful," said he.

"It is. Very beautiful. My grandfather built this house by the sea many years ago, after the Great Hurricane of 1900. It came without warning and wiped out the entire city—killed over 10,000."

"Yes, I've read about it—the worst natural disaster in American history."

"You know," said she after a long pause, "without the effort of all three of you—Judy, of course, but you and Amber as well— my brother would never have survived. He was slowly dying in that hell-hole of a County jail, and his future looked so dark."

Robin shook his head. "You are kind to give Amber and me some credit, but I have to say—it was all Judy. Without her efforts, her concern for justice, her imagination and resourcefulness, your brother would have faced a terrible fate. All I did was let Judy come down to Houston on behalf of our Exoneration Clinic—at her own expense, I might add. And Amber—well she did all she could—but her efforts would have come to naught had Judy not tracked down the information that she could use to get your brother released."

"I realize that, but thank you and Amber all the same."

"Susan, I have a personal question to ask, if you would permit."

"Yes, of course."

"I received some information about your brother's health, and was wondering if it might be true."

"You're asking about his cancer—his pancreas."

"Yes, I'm sorry."

"No it's all right. It's true. He has been so diagnosed. And of course many of us think that such a diagnosis is the equivalent of a death sentence—we think Steve Jobs, or Patrick Swayze. But it turns out that Roger was fortunate in one respect. His symptoms manifested themselves very early. As his doctor explained it to me, the most deadly type of pancreatic cancer originates in that part of the pancreas which shows no early symptoms. When symptoms finally reveal themselves in such cases, it is usually too late to treat the cancer. In Roger's case, however, the cancer originated in that part of the pancreas in which symptoms appear early, often in time for treatment."

"So there is hope for him?"

"Yes, some, although of course the doctors can make no guarantee. But they say he has a chance, especially now that he's out of jail and getting the proper treatment."

"I'm glad to hear that. I hope it works out for him."

"As do I."

"Well, shall we return to our friends and join them for what I anticipate is a most delicious roast?"

"Yes, let us go."

******

The dinner that night was filled with happy conversation and amusing stories. Even the Doctor seemed of good cheer, and weighed in with his own amusing anecdotes. Left unsaid, but understood by all, was that there would be no allusions to the traumatic events of the last month. No one wanted to spoil a festive evening. There would be time enough later to tie the ribbon on any unresolved matters relating to those events.

As Judy sipped a glass of wine, she became more animated and responded enthusiastically to Susan's question about how she had liked Paris on her recent trip, especially since her question was neatly couched to suggest that she was only asking about her impressions as a tourist—and nothing more.

"Oh, Paris was wonderful!" Judy enthused. "I only regret that I did not have time to visit the Eiffel Tower or the Louvre. But I did one better and had a wonderful time at a party to which I was invited at the Danish Embassy."

"I'd like to hear more about that," said Roger. "But what part of France did you most enjoy?" Roger asked.

"Well, Mont St. Michel, of course, but I won't talk about that now. I would love to tell you about the most charming little village in Southern France—the little medieval village of Saint Jeanette. Absolutely enchanting. I would so like to visit there again."

There was a silence as everyone seemed to sense that Judy had more to say, and waited.

Finally, looking at Robin, she said, "I was hoping that perhaps Professor Hammond might take me there. There is the cutest little hotel—Le Moulin Camoula—overlooking the village square. "

There were knowing smiles all around as all eyes were now on the Professor.

For a moment, Robin could only manage a stutter, as for the moment he was speechless.

He recovered to say, "I would love to, of course. Who wouldn't want to see Saint Jeanette?"

******

After dinner as the five retired to the living room for dessert, Robin asked his hosts if they would excuse Judy and him for a little while so he could show Judy the path by the sea that Susan had shown him just a short while before.

"Of course!" said Roger. "Take your time, you two lovebirds!" At this both Robin and Judy in unison turned a light shade of pink.

"We'll be back soon," Robin said sheepishly.

Along the path by the sea, the two stopped on a bench and looked out at the full moon.

After several minutes, Robin said, "Were you teasing me in there?"

"Whatever makes you think that," Judy said innocently. "Have I done anything to make you think I'm a teaser?"

He looked into her Nerfertiti eyes and the moon's reflection in each. "No, nothing," he managed.

"So, that's all you can say?"

"You really would let me take you to this..."

"Yes, Saint Jeanette. A lovely village in the Cote d'Azur."

"I'm sure it is."

"You'd rather go there than, say, Mont St. Michel?"

"I'd like to go back there too, but not for a while. Perhaps you'd like to take me there later."

"I would."

And then he kissed her.

END OF
STORY

www.ingramcontent.com/pod-product-compliance
Lightning Source LLC
Chambersburg PA
CBHW061537170626
46811CB00001B/4